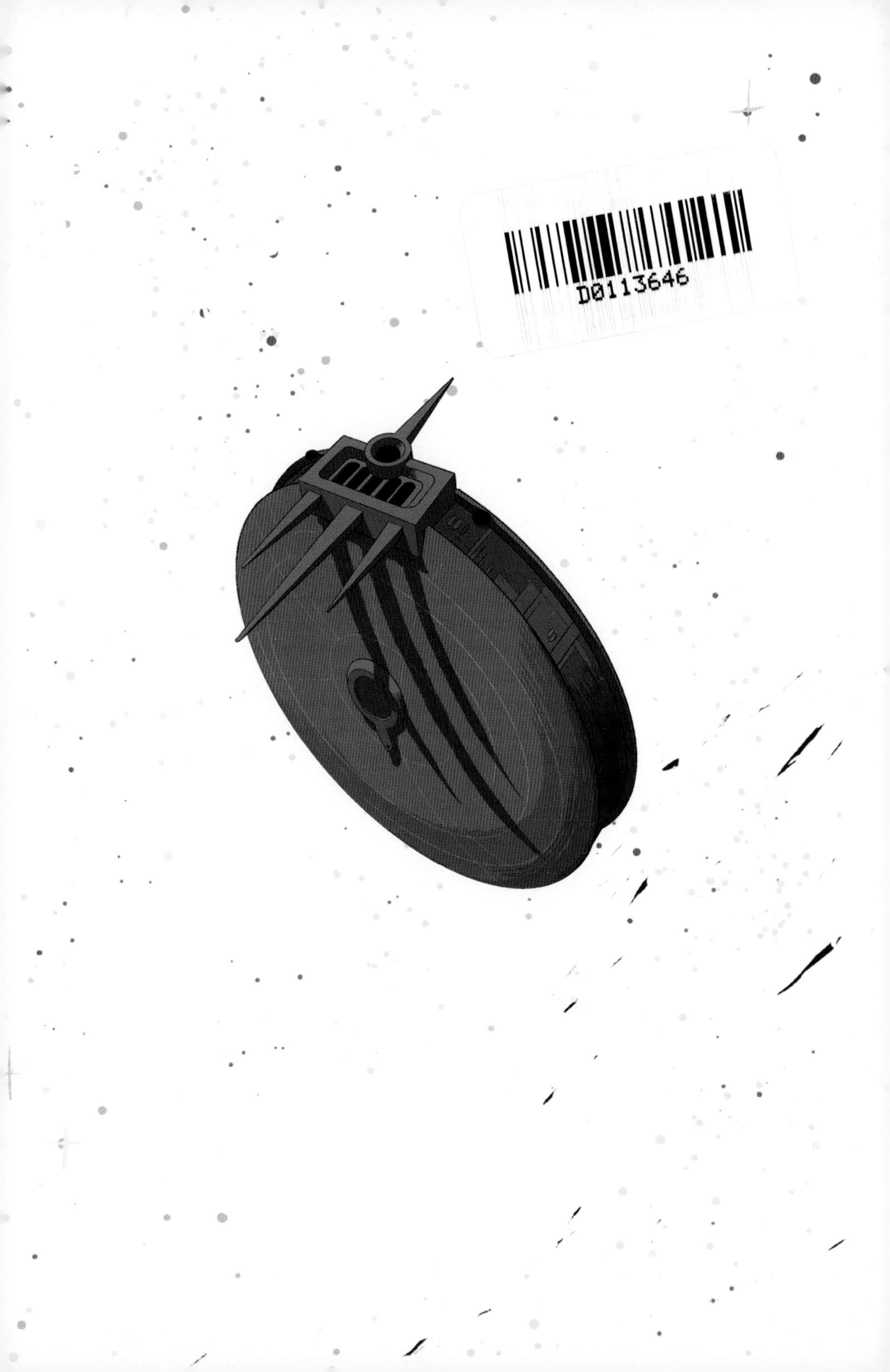

Stephen McCranie's

SPACE
BOY

VOLUME 11

Written and illustrated by
STEPHEN McCRANIE

DARK HORSE BOOKS

President and Publisher **Mike Richardson**
Editor **Shantel LaRocque**
Associate Editor **Brett Israel**
Assistant Editor **Sanjay Dharawat**
Designer **Anita Magaña**
Digital Art Technician **Allyson Haller**

STEPHEN MCCRANIE'S SPACE BOY VOLUME 11
Space Boy™ © 2021 Stephen McCranie. All rights reserved. Dark Horse
Books® and the Dark Horse logo are registered trademarks of Dark Horse
Comics LLC. All rights reserved. No portion of this publication may be
reproduced or transmitted, in any form or by any means, without the
express written permission of Dark Horse Comics LLC. Names, characters,
places, and incidents featured in this publication either are the product of
the author's imagination or are used fictitiously. Any resemblance to actual
persons (living or dead), events, institutions, or locales, without satiric
intent, is coincidental.

This book collects *Space Boy* episodes 160–175, previously published
online at WebToons.com.

Published by Dark Horse Books
A division of Dark Horse Comics LLC
10956 SE Main Street | Milwaukie, OR 97222
StephenMcCranie.com | DarkHorse.com

To find a comics shop in your area, visit comicshoplocator.com

First edition: October 2021
ISBN 978-1-50671-885-9
10 9 8 7 6 5 4 3 2 1
Printed in China

Neil Hankerson Executive Vice President • **Tom Weddle** Chief Financial
Officer • **Dale LaFountain** Chief Information Officer • **Tim Wiesch** Vice
President of Licensing • **Matt Parkinson** Vice President of Marketing •
Vanessa Todd-Holmes Vice President of Production and Scheduling •
Mark Bernardi Vice President of Book Trade and Digital Sales • **Ken Lizzi**
General Counsel • **Dave Marshall** Editor in Chief • **Davey Estrada** Editorial
Director • **Chris Warner** Senior Books Editor • **Cary Grazzini** Director of
Specialty Projects • **Lia Ribacchi** Art Director • **Matt Dryer** Director of
Digital Art and Prepress • **Michael Gombos** Senior Director of Licensed
Publications • **Kari Yadro** Director of Custom Programs • **Kari Torson**
Director of International Licensing • **Sean Brice** Director of Trade Sales •
Randy Lahrman Director of Product Sales

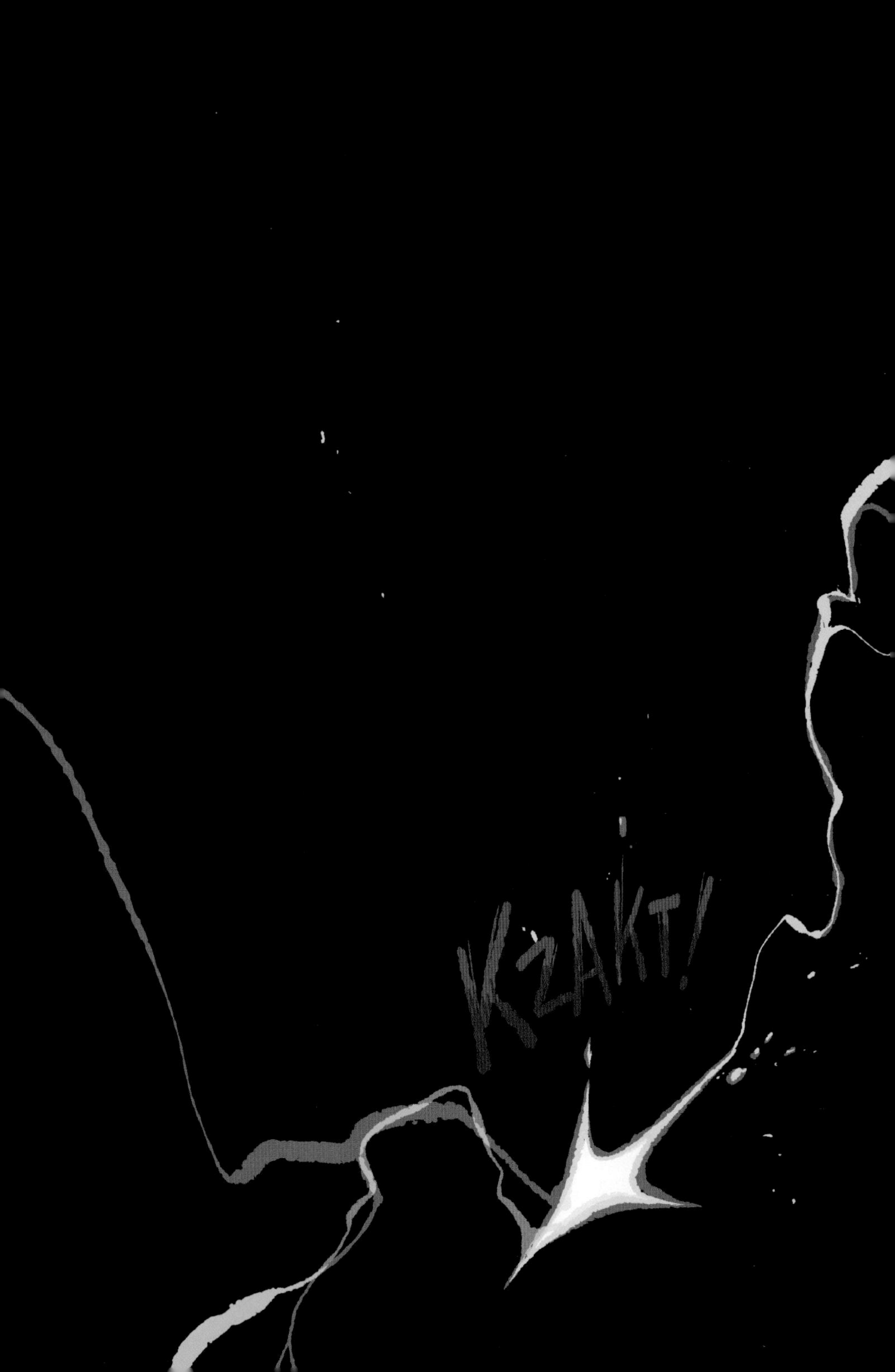
KZAKT!

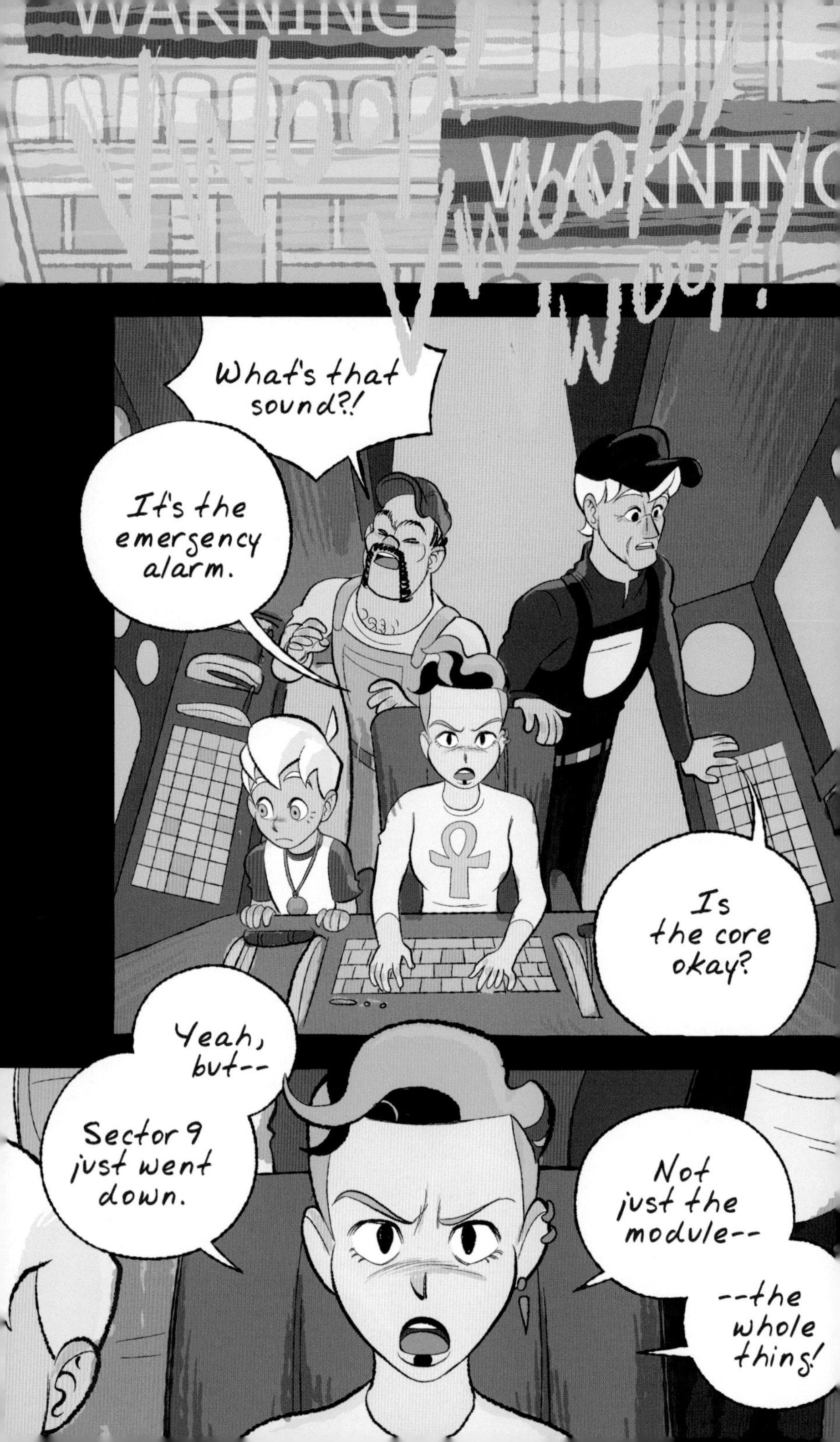
WARNING
Whoop!
WARNING
Whoop!
Whoop!
What's that sound?!
It's the emergency alarm.
Is the core okay?
Yeah, but--
Sector 9 just went down.
Not just the module--
--the whole thing!

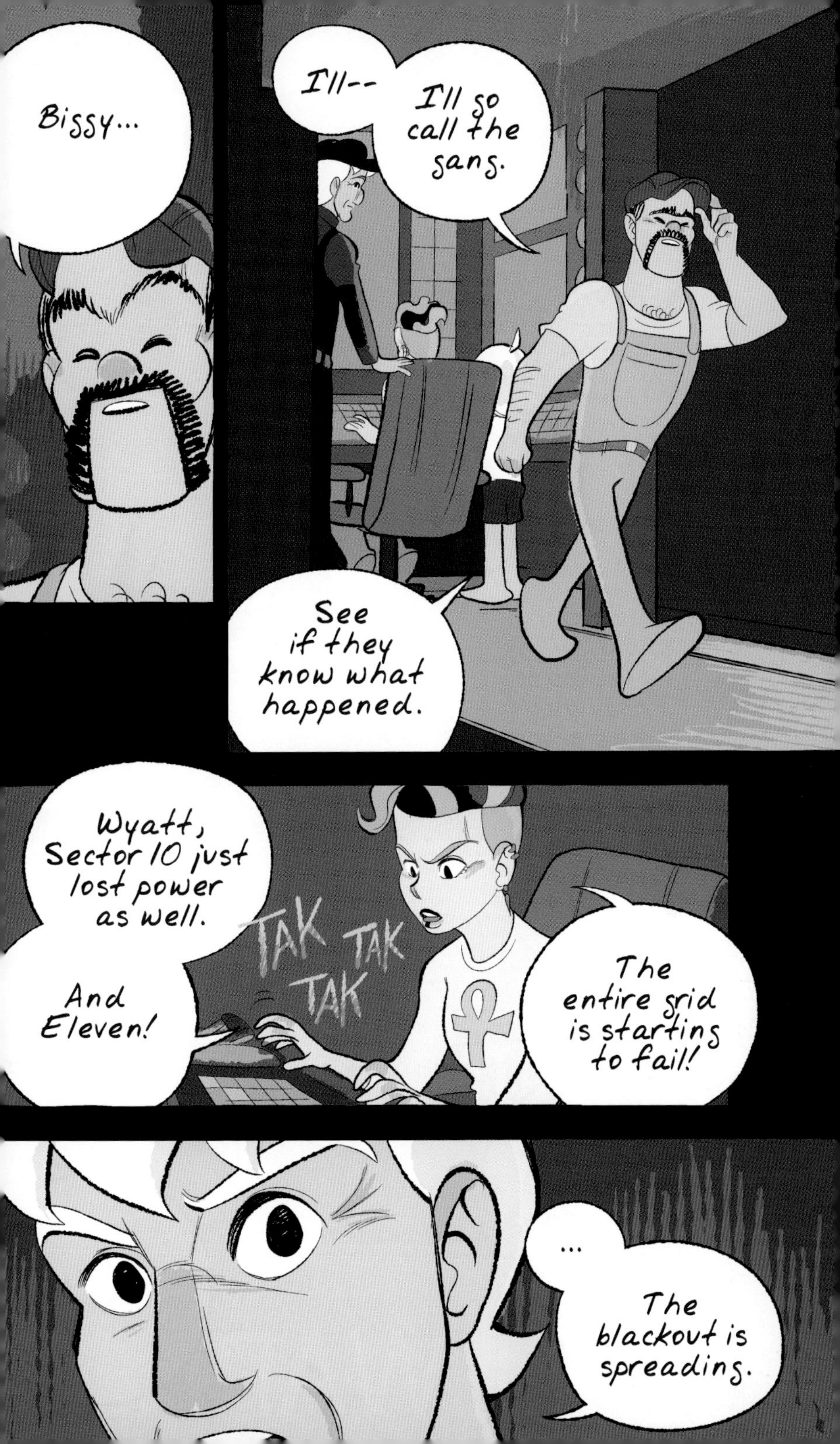
Bissy...
I'll--
I'll go call the gang.
See if they know what happened.
Wyatt, Sector 10 just lost power as well.
And Eleven!
TAK TAK TAK
The entire grid is starting to fail!
...
The blackout is spreading.

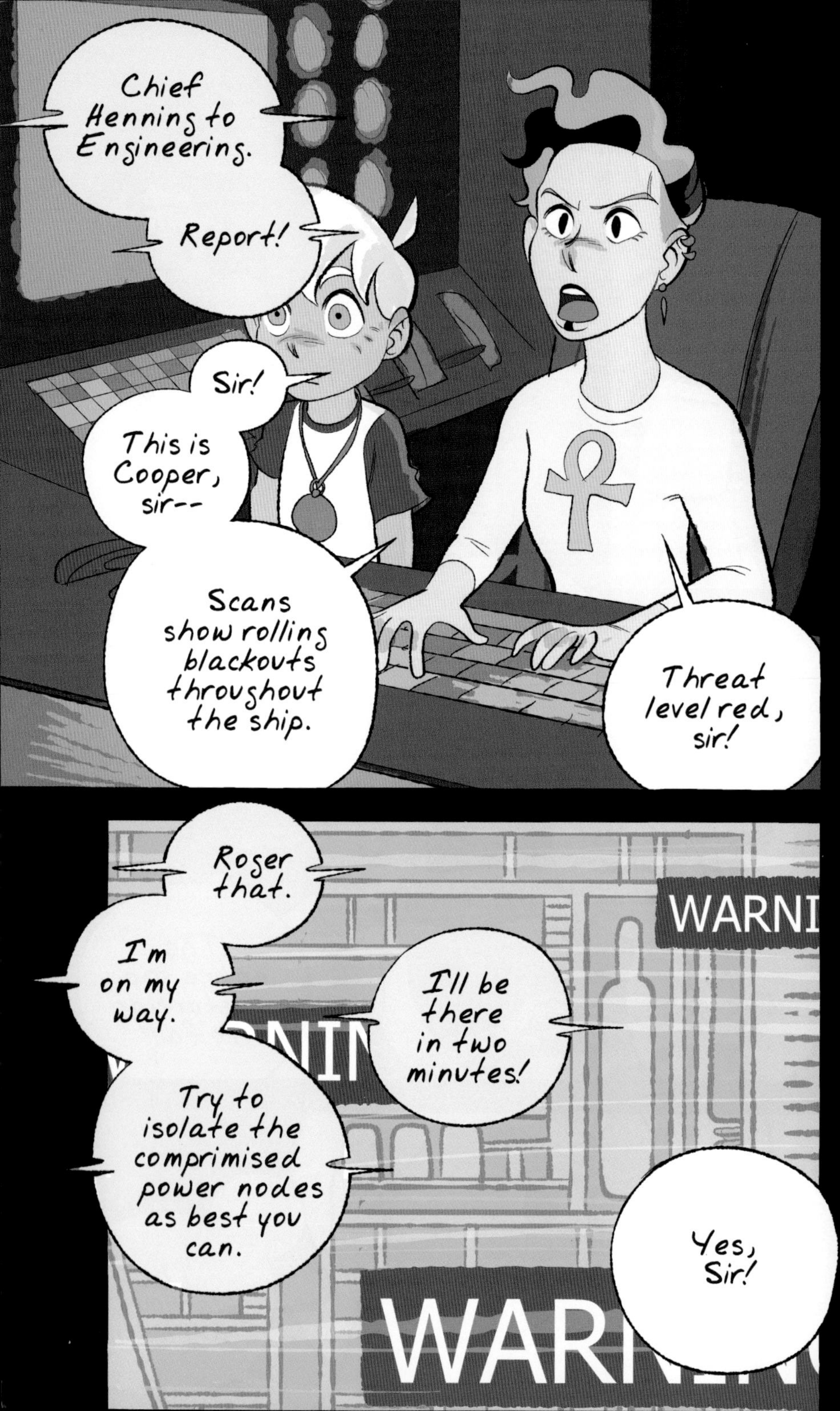
Chief Henning to Engineering.
Report!
Sir!
This is Cooper, sir--
Scans show rolling blackouts throughout the ship.
Threat level red, sir!
WARNI
Roger that.
I'm on my way.
I'll be there in two minutes!
Try to isolate the comprimised power nodes as best you can.
Yes, Sir!
WARN

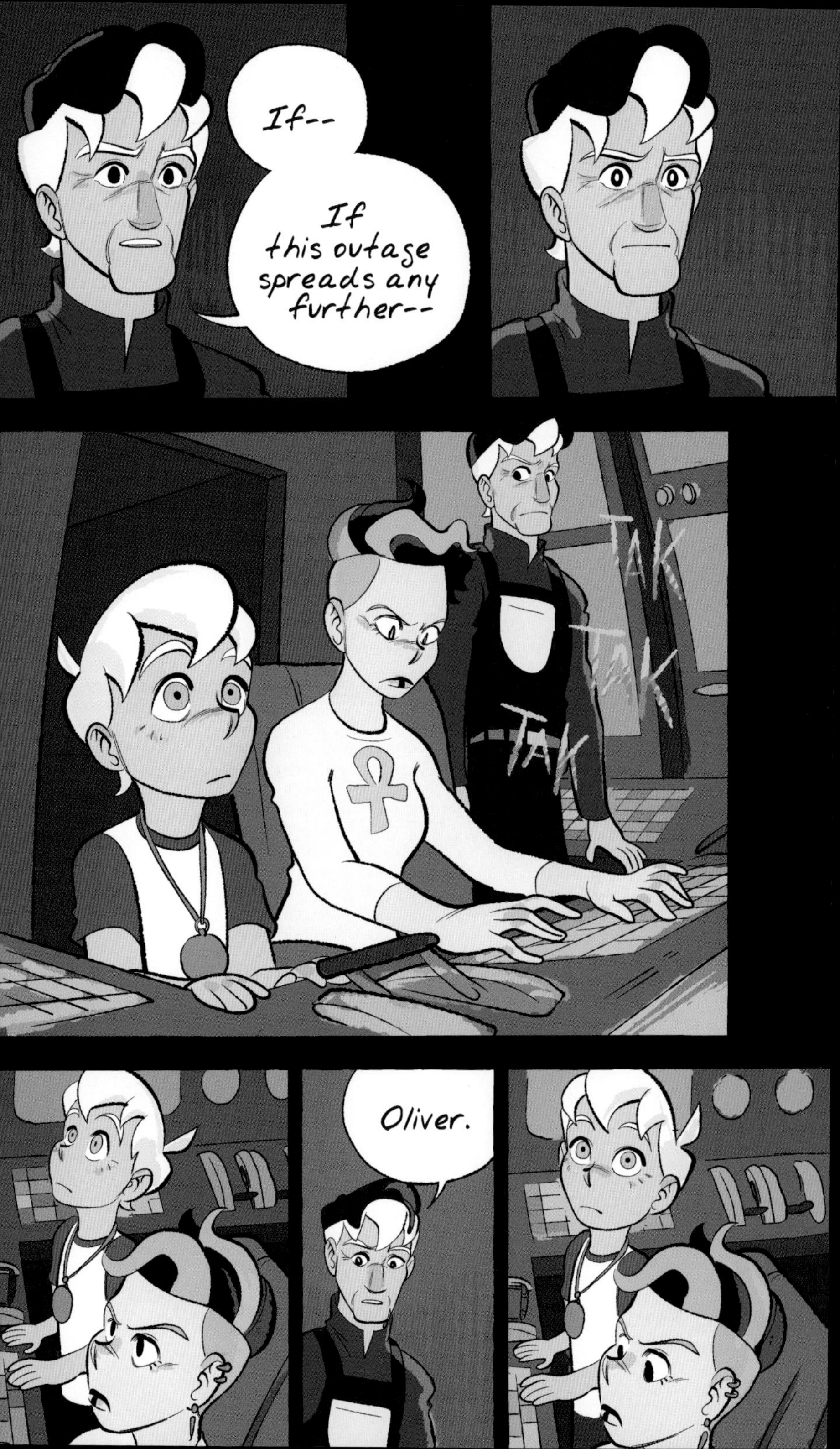
If--
If this outage spreads any further--
TAK TAK TAK
Oliver.

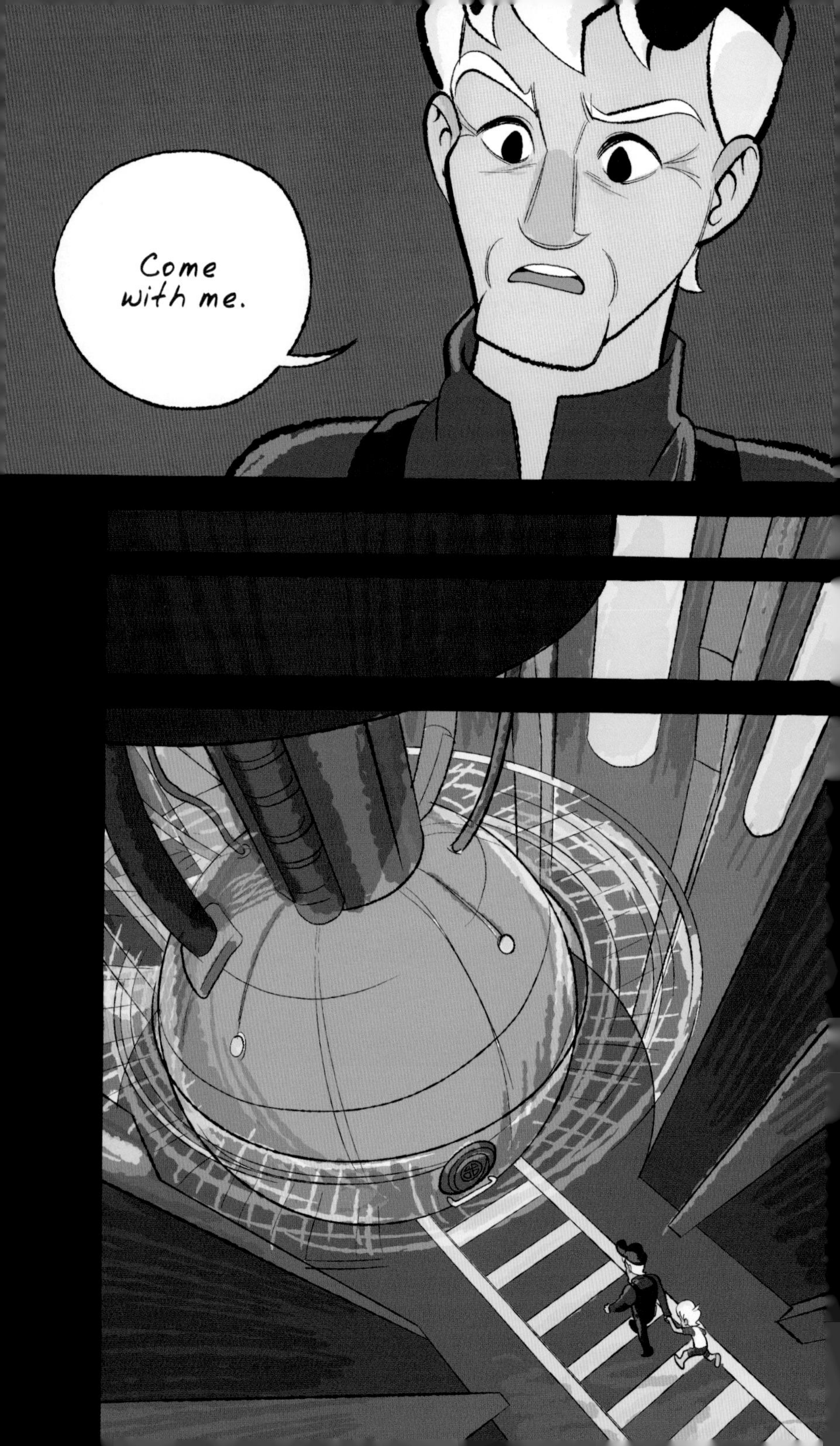
Come with me.

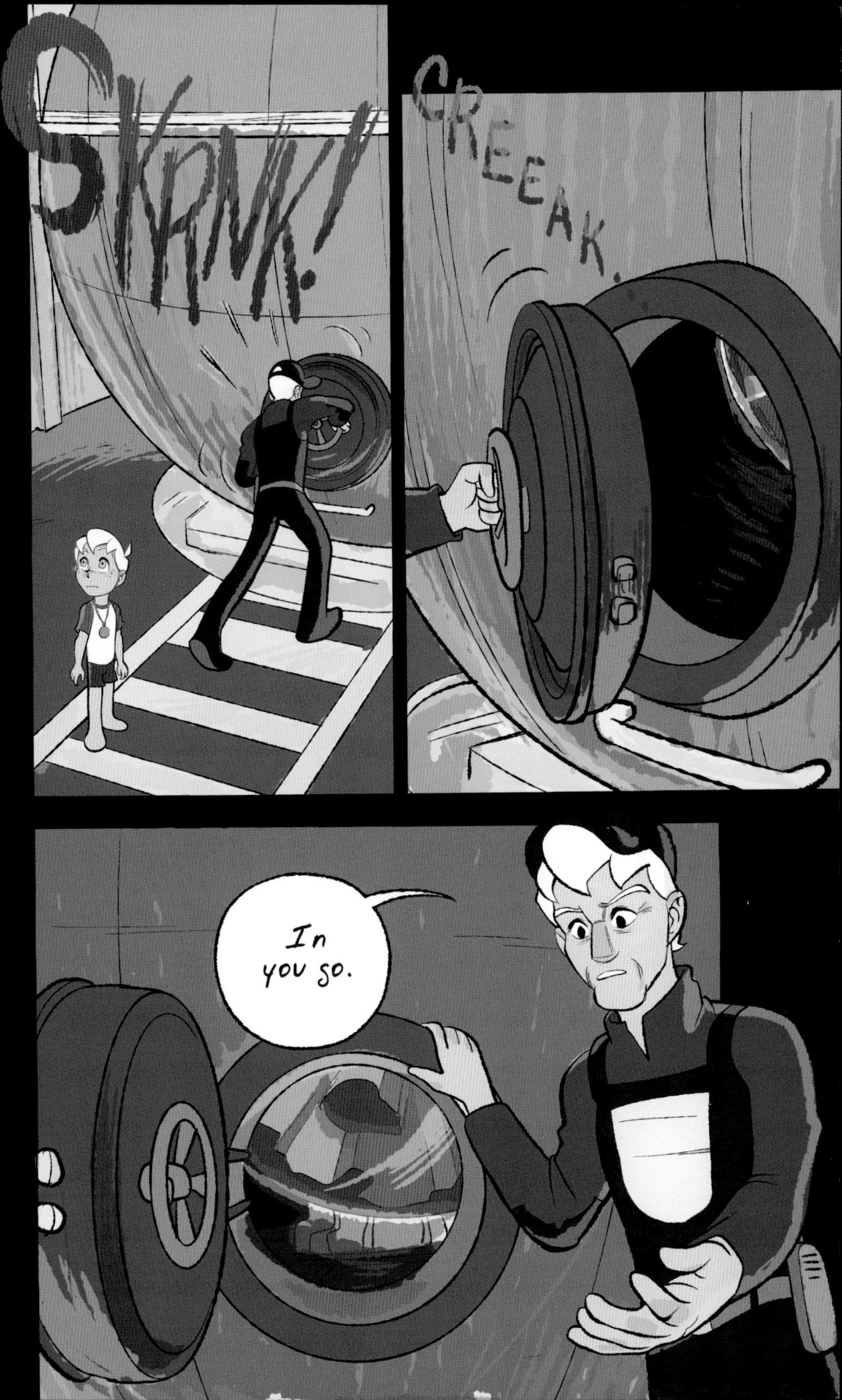
SKRNK!
CREEAK.
In you go.

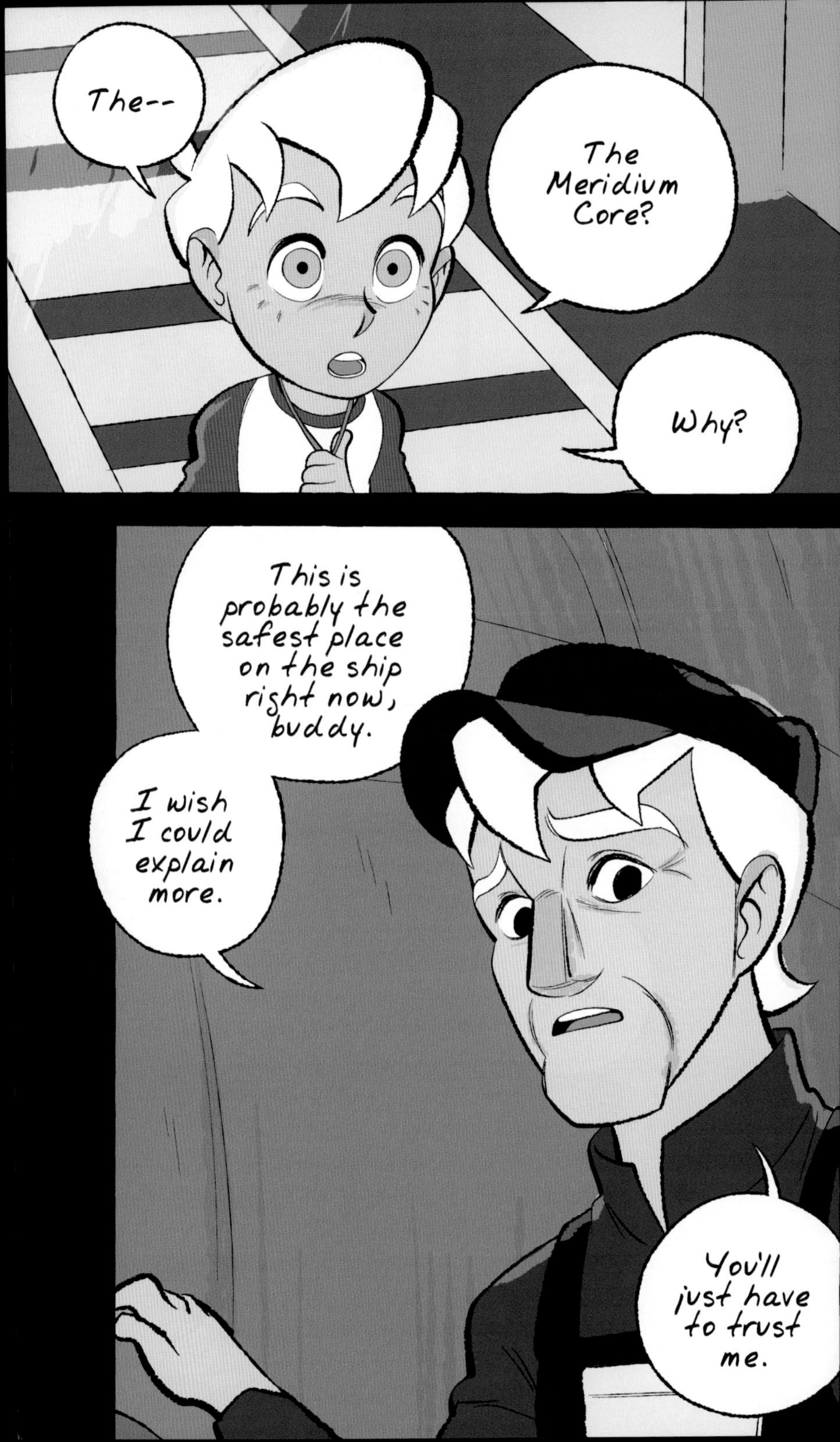
The--
The Meridium Core?
Why?
This is probably the safest place on the ship right now, buddy.
I wish I could explain more.
You'll just have to trust me.

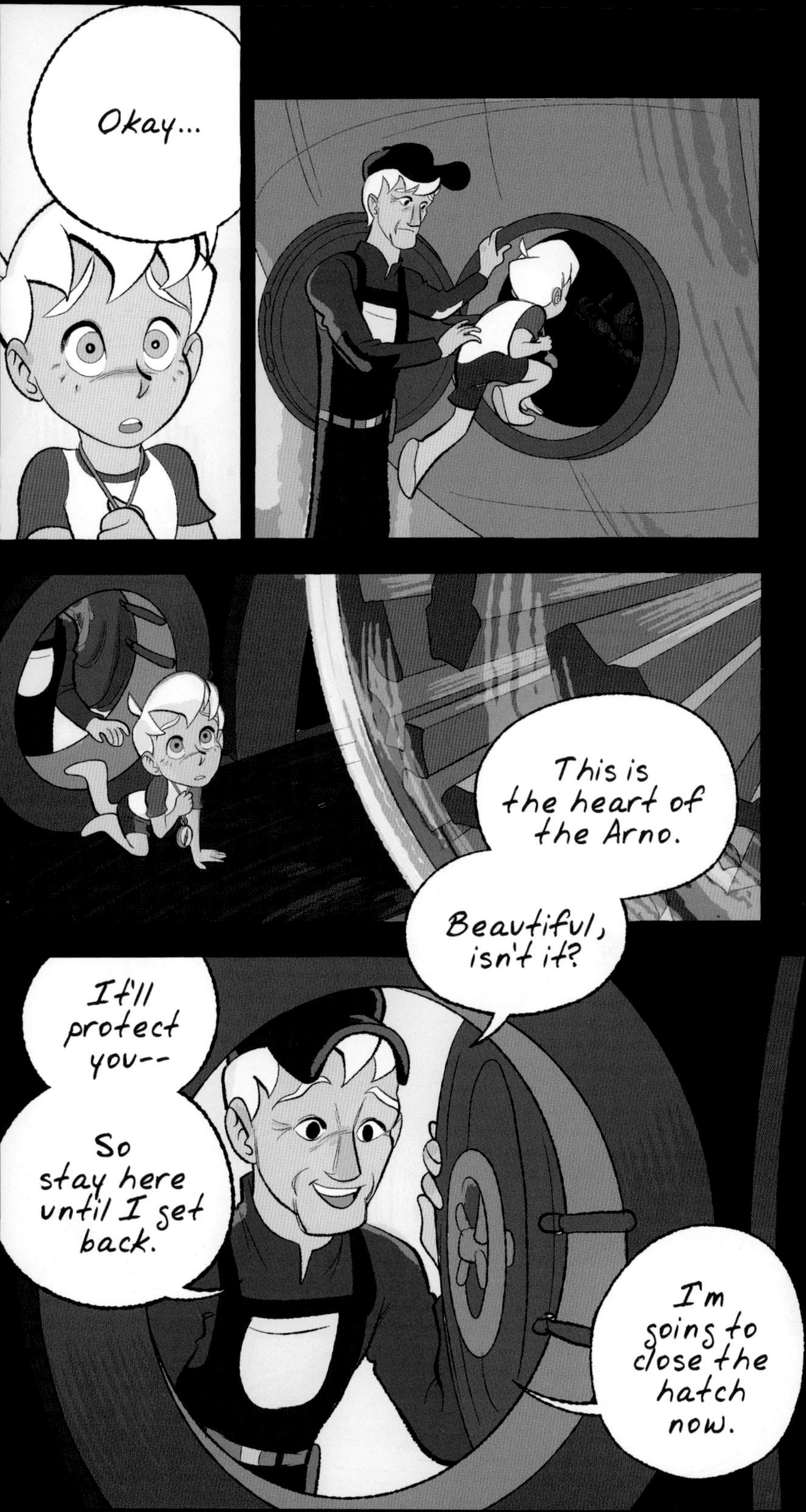

Okay...
This is the heart of the Arno.
Beautiful, isn't it?
It'll protect you--
So stay here until I get back.
I'm going to close the hatch now.

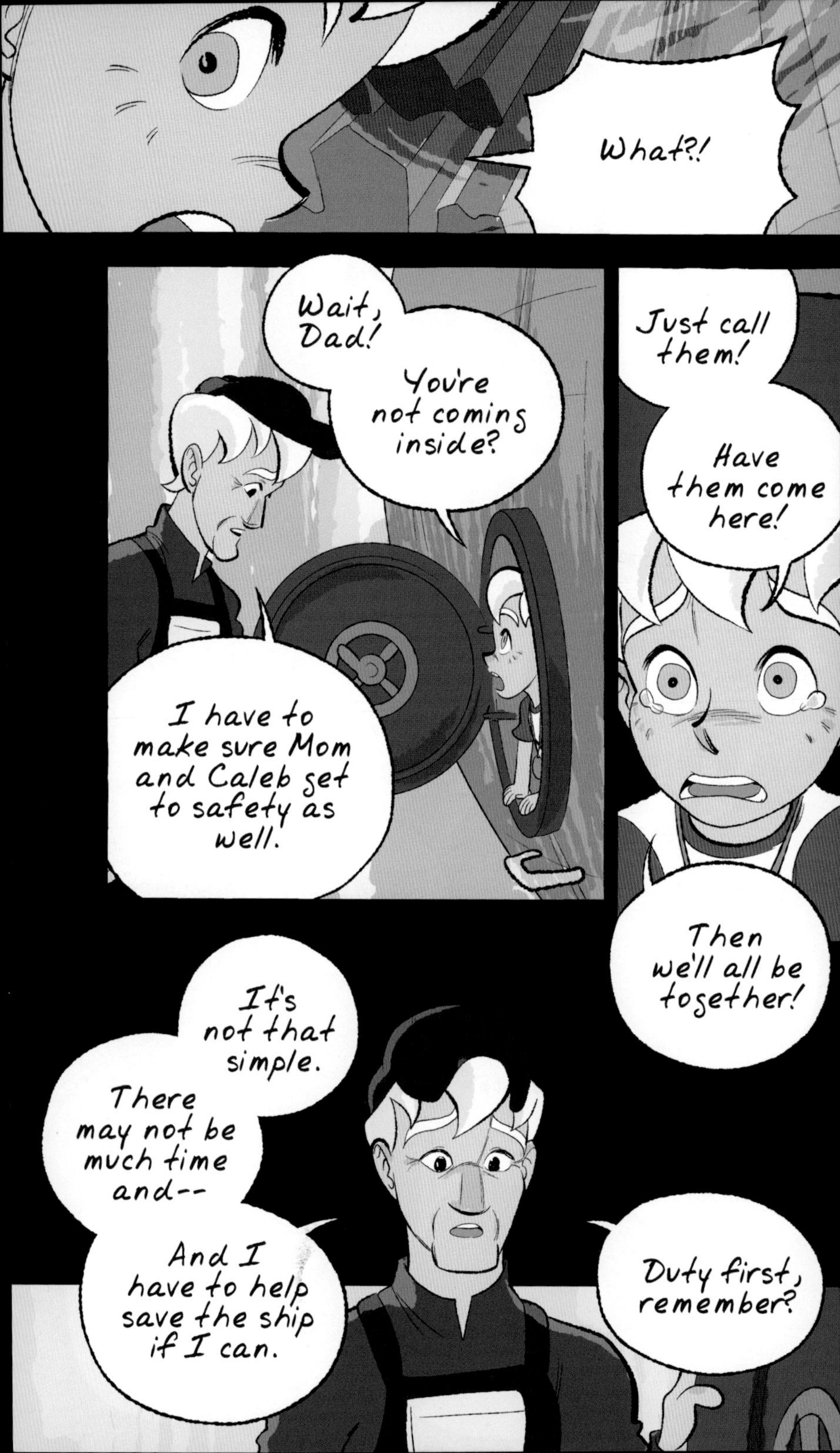
What?!
Wait, Dad!
You're not coming inside?
I have to make sure Mom and Caleb get to safety as well.
Just call them!
Have them come here!
Then we'll all be together!
It's not that simple.
There may not be much time and--
And I have to help save the ship if I can.
Duty first, remember?

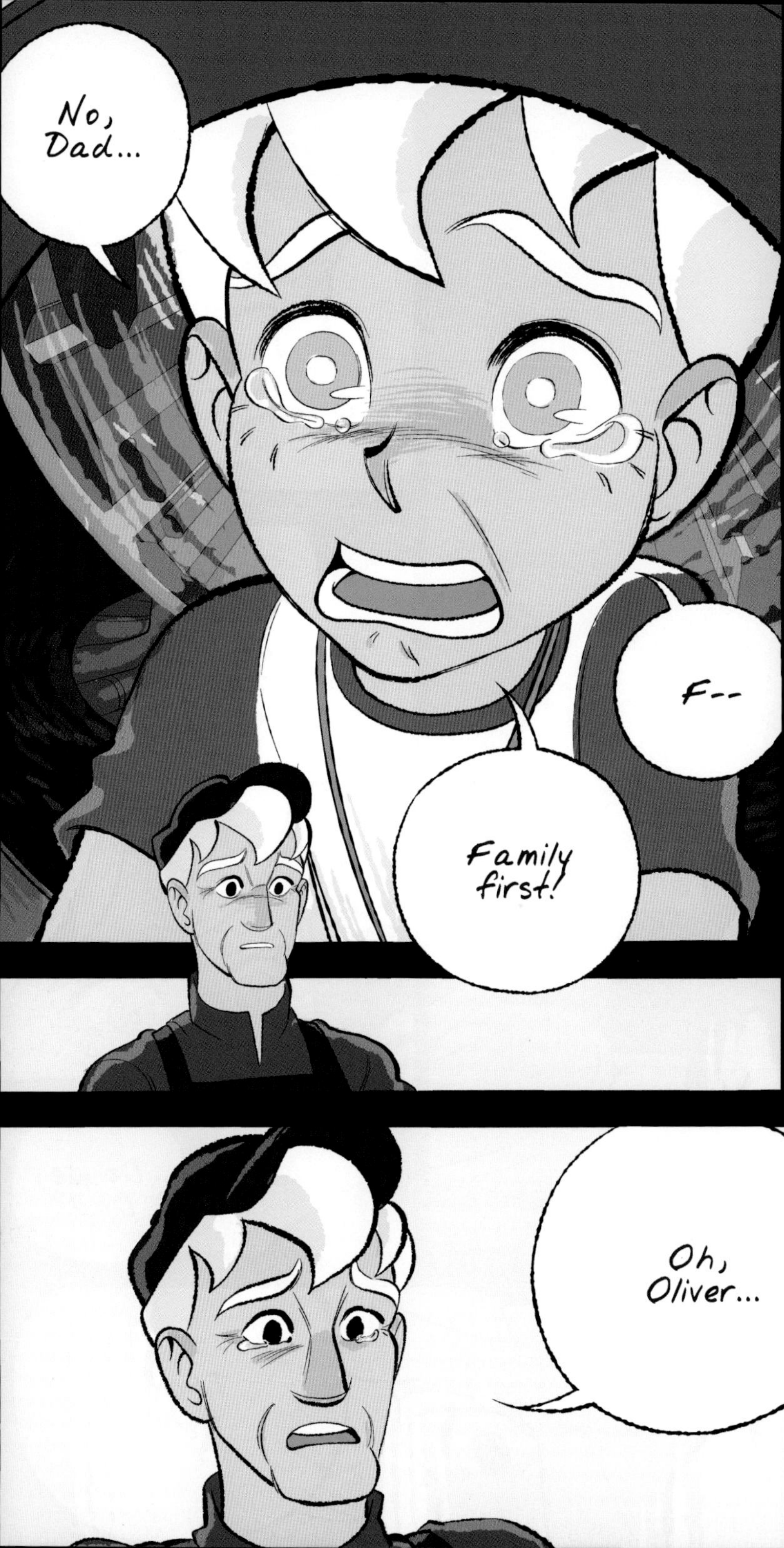
No, Dad...
F--
Family first!
Oh, Oliver...

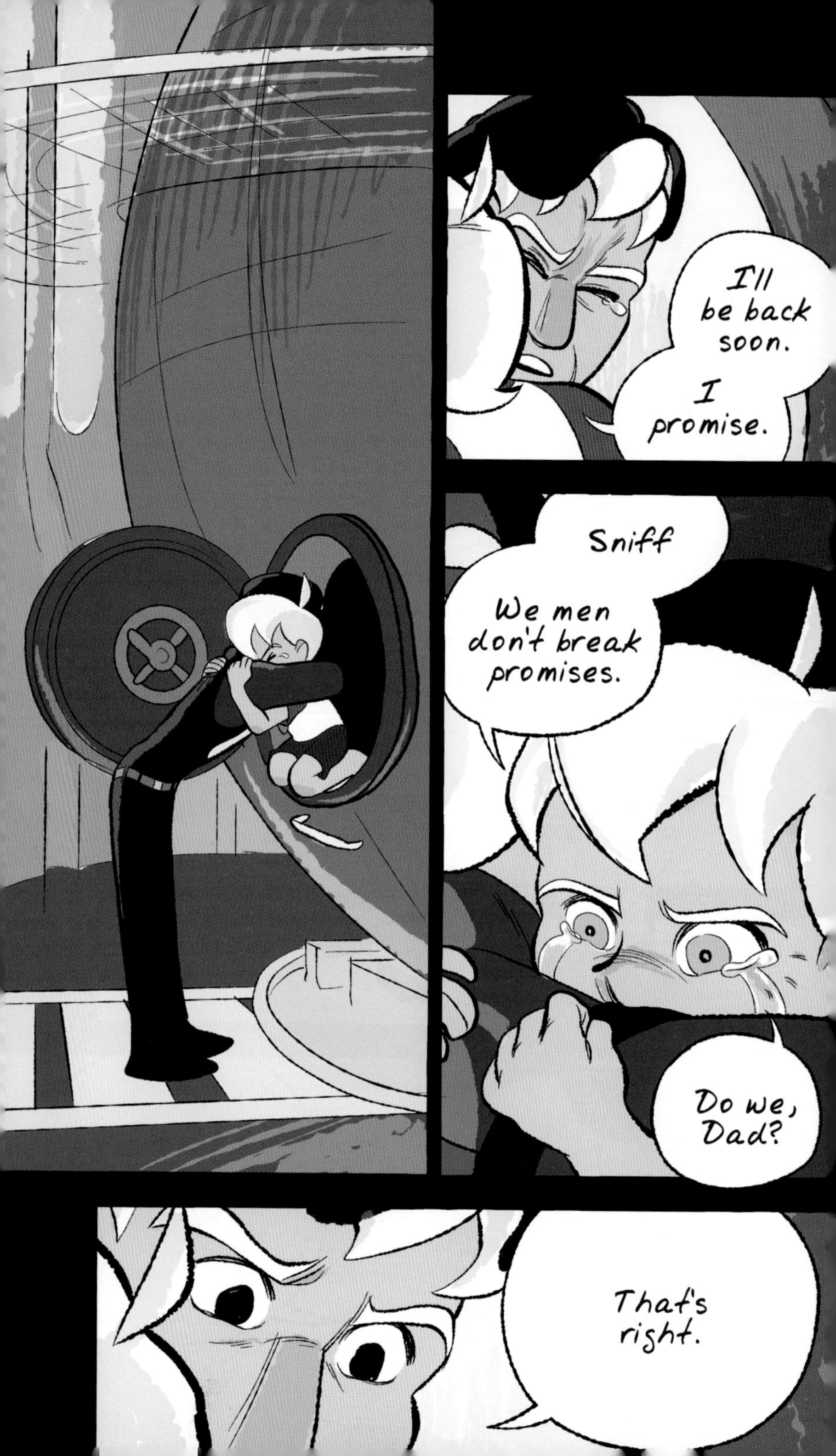
I'll be back soon.
I promise.
Sniff
We men don't break promises.
Do we, Dad?
That's right.

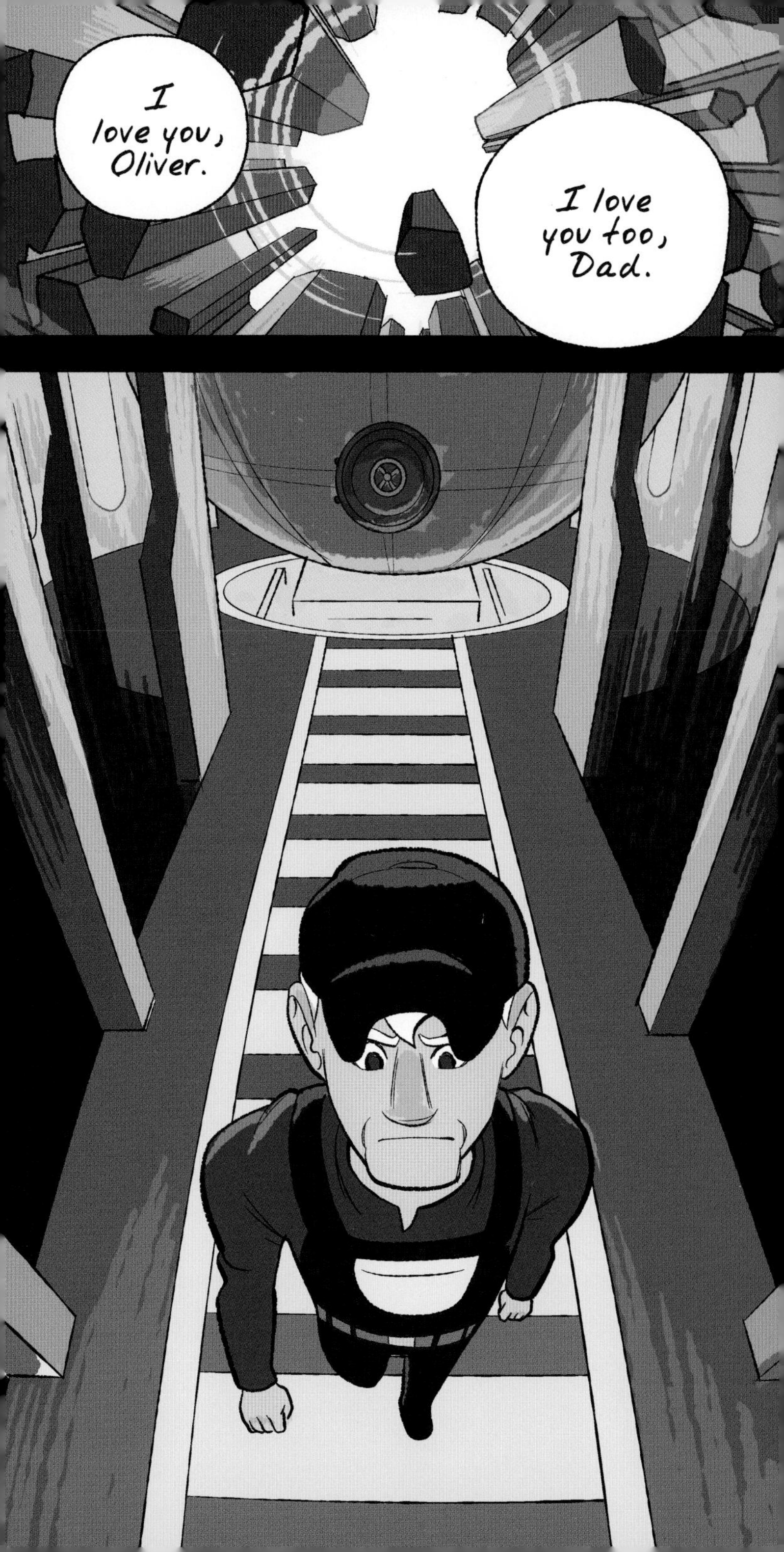
I love you, Oliver.
I love you too, Dad.

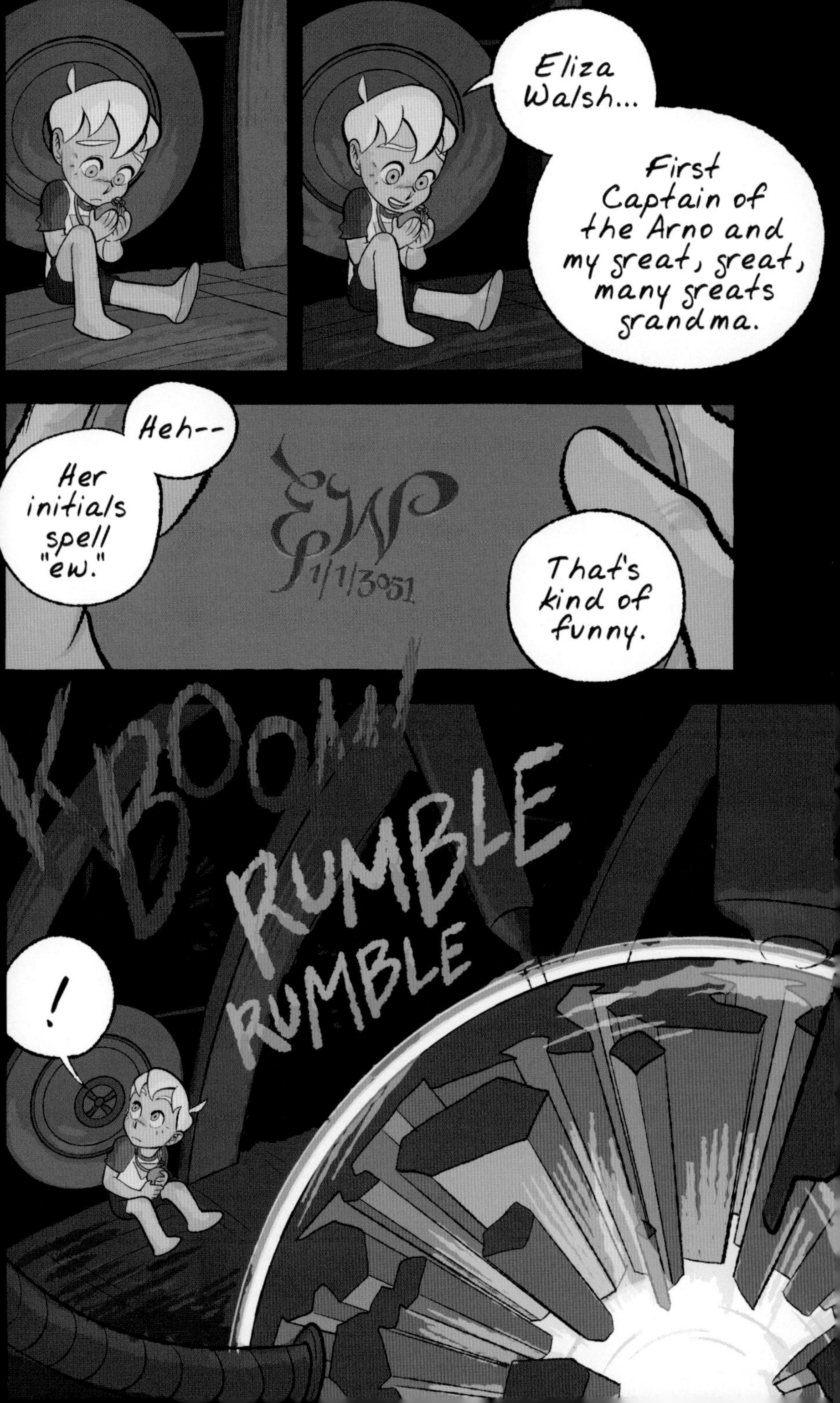
Eliza Walsh...
First Captain of the Arno and my great, great, many greats grandma.
Heh--
Her initials spell "ew."
EW
1/1/3051
That's kind of funny.
KBOOM!
RUMBLE
RUMBLE
!

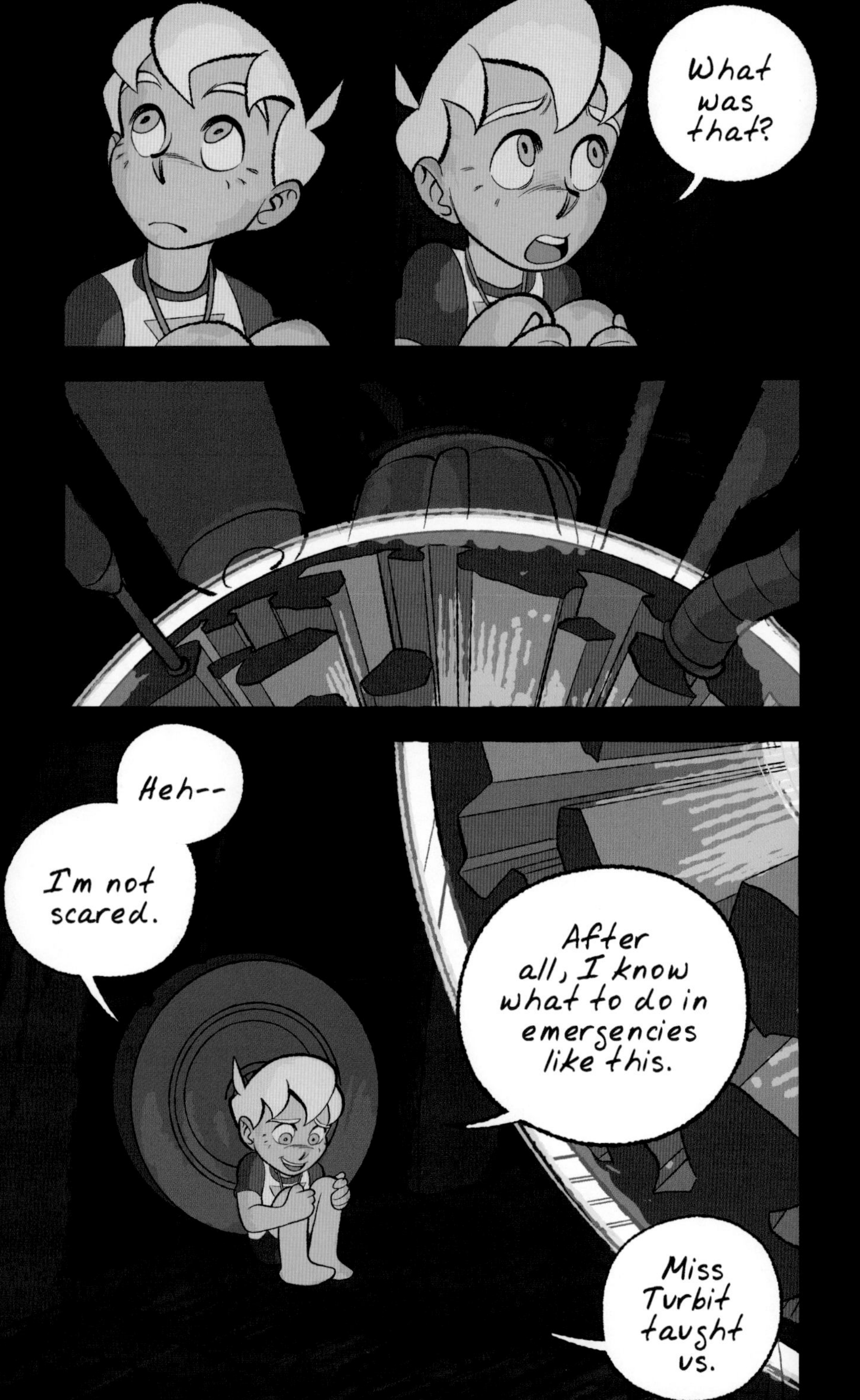
What was that?
Heh--
I'm not scared.
After all, I know what to do in emergencies like this.
Miss Turbit taught us.

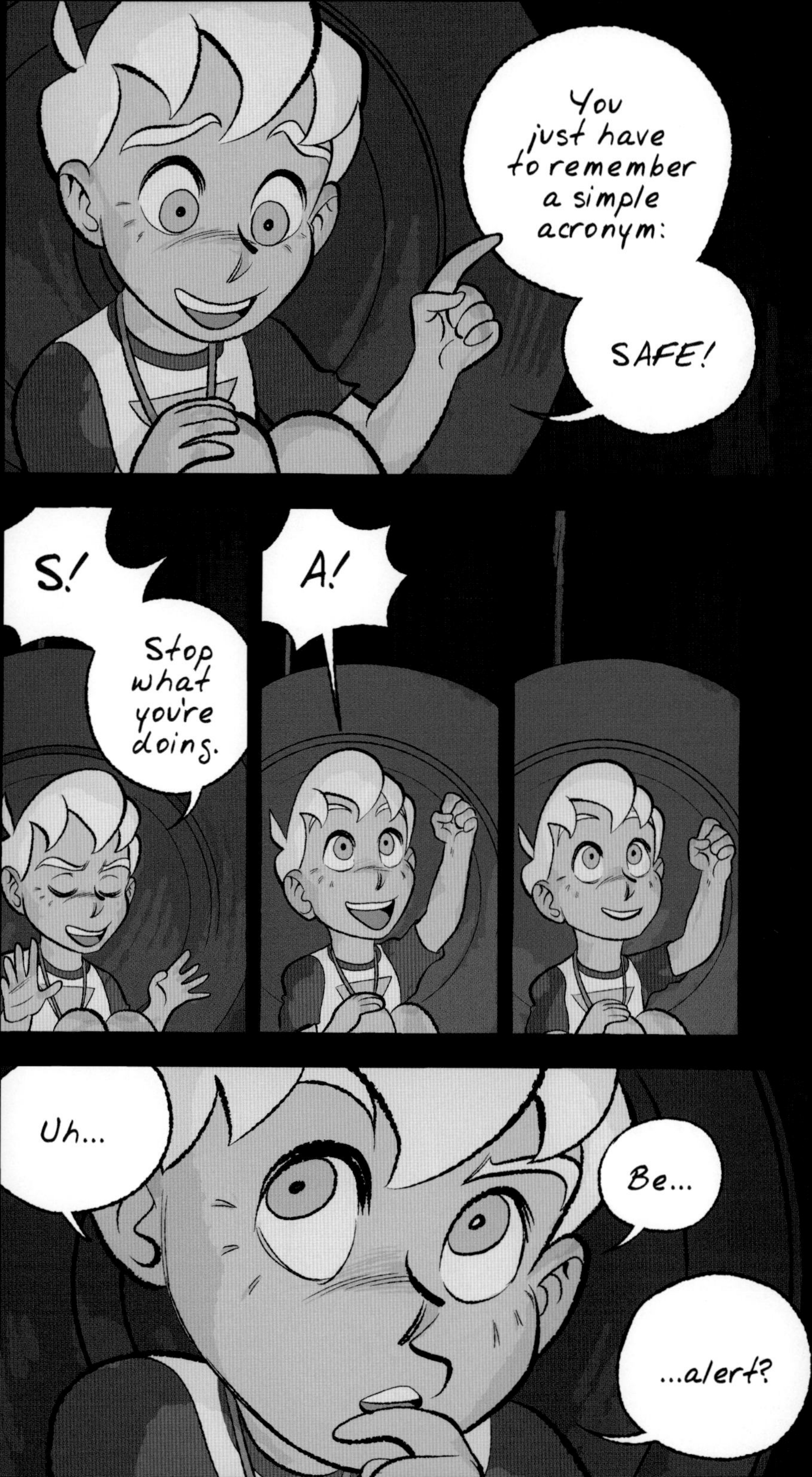
You just have to remember a simple acronym:
SAFE!
S!
Stop what you're doing.
A!
Uh...
Be...
...alert?

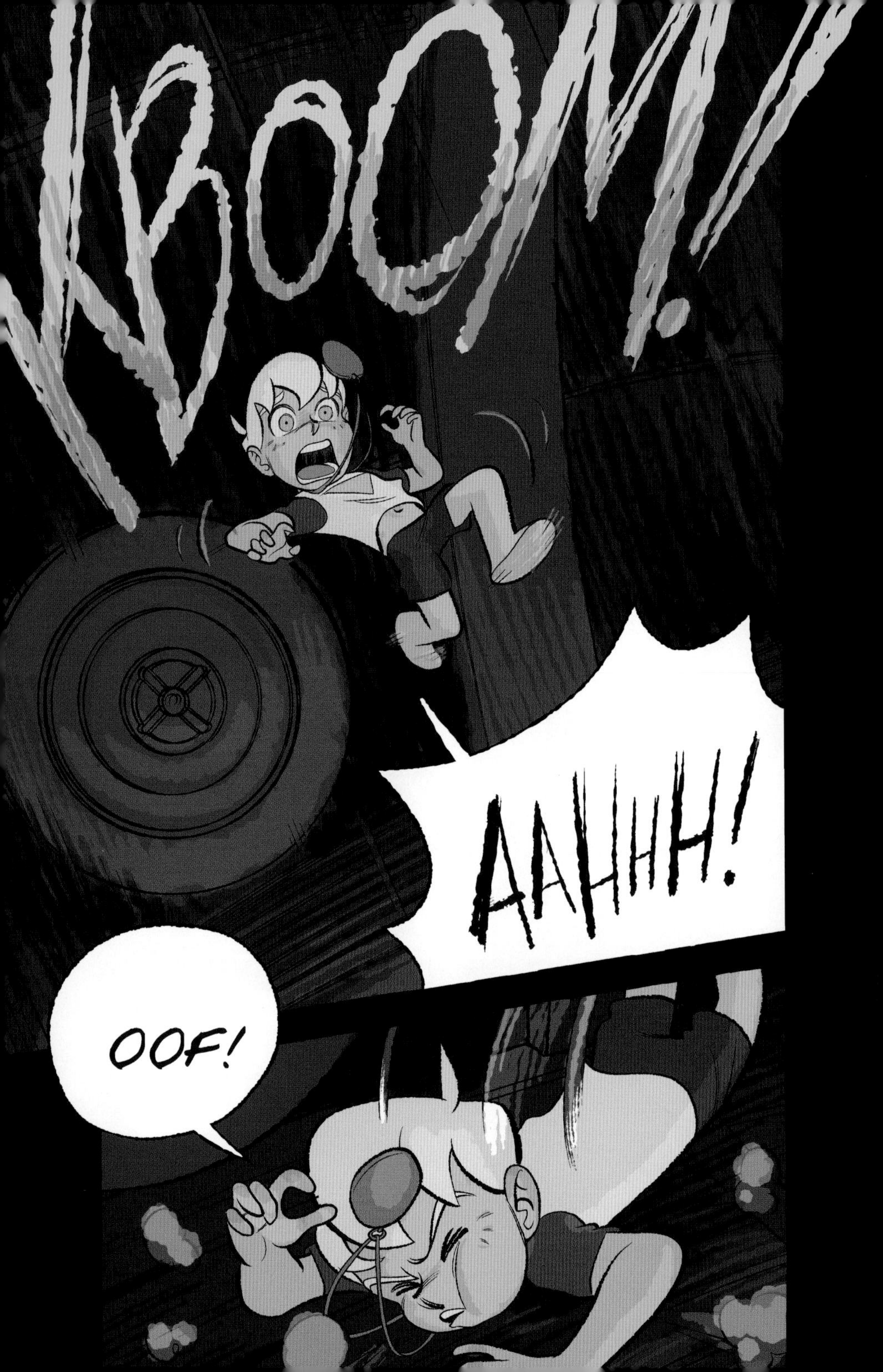
KABOOM!
AAHHH!
OOF!

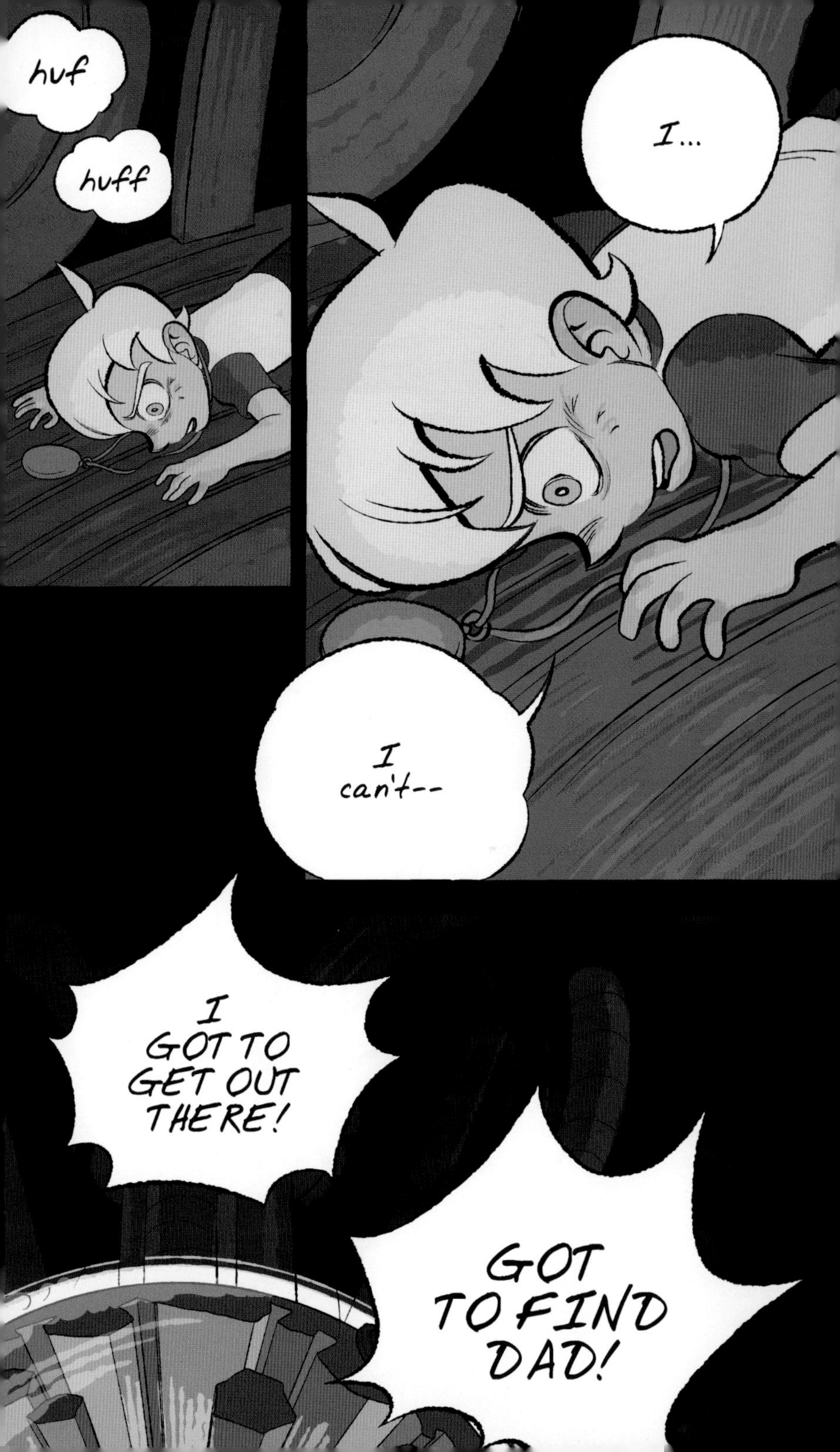
huf
huff
I...
I can't--
I GOT TO GET OUT THERE!
GOT TO FIND DAD!

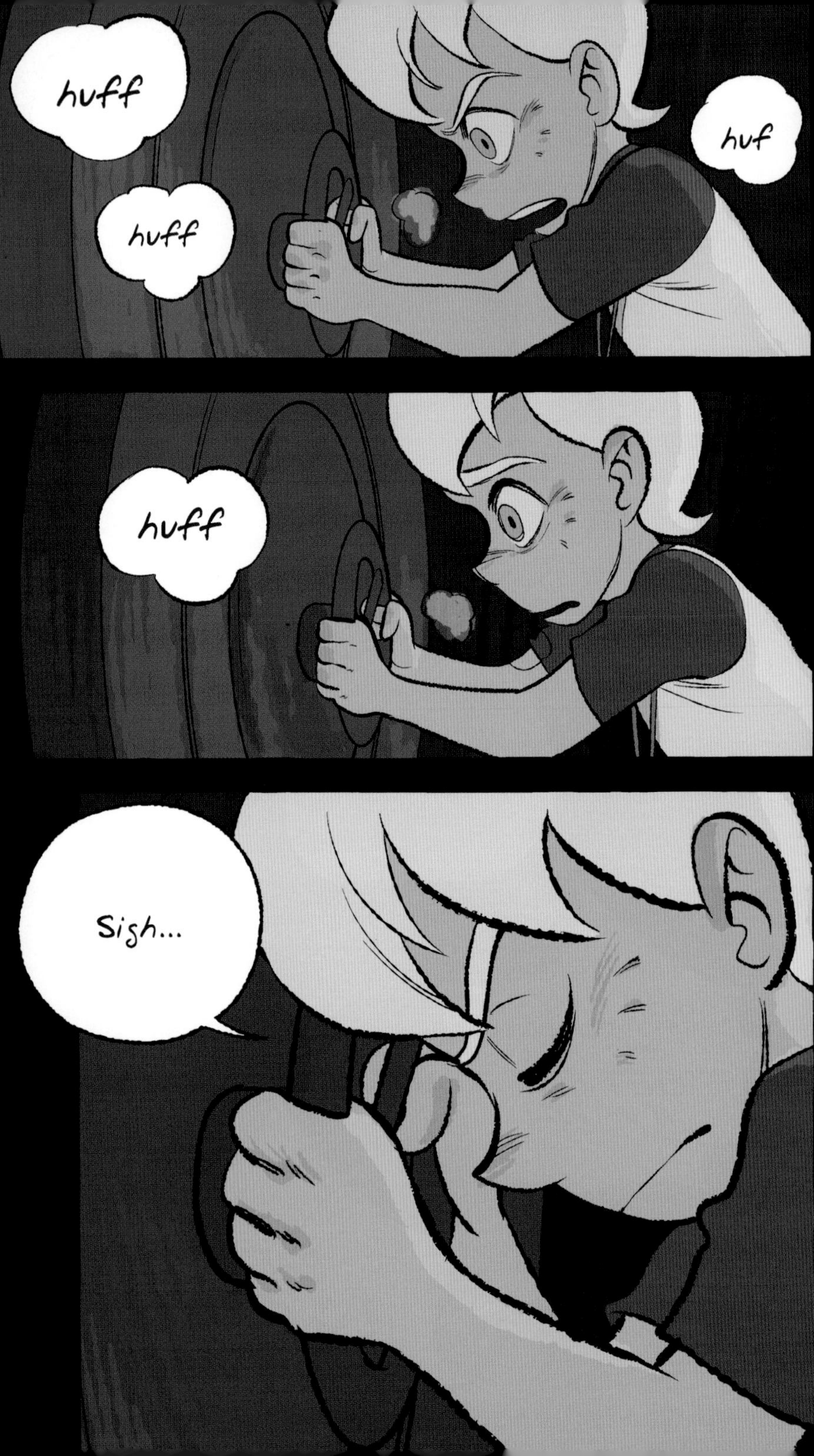
huff
huf
huff
huff
Sigh...

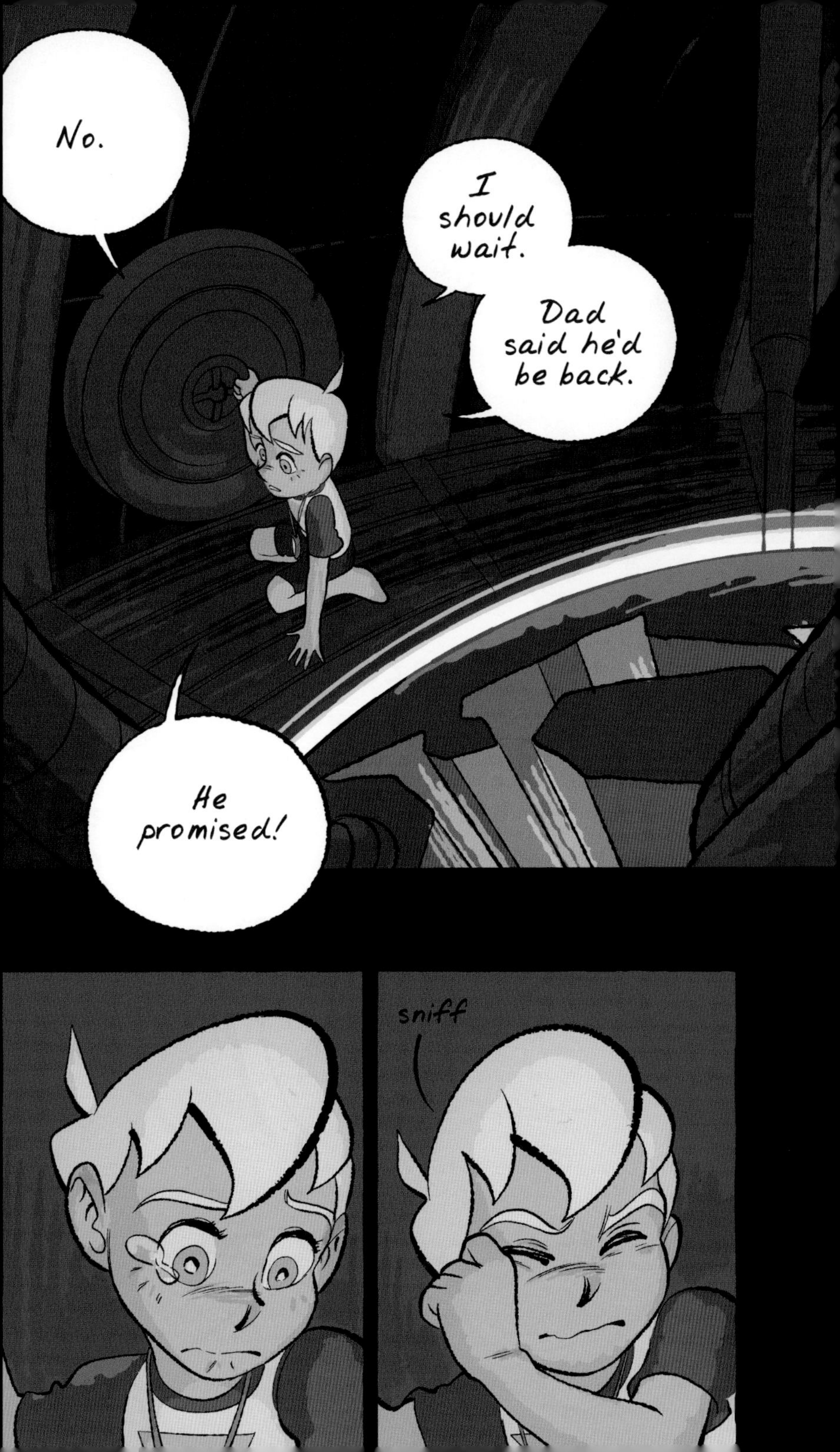
No.
I should wait.
Dad said he'd be back.
He promised!
sniff

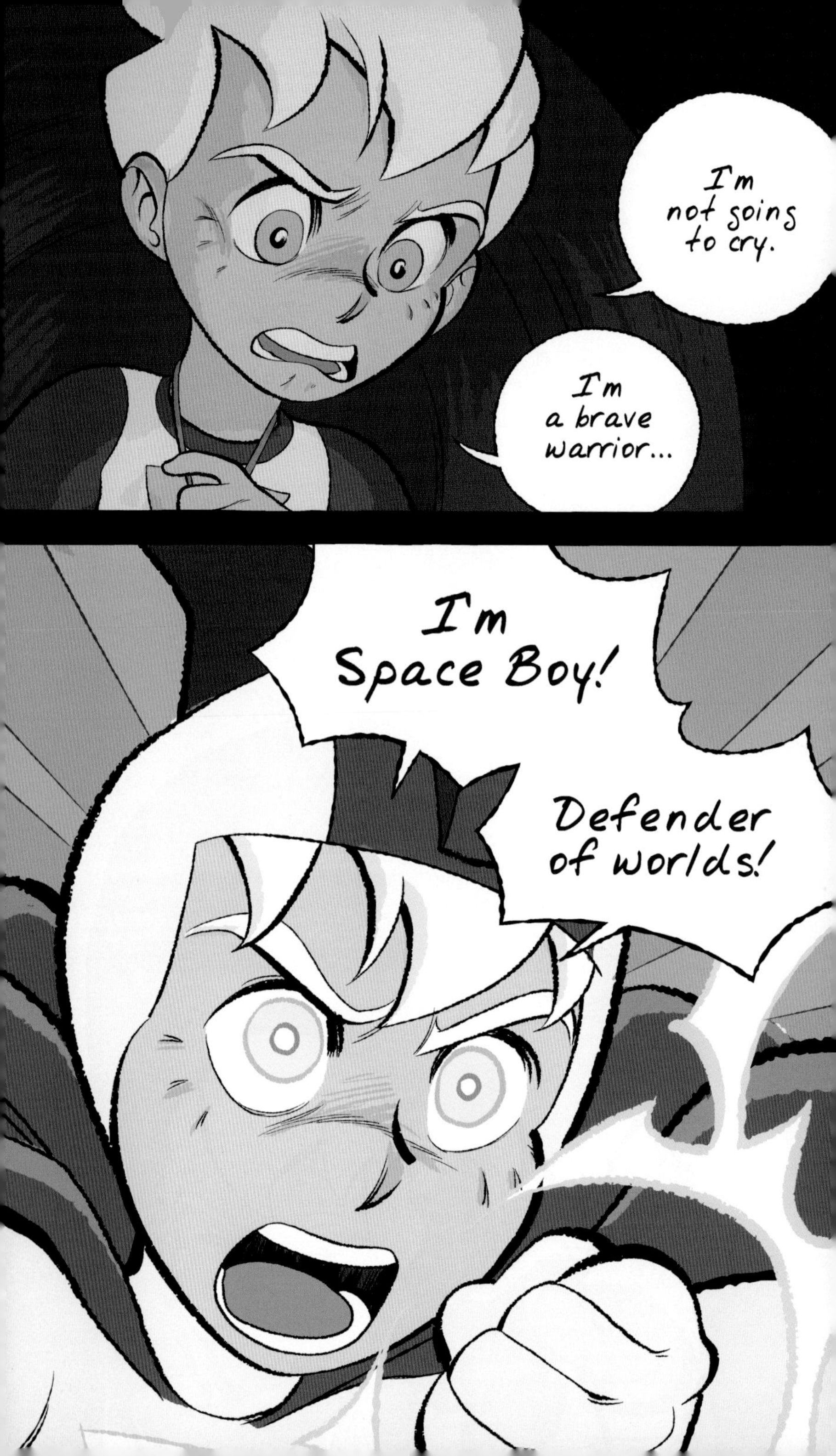
I'm not goins to cry.
I'm a brave warrior...
I'm Space Boy!
Defender of worlds!

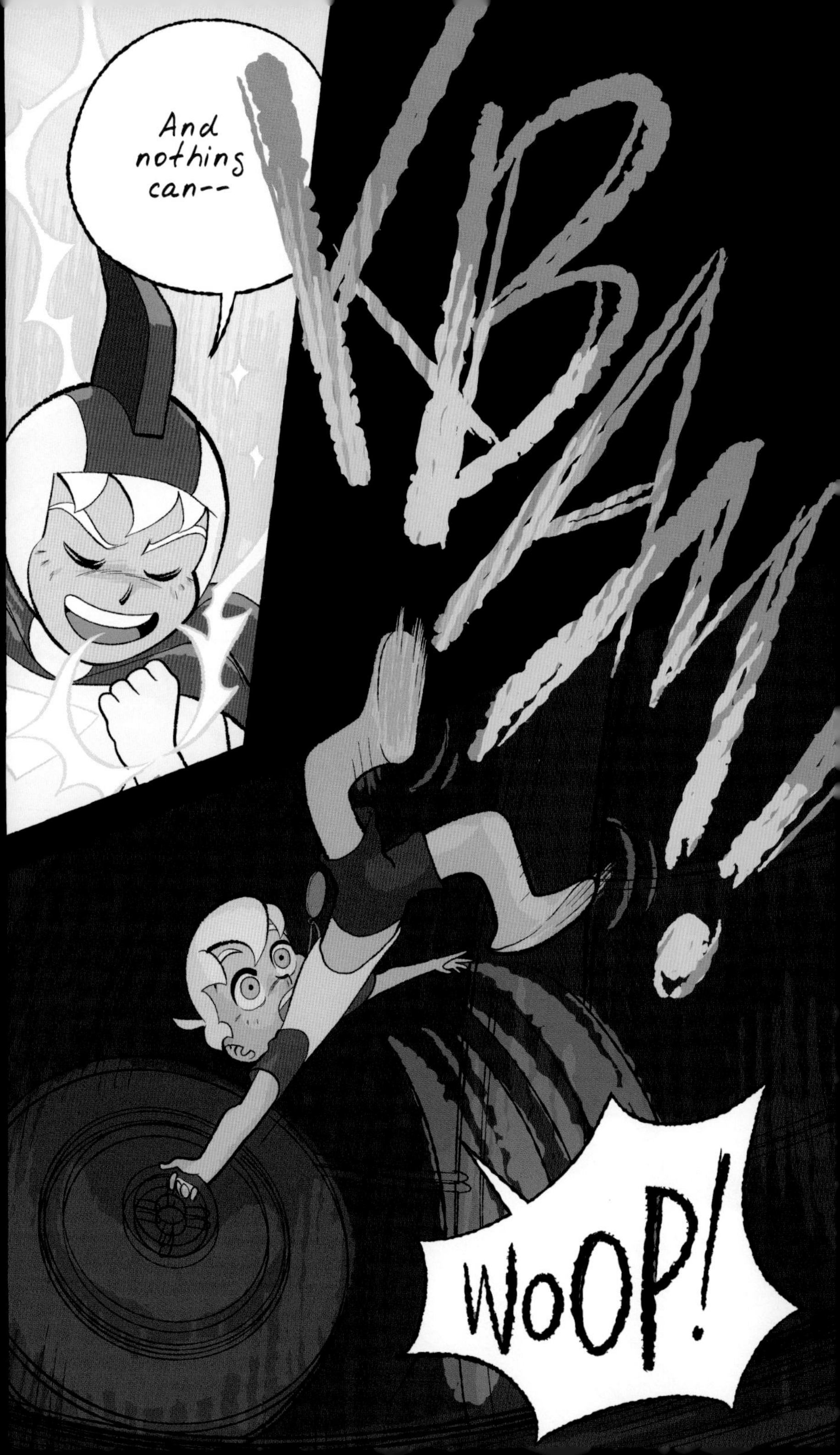
And nothing can--
KBAMM!!!
WOOP!

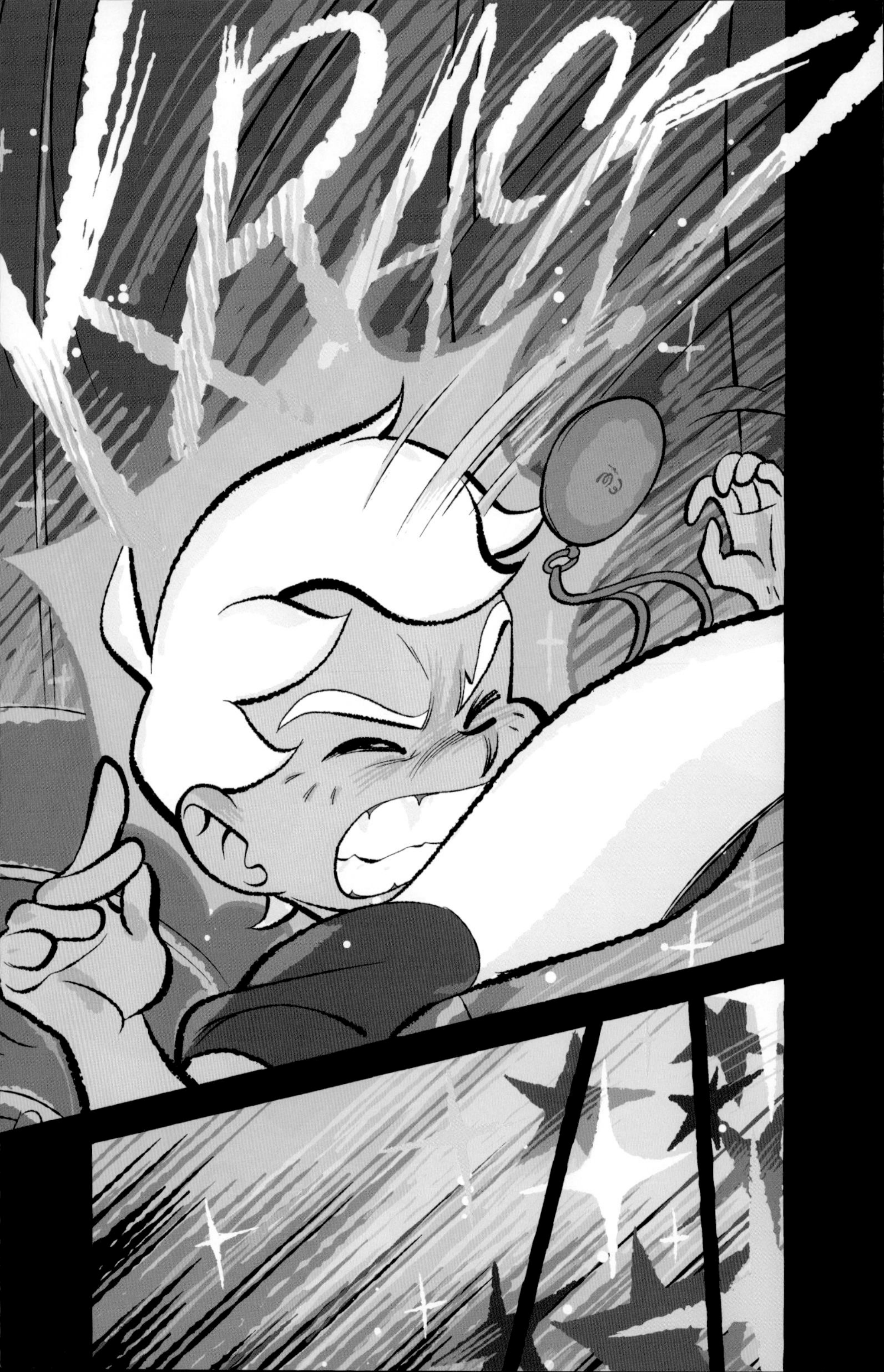
WHACK

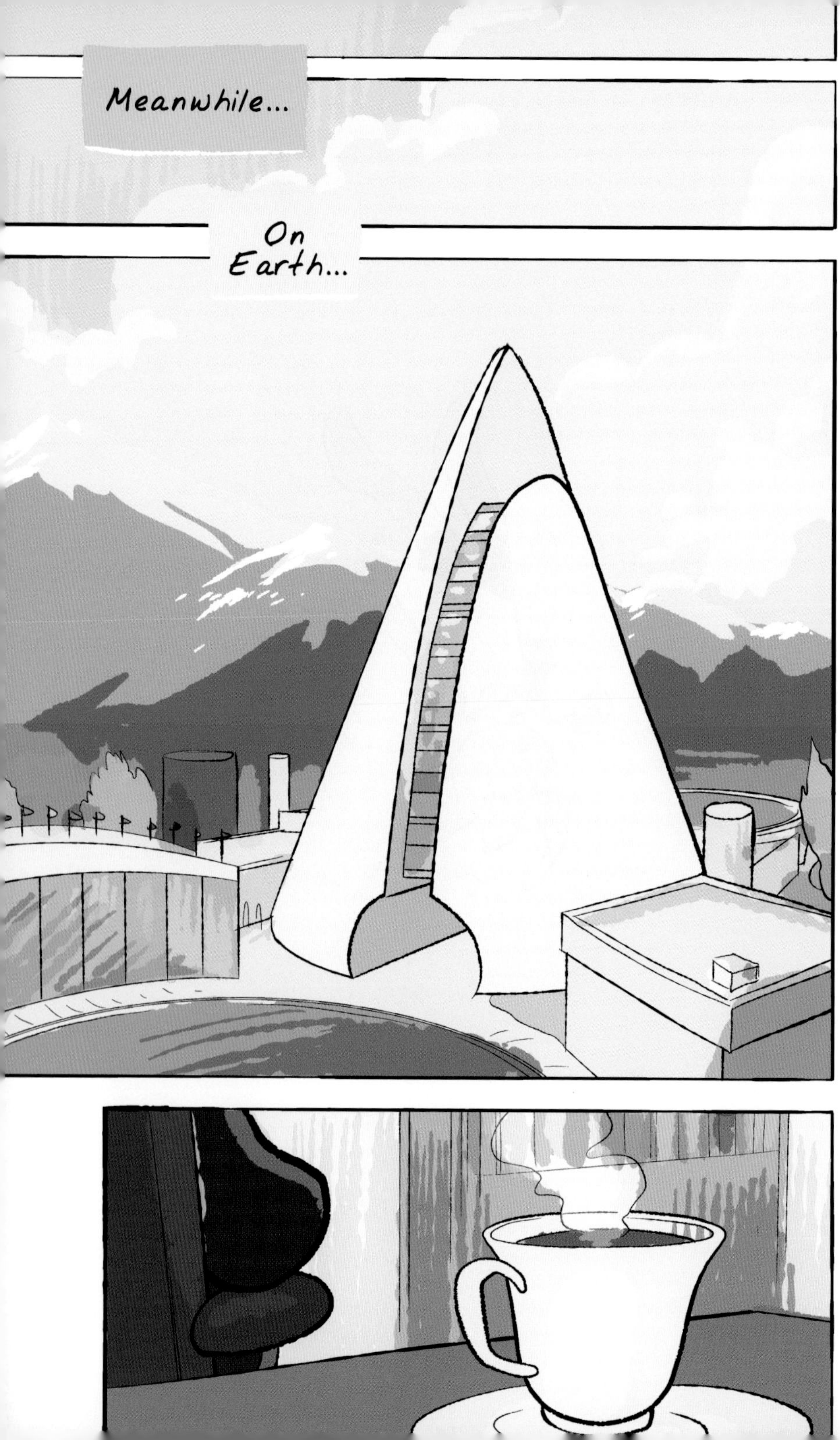
Meanwhile...
On Earth...

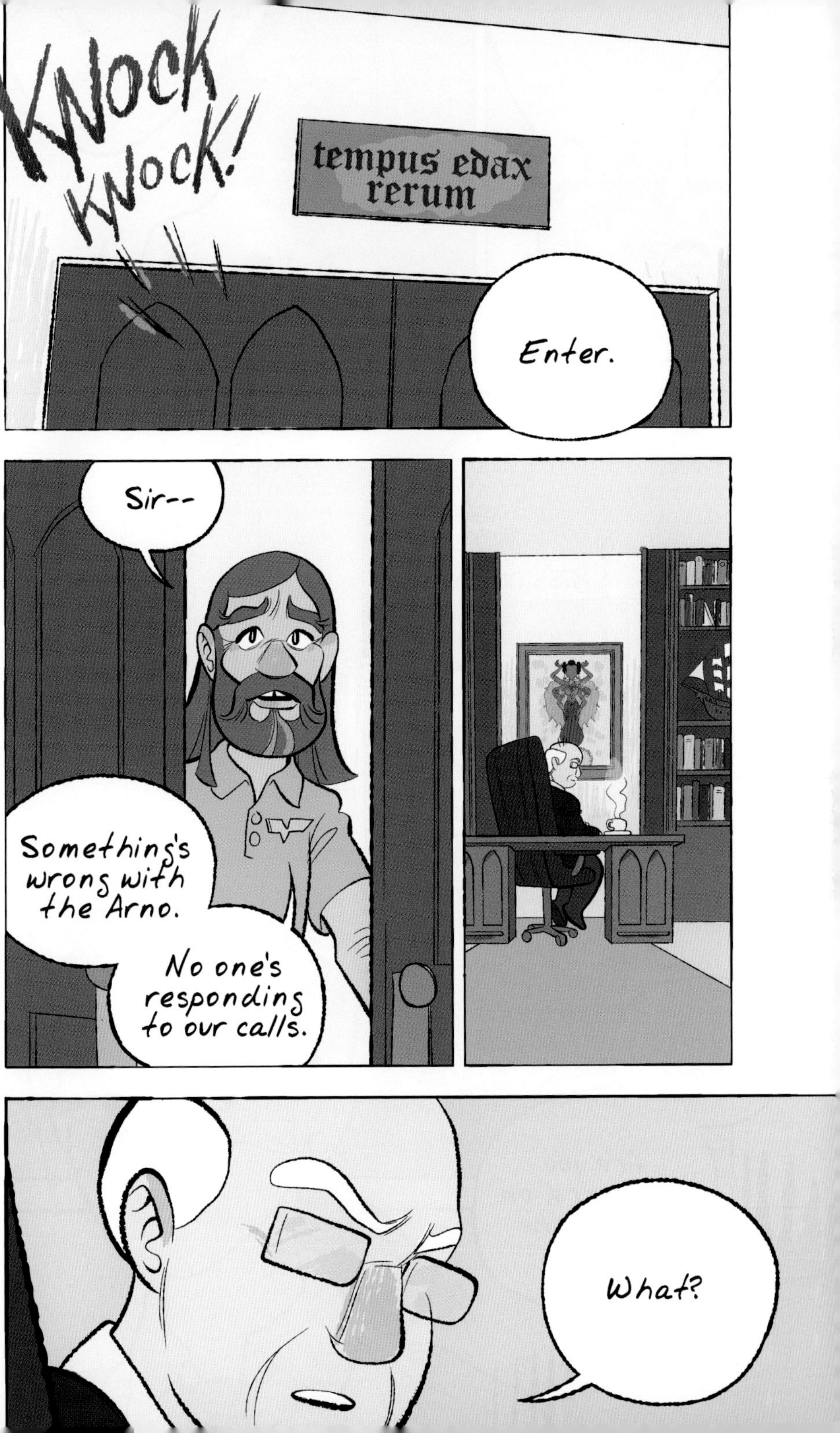
KNOCK KNOCK!
tempus edax rerum
Enter.
Sir--
Something's wrong with the Arno.
No one's responding to our calls.
What?

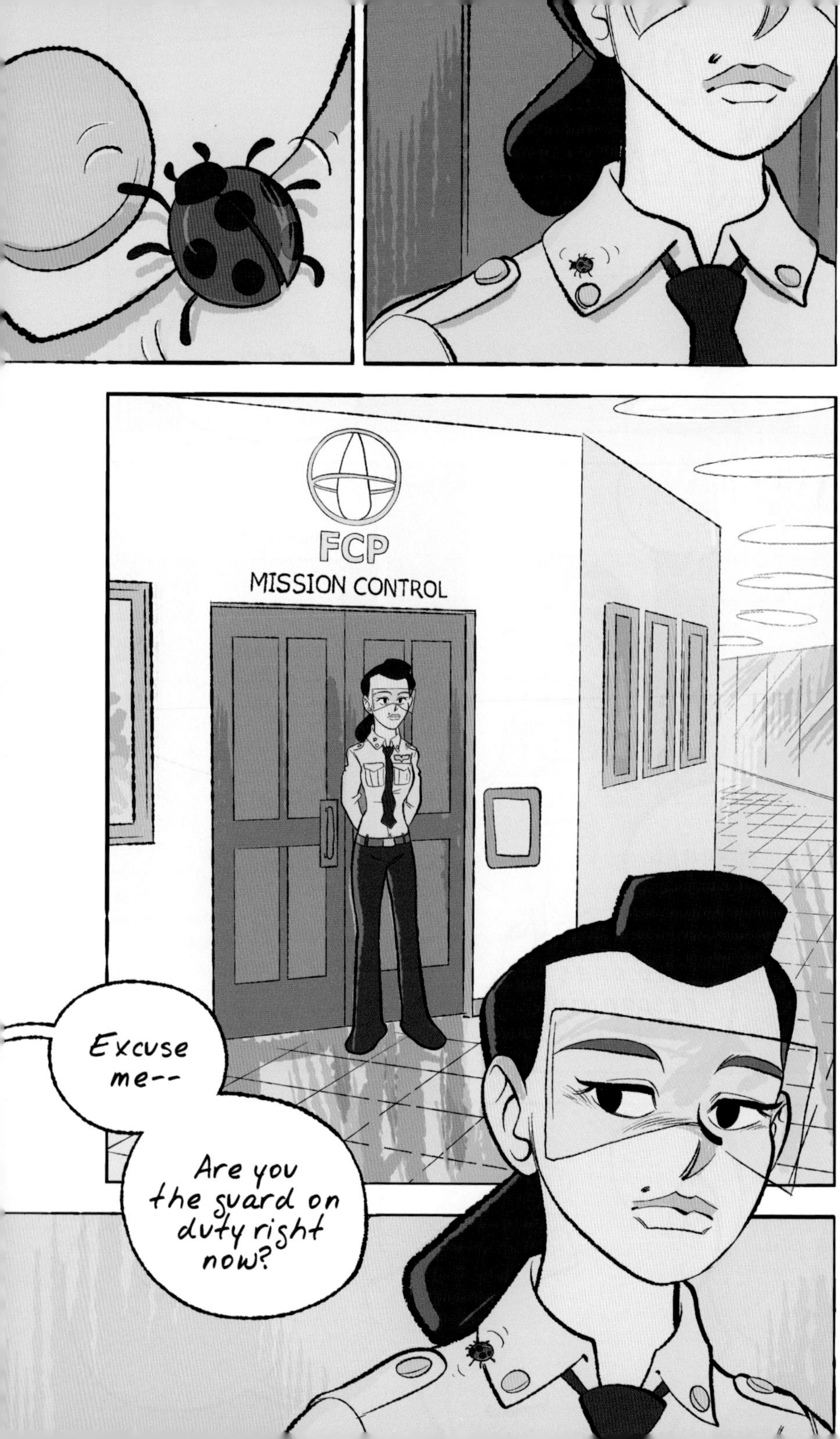
FCP
MISSION CONTROL
Excuse me--
Are you the guard on duty right now?

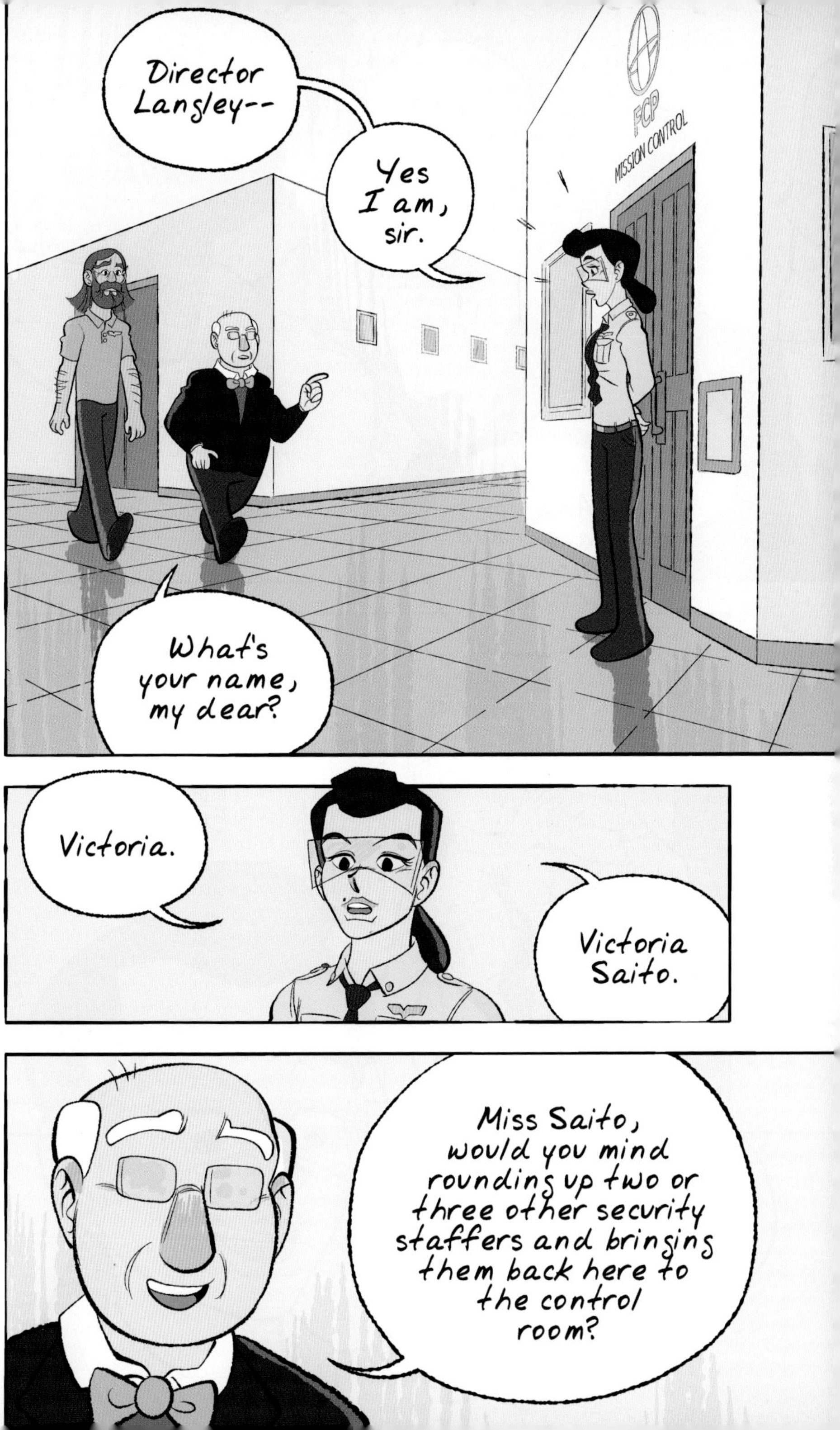
FCP
MISSION CONTROL
Director Langley--
Yes I am, sir.
What's your name, my dear?
Victoria.
Victoria Saito.
Miss Saito, would you mind rounding up two or three other security staffers and bringing them back here to the control room?

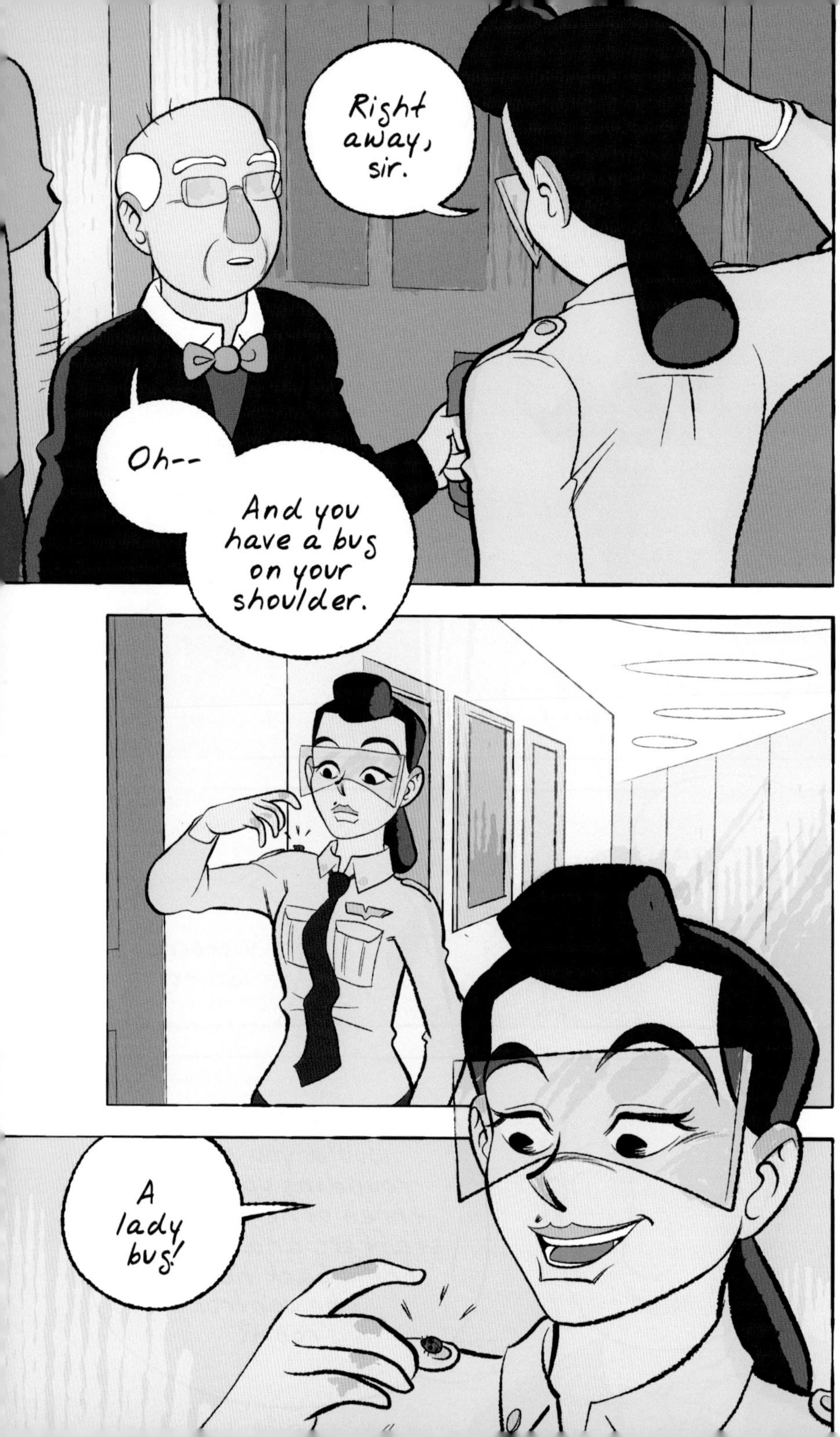
Right away, sir.
Oh--
And you have a bug on your shoulder.
A lady bug!

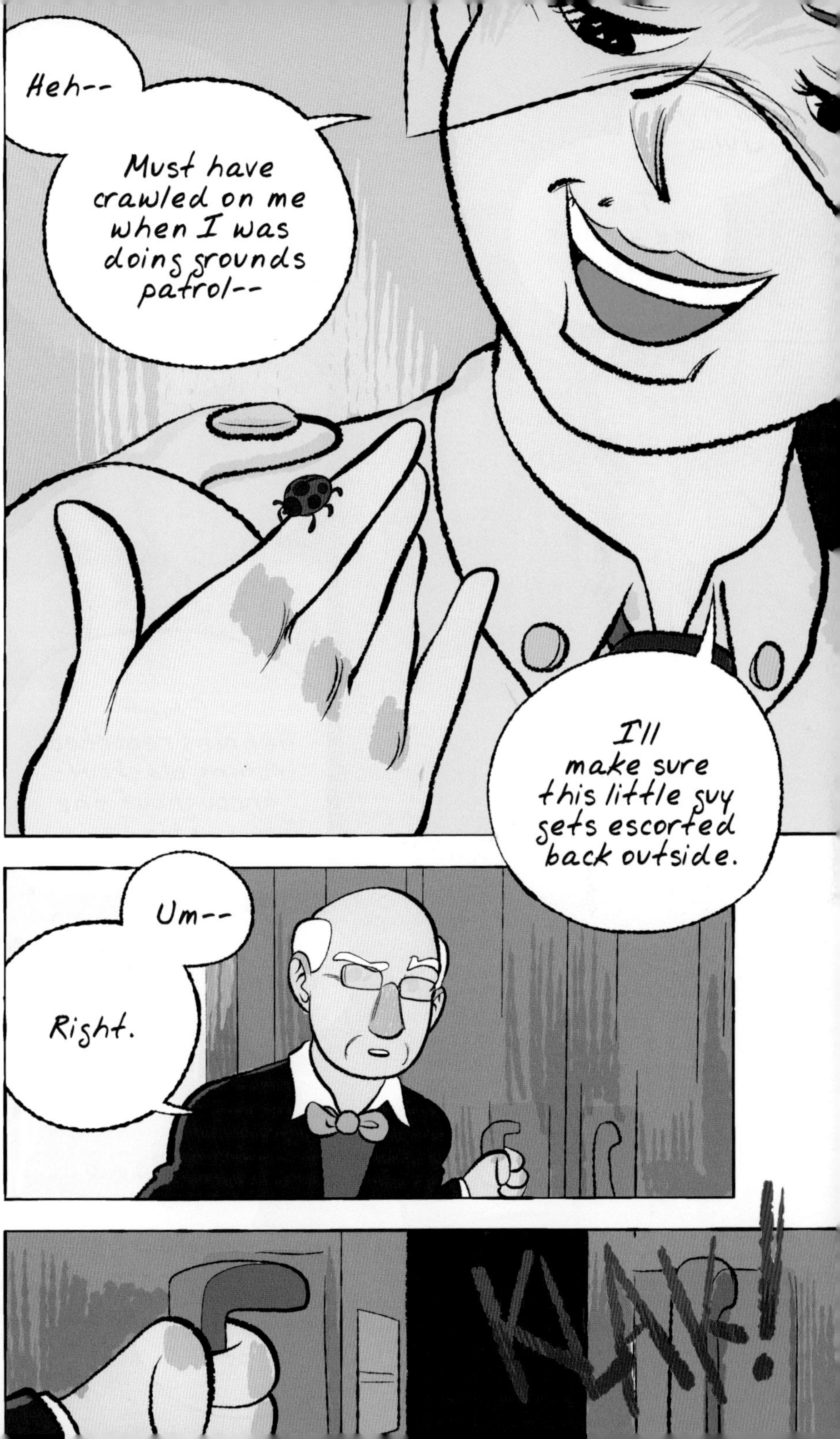
Heh--
Must have crawled on me when I was doing grounds patrol--
I'll make sure this little guy gets escorted back outside.
Um--
Right.
KLAK!

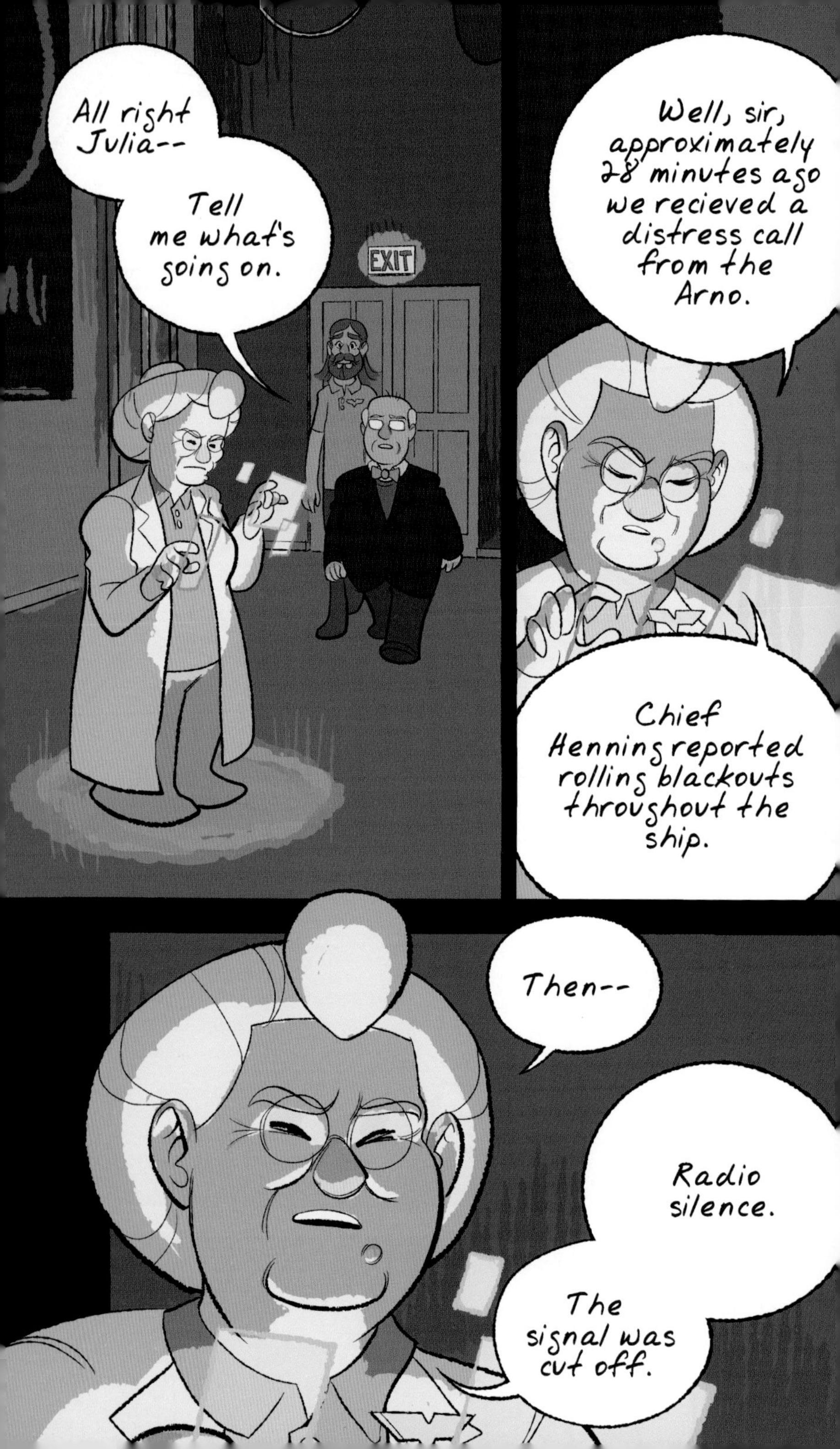

All right Julia--
Tell me what's going on.
EXIT
Well, sir, approximately 28 minutes ago we recieved a distress call from the Arno.
Chief Henning reported rolling blackouts throughout the ship.
Then--
Radio silence.
The signal was cut off.

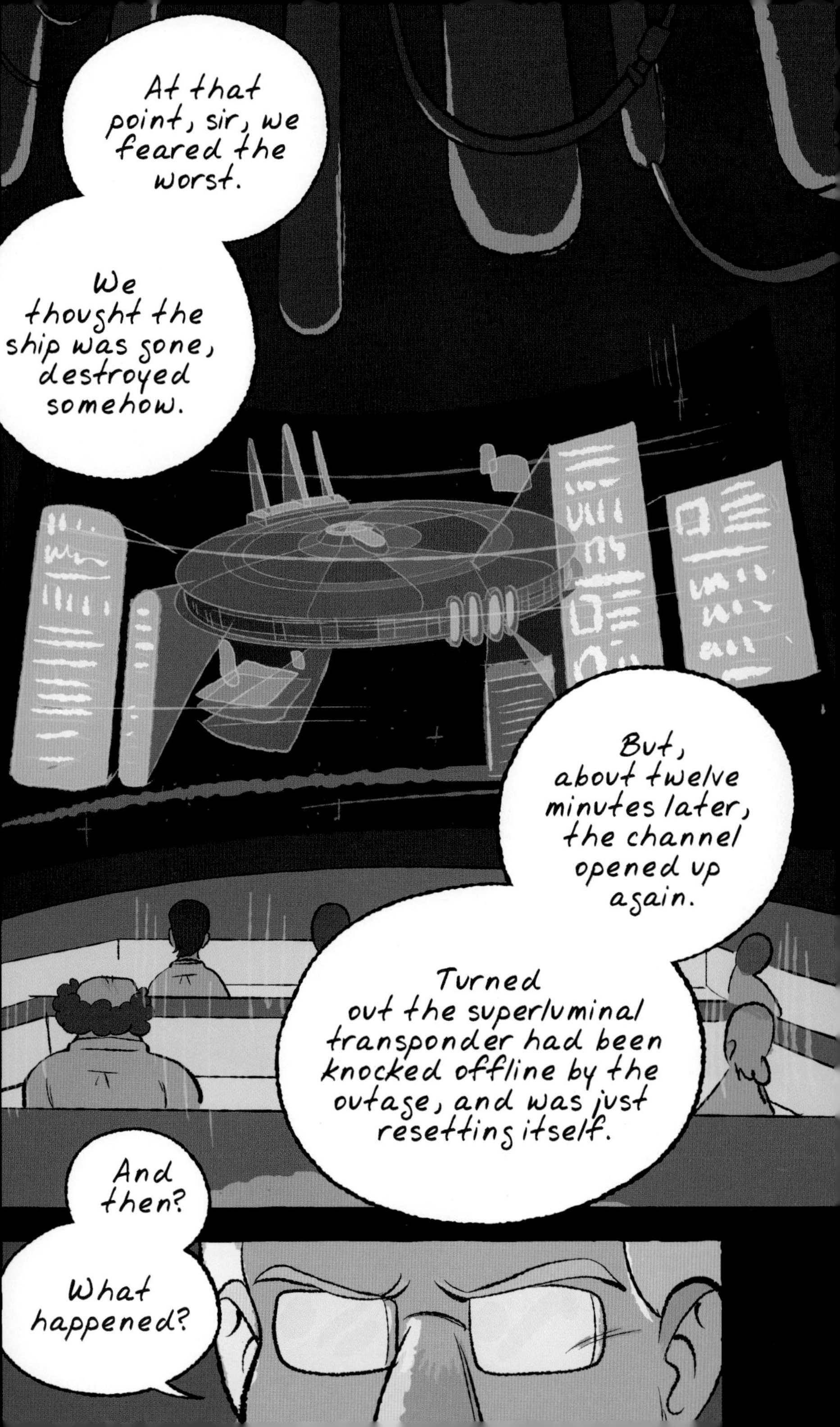
At that point, sir, we feared the worst.
We thought the ship was gone, destroyed somehow.
But, about twelve minutes later, the channel opened up again.
Turned out the superluminal transponder had been knocked offline by the outage, and was just resetting itself.
And then?
What happened?

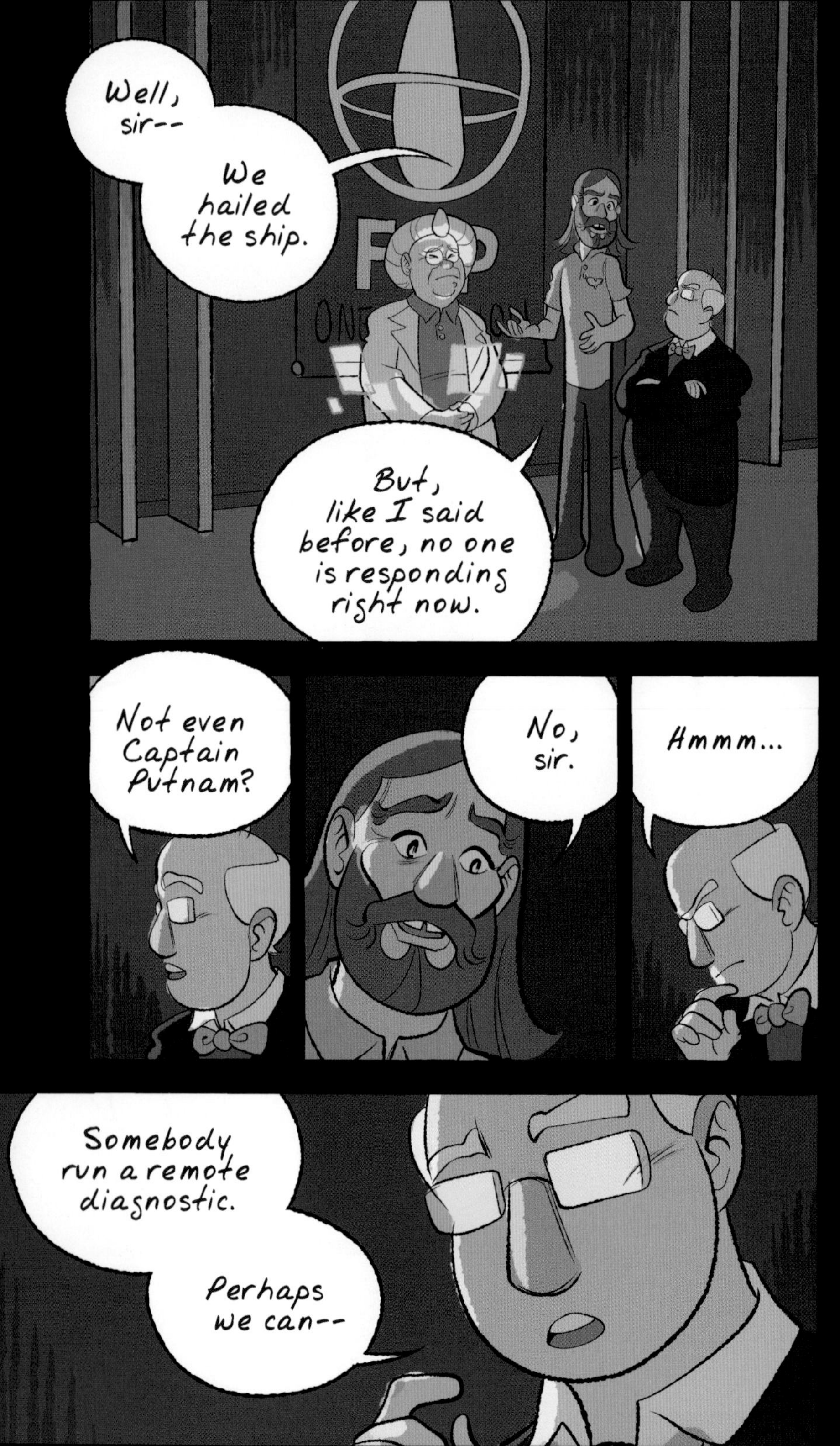
Well, sir--
We hailed the ship.
FEP
But, like I said before, no one is responding right now.
Not even Captain Putnam?
No, sir.
Hmmm...
Somebody run a remote diagnostic.
Perhaps we can--

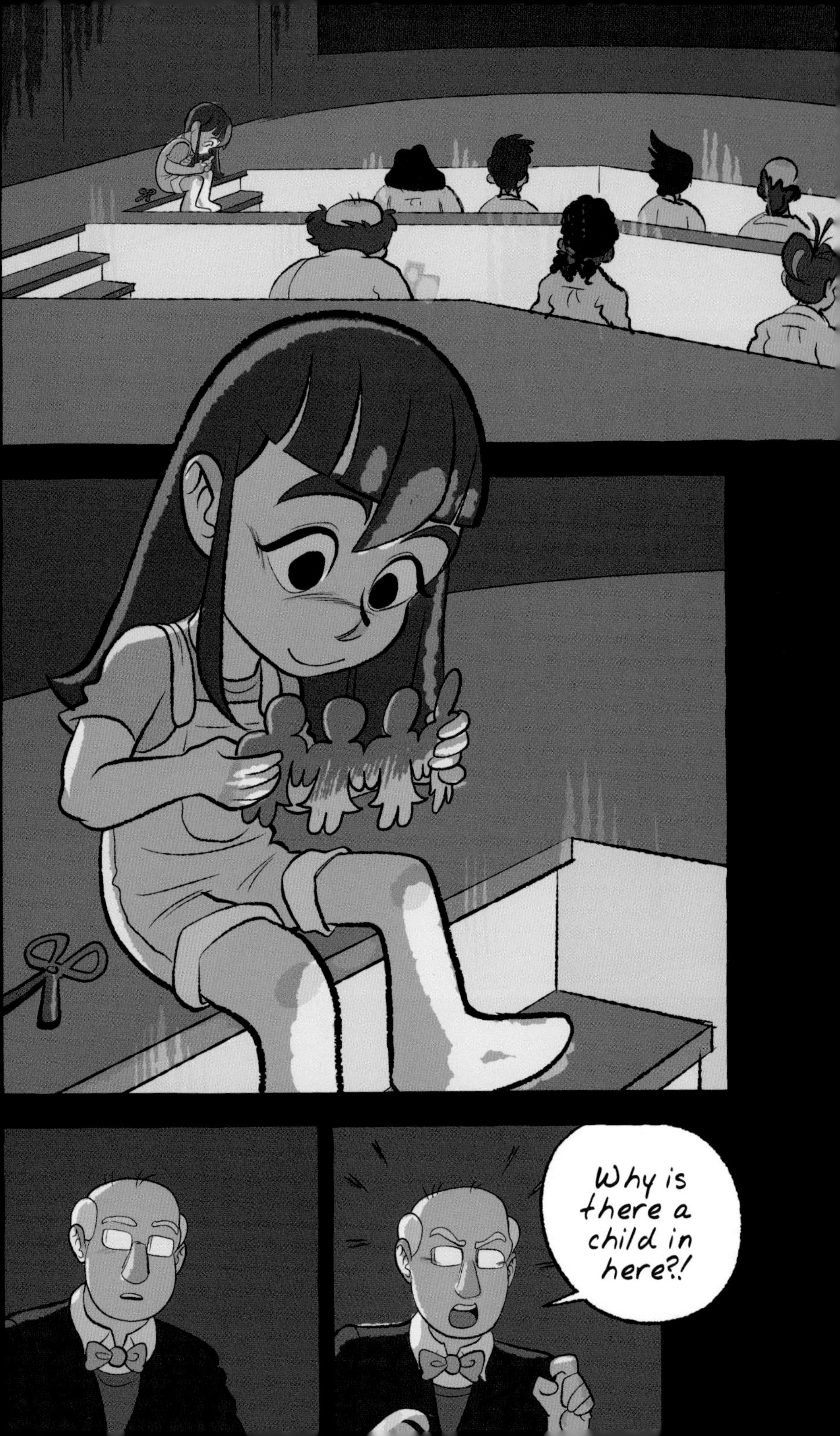
Why is there a child in here?!

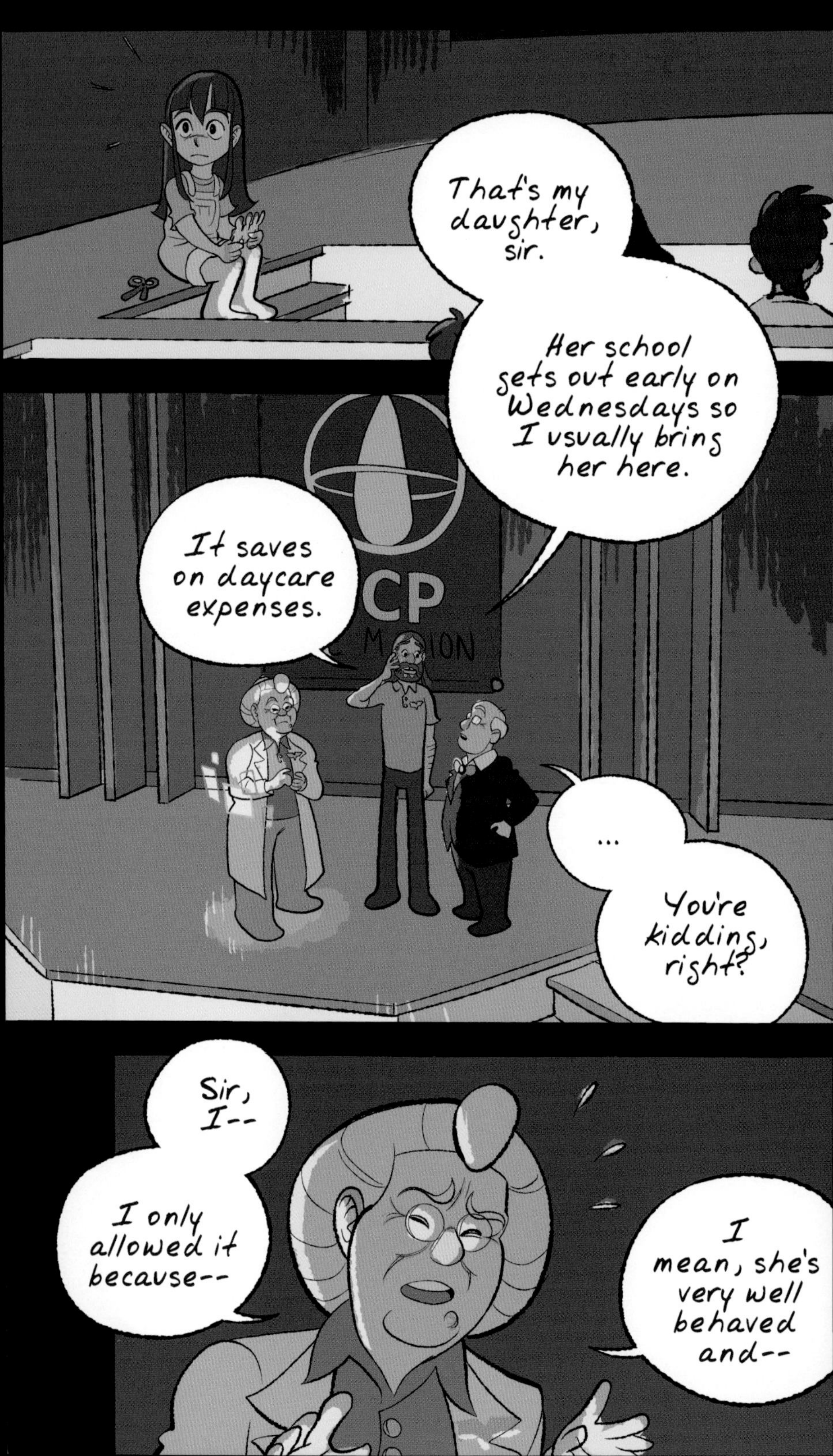

That's my daughter, sir.
Her school gets out early on Wednesdays so I usually bring her here.
It saves on daycare expenses.
CP
...
You're kidding, right?
Sir, I--
I only allowed it because--
I mean, she's very well behaved and--

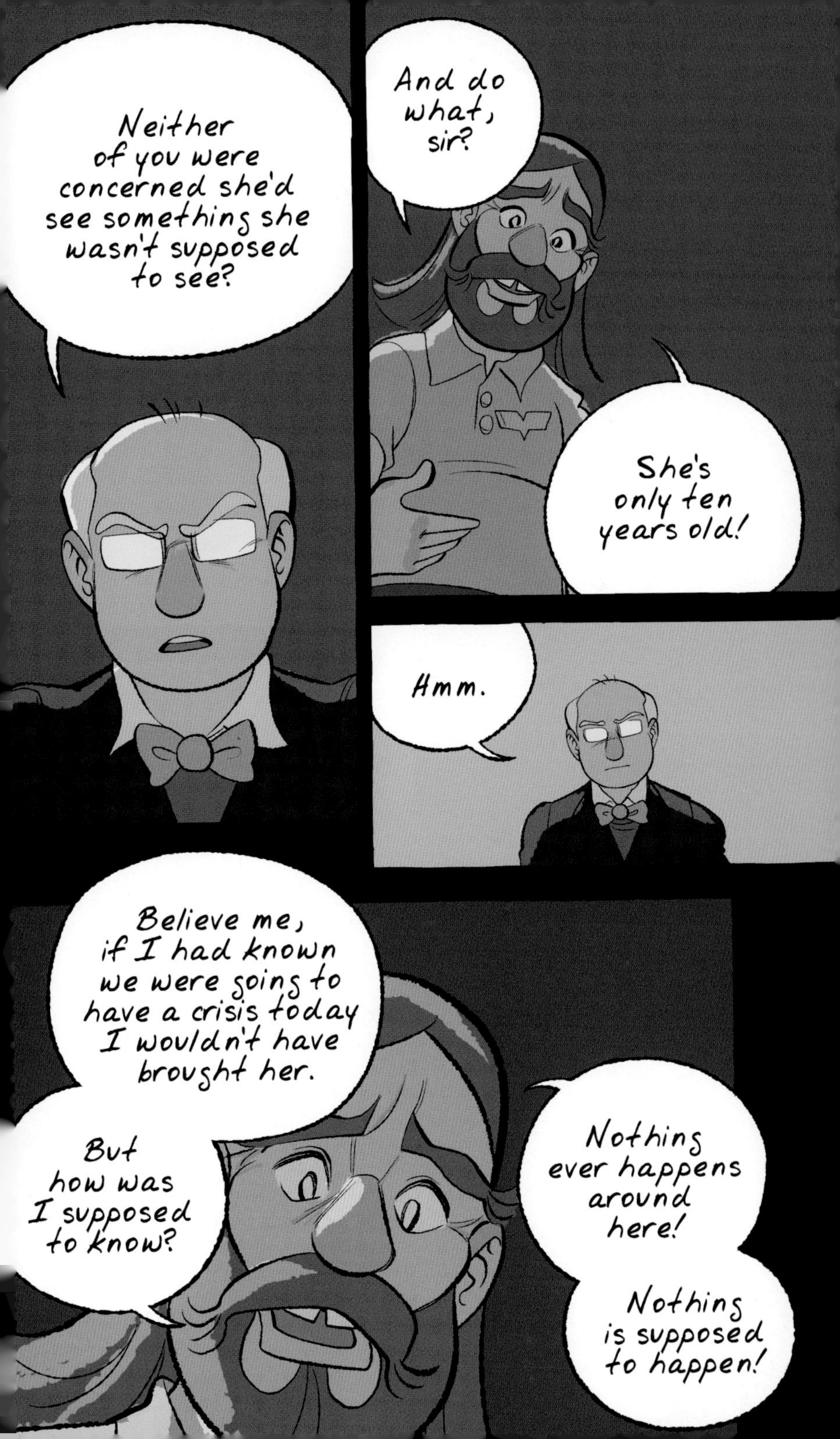
Neither of you were concerned she'd see something she wasn't supposed to see?
And do what, sir?
She's only ten years old!
Hmm.
Believe me, if I had known we were going to have a crisis today I wouldn't have brought her.
But how was I supposed to know?
Nothing ever happens around here!
Nothing is supposed to happen!

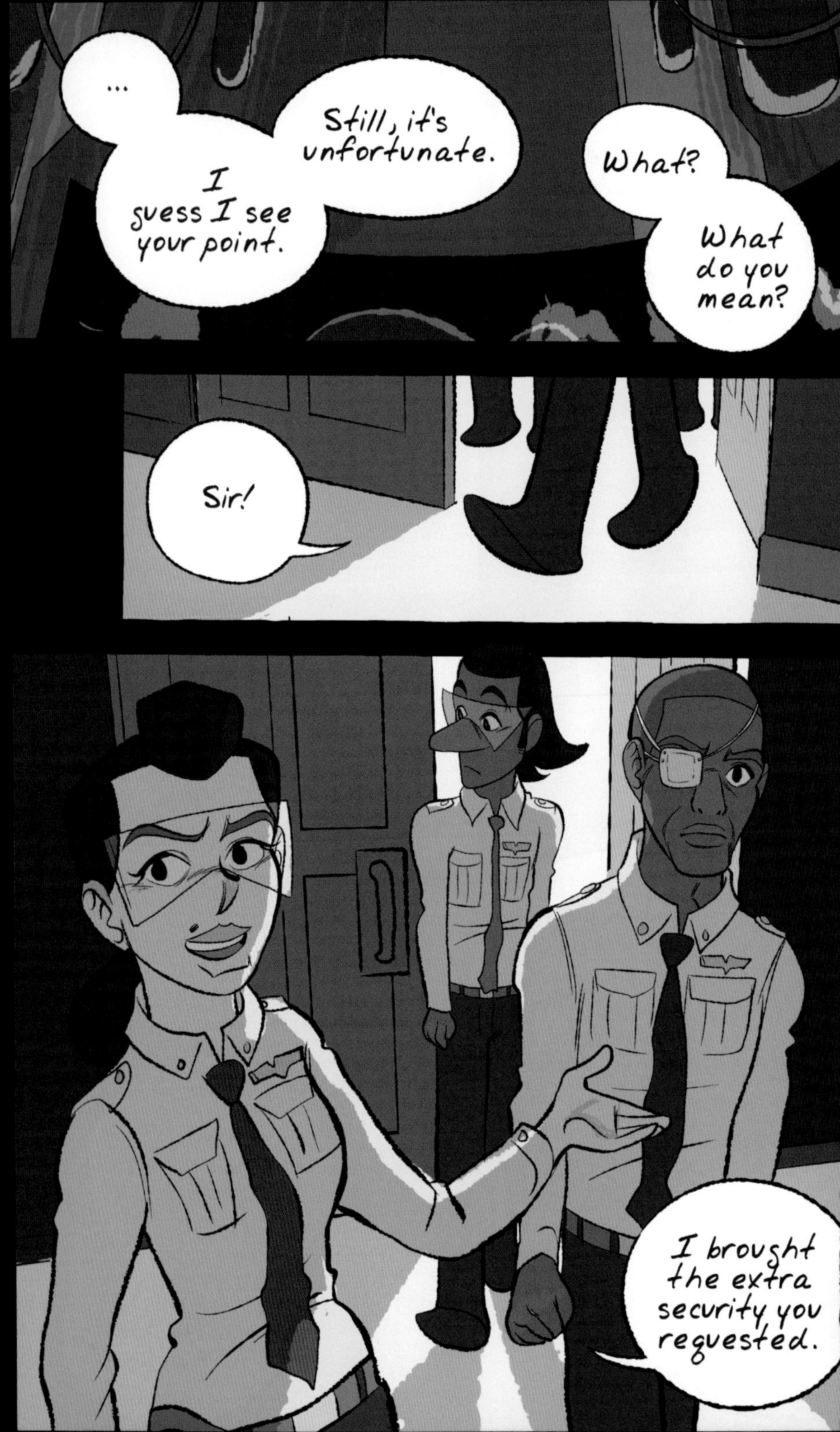
...
I guess I see your point.
Still, it's unfortunate.
What?
What do you mean?
Sir!
I brought the extra security you requested.

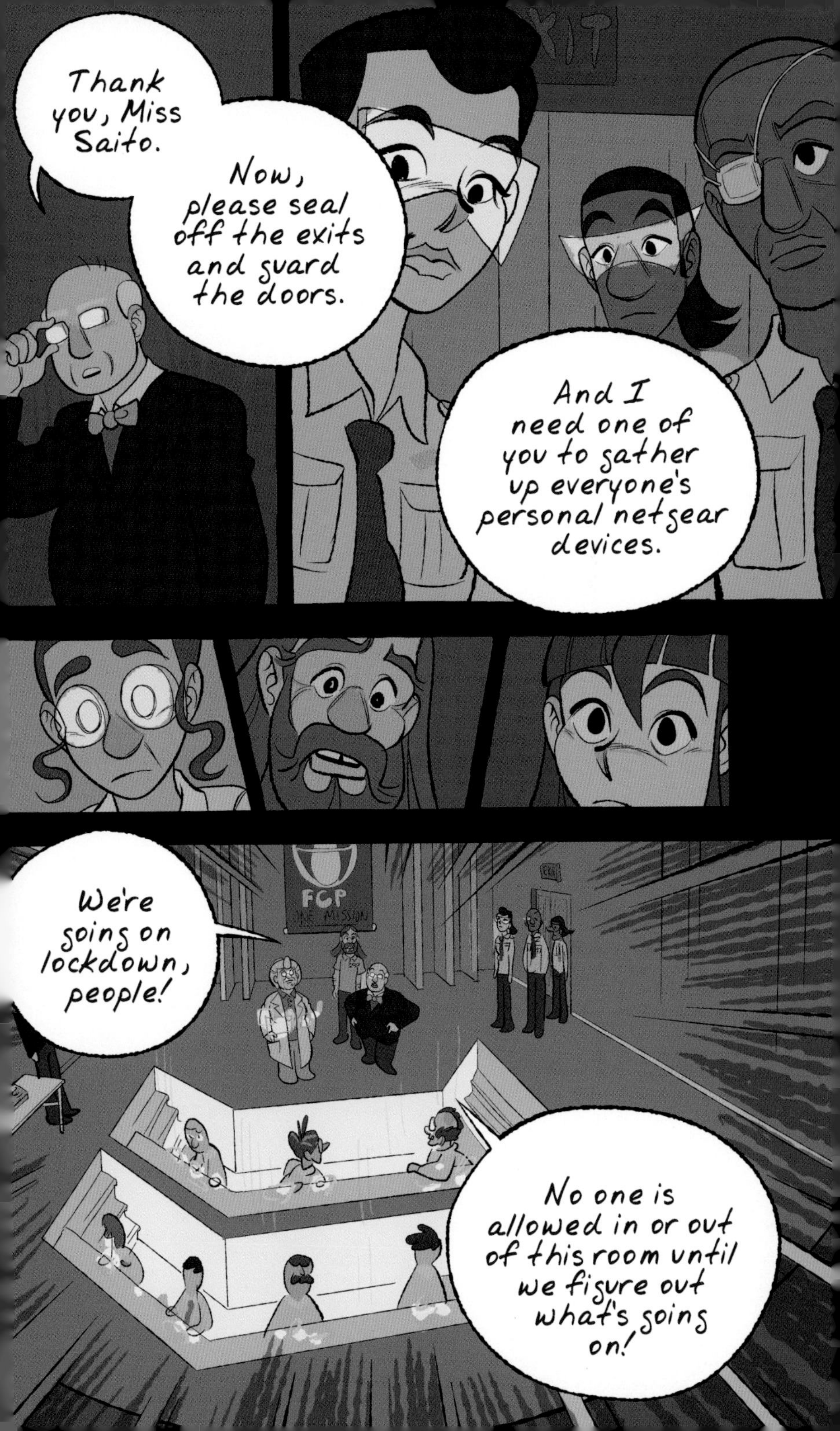

Thank you, Miss Saito.
Now, please seal off the exits and guard the doors.
EXIT
And I need one of you to gather up everyone's personal netgear devices.
We're going on lockdown, people!
FGP
THE MISSION
EXIT
No one is allowed in or out of this room until we figure out what's going on!

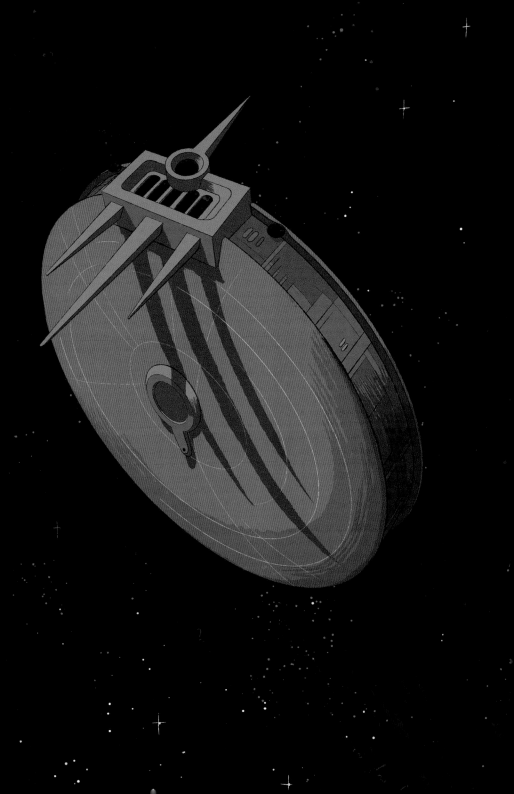

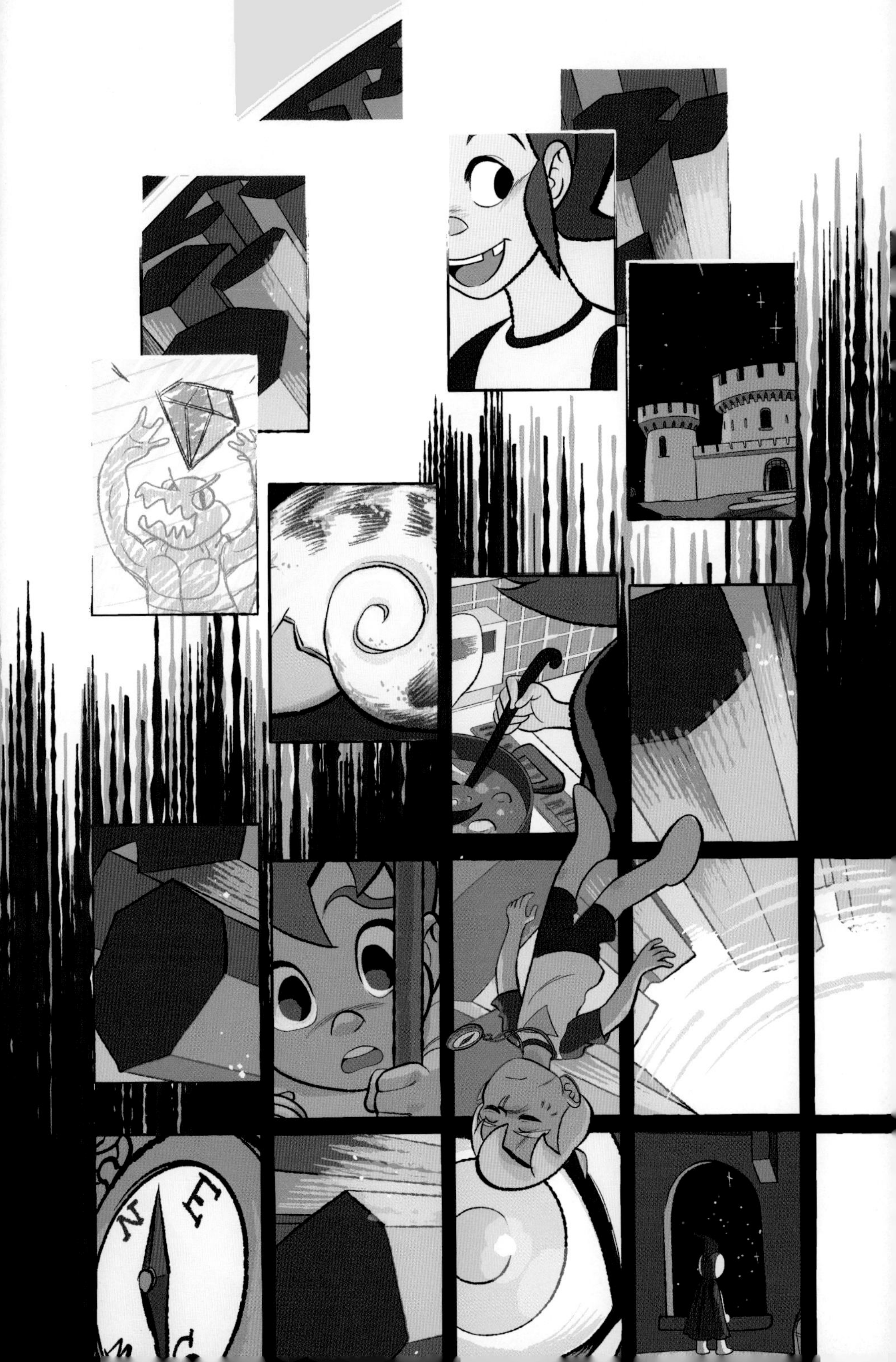
N
E

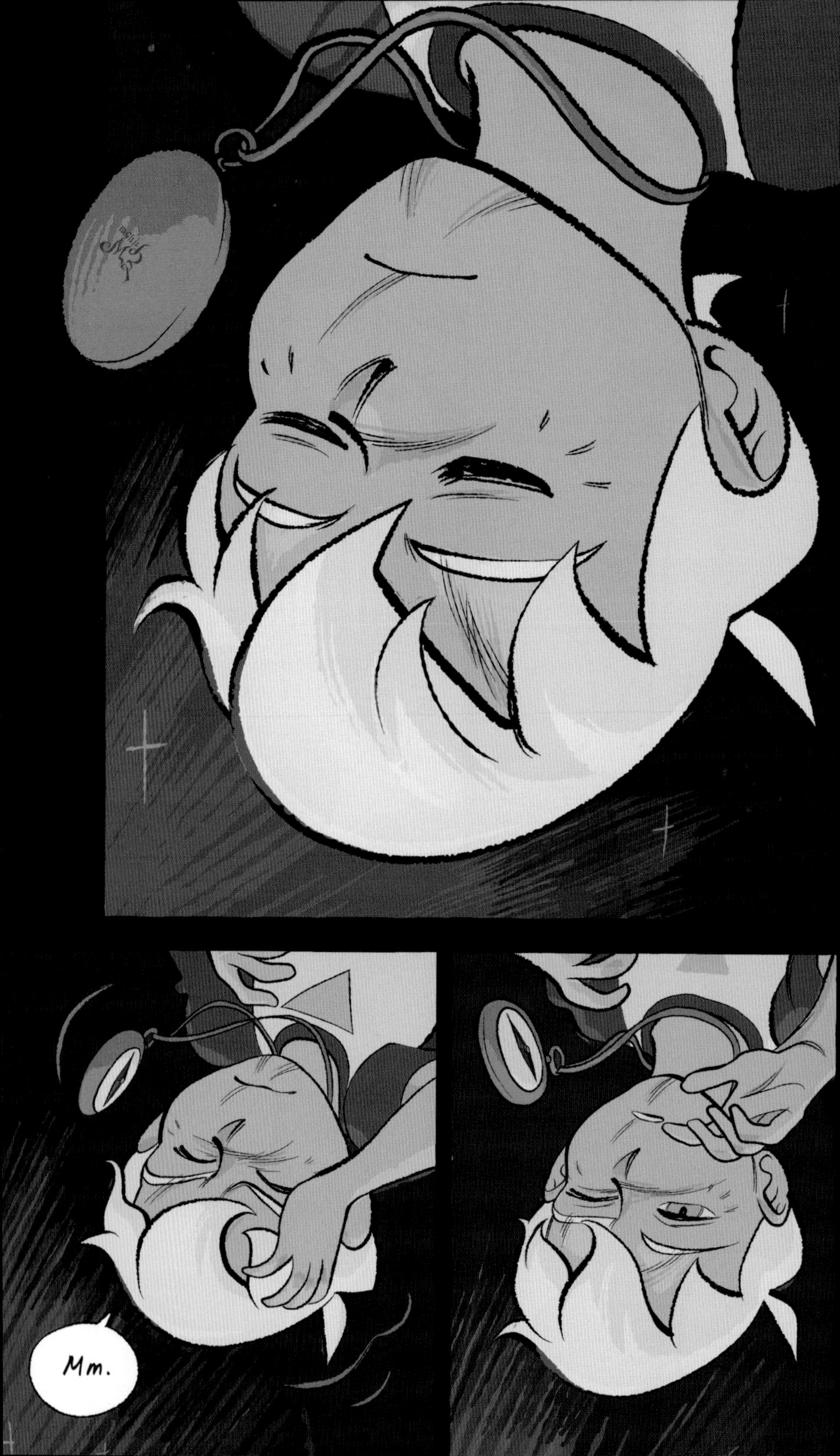
Mm.

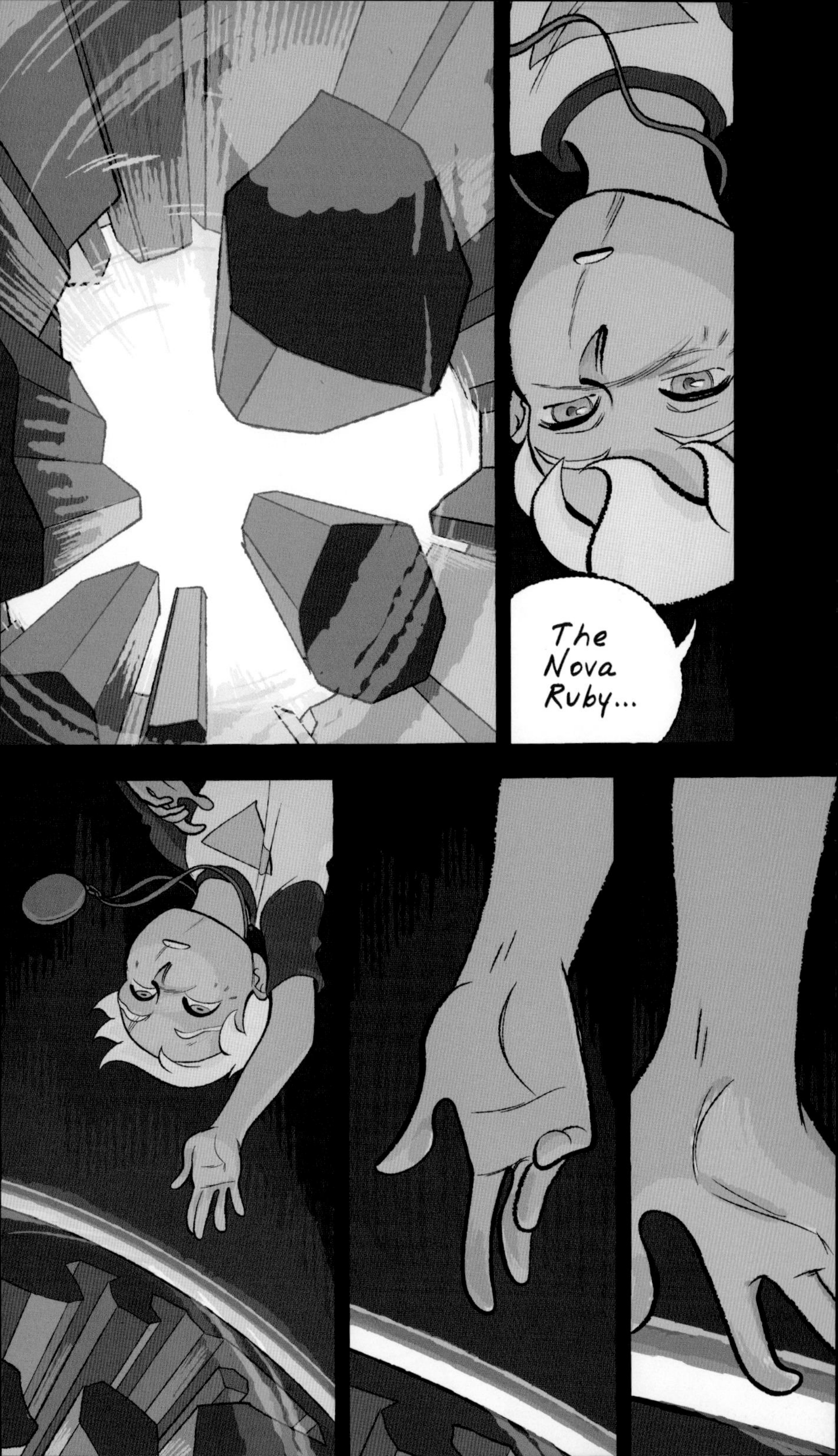
The Nova Ruby...

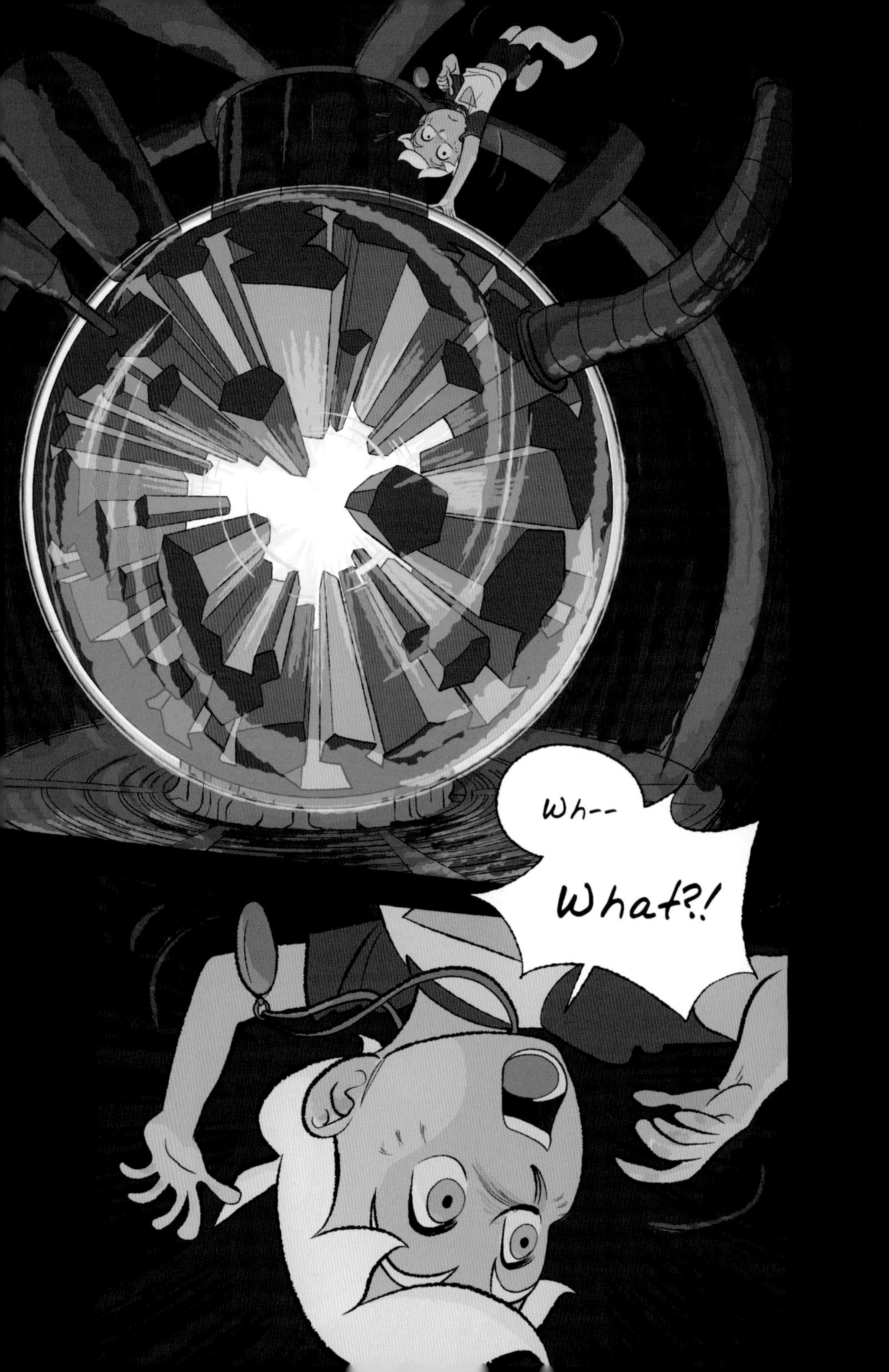
Wh--
What?!

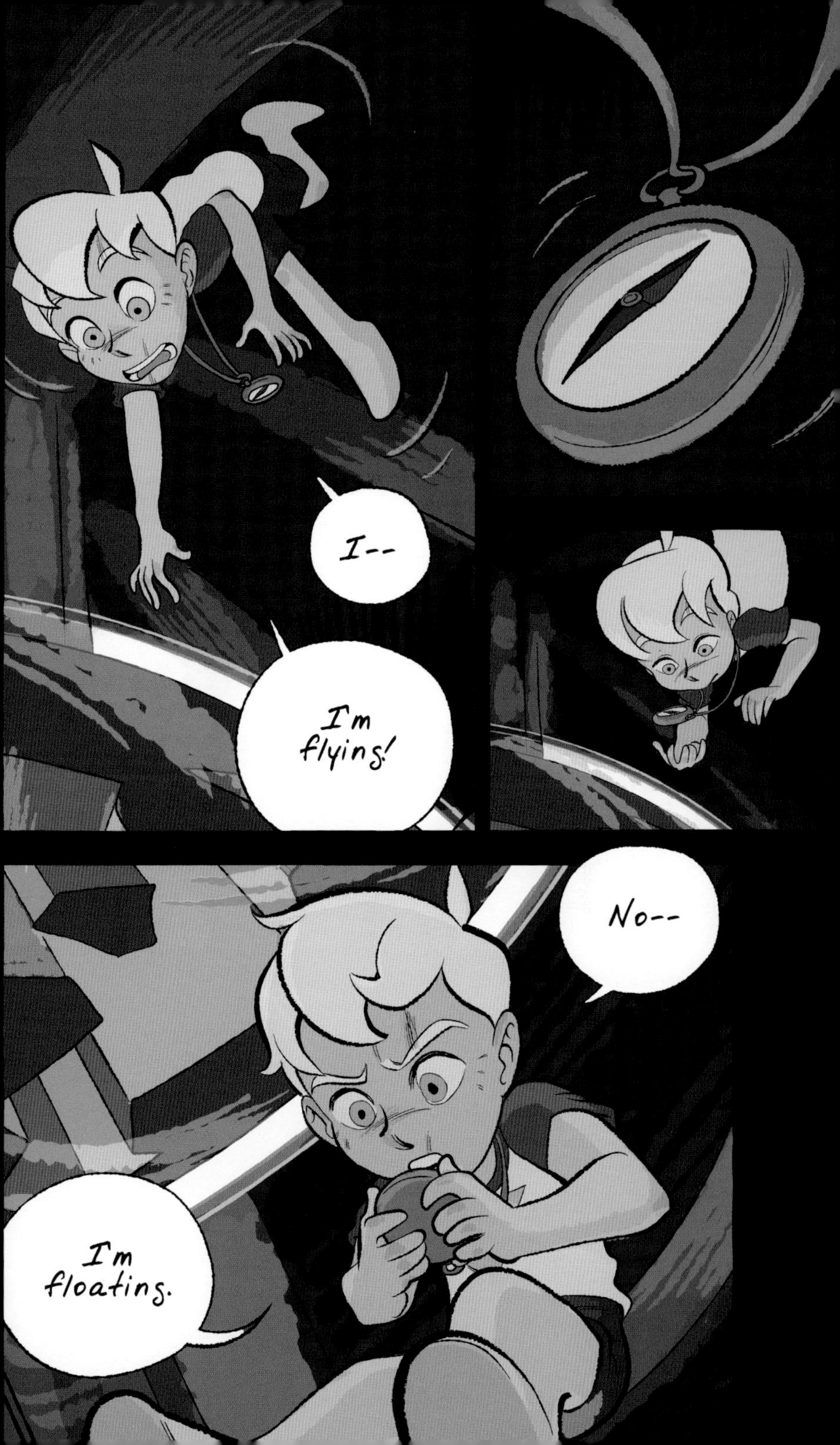
I--
I'm flying!
No--
I'm floating.

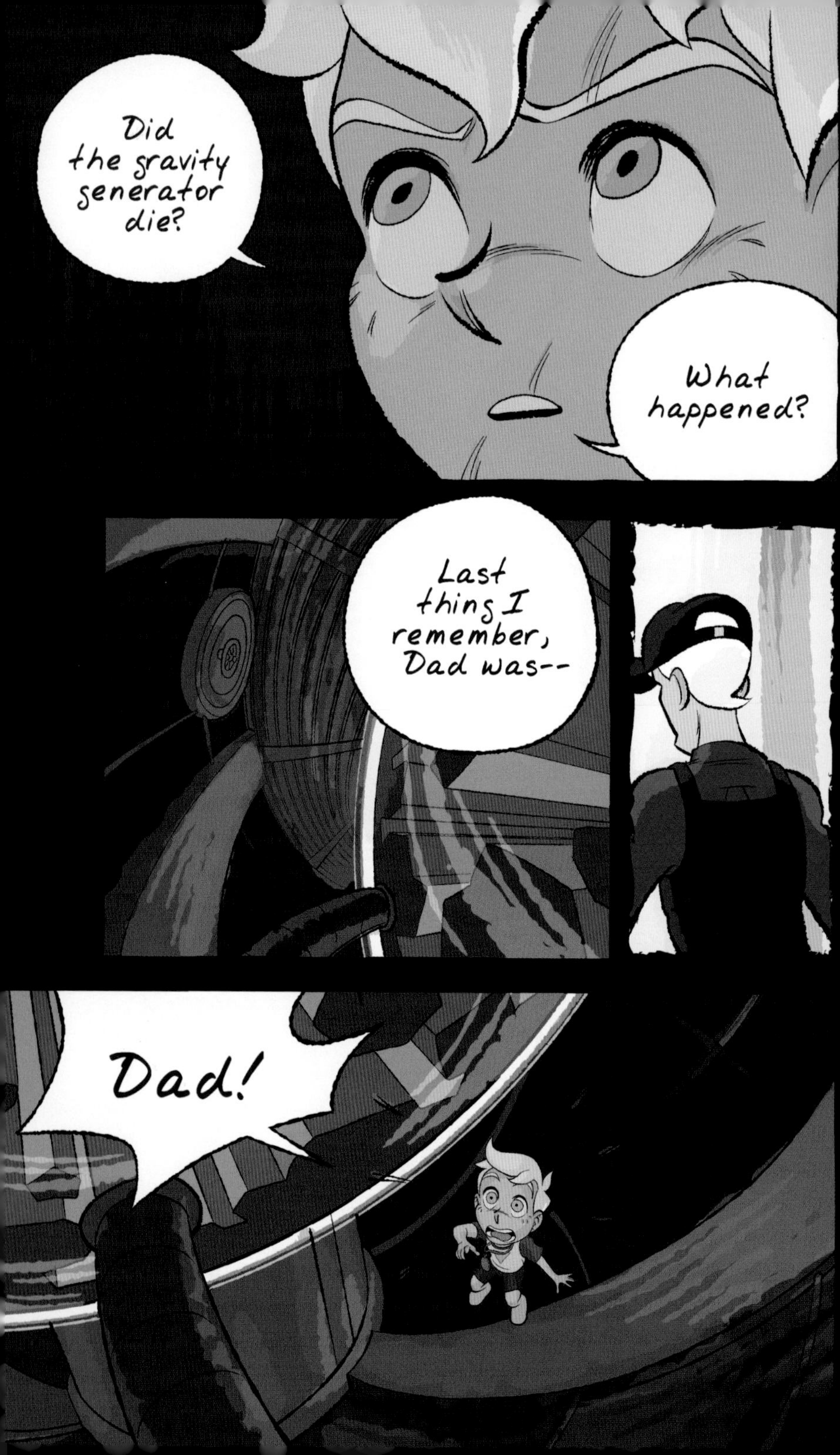
Did the gravity generator die?
What happened?
Last thing I remember, Dad was--
Dad!

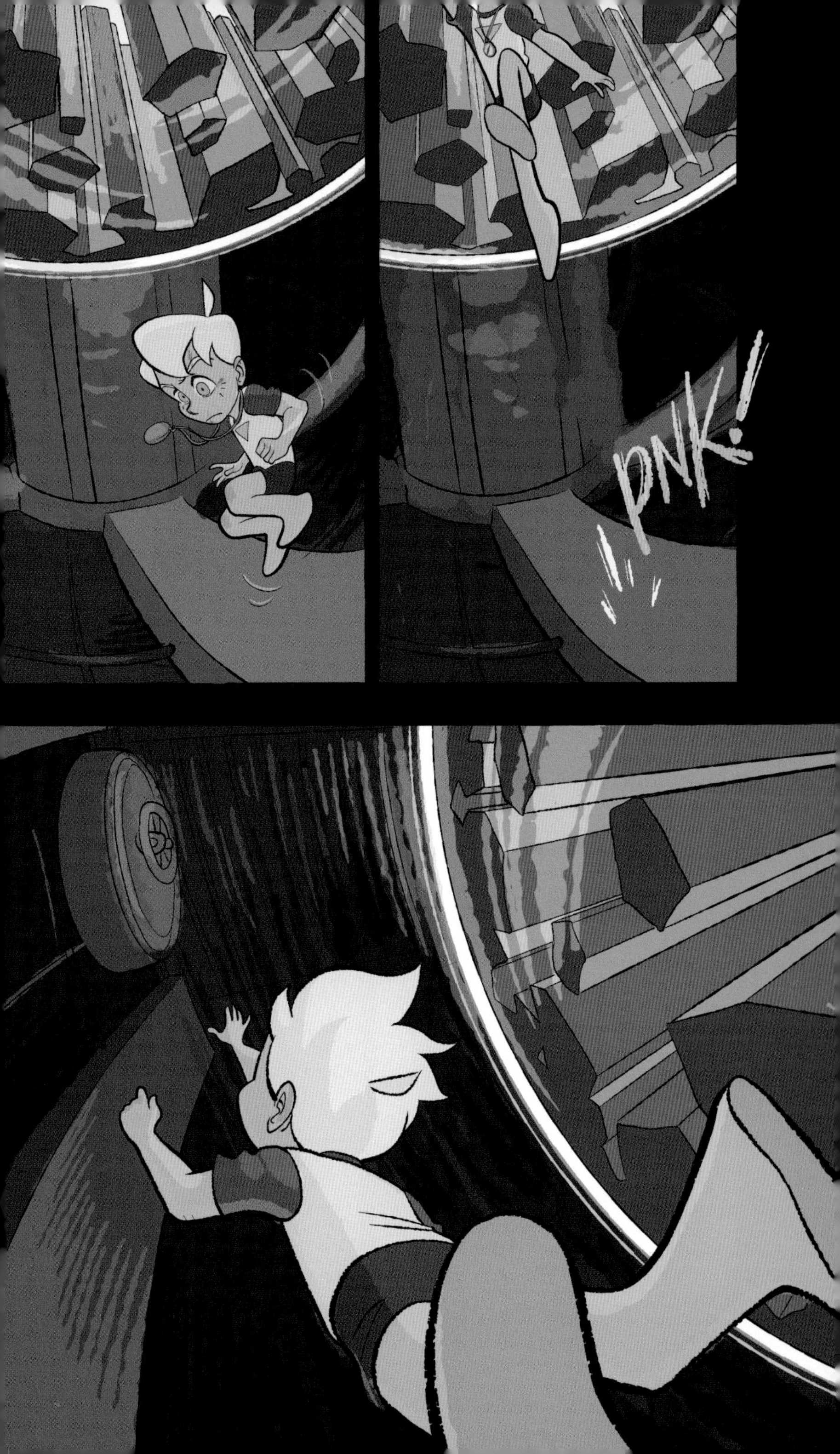
PNK!

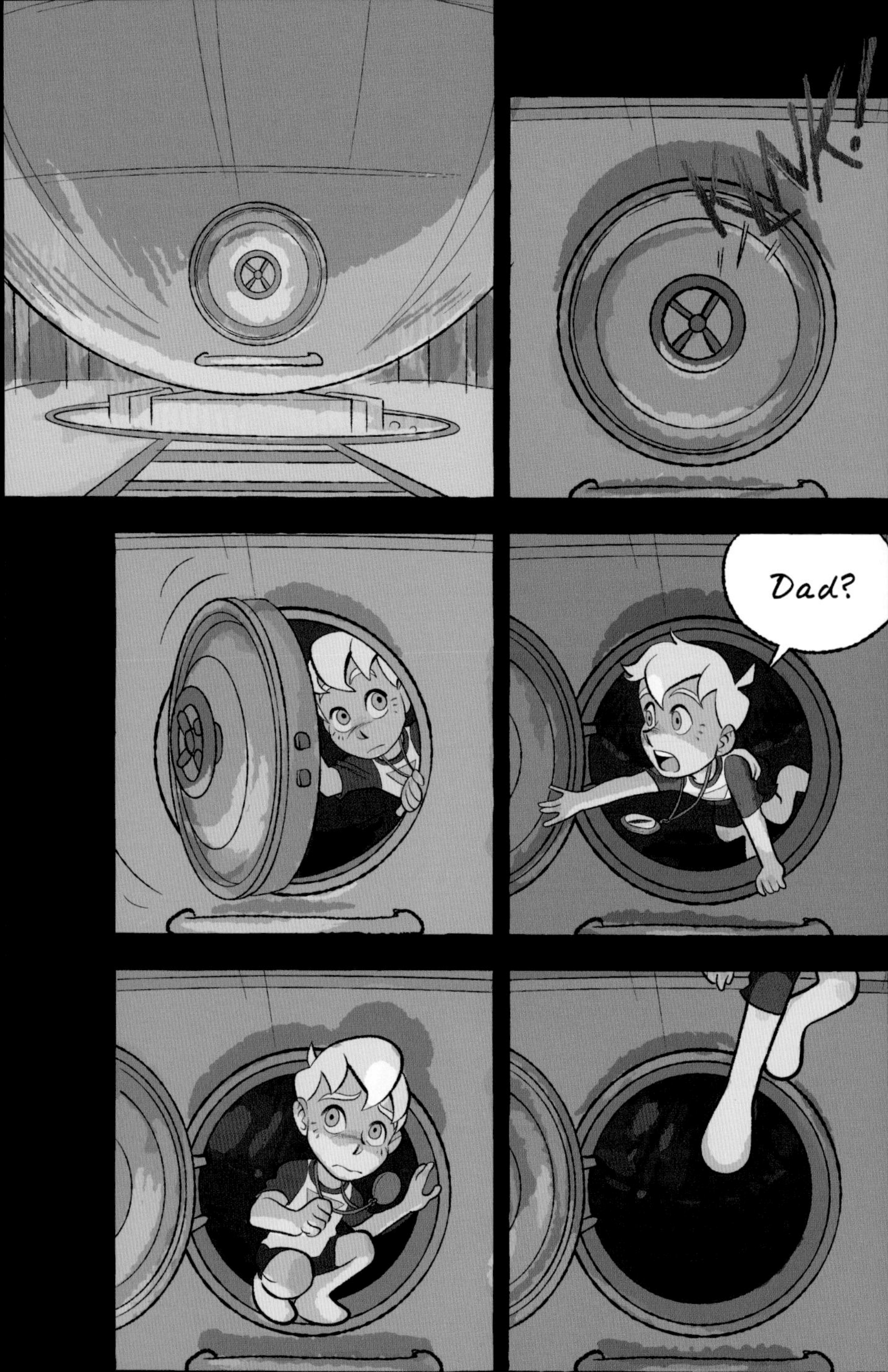
KLUNK!!
Dad?

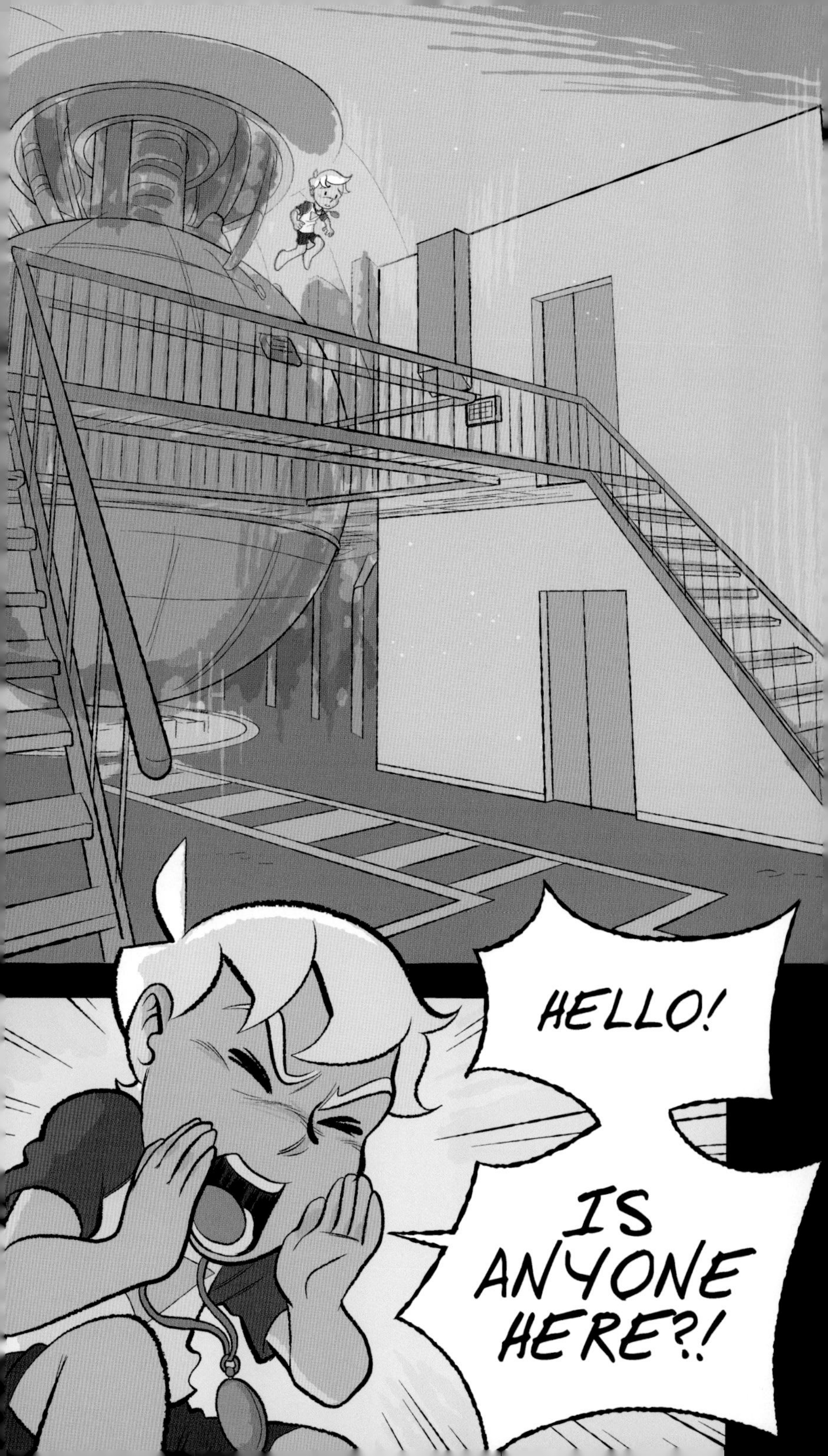
HELLO!
IS ANYONE HERE?!

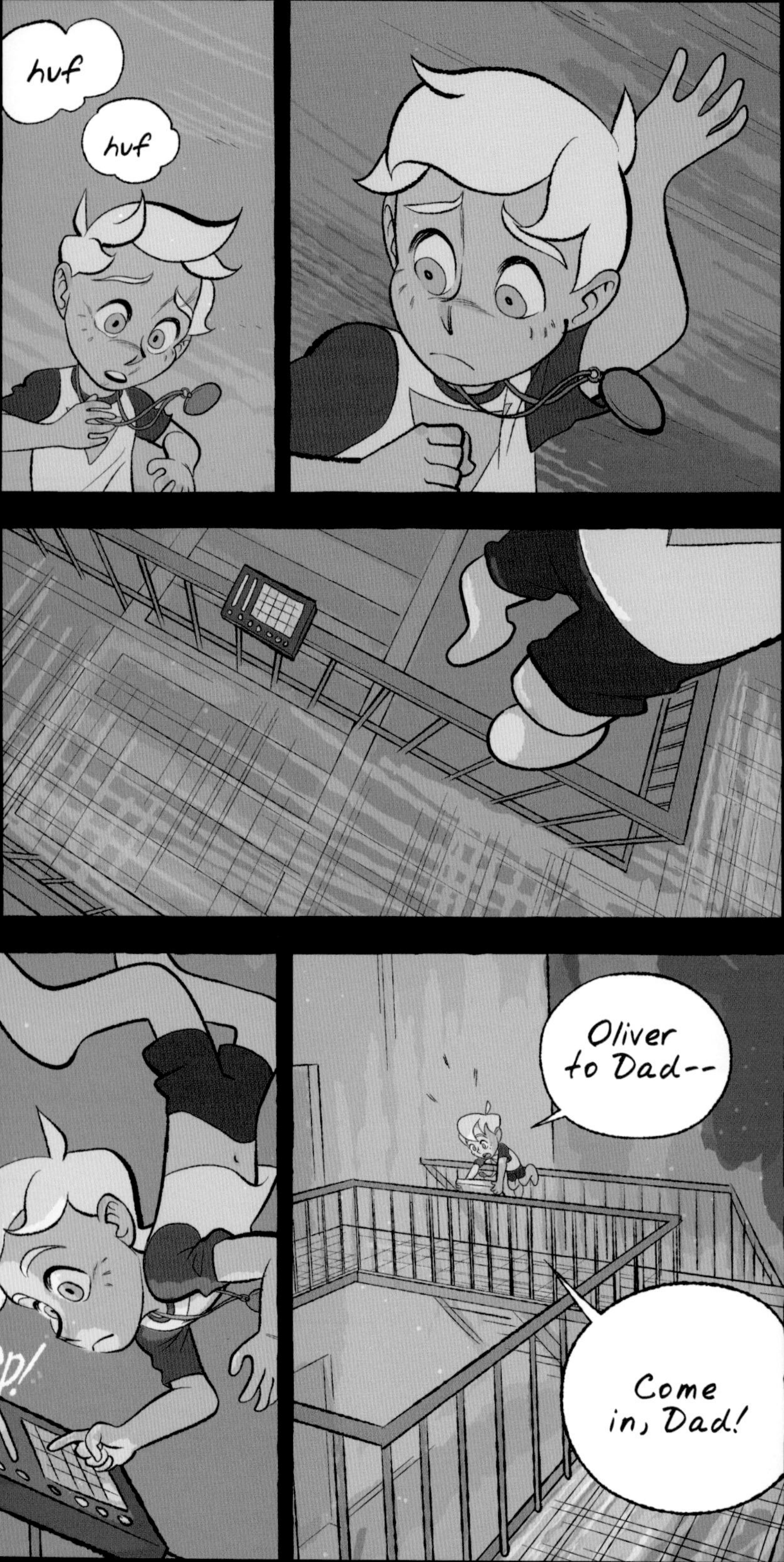
huf
huf
beep!
Oliver to Dad--
Come in, Dad!

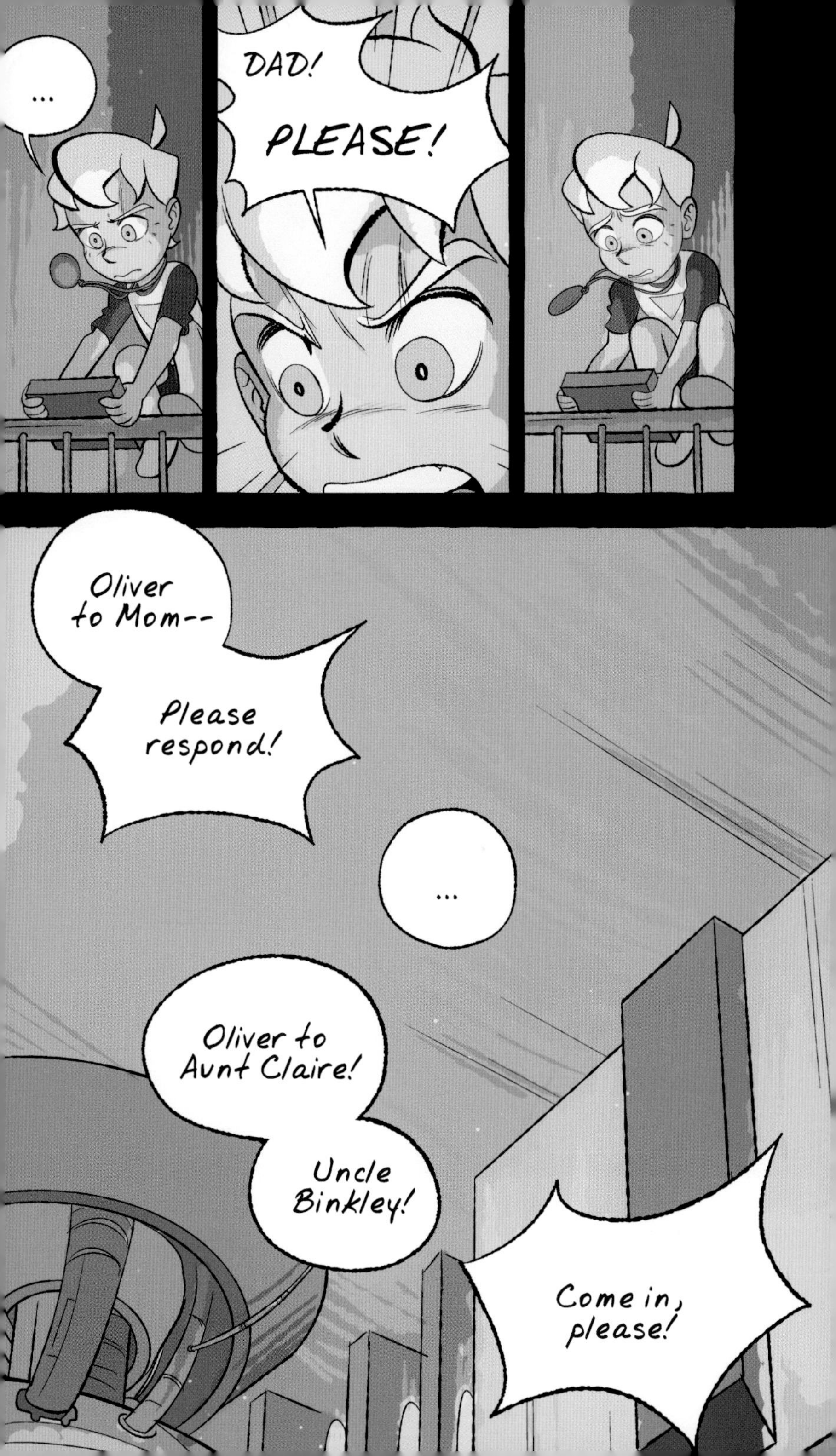
...
DAD!
PLEASE!
Oliver to Mom--
Please respond!
...
Oliver to Aunt Claire!
Uncle Binkley!
Come in, please!

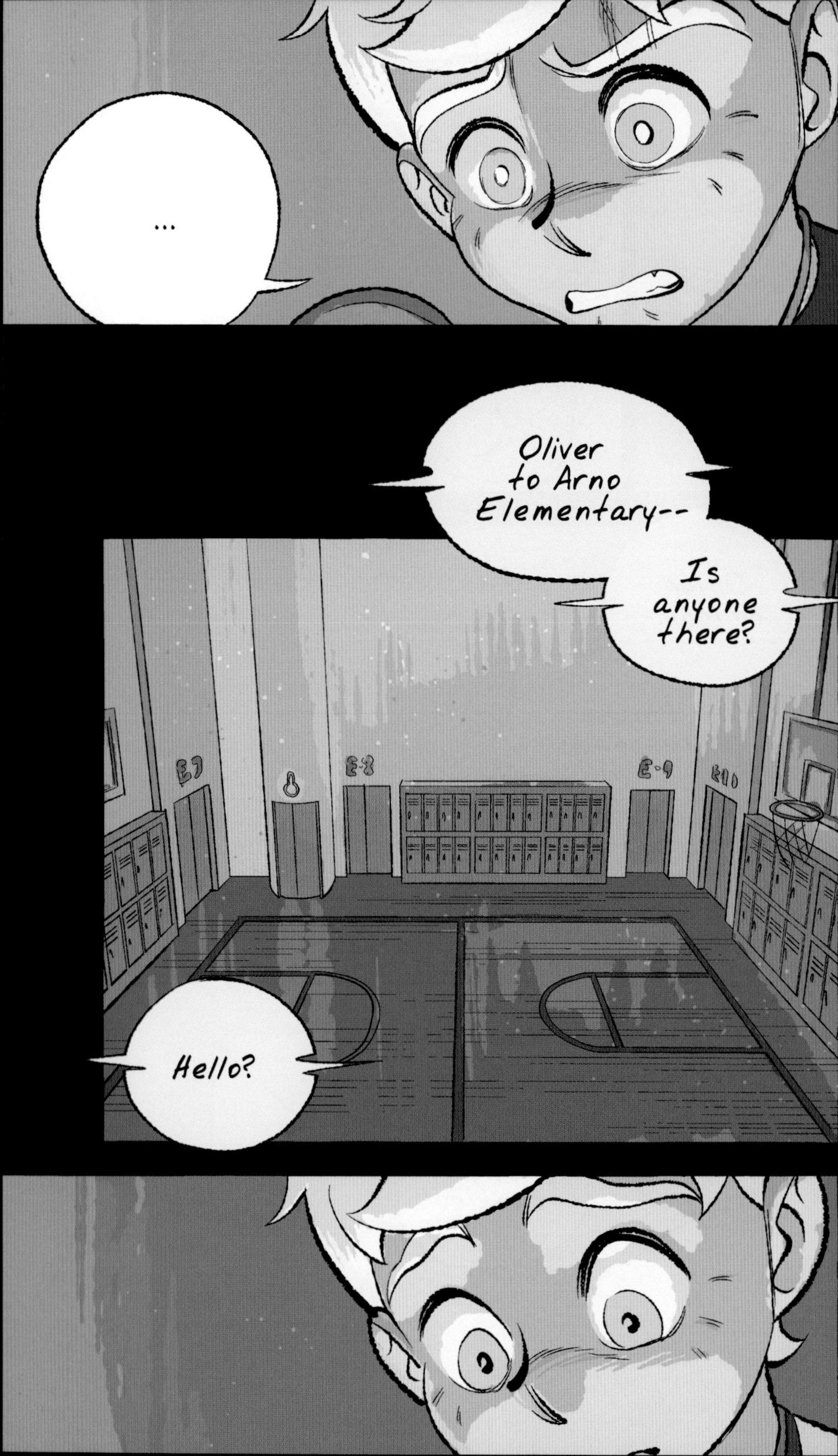
...
Oliver to Arno Elementary--
Is anyone there?
Hello?

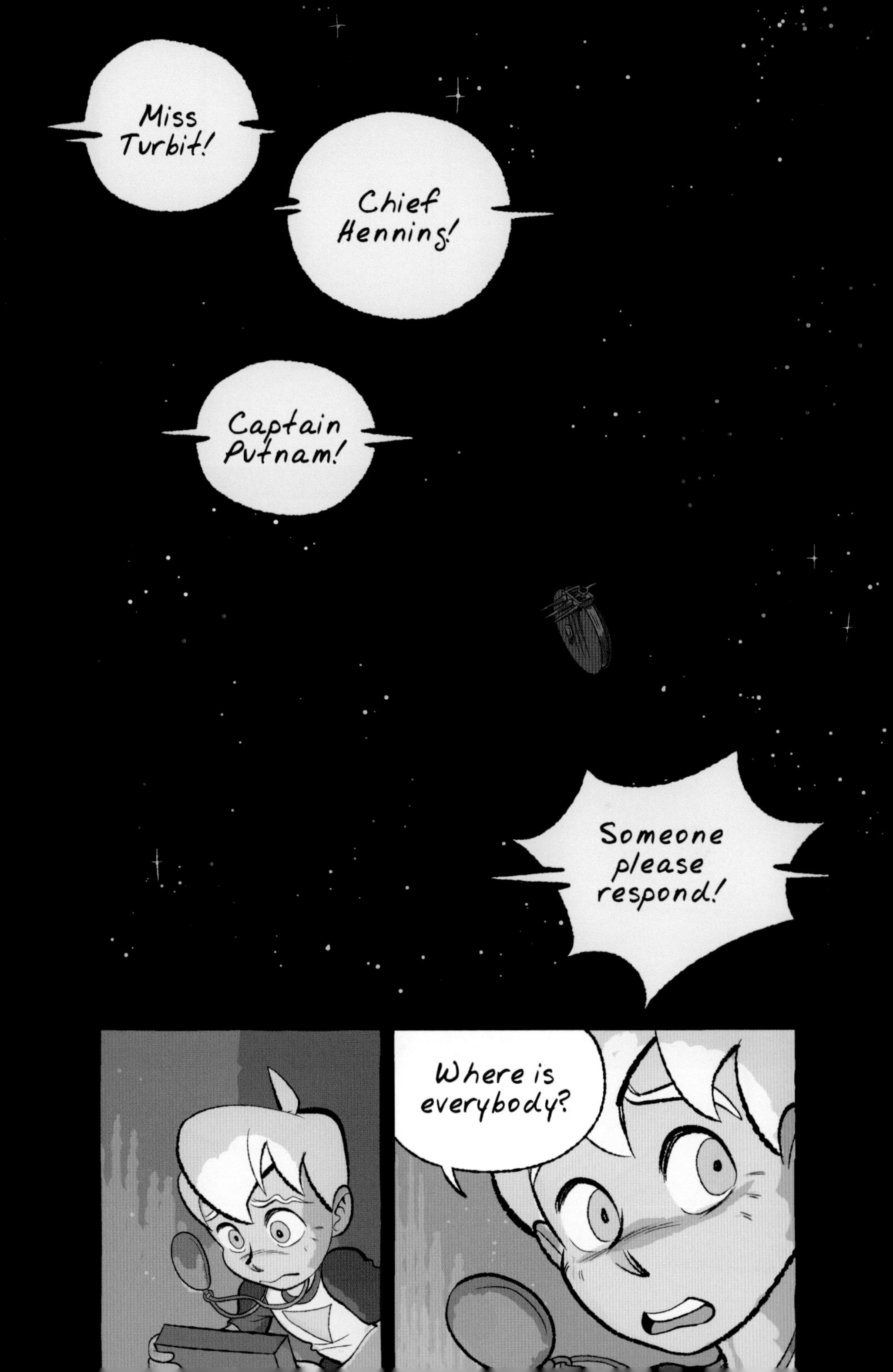
Miss Turbit!
Chief Hennings!
Captain Putnam!
Someone please respond!
Where is everybody?

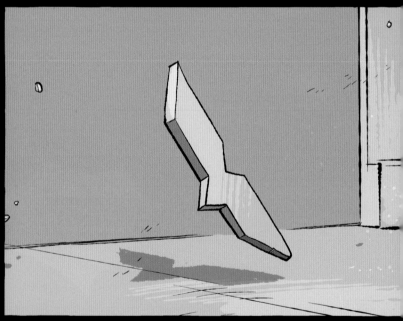

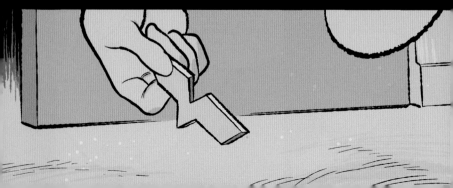

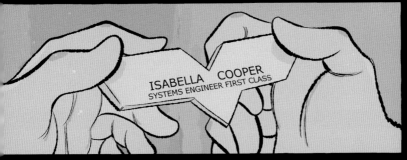

ISABELLA COOPER
SYSTEMS ENGINEER FIRST CLASS

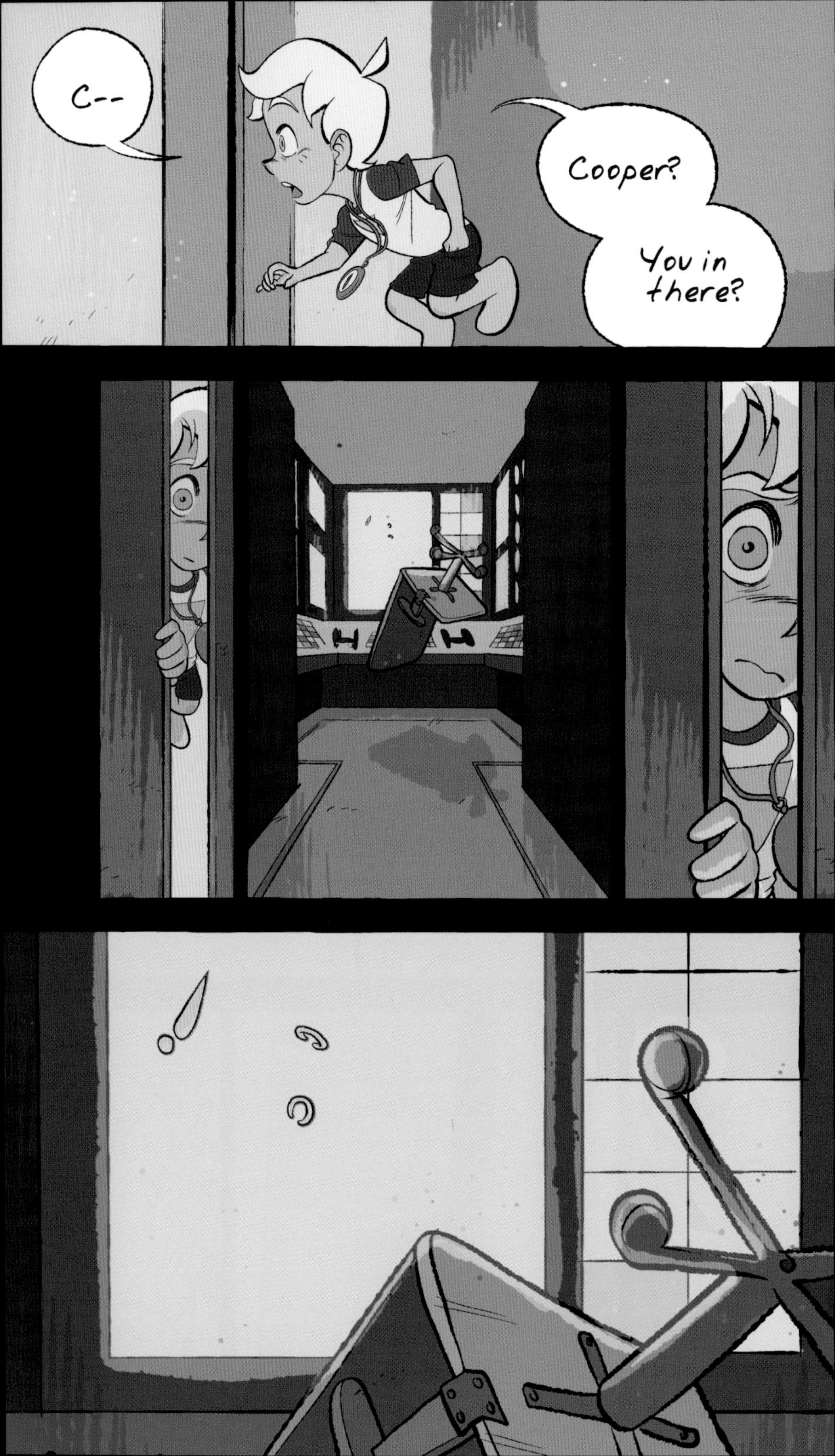
C--
Cooper?
You in there?

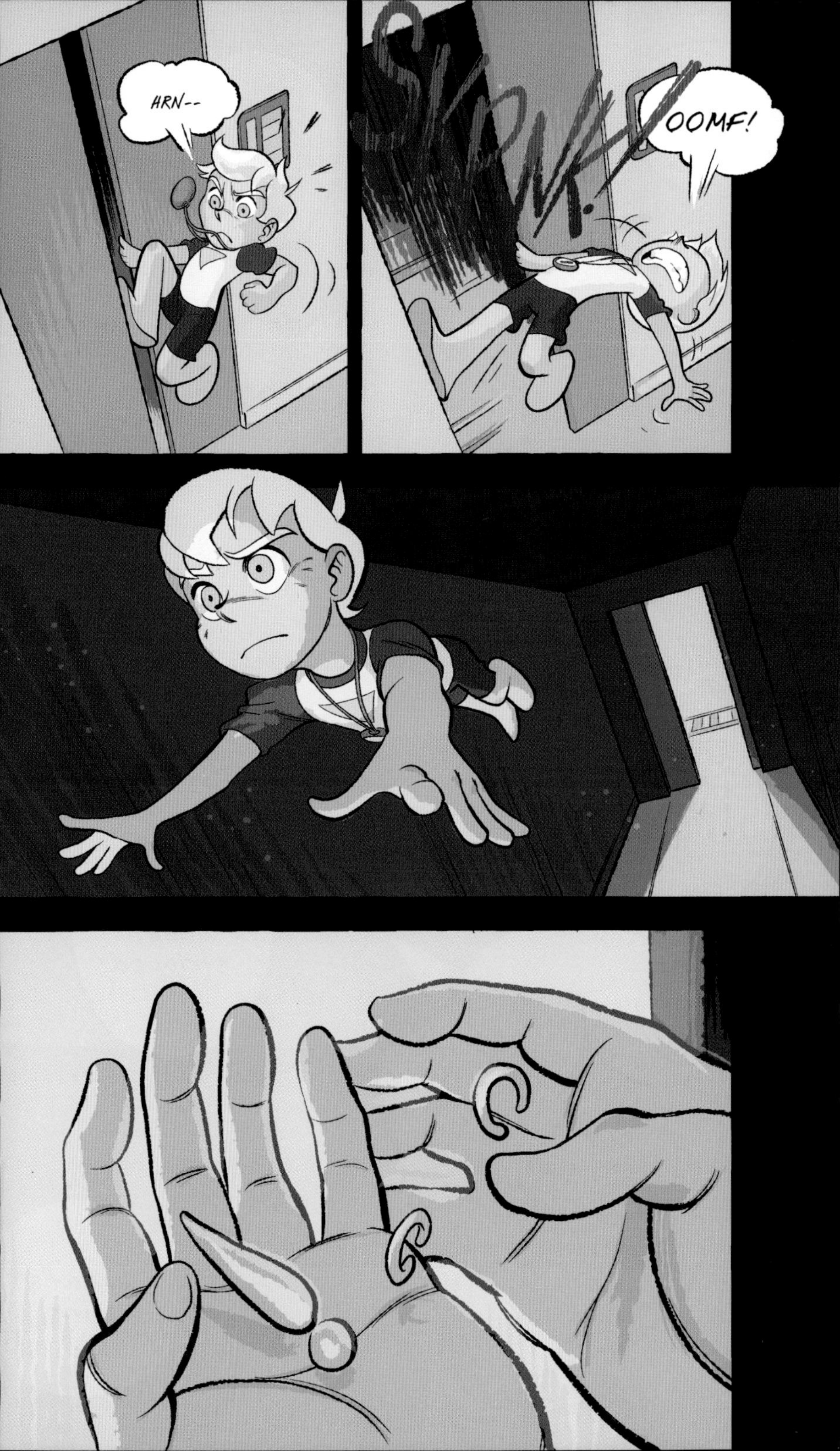
HRN--
SHWAM!
OOMF!

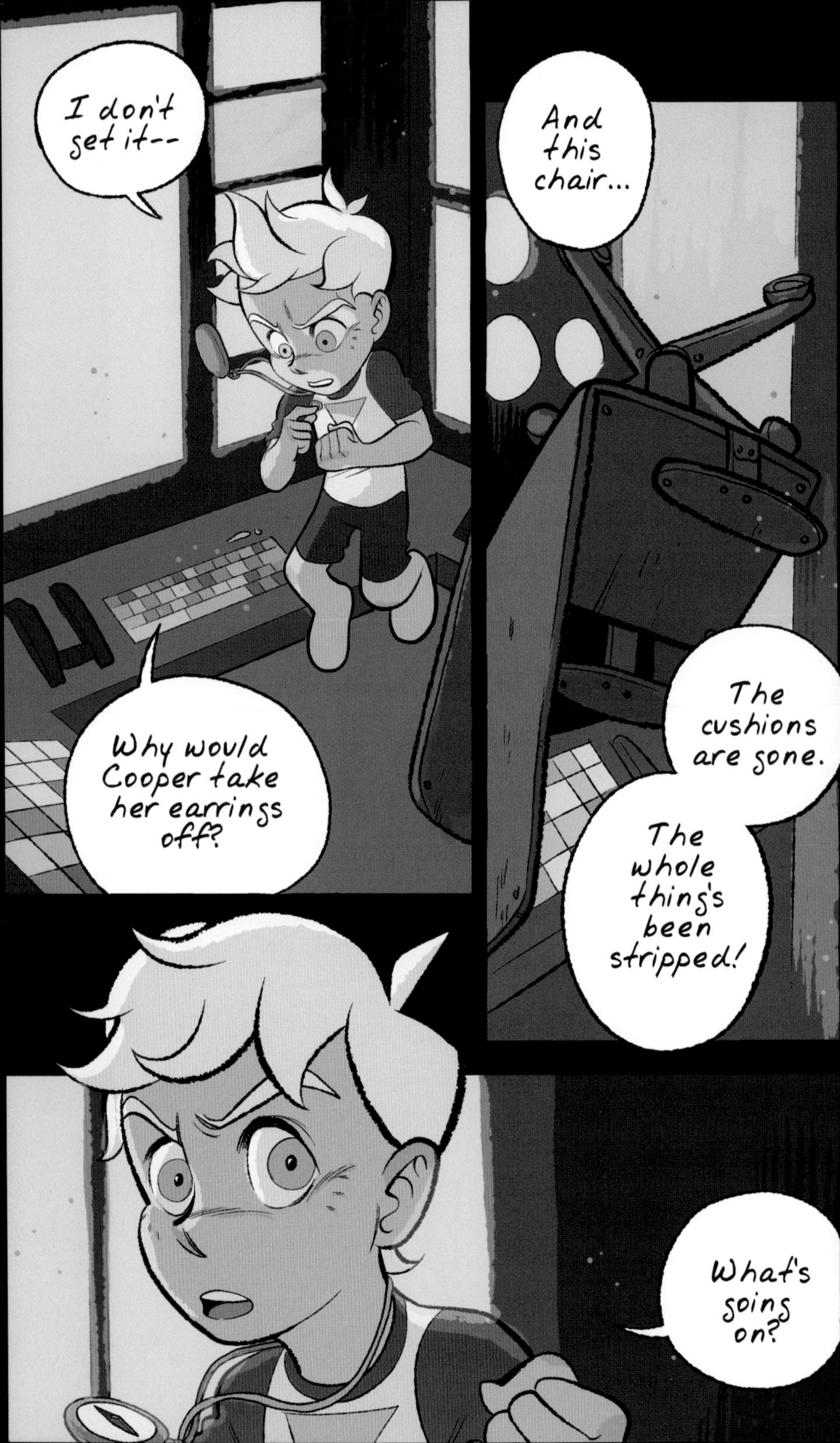
I don't get it--
Why would Cooper take her earrings off?
And this chair...
The cushions are gone.
The whole thing's been stripped!
What's going on?

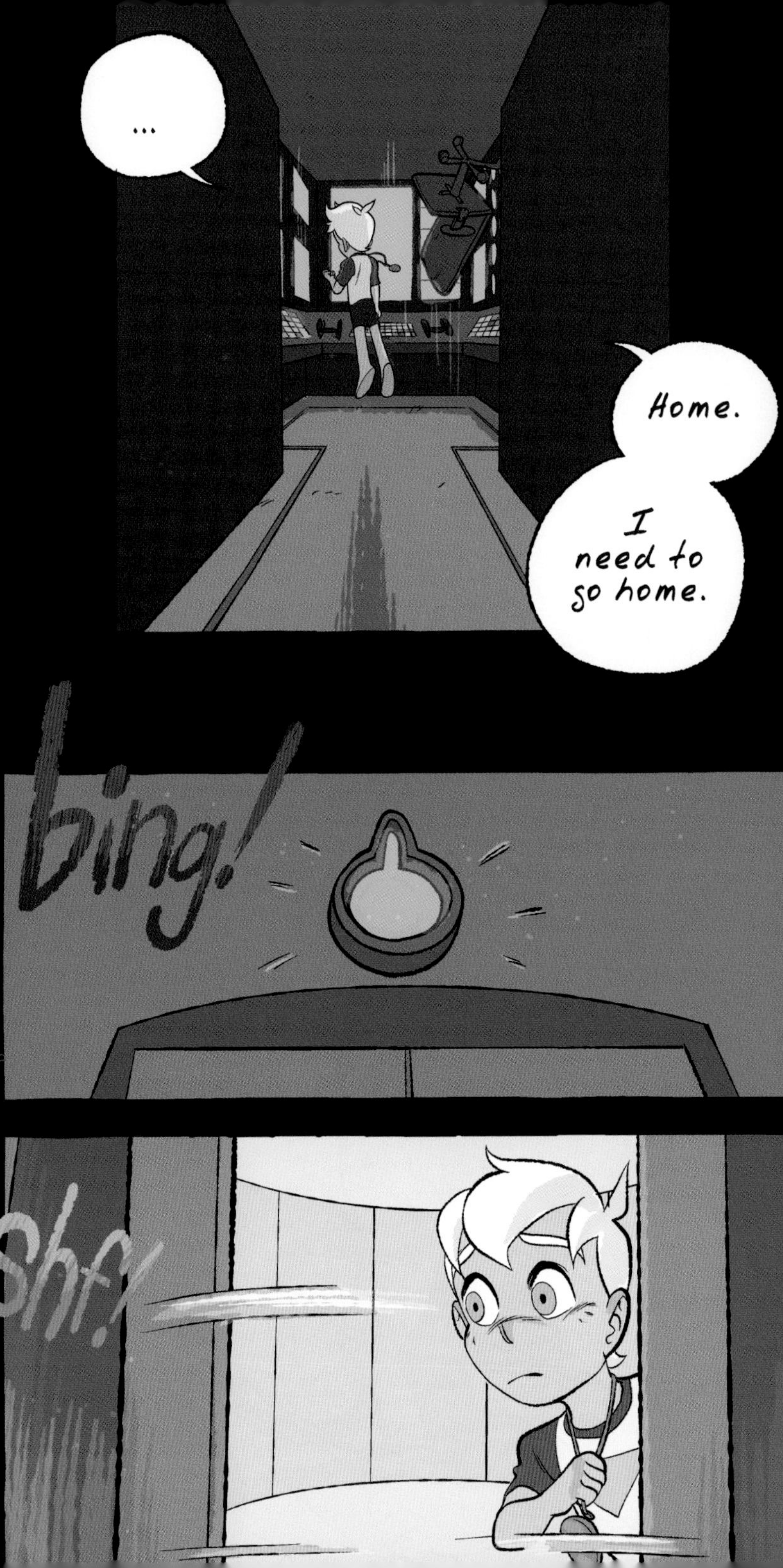
...
Home.
I need to go home.
bing!
Shf!

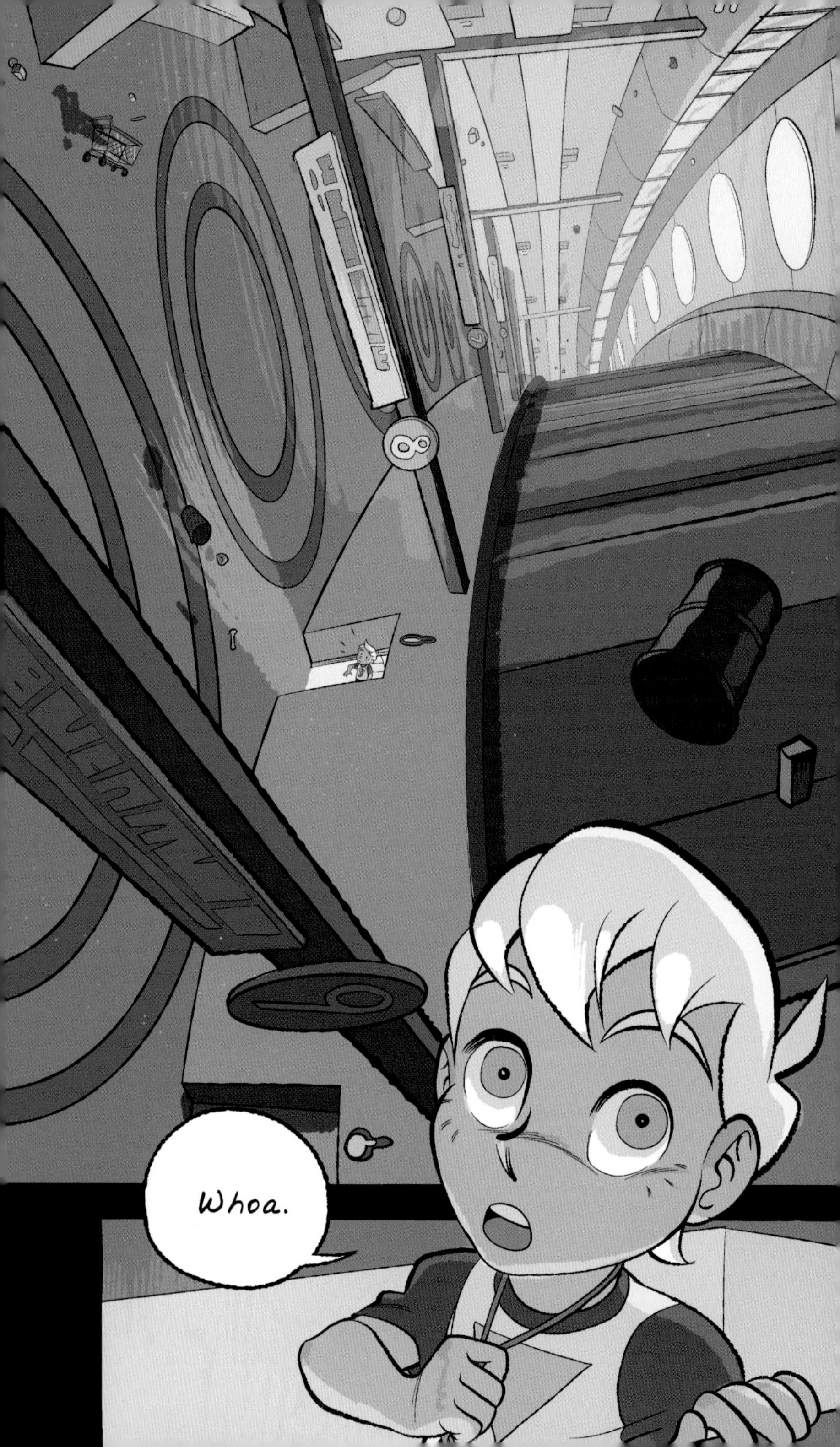
Whoa.

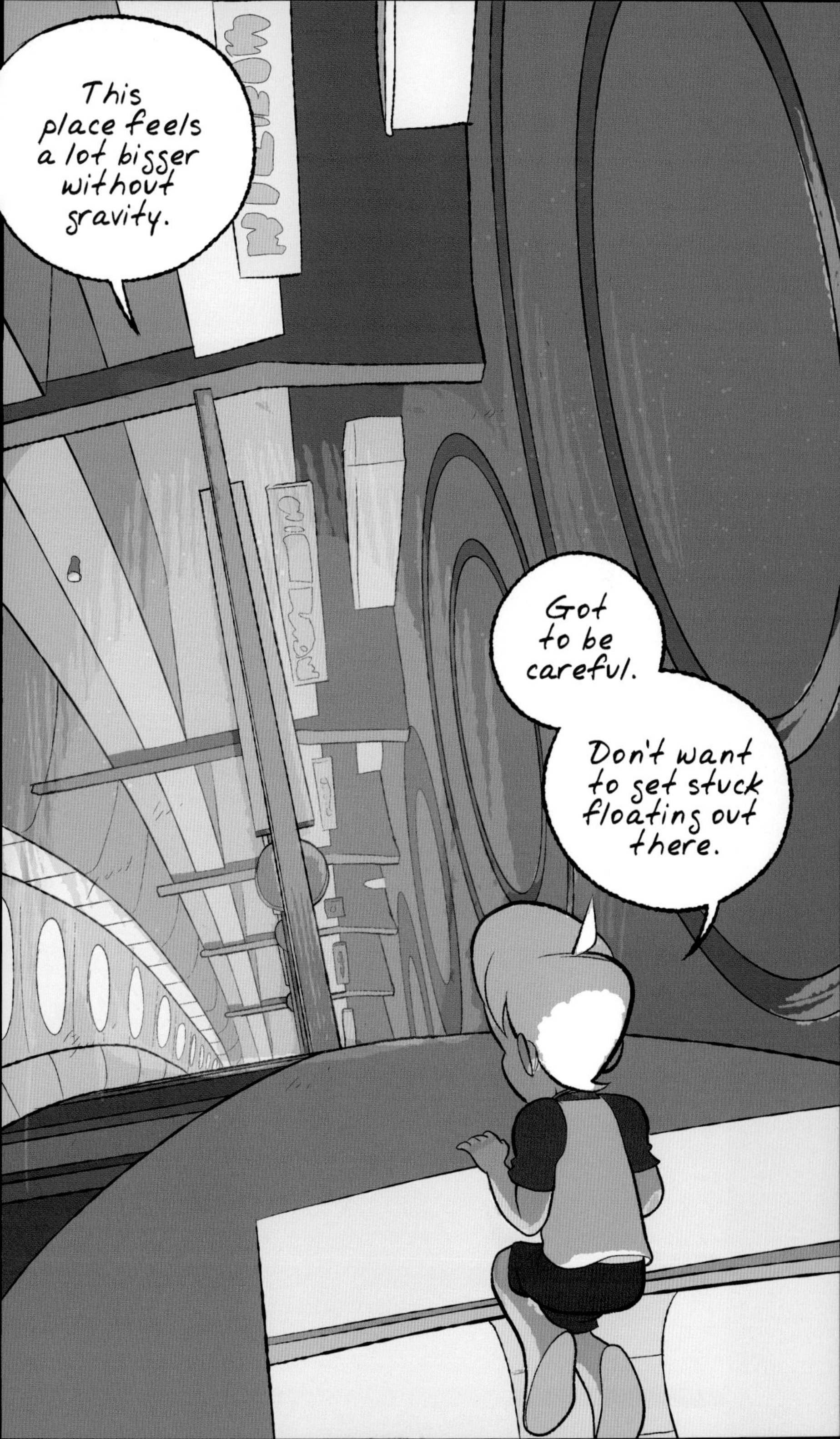
This place feels a lot bigger without gravity.
Got to be careful.
Don't want to get stuck floating out there.

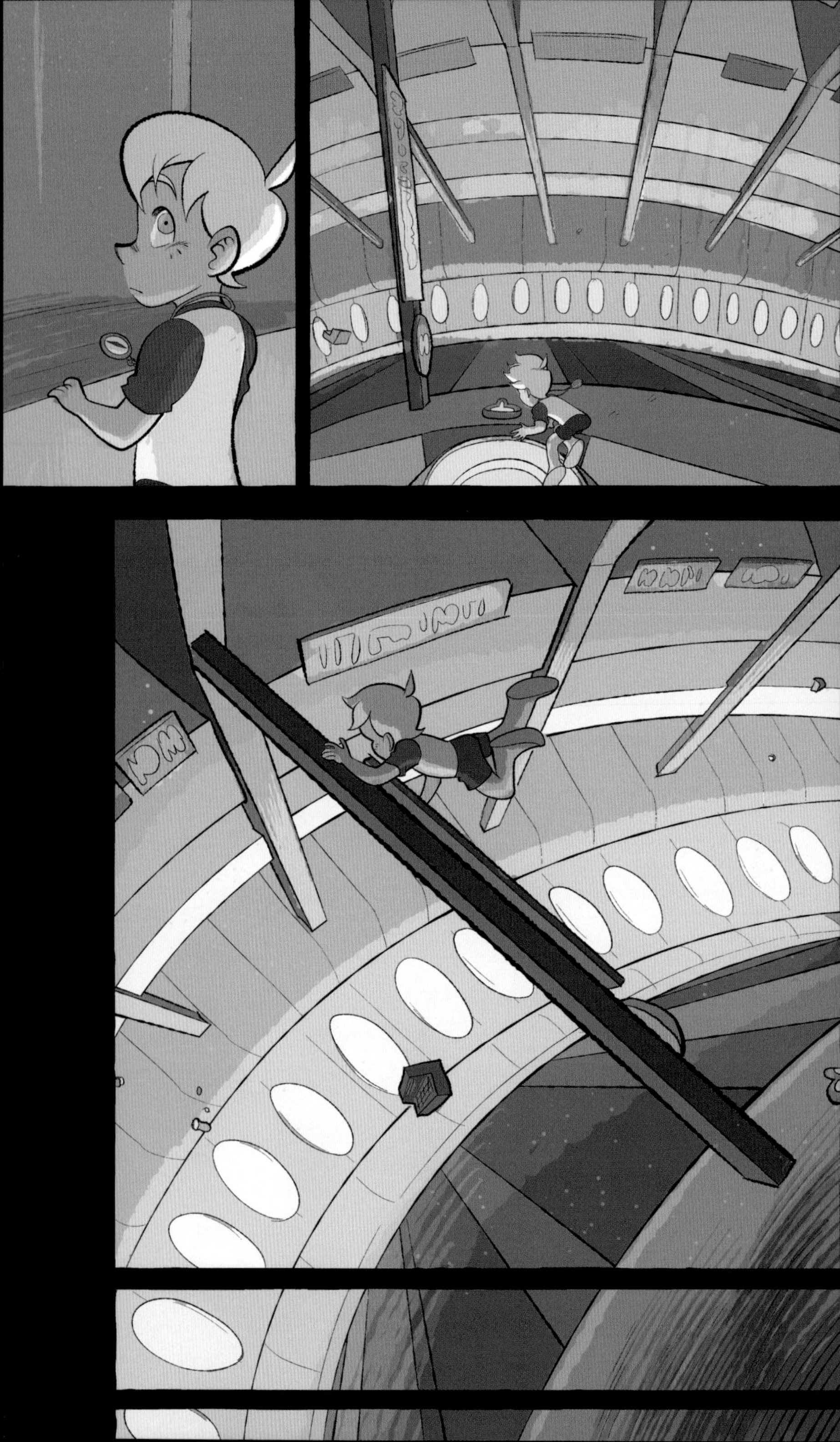

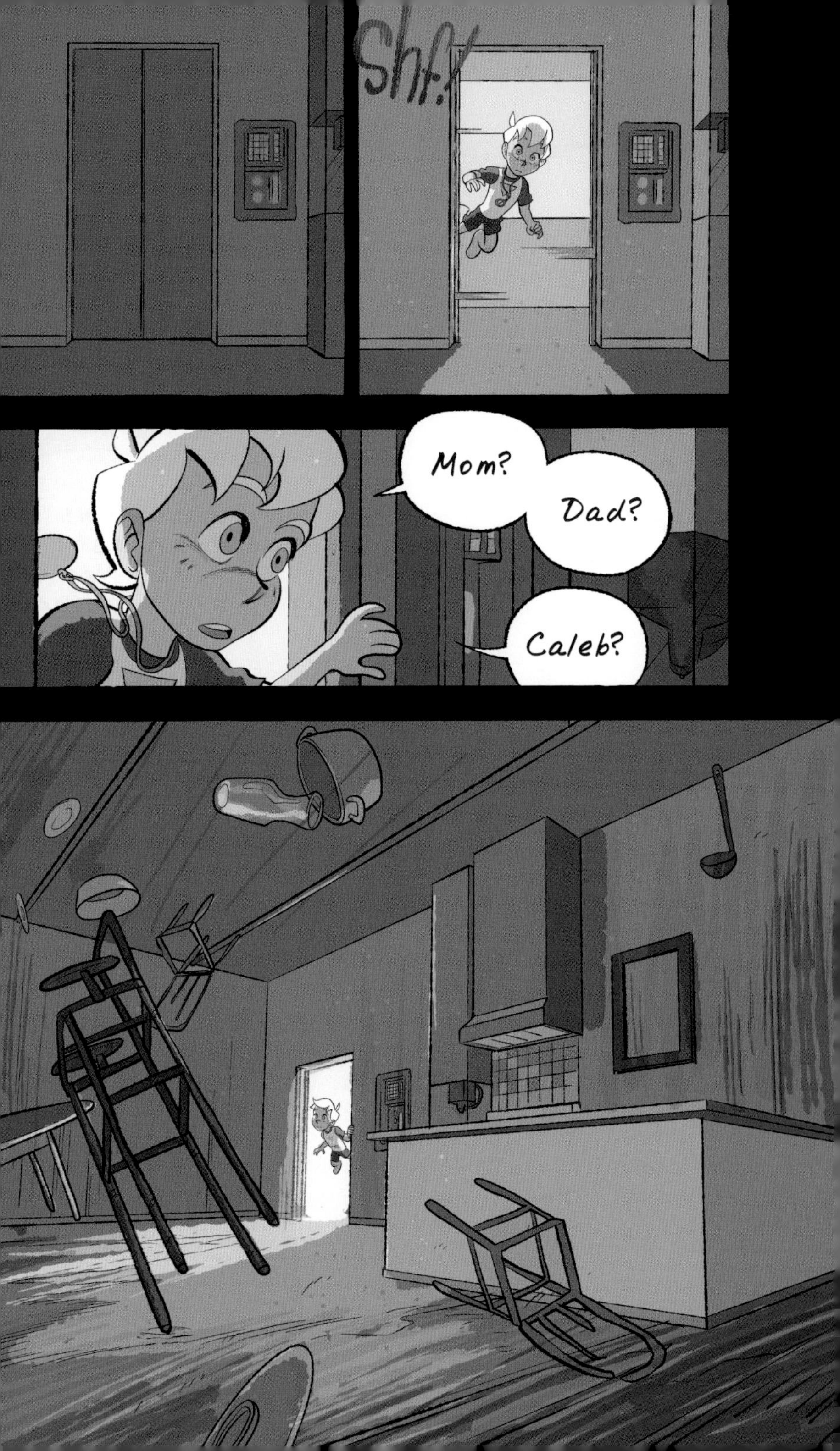
Shf!
Mom?
Dad?
Caleb?

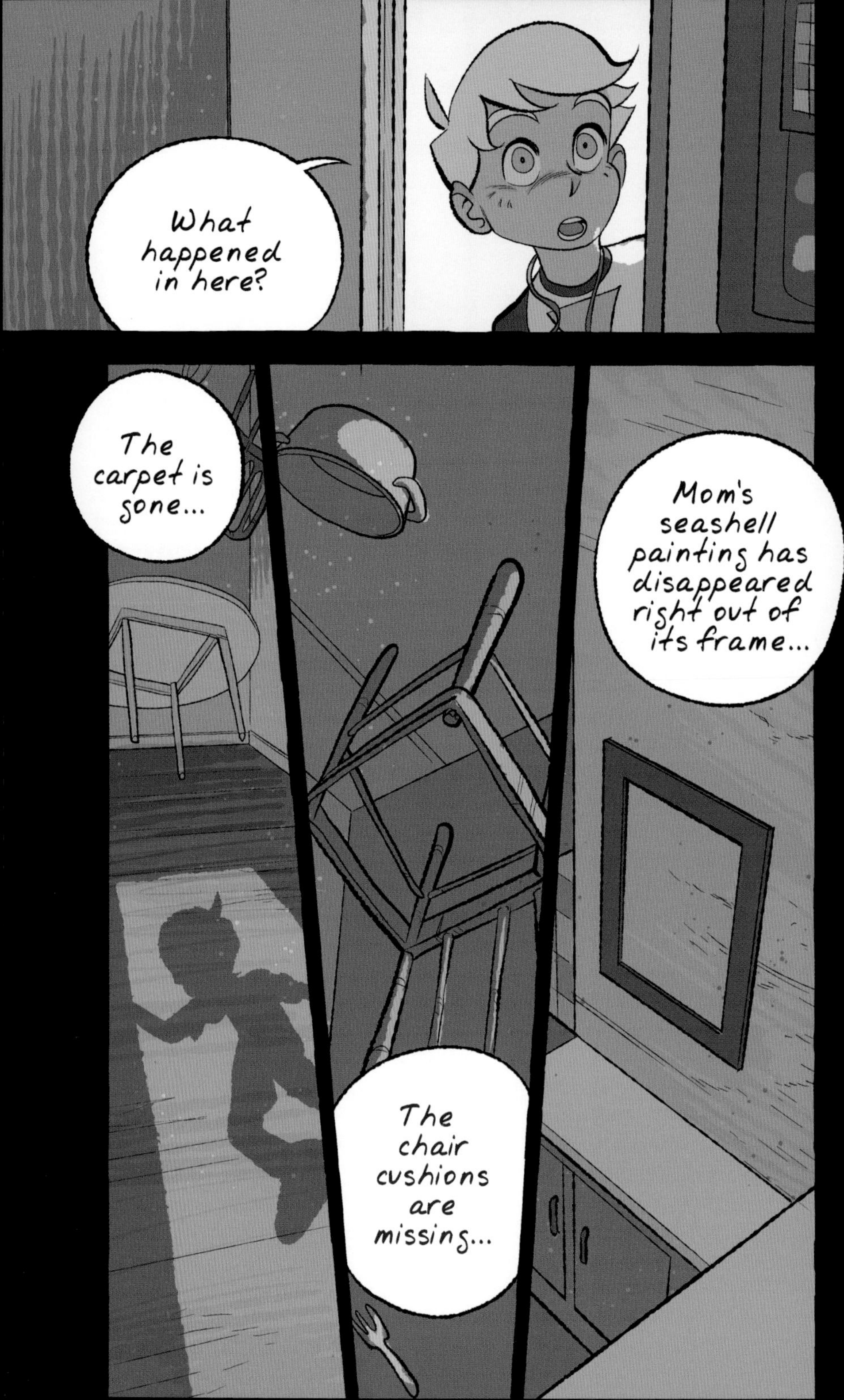
What happened in here?
The carpet is gone...
Mom's seashell painting has disappeared right out of its frame...
The chair cushions are missing...

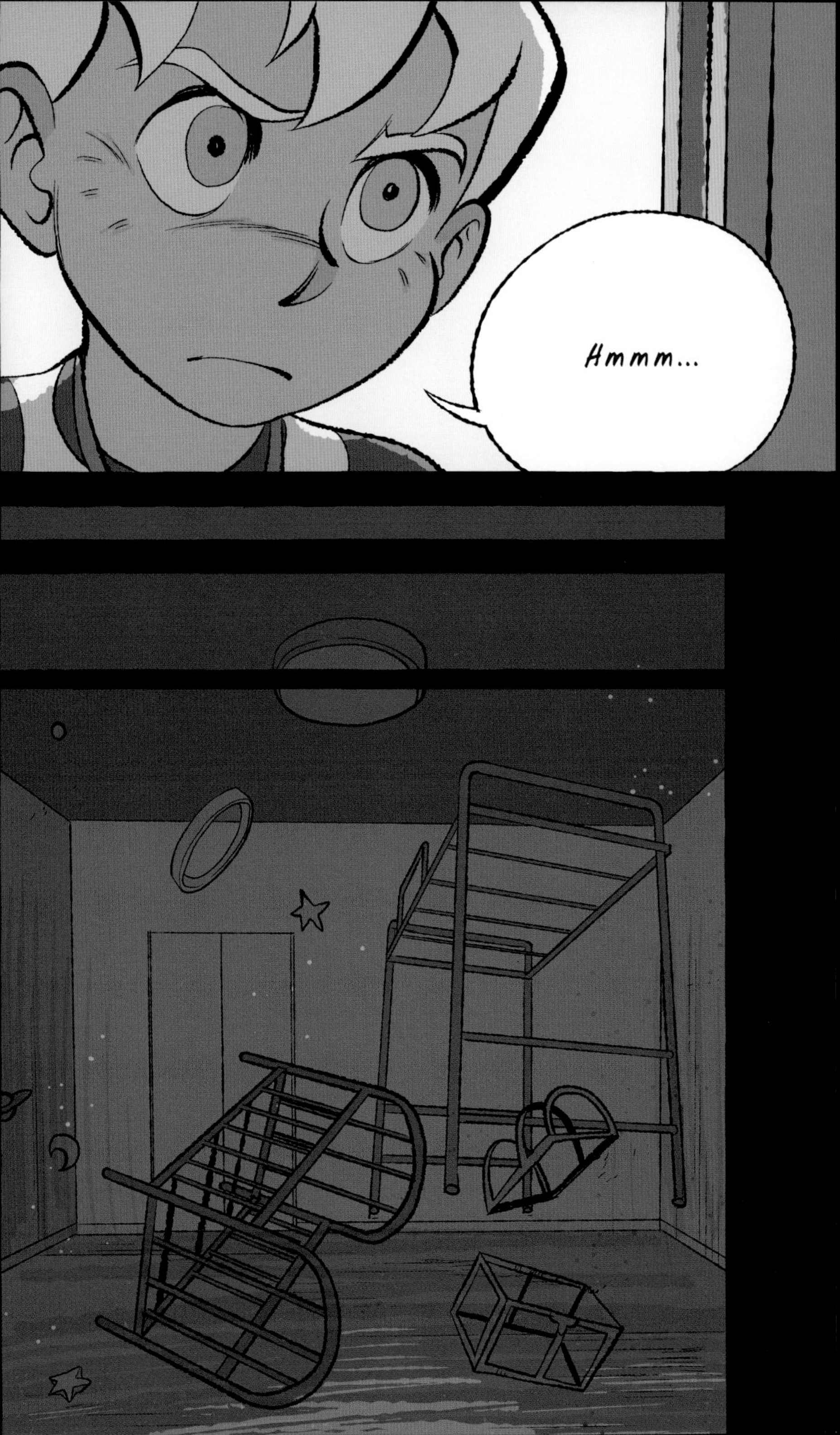
Hmmm...

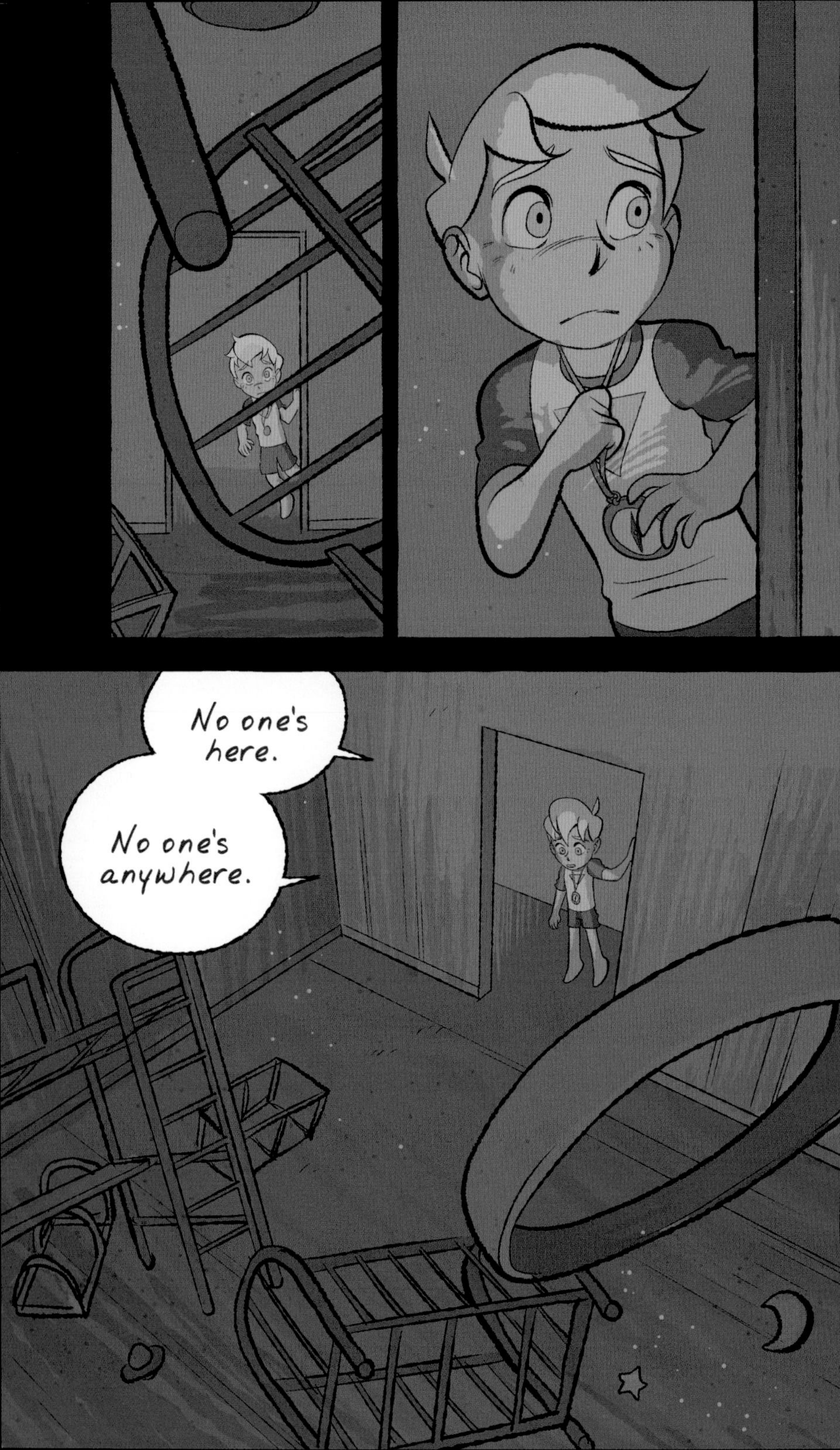
No one's here.
No one's anywhere.

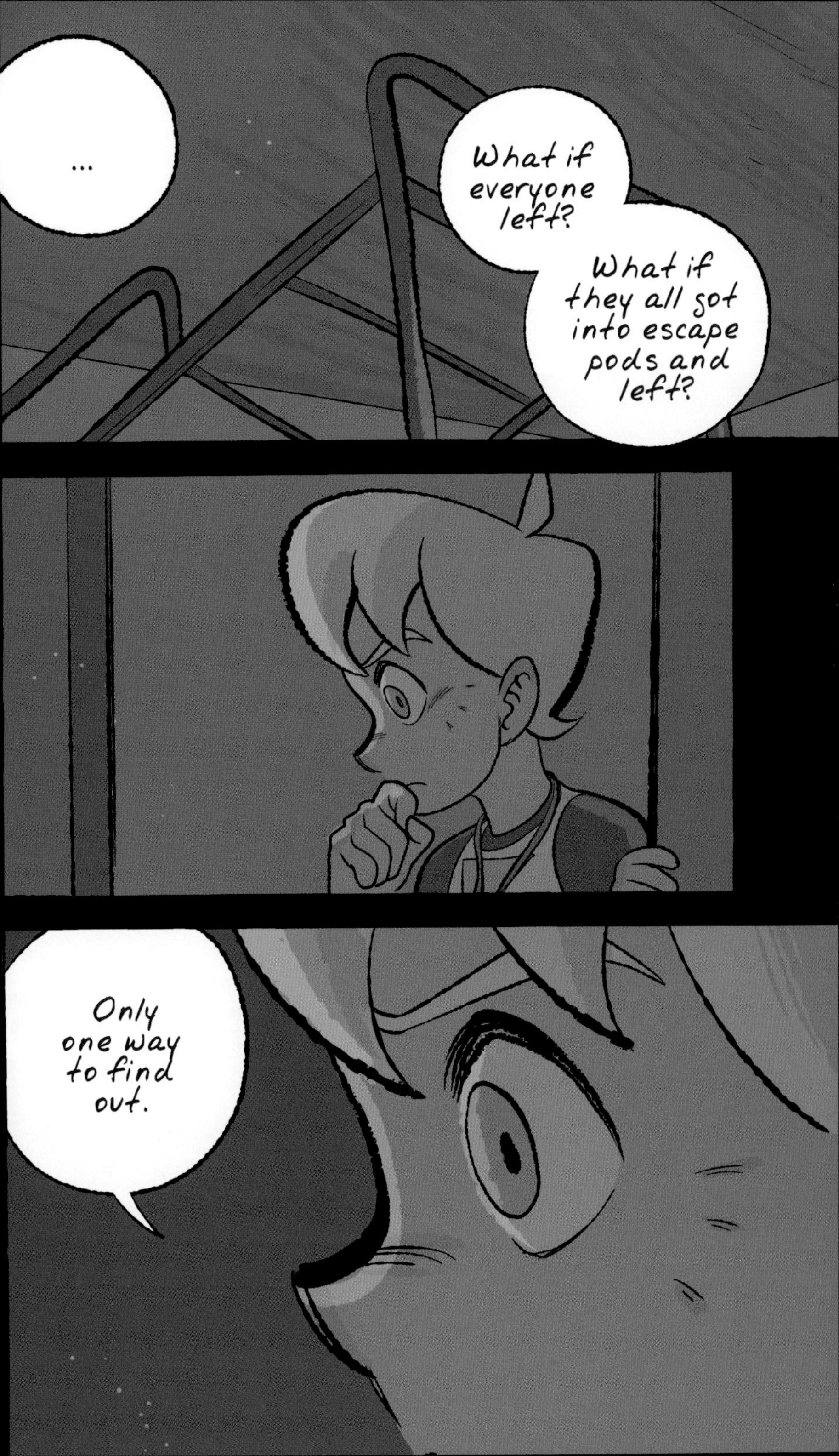
...
What if everyone left?
What if they all got into escape pods and left?
Only one way to find out.

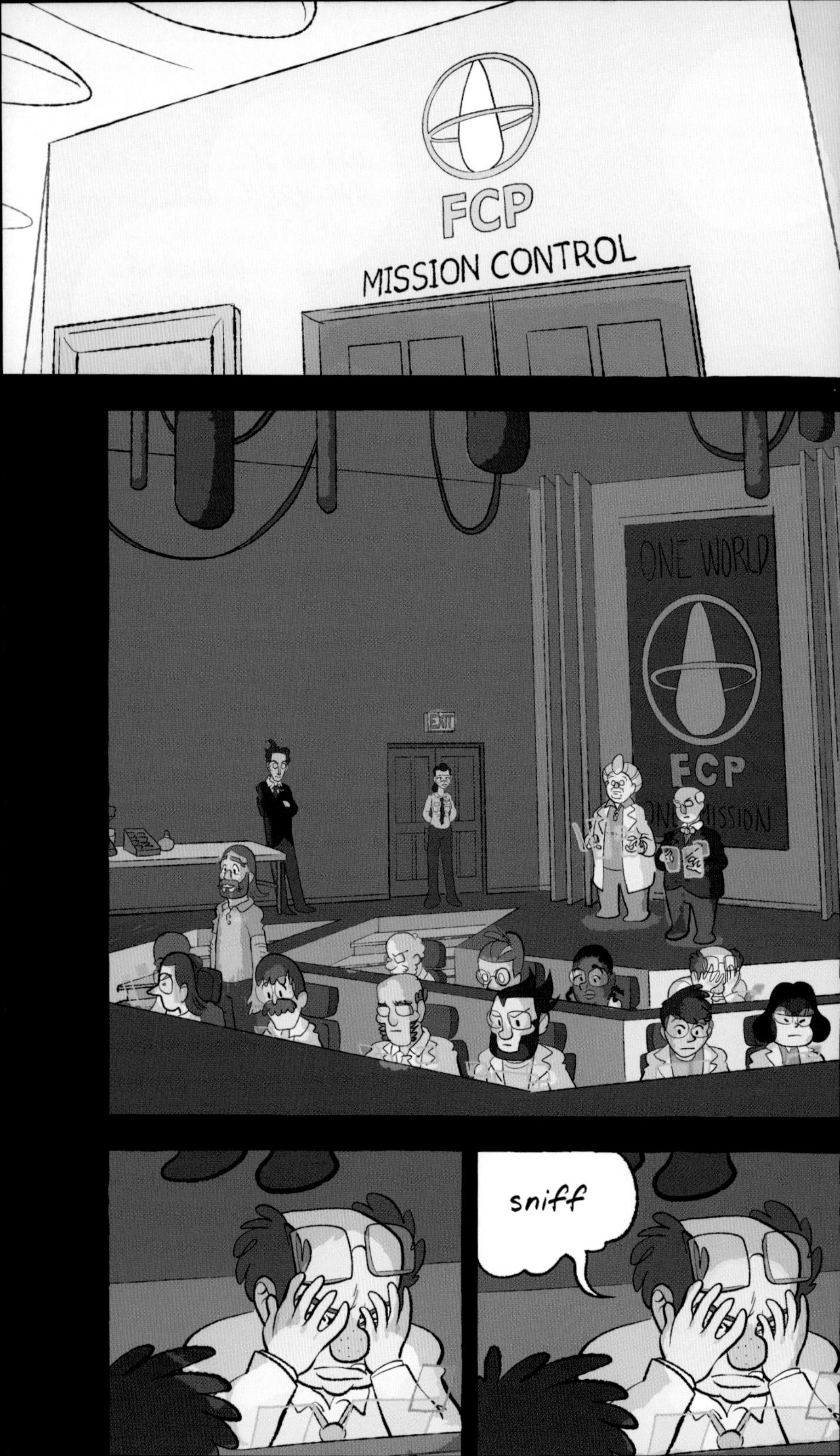
FCP
MISSION CONTROL
ONE WORLD
FCP
ONE MISSION
EXIT
sniff

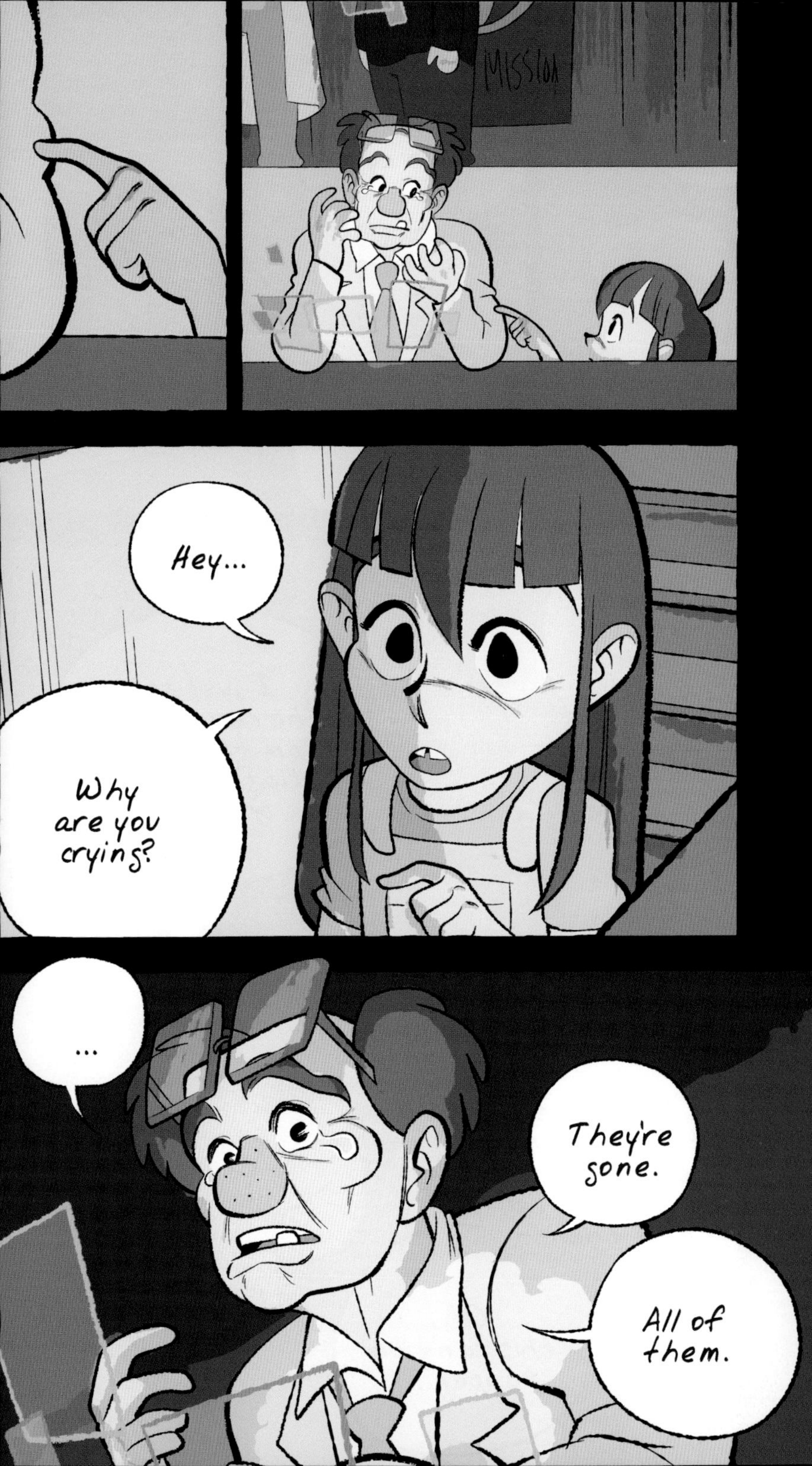
Hey...
Why are you crying?
...
They're gone.
All of them.

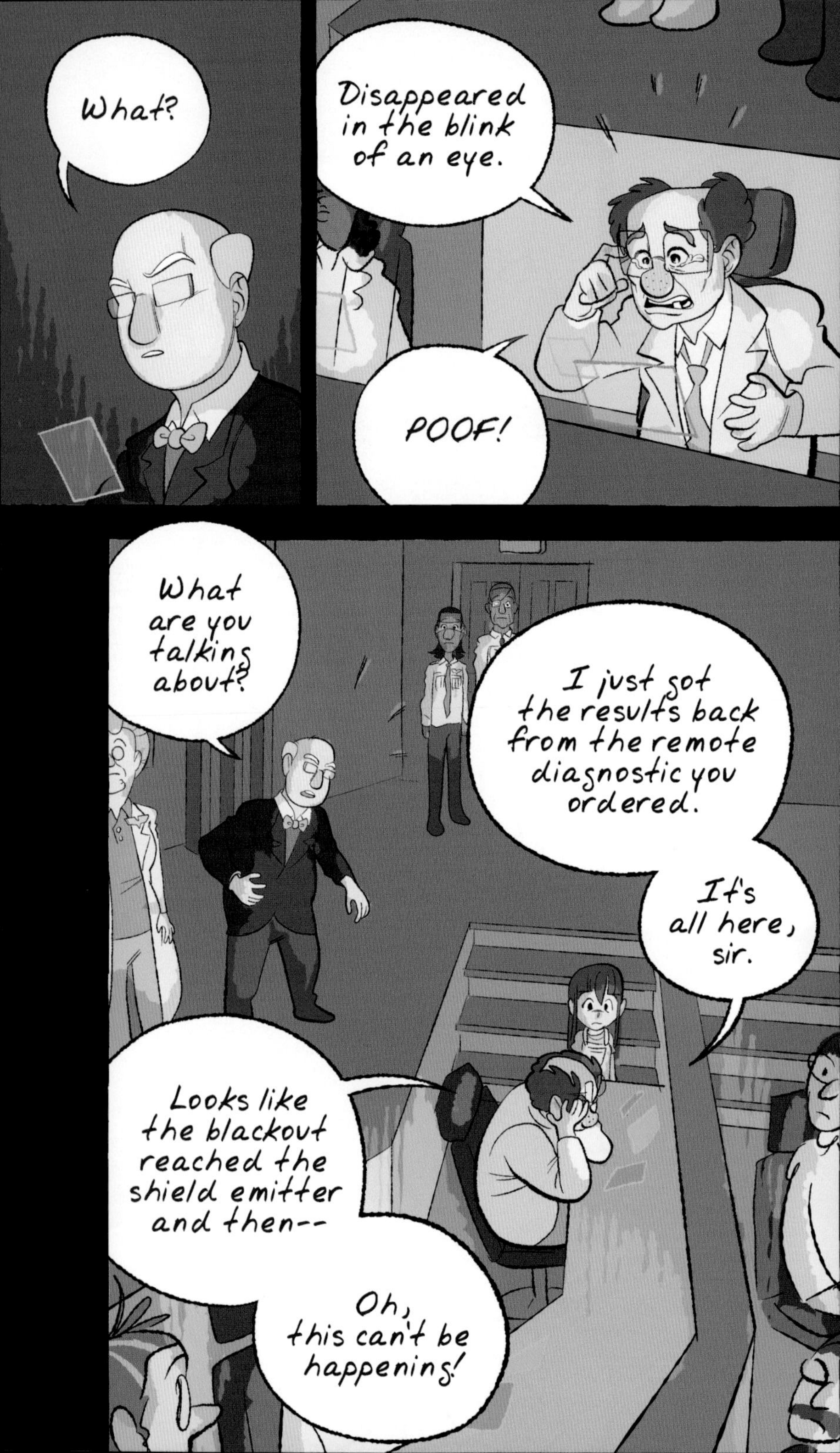
What?
Disappeared in the blink of an eye.
POOF!
What are you talking about?
I just got the results back from the remote diagnostic you ordered.
It's all here, sir.
Looks like the blackout reached the shield emitter and then--
Oh, this can't be happening!

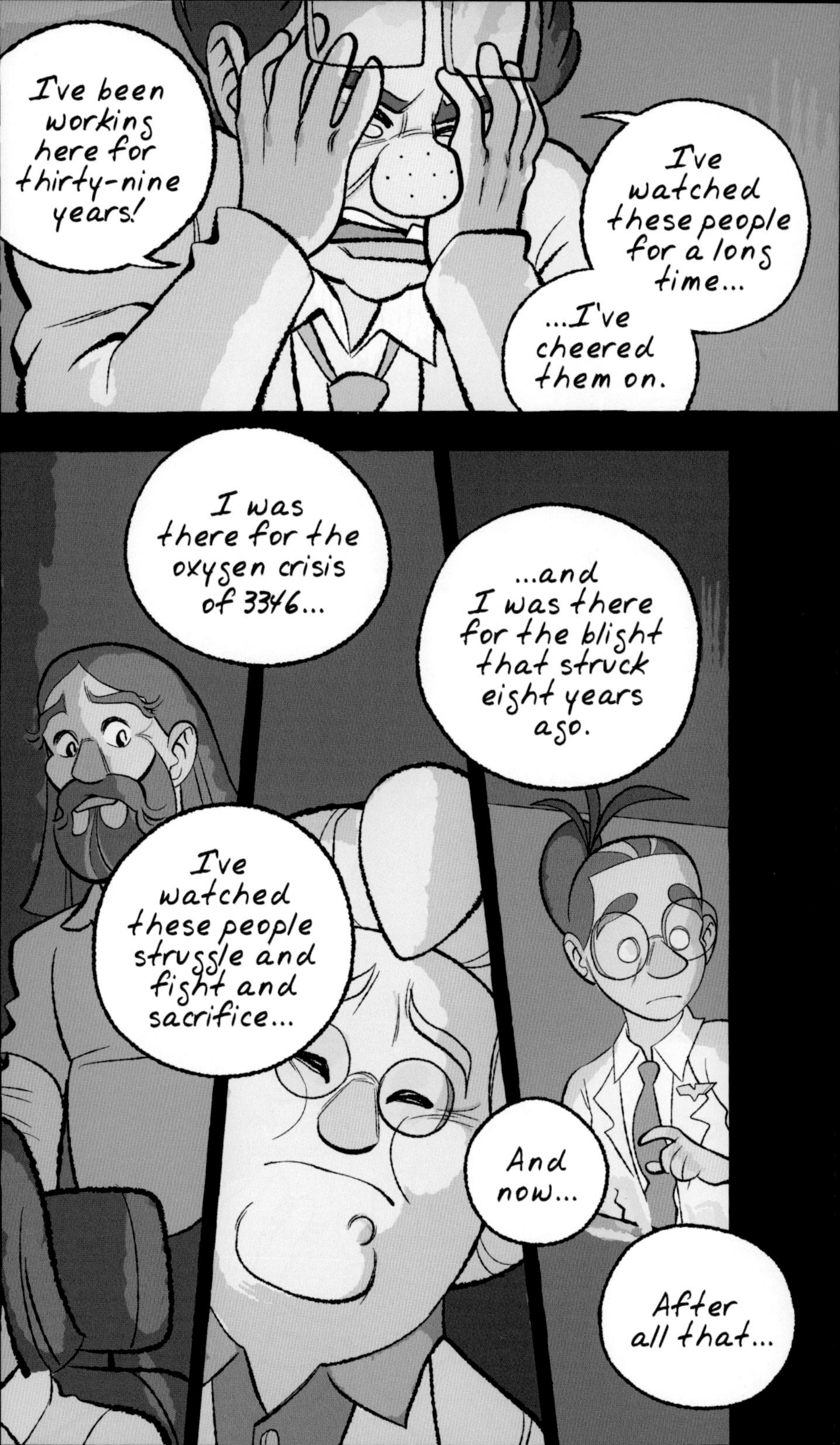
I've been working here for thirty-nine years!
I've watched these people for a long time...
...I've cheered them on.
I was there for the oxygen crisis of 3346...
...and I was there for the blight that struck eight years ago.
I've watched these people struggle and fight and sacrifice...
And now...
After all that...

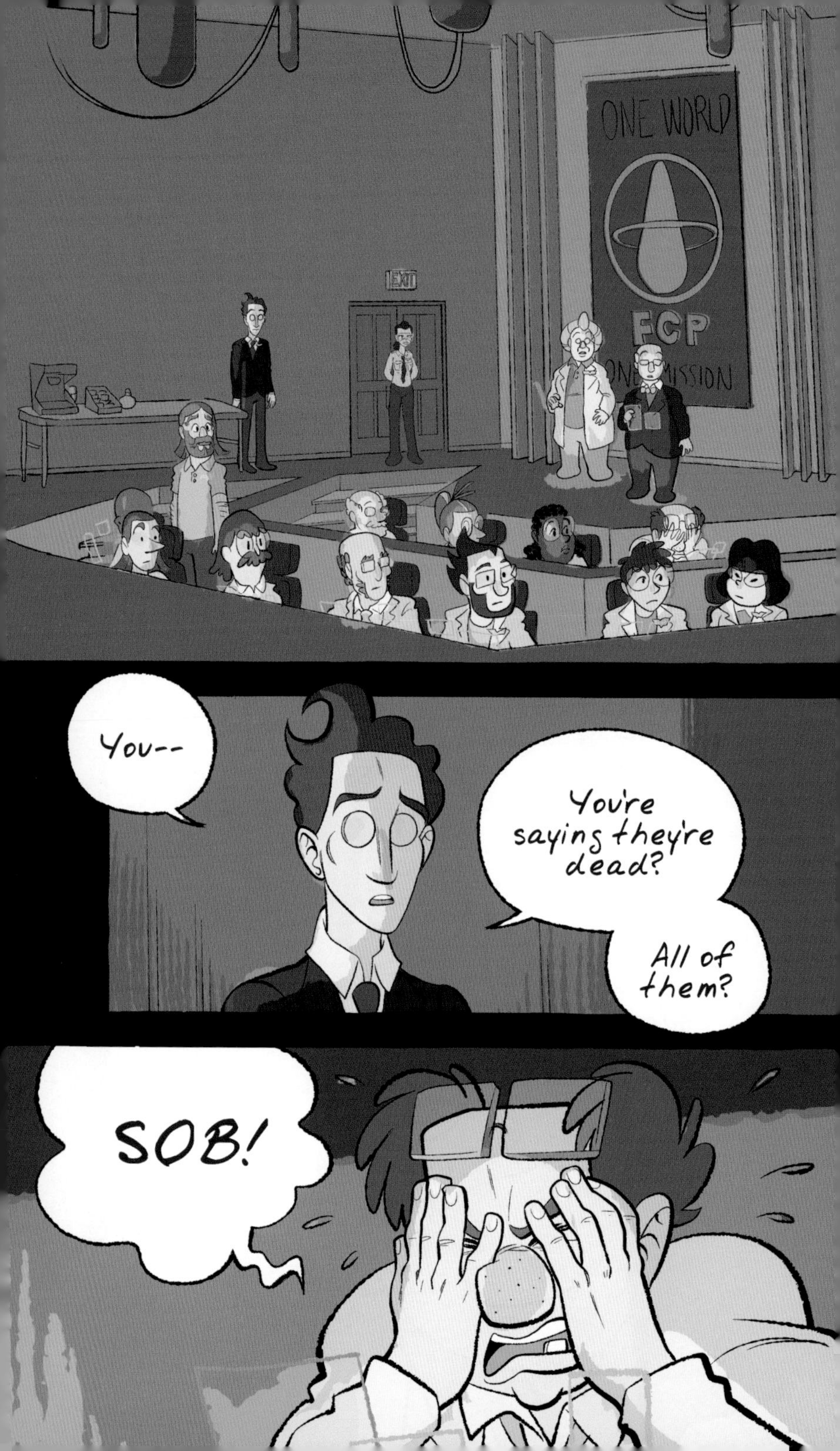
ONE WORLD
FCP
ONE MISSION
EXIT
You--
You're saying they're dead?
All of them?
SOB!

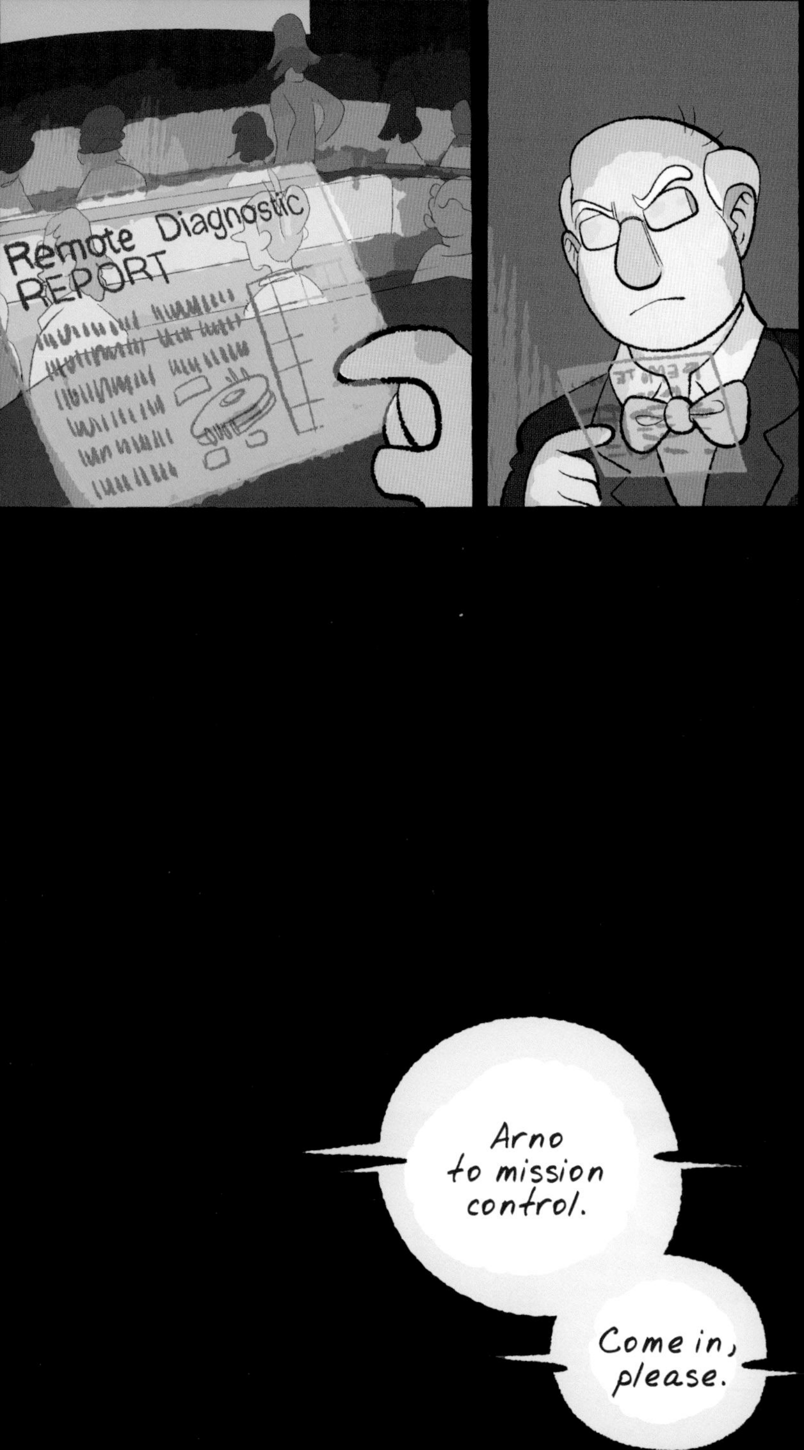
Remote Diagnostic REPORT
Arno to mission control.
Come in, please.

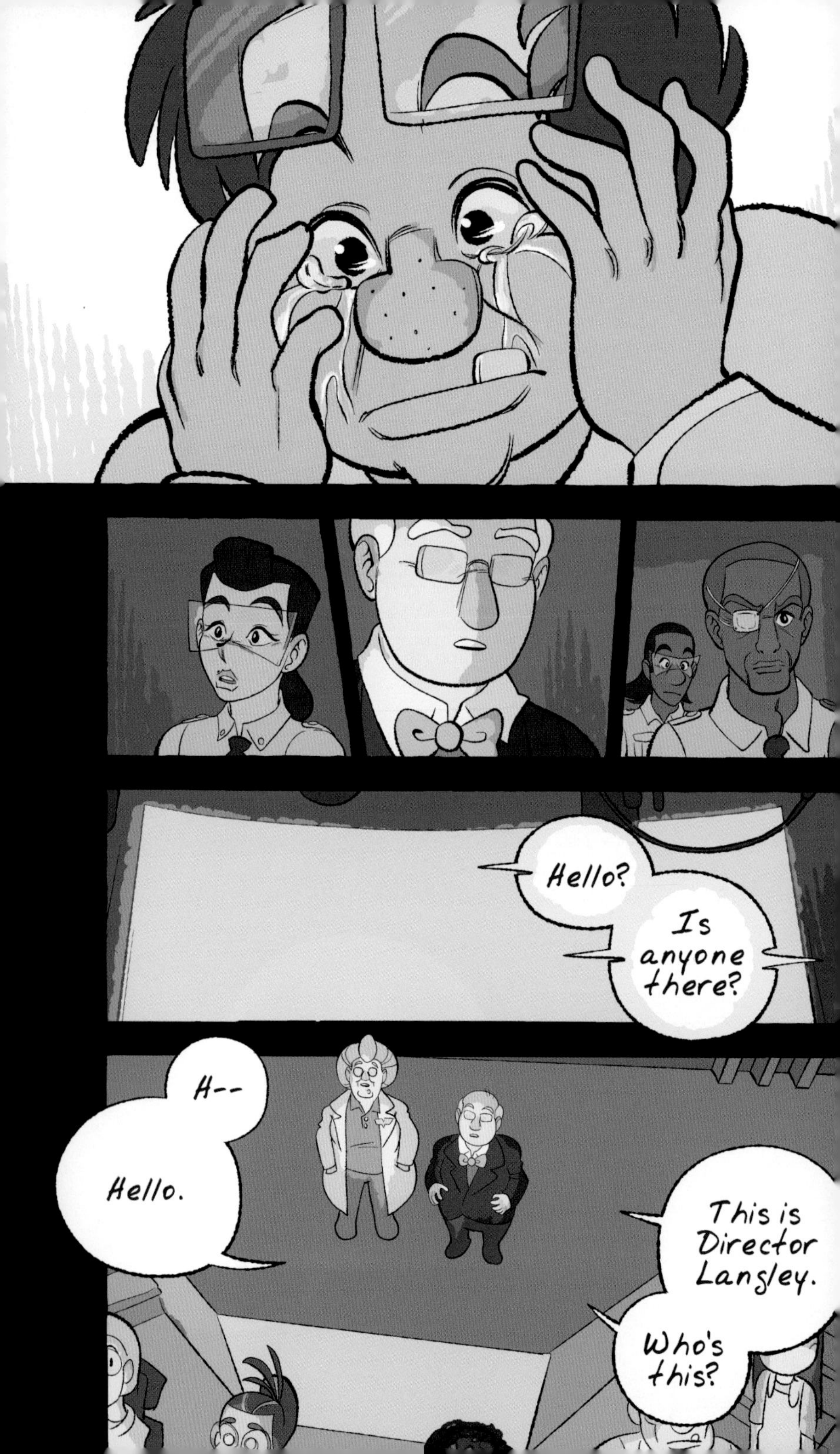
Hello?
Is anyone there?
H--
Hello.
This is Director Langley.
Who's this?

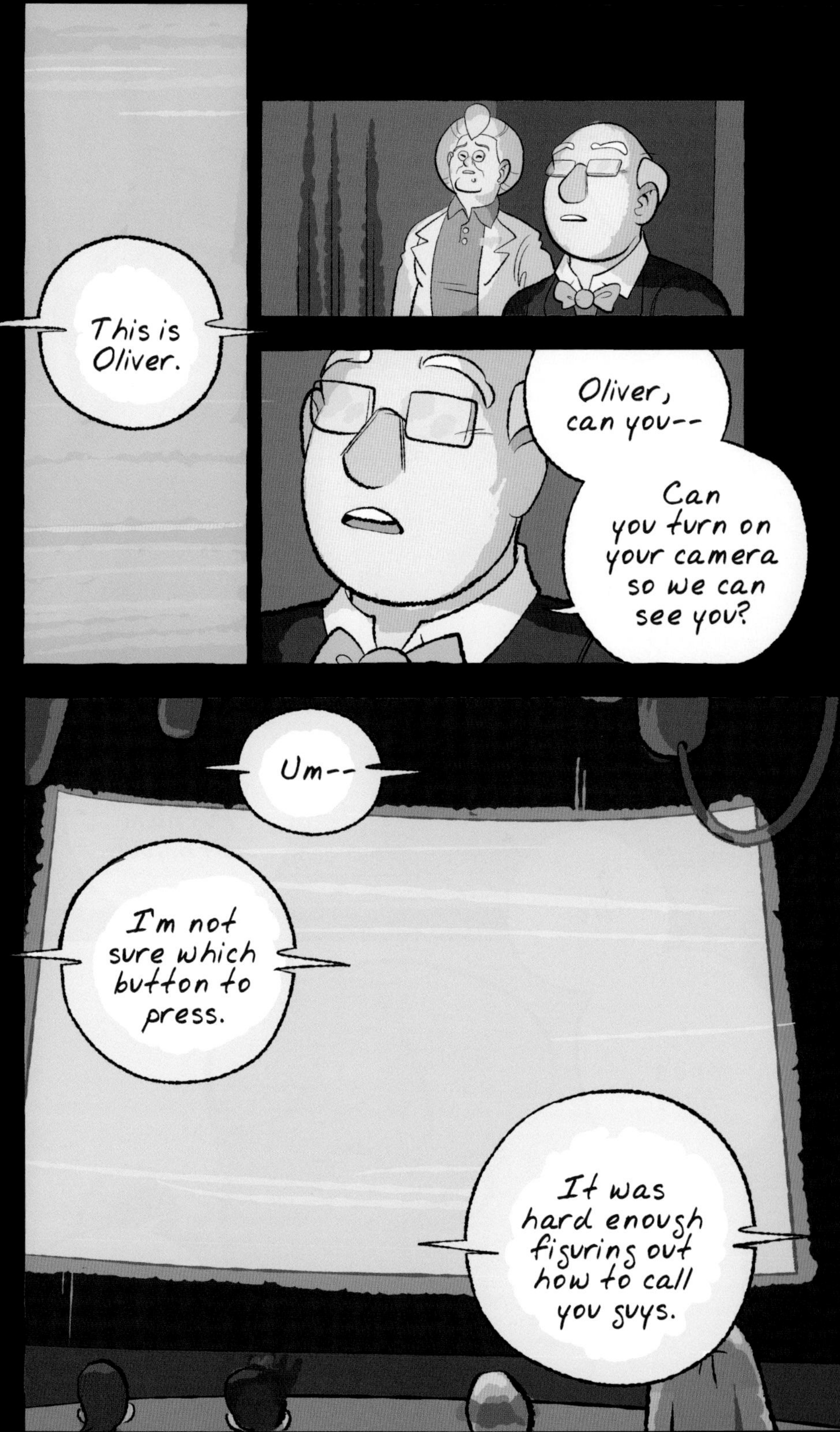
This is Oliver.
Oliver, can you--
Can you turn on your camera so we can see you?
Um--
I'm not sure which button to press.
It was hard enough figuring out how to call you guys.

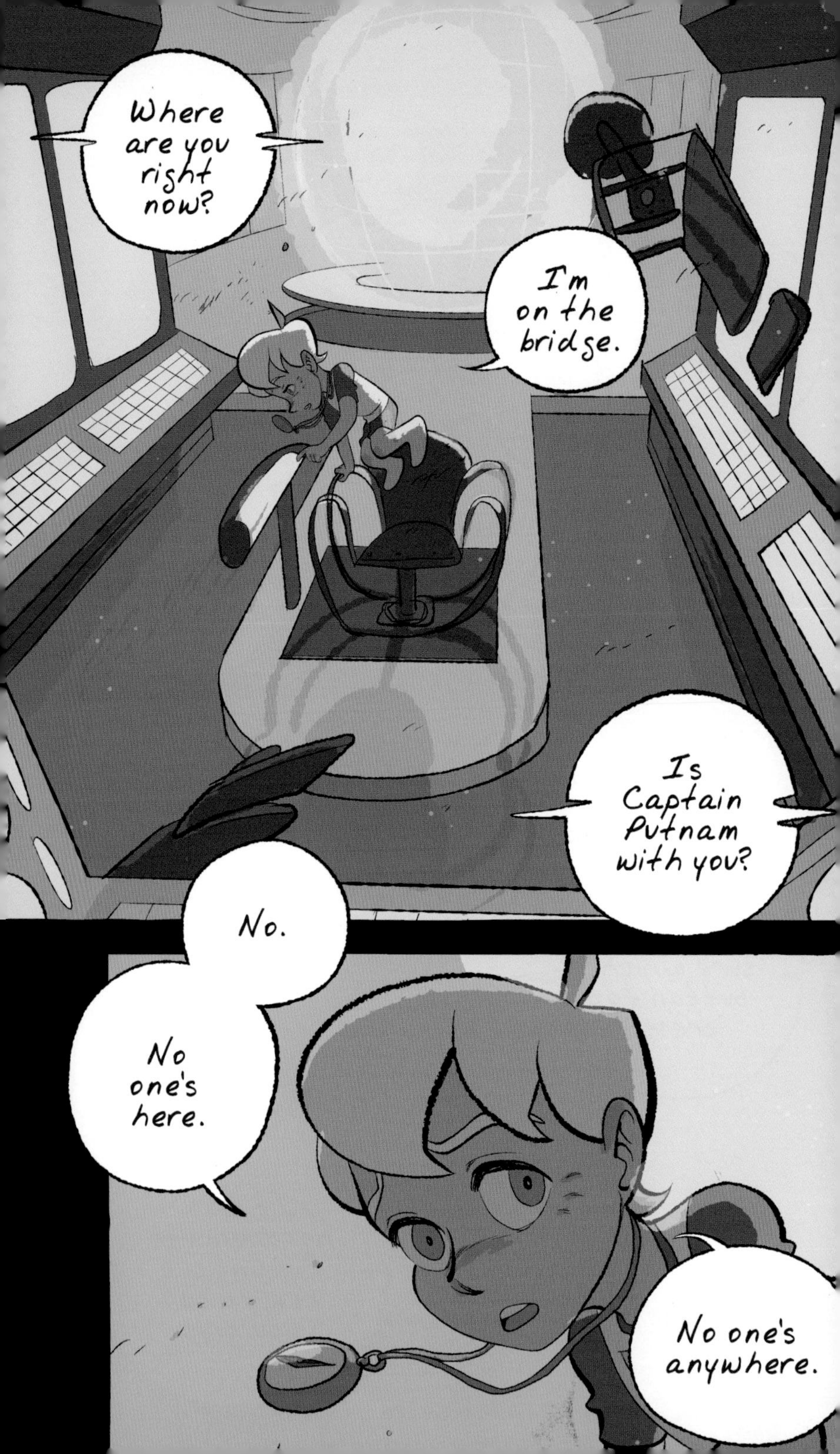
Where are you right now?
I'm on the bridge.
Is Captain Putnam with you?
No.
No one's here.
No one's anywhere.

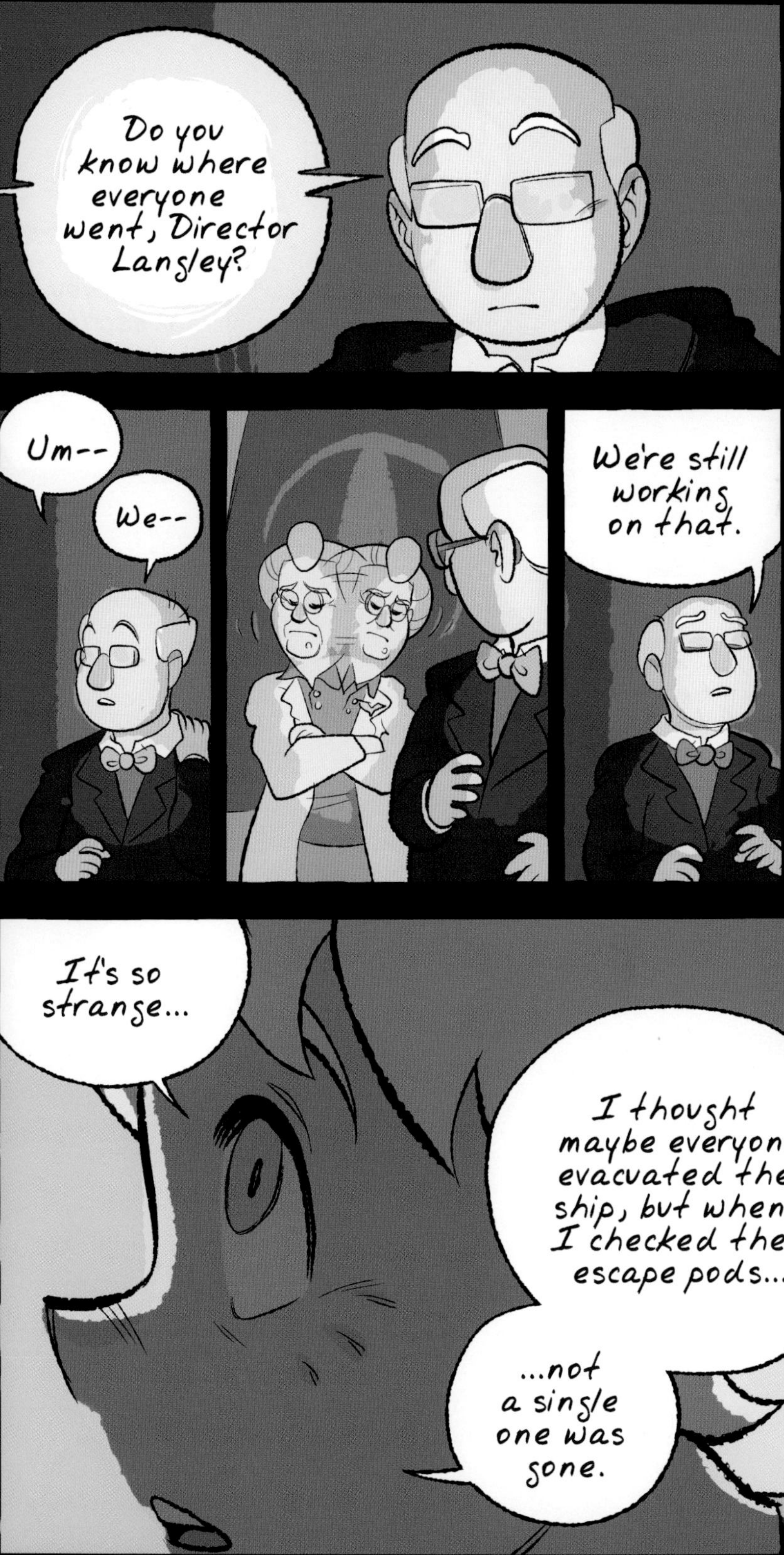
Do you know where everyone went, Director Langley?
Um--
We--
We're still working on that.
It's so strange...
I thought maybe everyone evacuated the ship, but when I checked the escape pods...
...not a single one was gone.

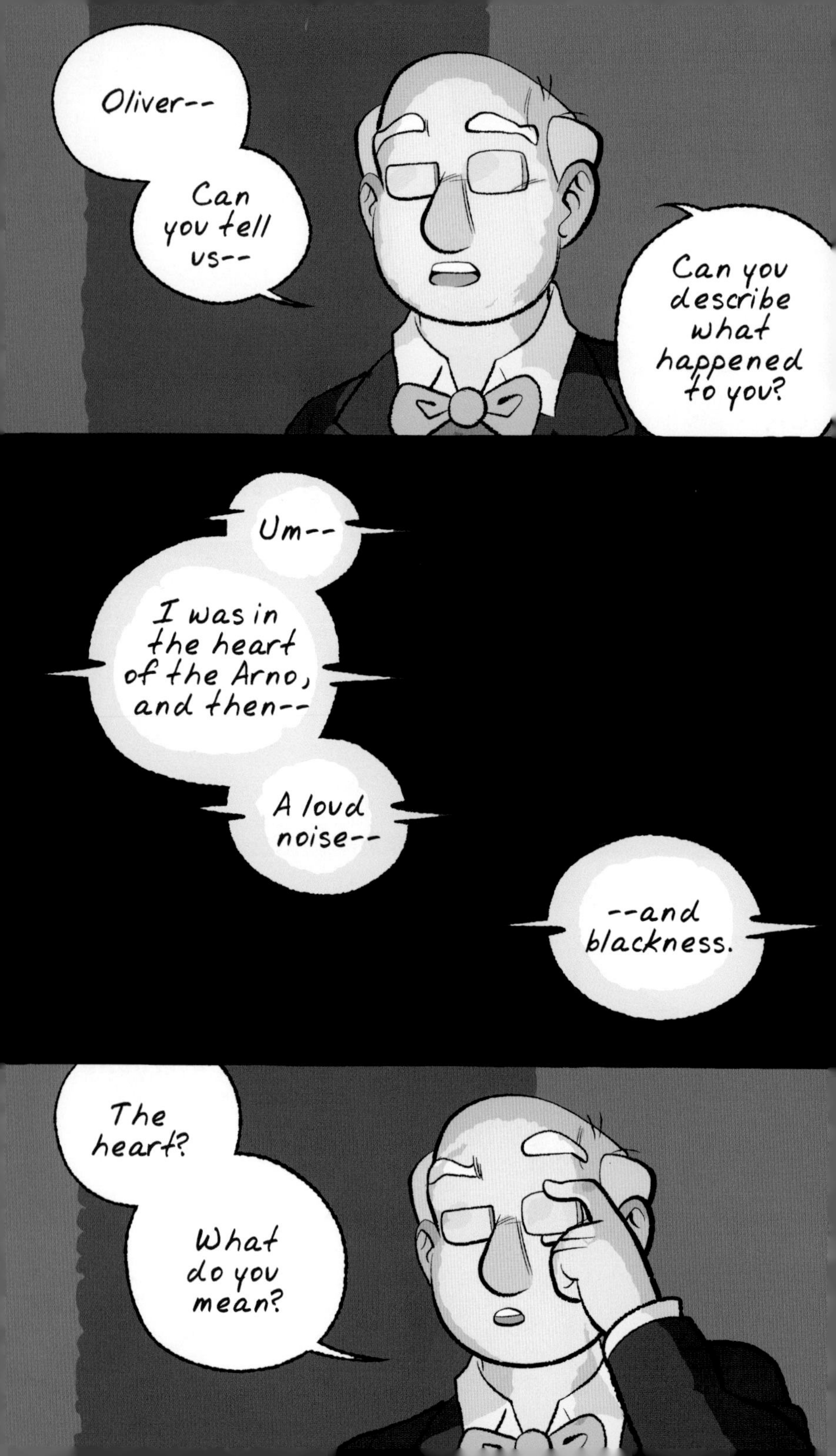

Oliver--
Can you tell us--
Can you describe what happened to you?
Um--
I was in the heart of the Arno, and then--
A loud noise--
--and blackness.
The heart?
What do you mean?

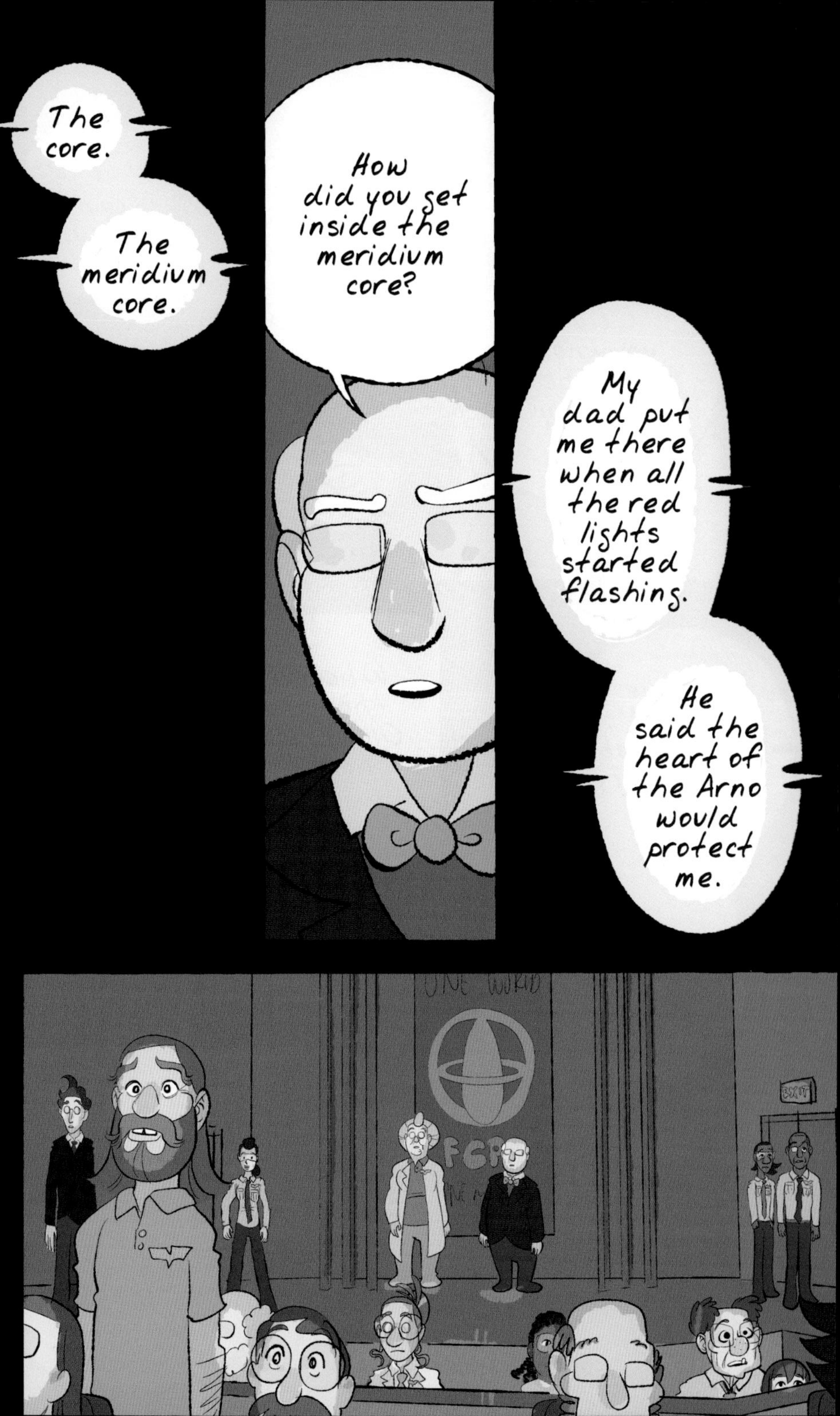
The core.
The meridium core.
How did you get inside the meridium core?
My dad put me there when all the red lights started flashing.
He said the heart of the Arno would protect me.

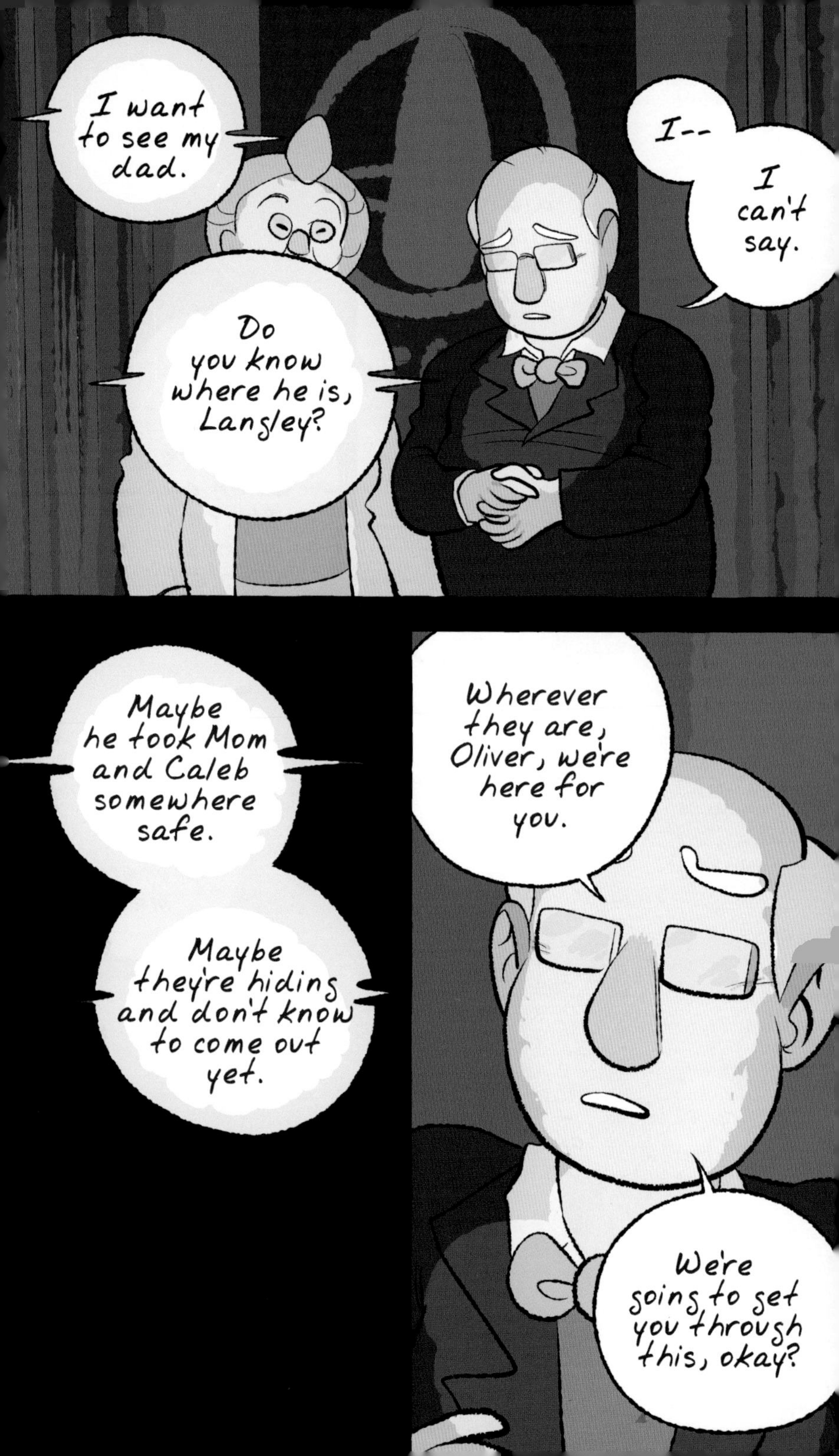
I want to see my dad.
Do you know where he is, Langley?
I--
I can't say.
Maybe he took Mom and Caleb somewhere safe.
Maybe they're hiding and don't know to come out yet.
Wherever they are, Oliver, we're here for you.
We're going to get you through this, okay?

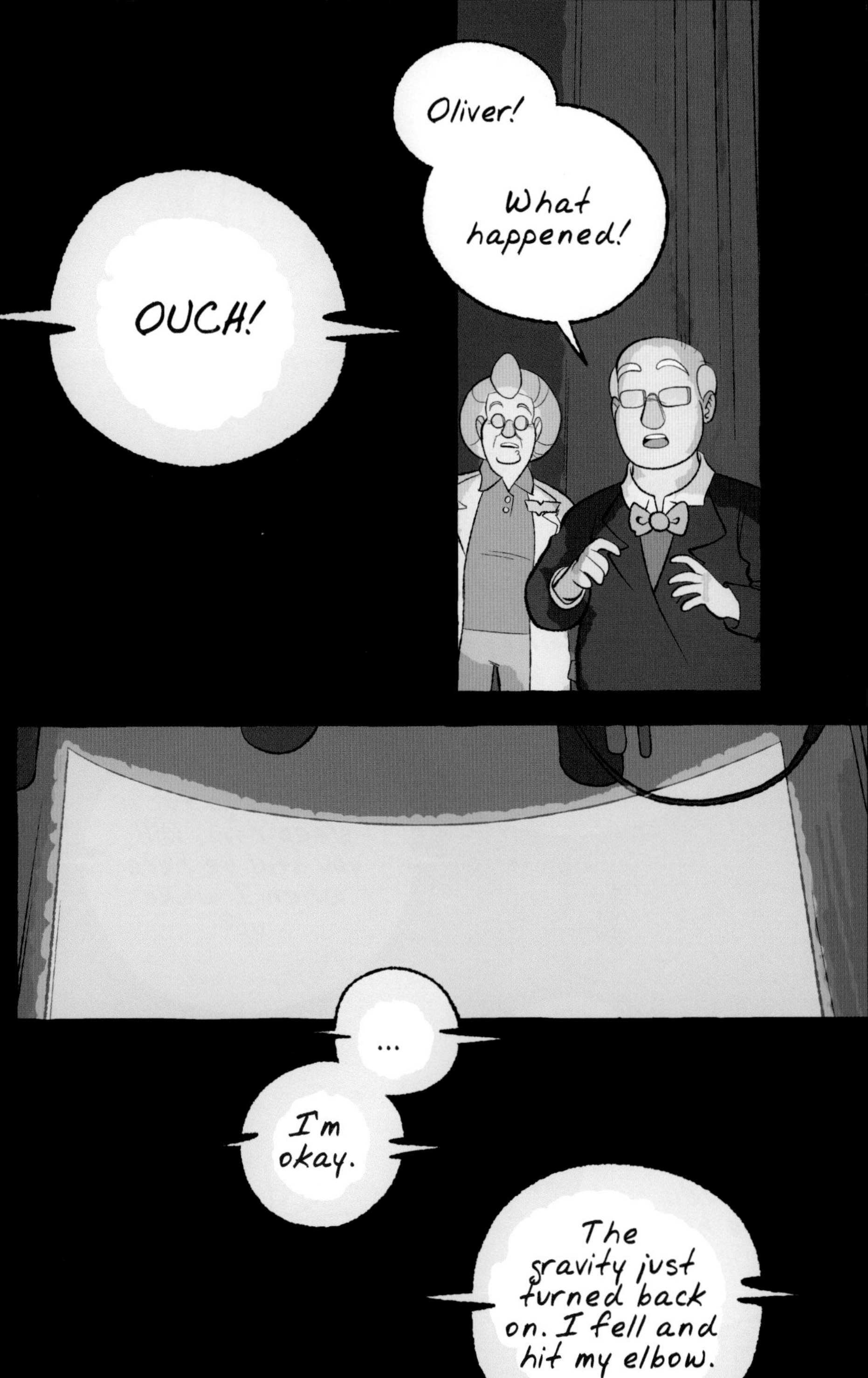
Oliver!
What happened!
OUCH!
...
I'm okay.
The gravity just turned back on. I fell and hit my elbow.

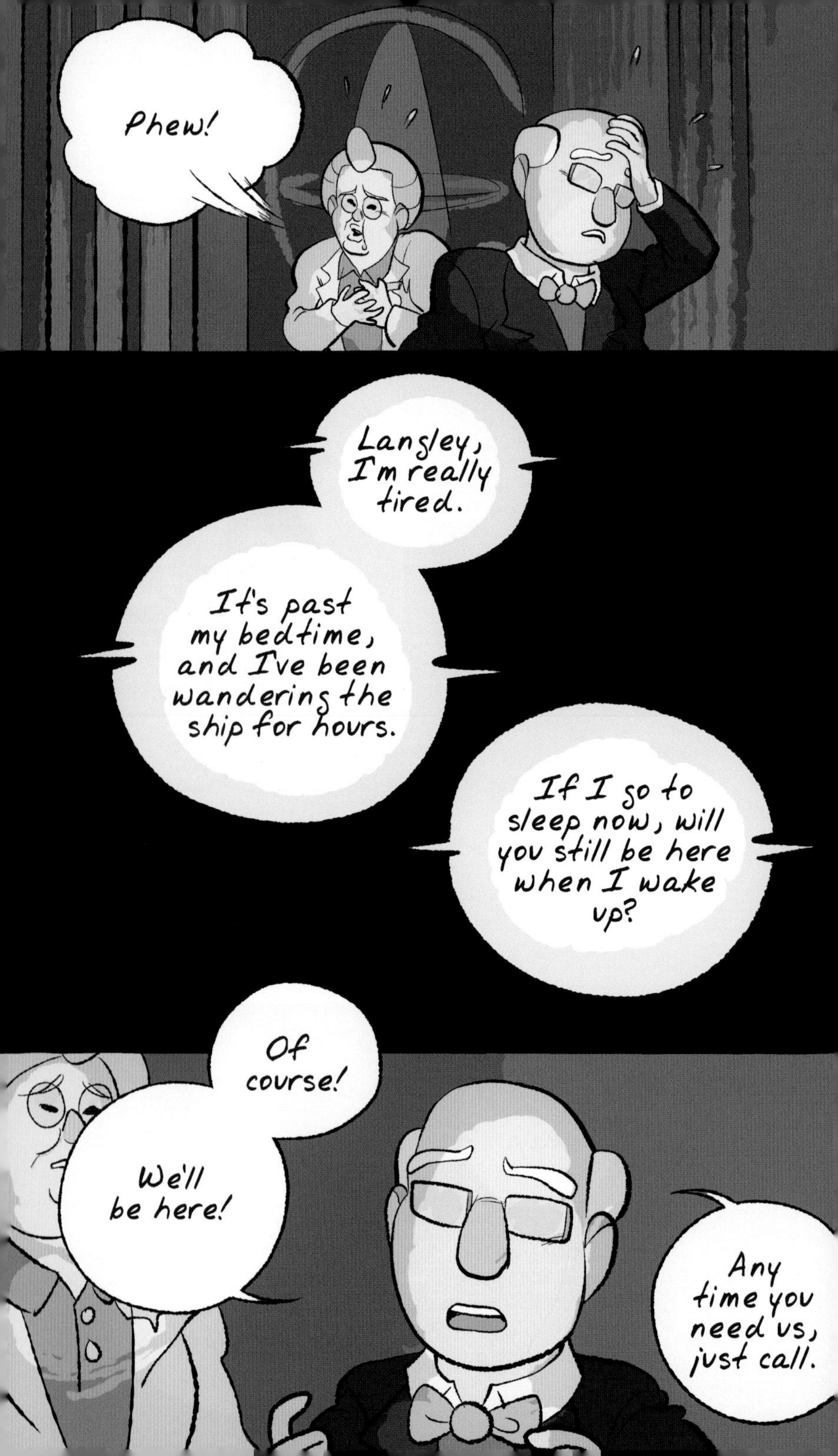
Phew!
Langley, I'm really tired.
It's past my bedtime, and I've been wandering the ship for hours.
If I go to sleep now, will you still be here when I wake up?
Of course!
We'll be here!
Any time you need us, just call.

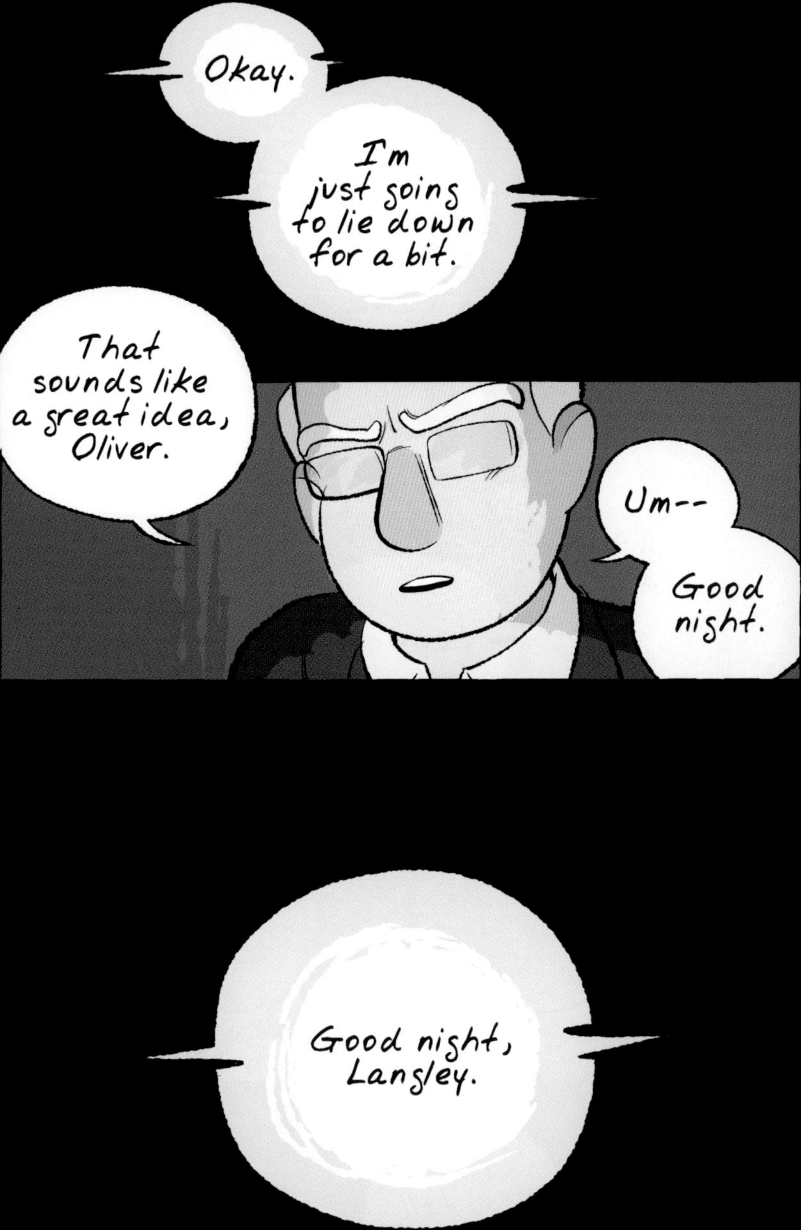
Okay.
I'm just going to lie down for a bit.
That sounds like a great idea, Oliver.
Um--
Good night.
Good night, Langley.

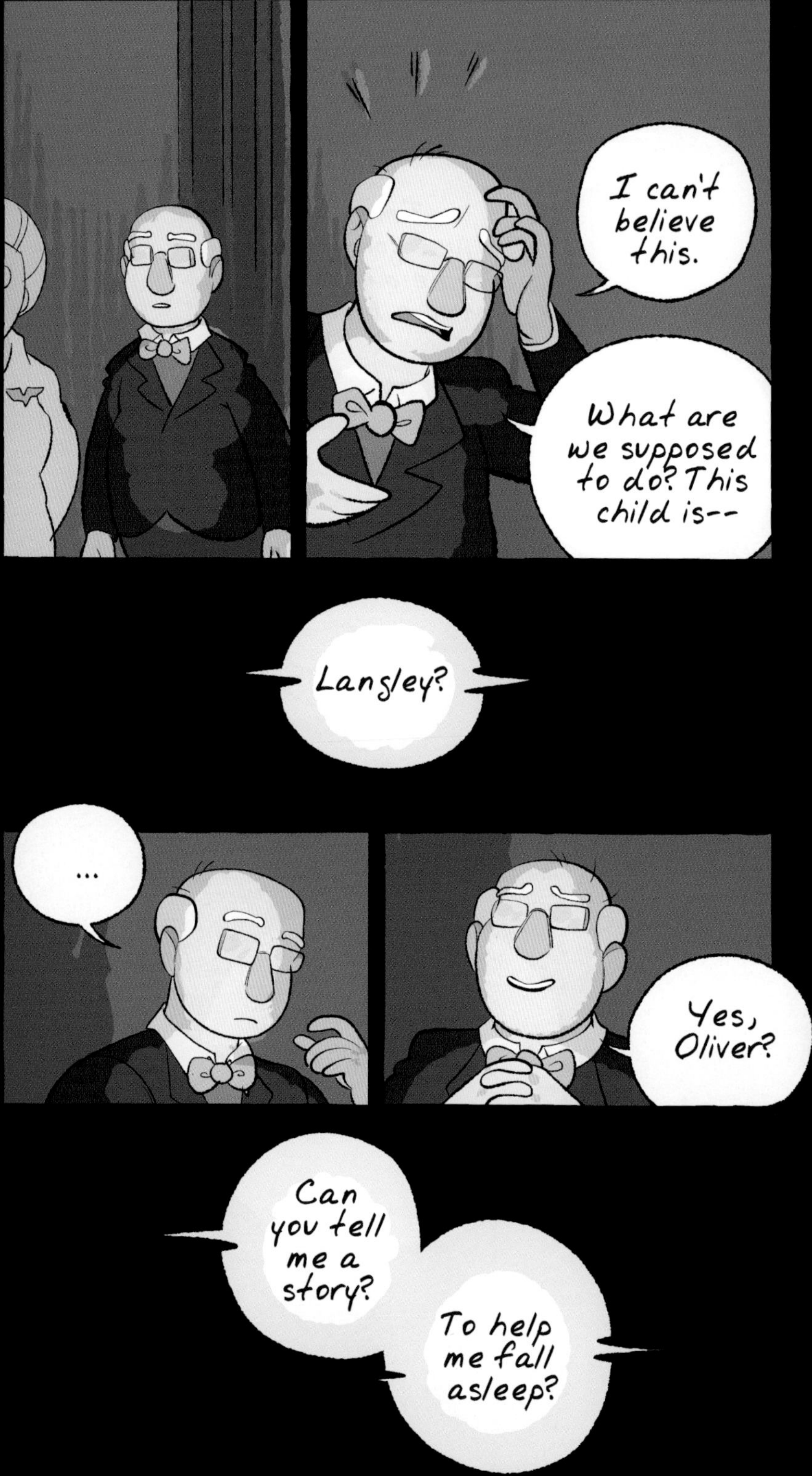
I can't believe this.
What are we supposed to do? This child is--
Langley?
...
Yes, Oliver?
Can you tell me a story?
To help me fall asleep?

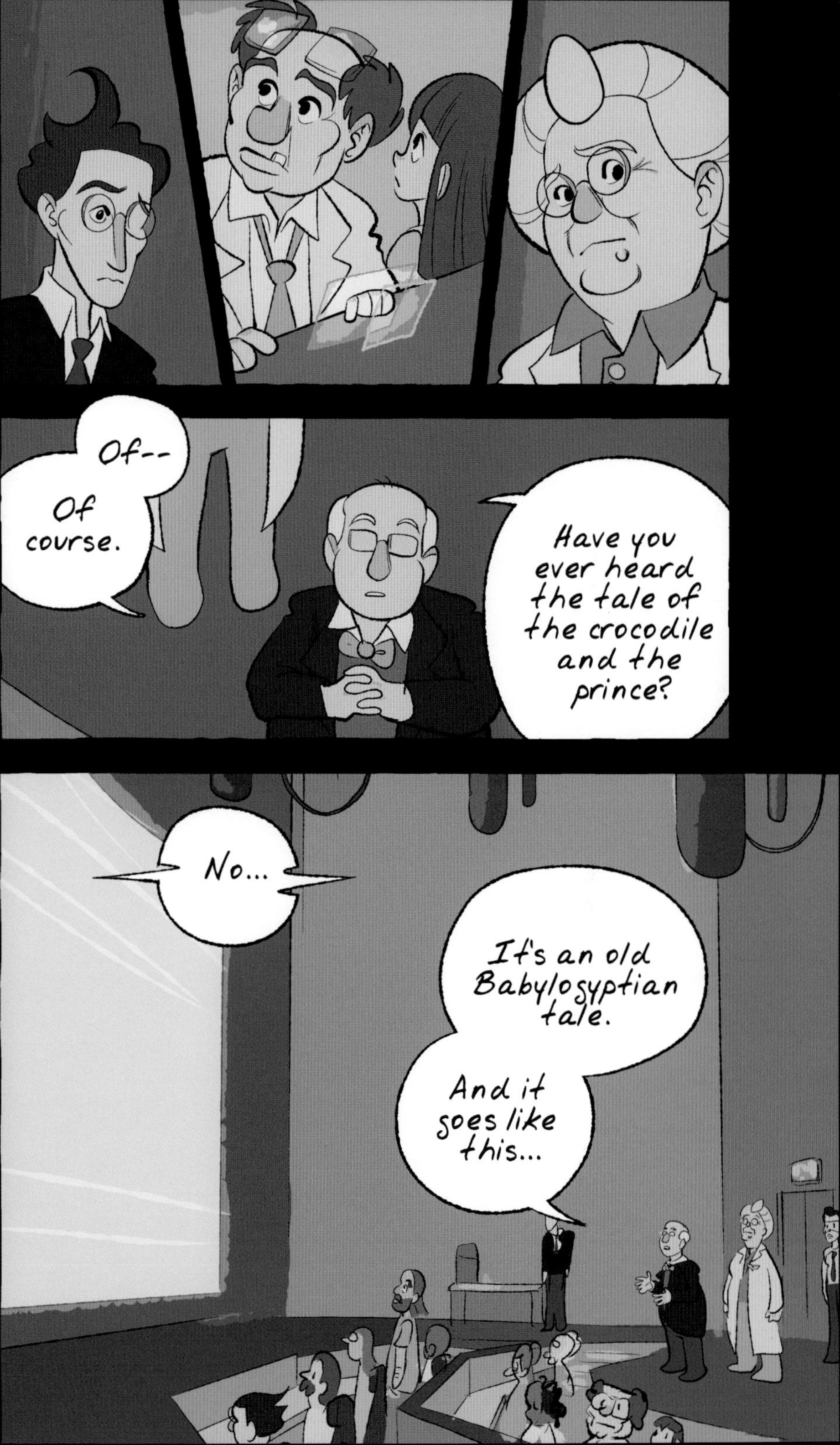
Of--
Of course.
Have you ever heard the tale of the crocodile and the prince?
No...
It's an old Babylosyptian tale.
And it goes like this...

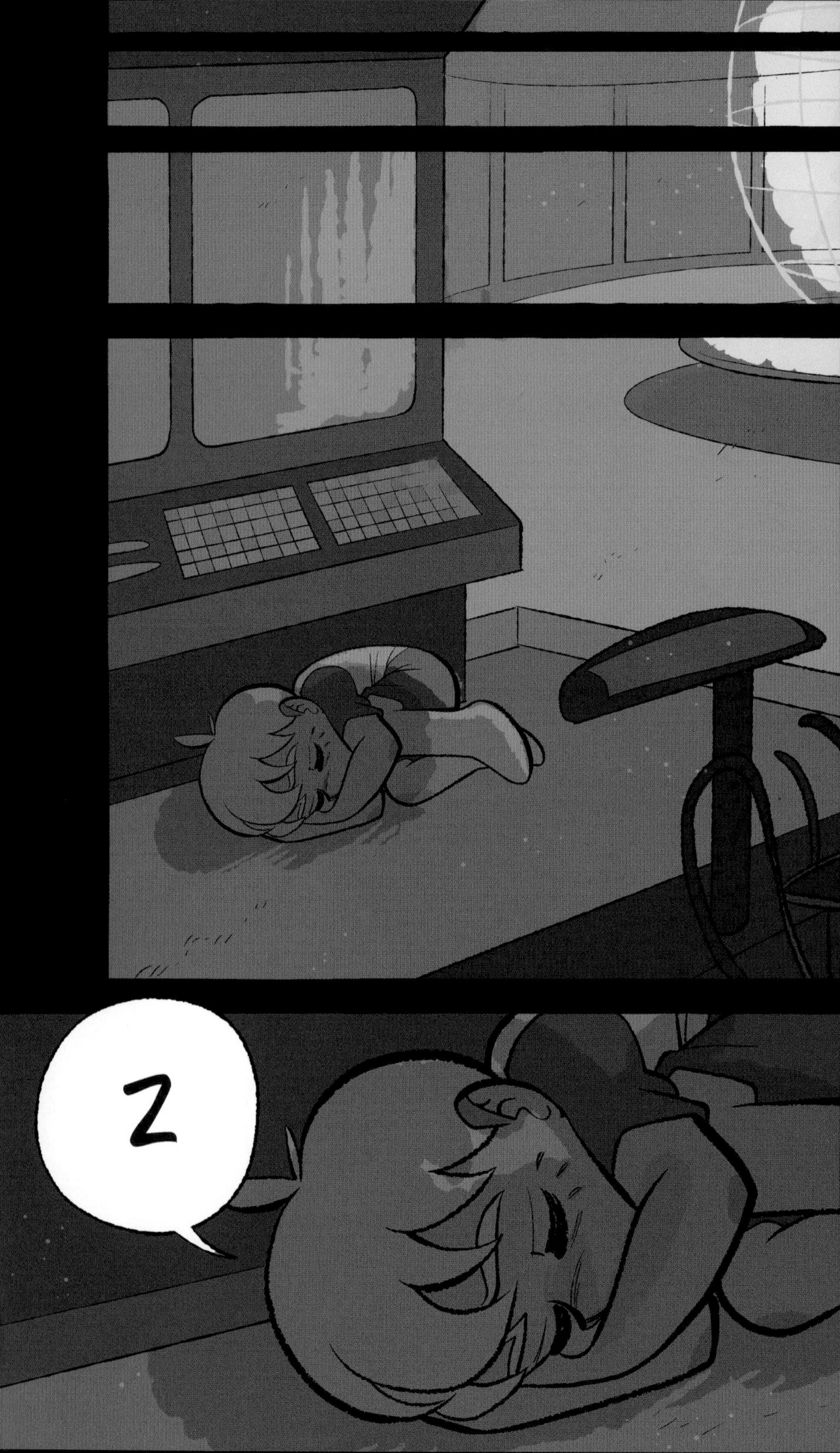
Z

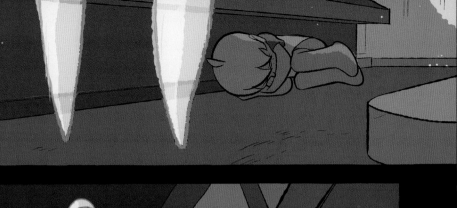

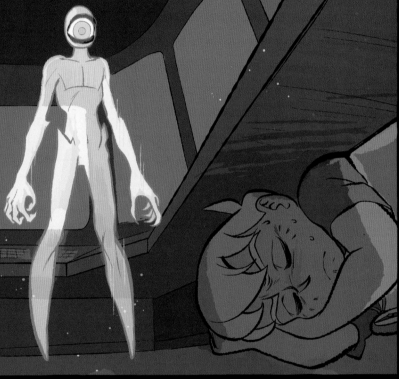

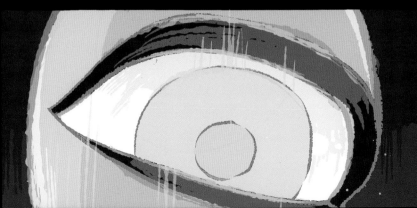

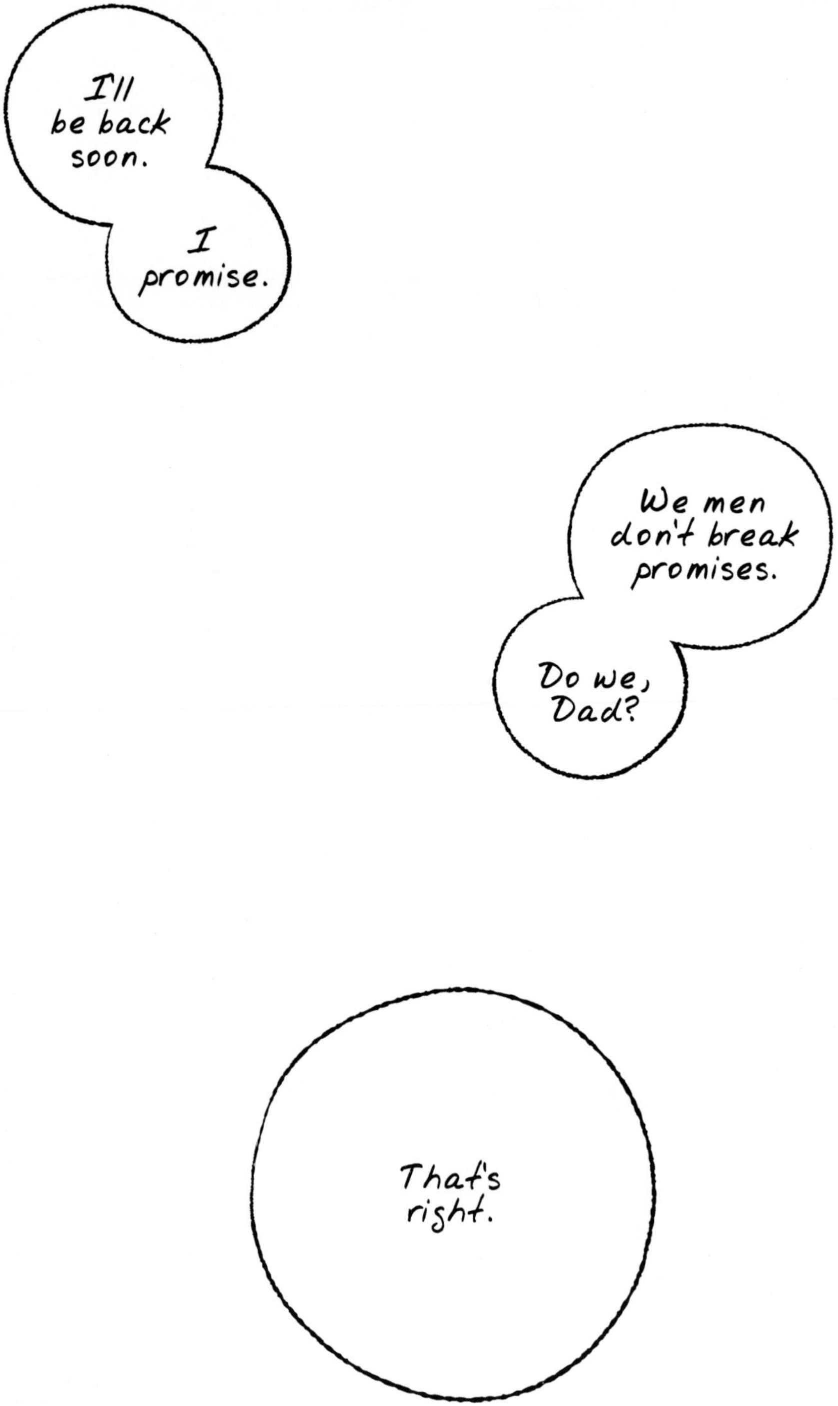
I'll be back soon.
I promise.
We men don't break promises.
Do we, Dad?
That's right.

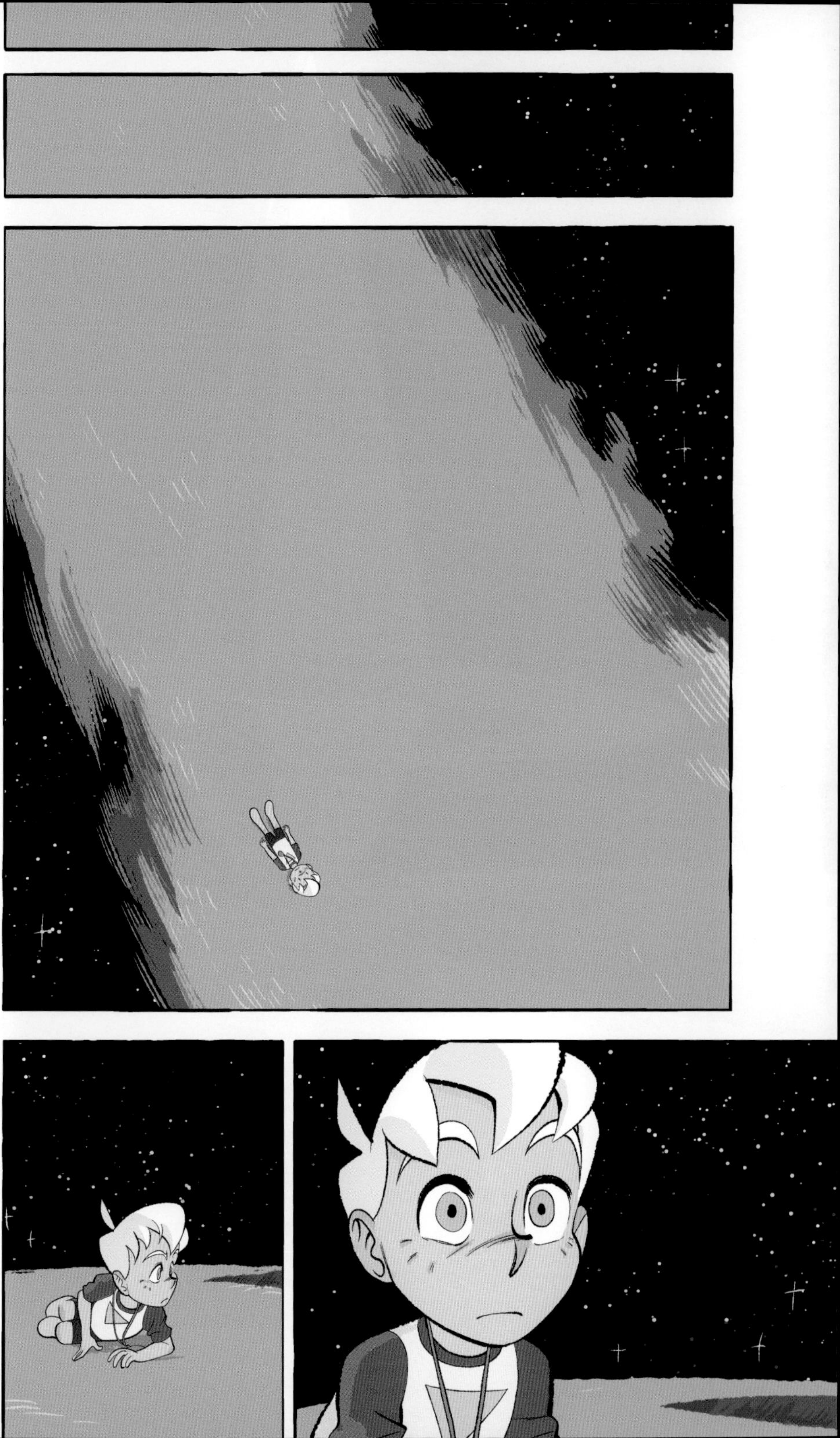

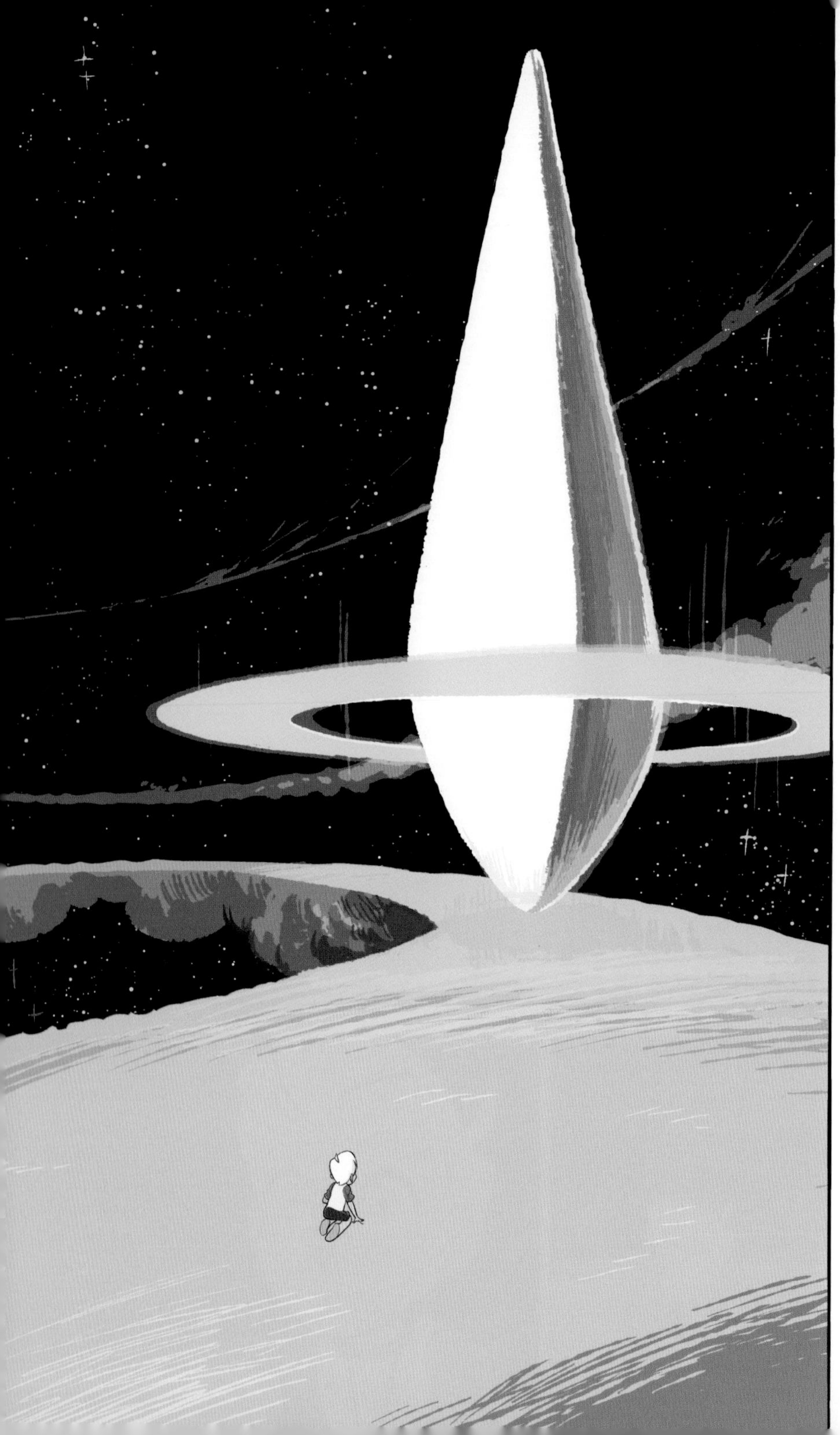

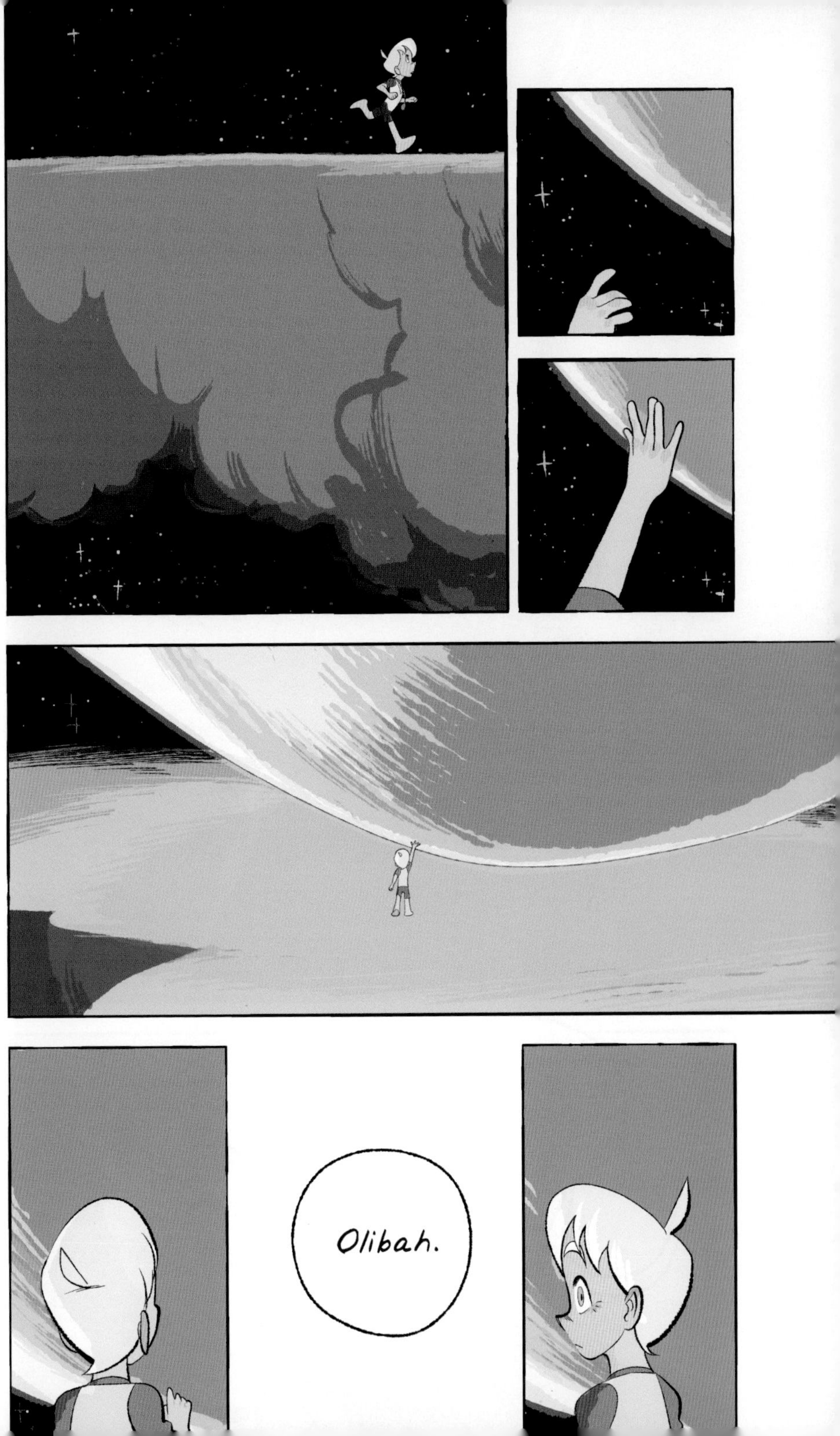
Olibah.

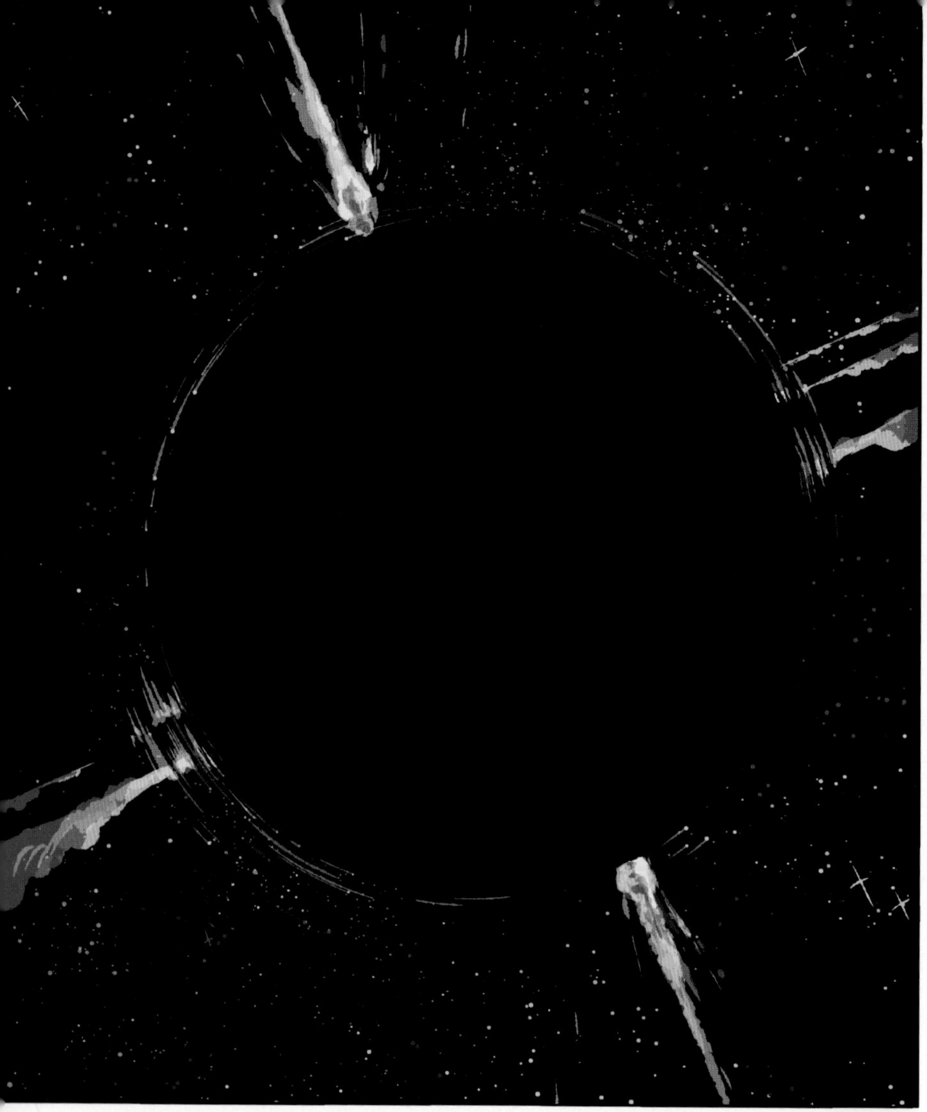

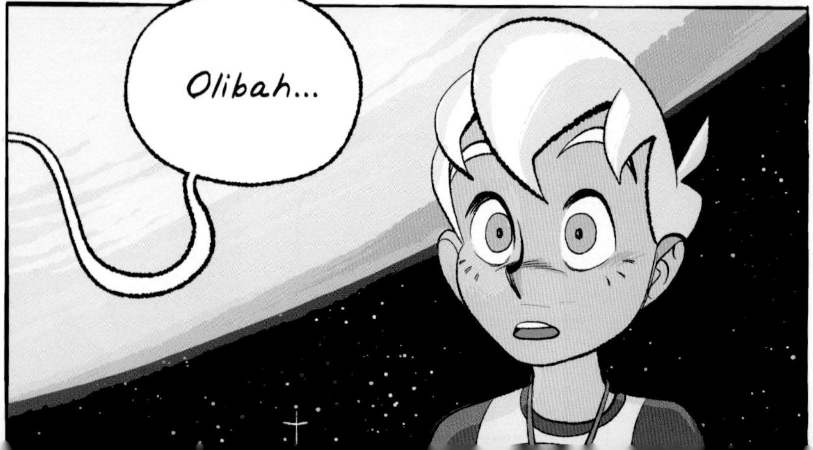
Olibah...

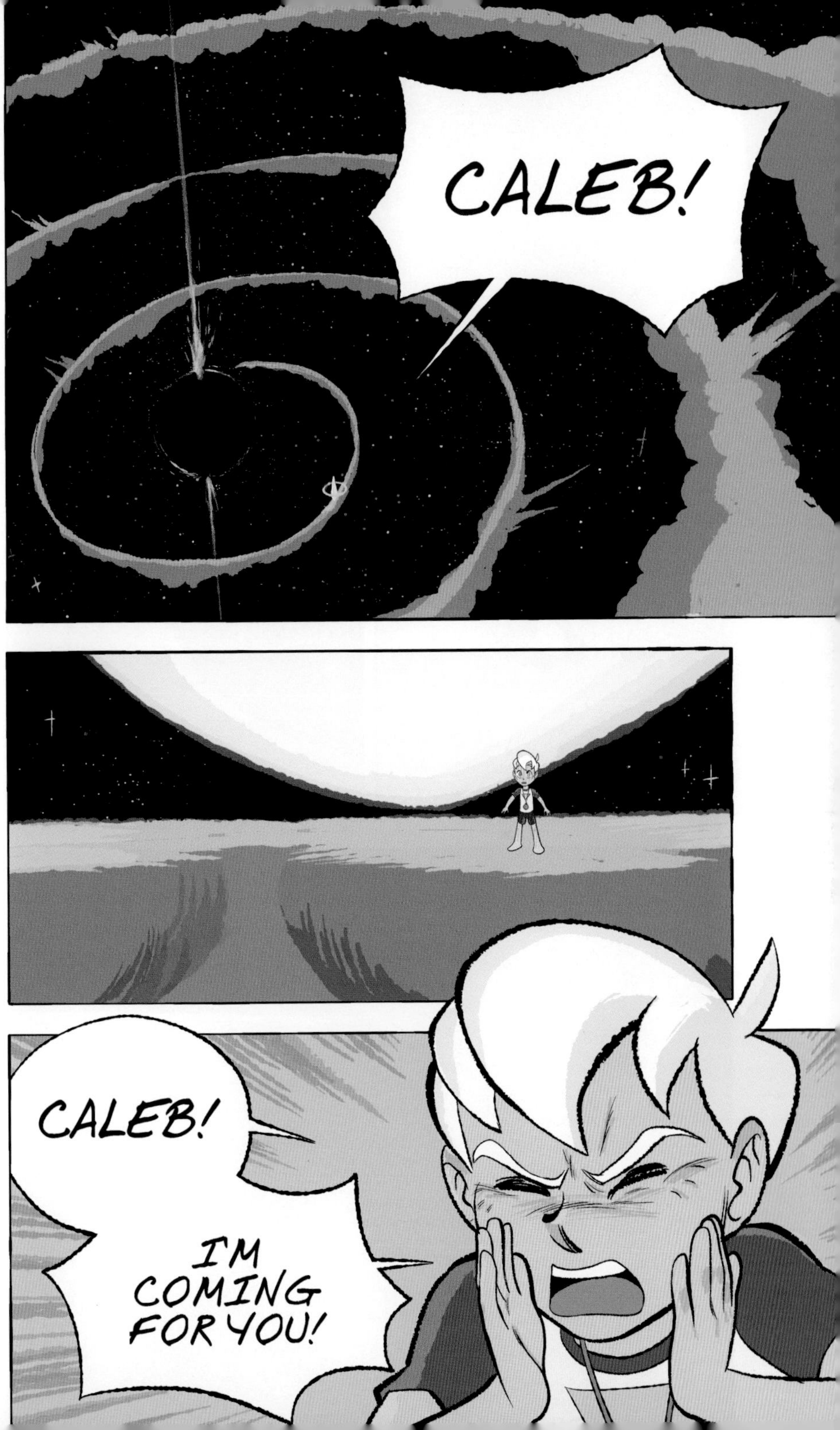
CALEB!
CALEB!
I'M COMING FOR YOU!

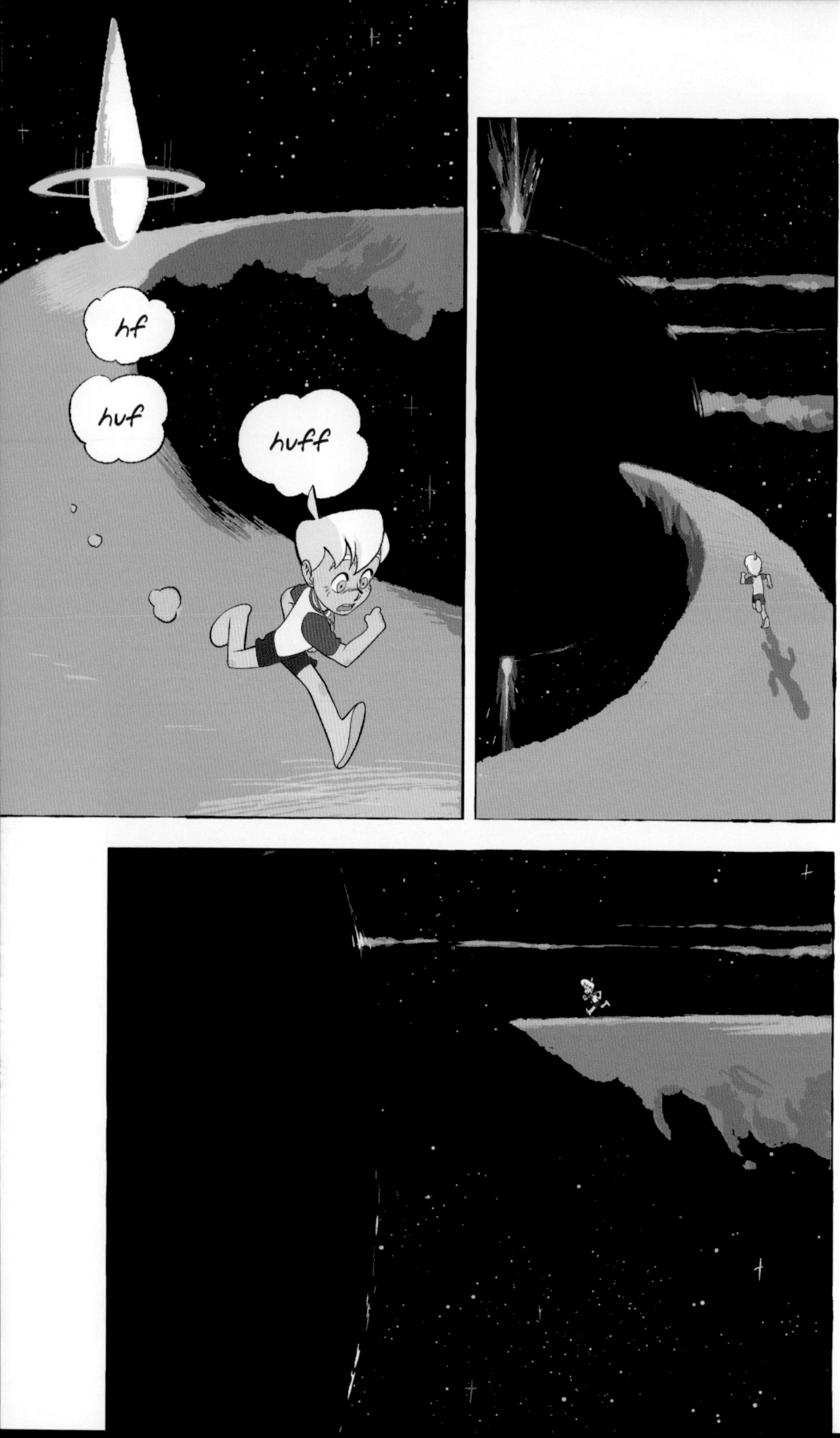

hf
huf
huff

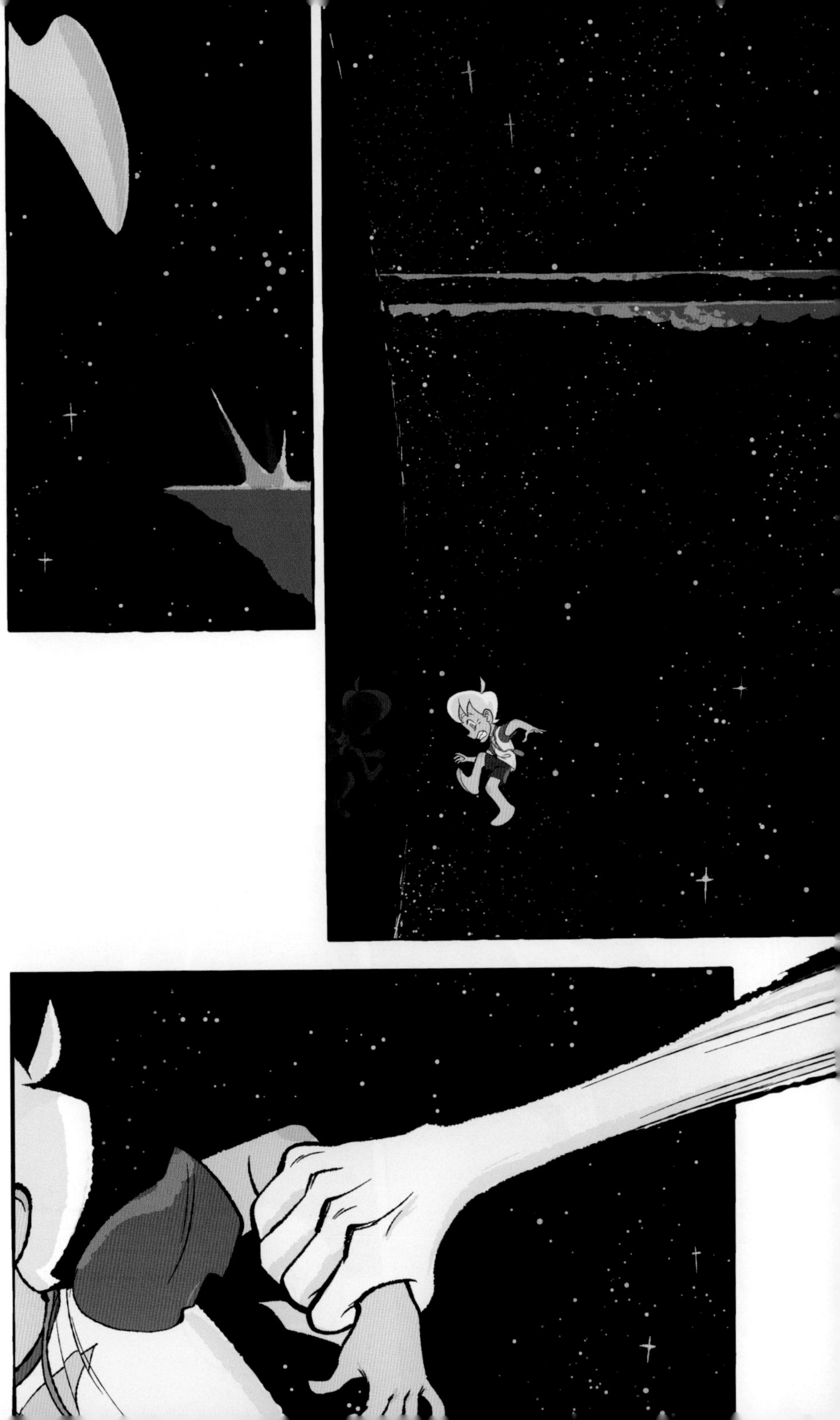

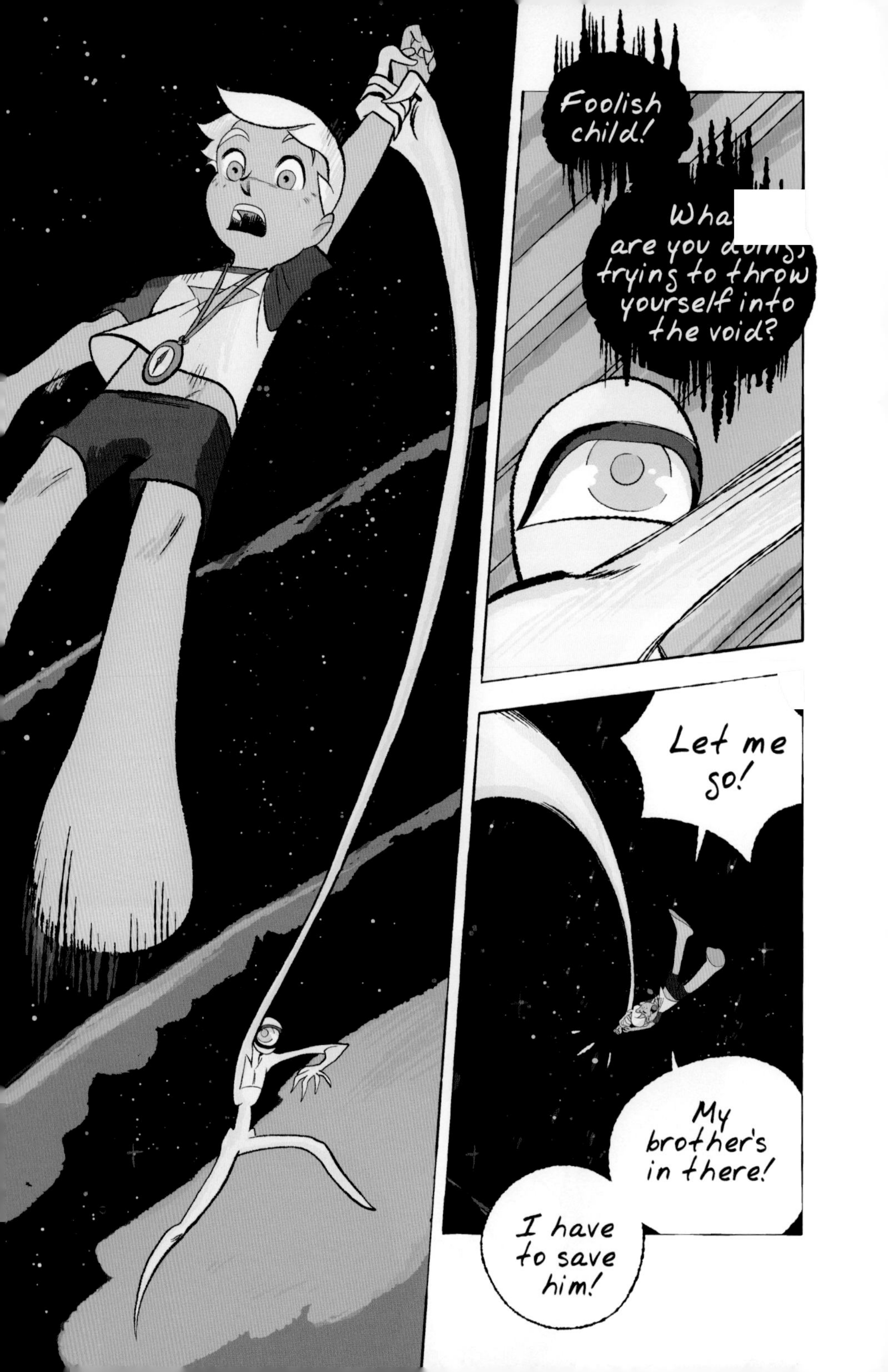
Foolish child!
Wha
are you doing, trying to throw yourself into the void?
Let me go!
My brother's in there!
I have to save him!

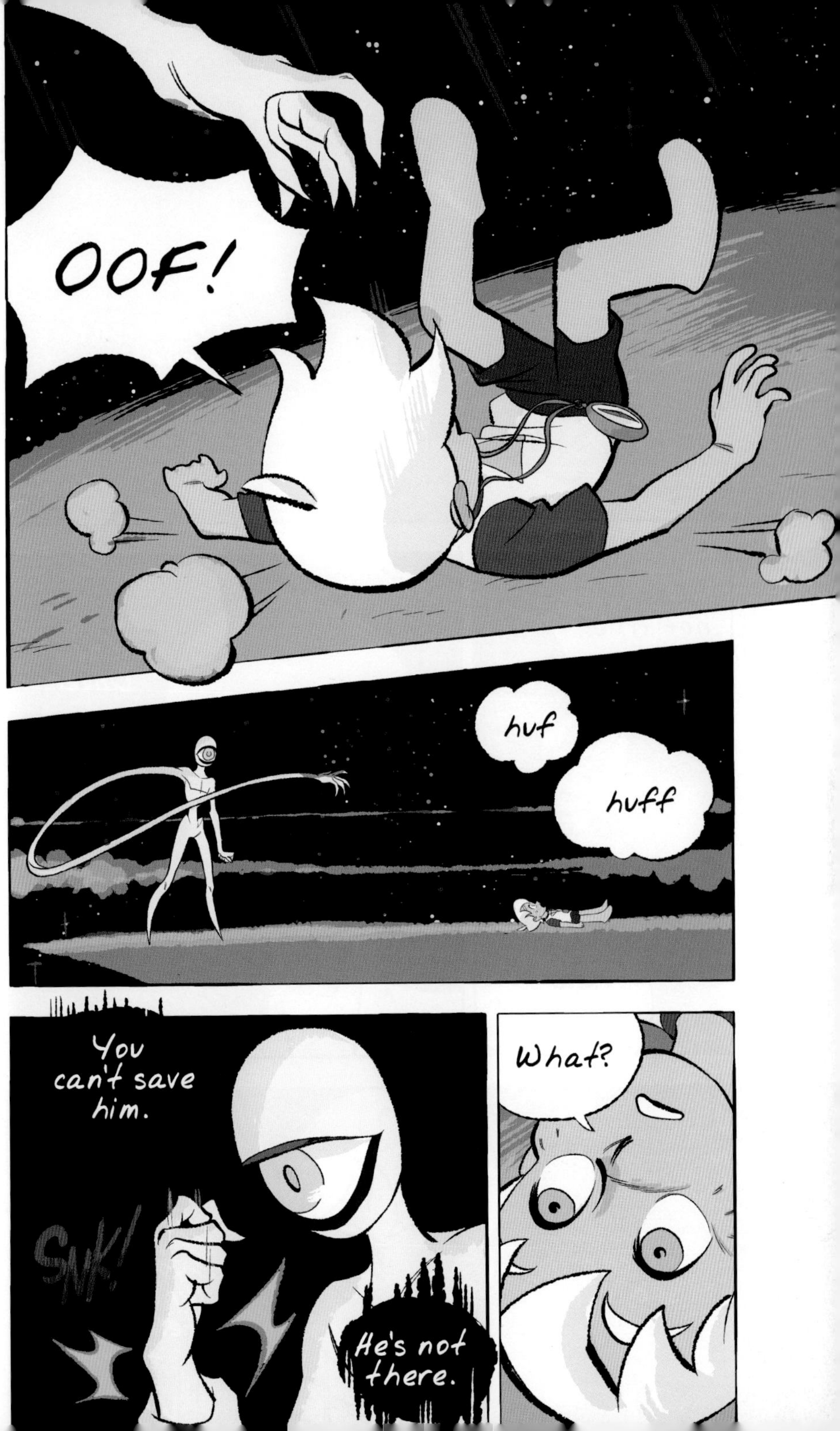
OOF!
huf
huff
You can't save him.
SNK!
He's not there.
What?

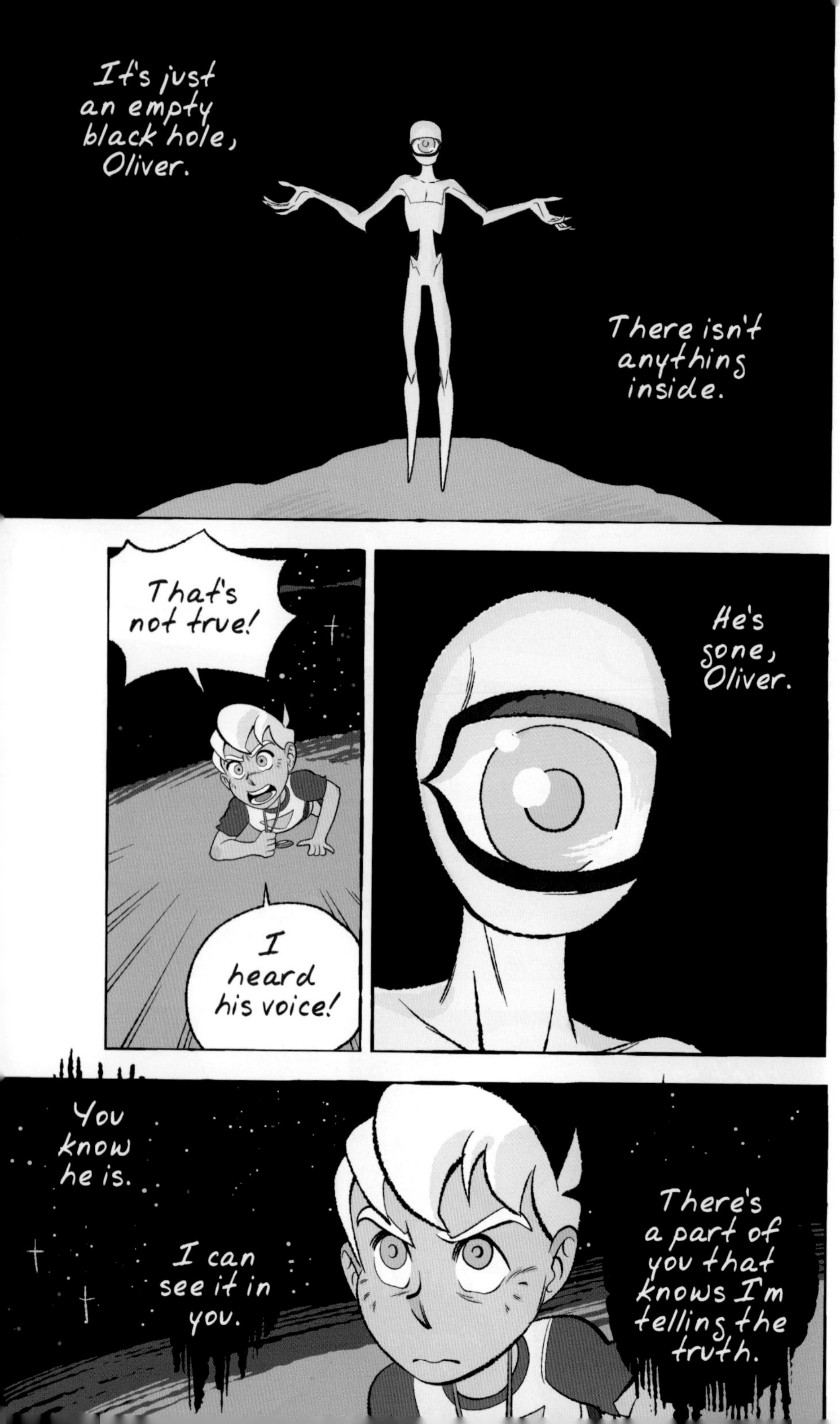
It's just an empty black hole, Oliver.
There isn't anything inside.
That's not true!
I heard his voice!
He's gone, Oliver.
You know he is.
I can see it in you.
There's a part of you that knows I'm telling the truth.

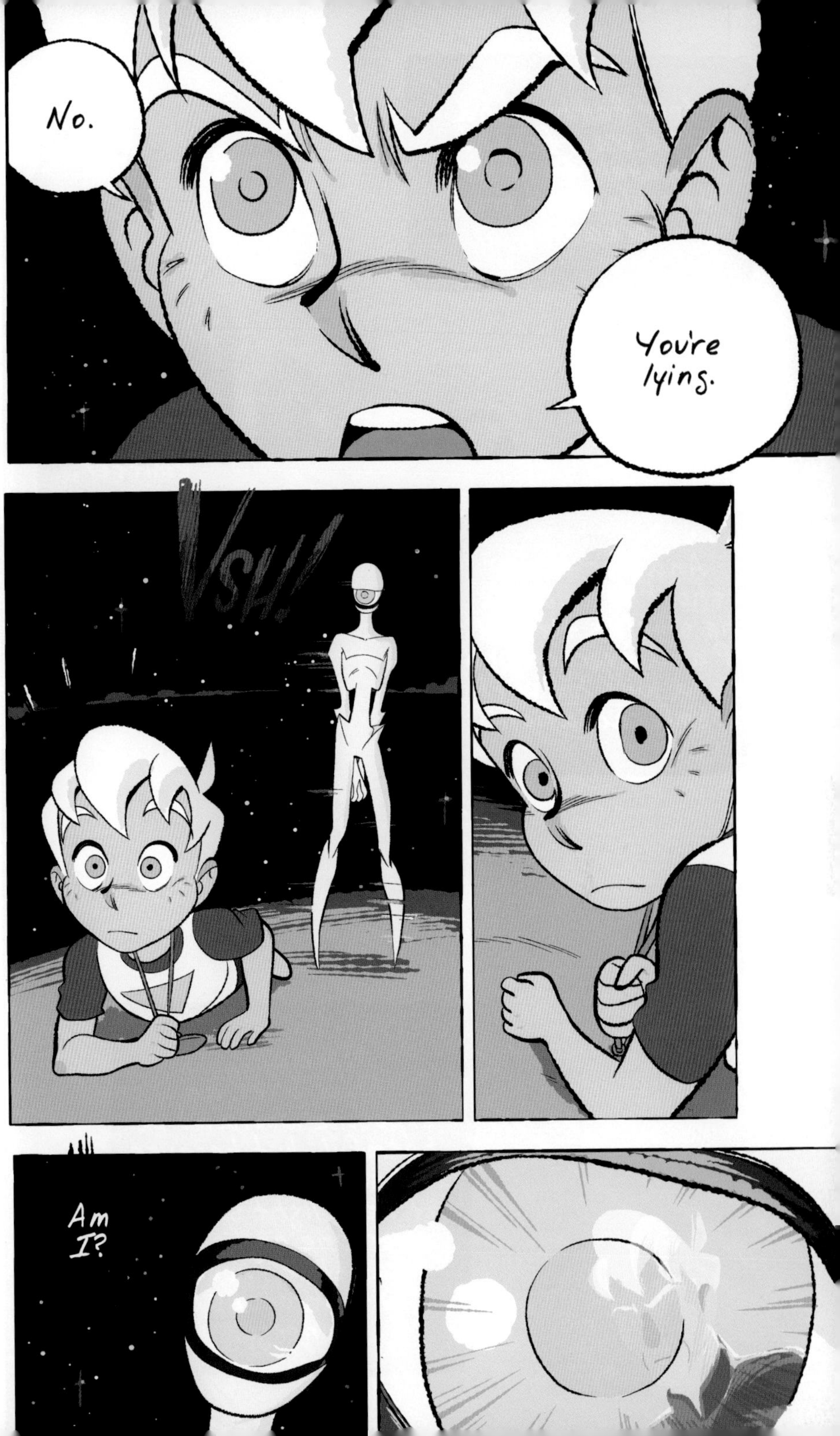
No.
You're lying.
VSH!
Am I?

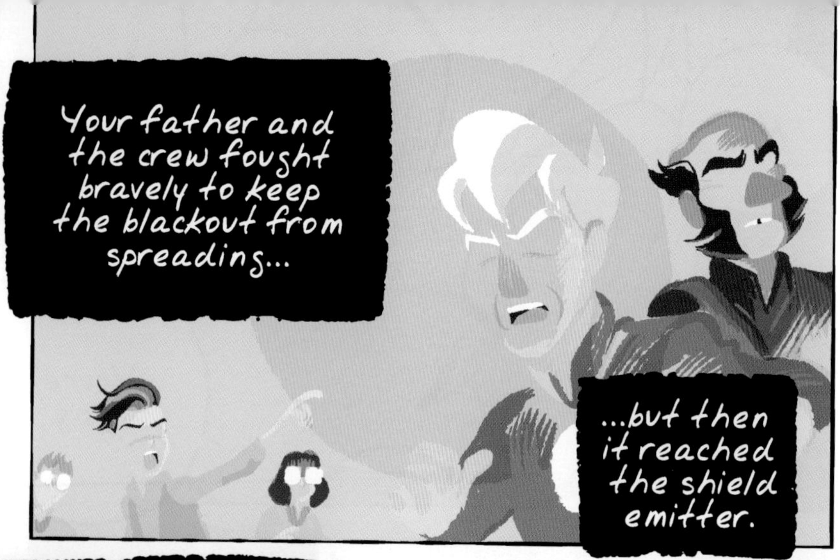
Your father and the crew fought bravely to keep the blackout from spreading...
...but then it reached the shield emitter.

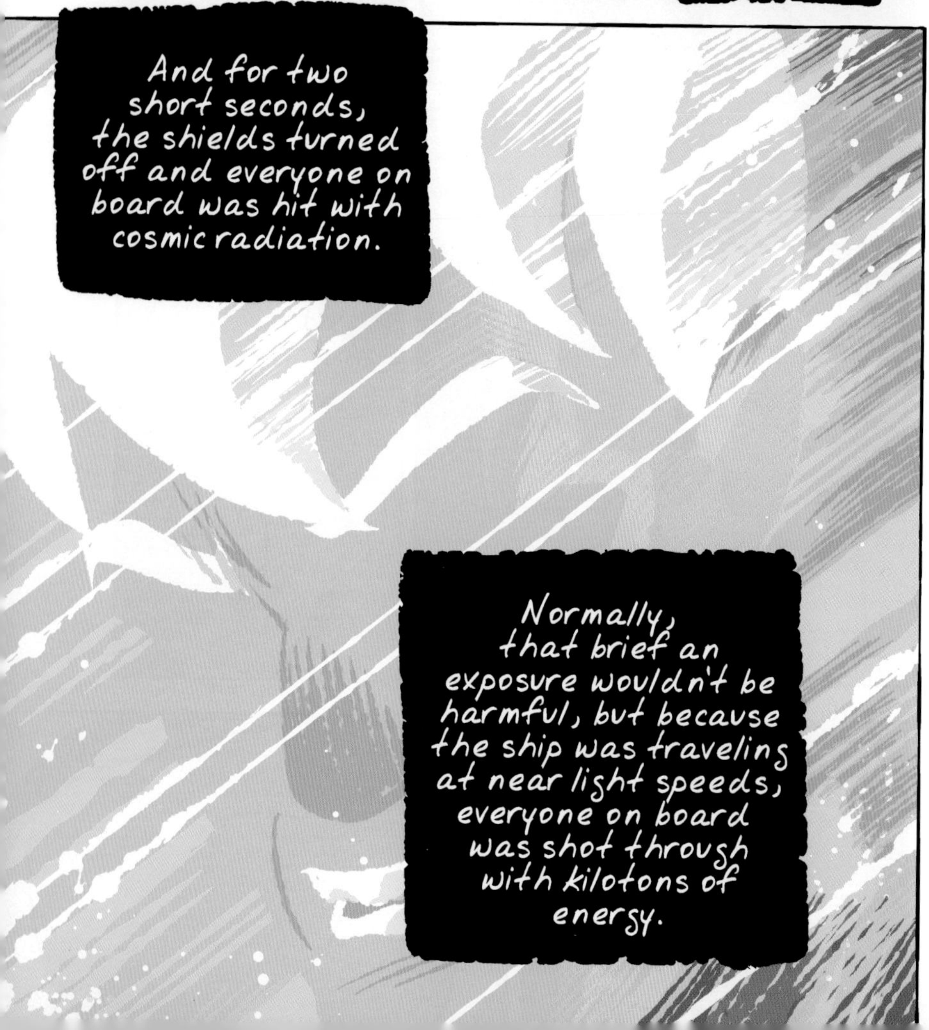
And for two short seconds, the shields turned off and everyone on board was hit with cosmic radiation.
Normally, that brief an exposure wouldn't be harmful, but because the ship was traveling at near light speeds, everyone on board was shot through with kilotons of energy.

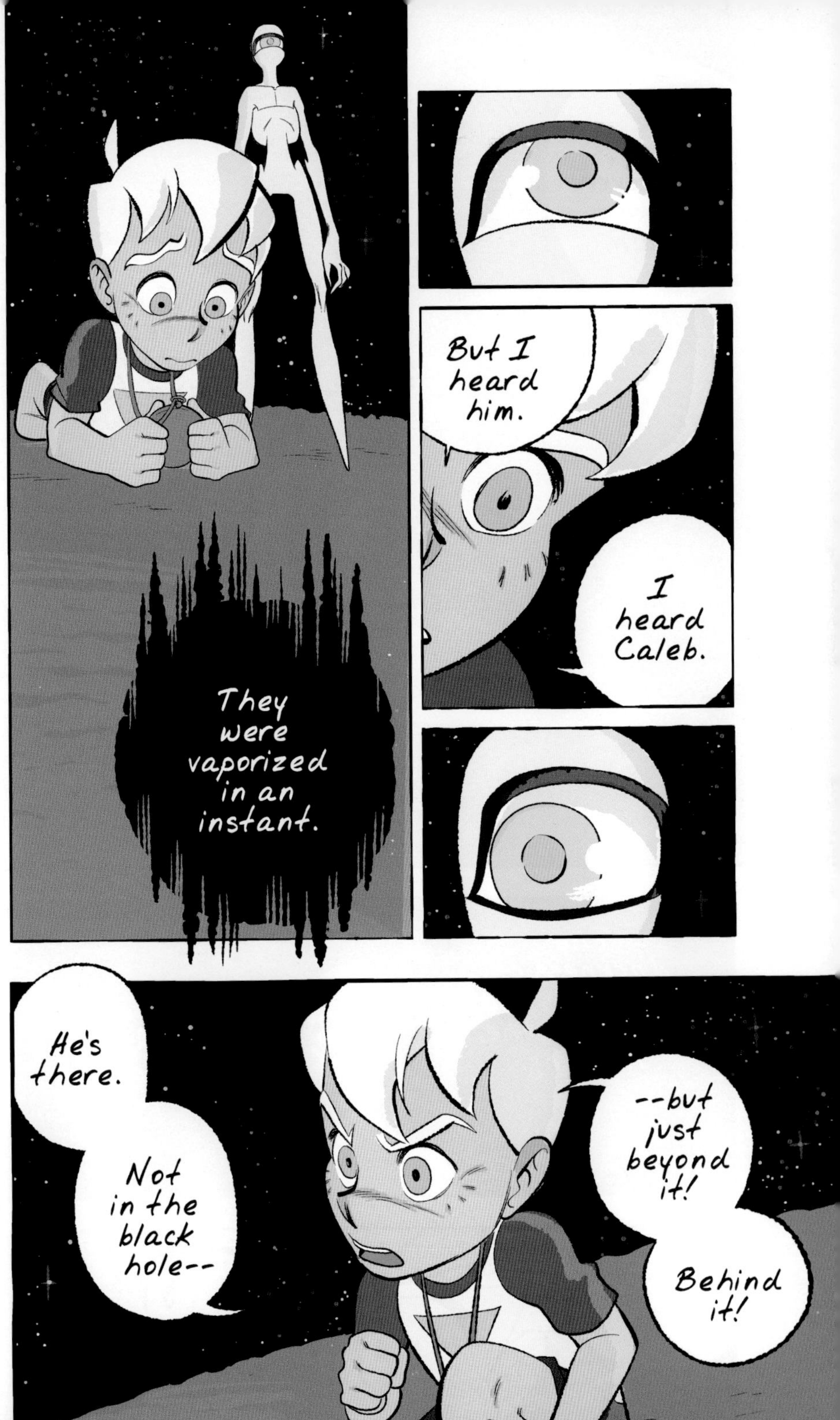
They were vaporized in an instant.
But I heard him.
I heard Caleb.
He's there.
Not in the black hole--
--but just beyond it!
Behind it!

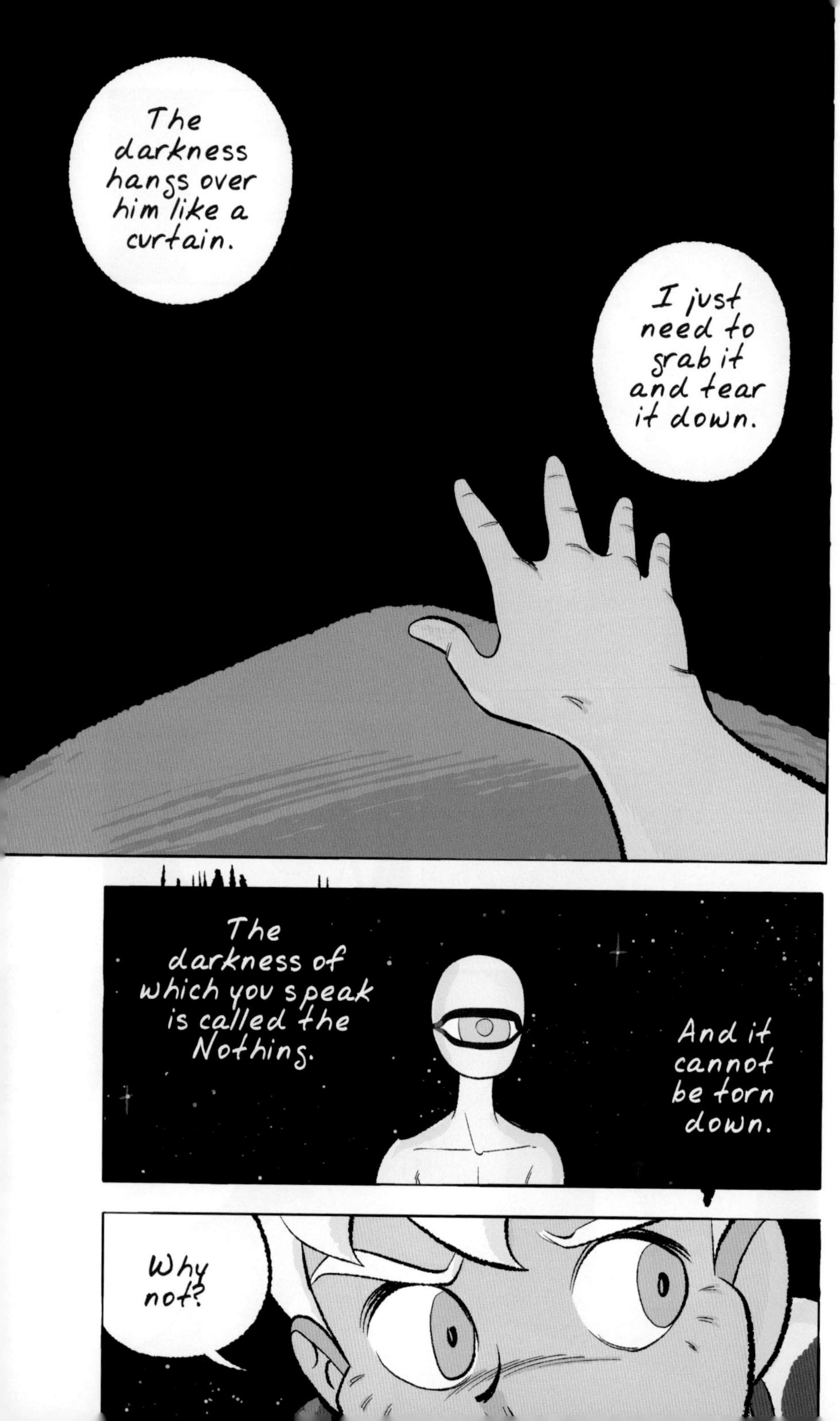
The darkness hangs over him like a curtain.
I just need to grab it and tear it down.
The darkness of which you speak is called the Nothing.
And it cannot be torn down.
Why not?

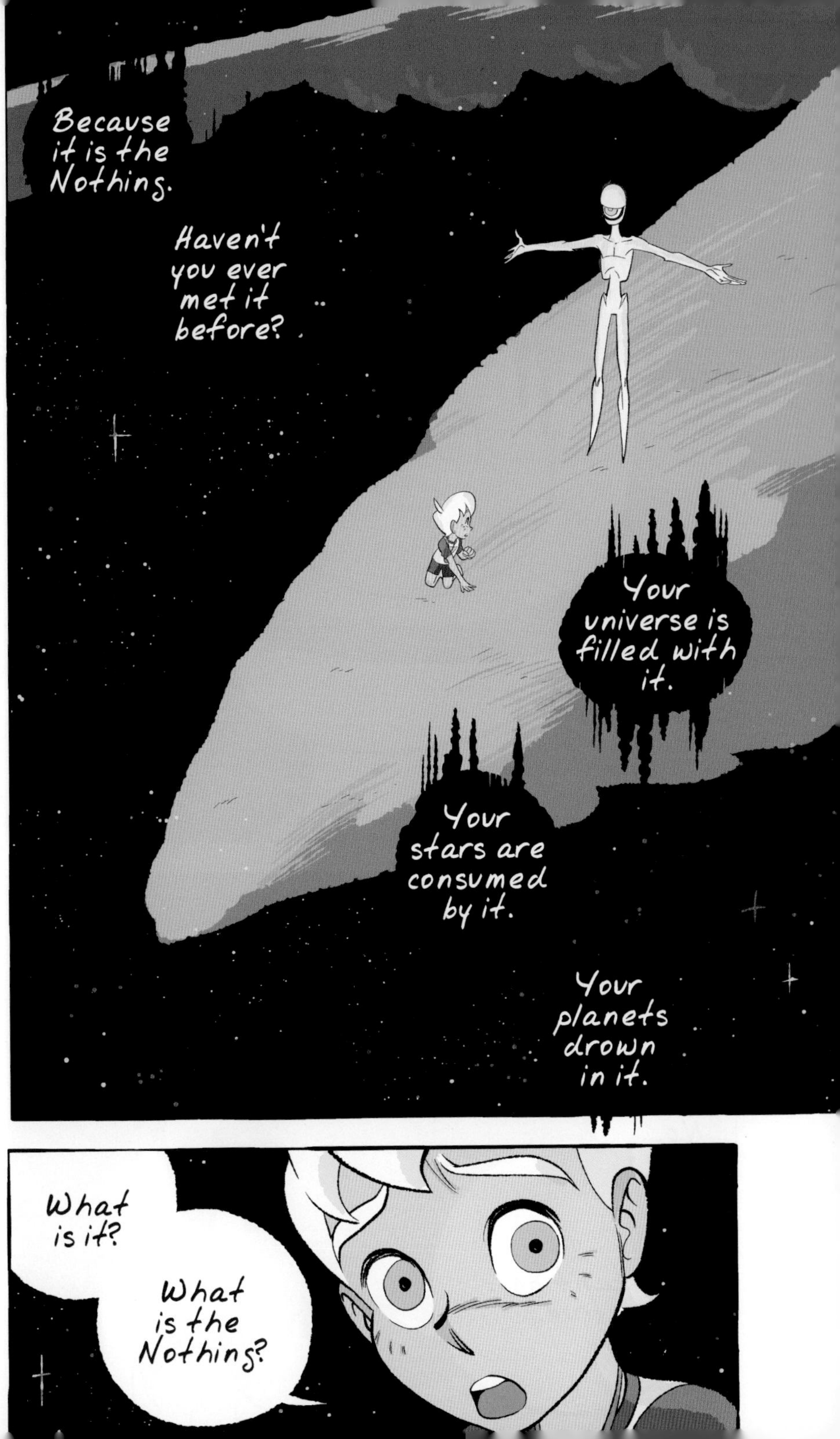
Because it is the Nothing.
Haven't you ever met it before?
Your universe is filled with it.
Your stars are consumed by it.
Your planets drown in it.
What is it?
What is the Nothing?

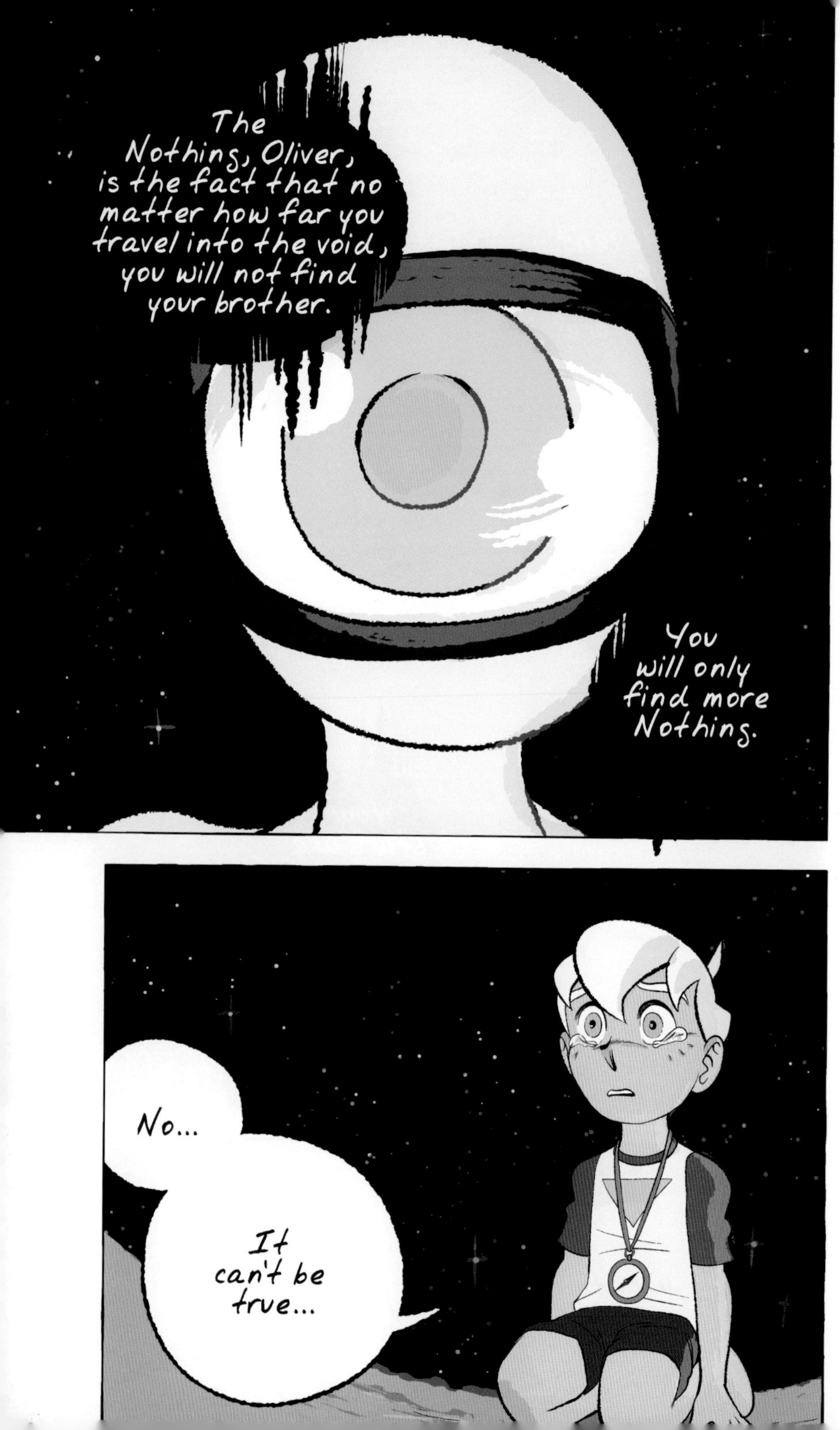
The Nothing, Oliver, is the fact that no matter how far you travel into the void, you will not find your brother.
You will only find more Nothing.
No...
It can't be true...

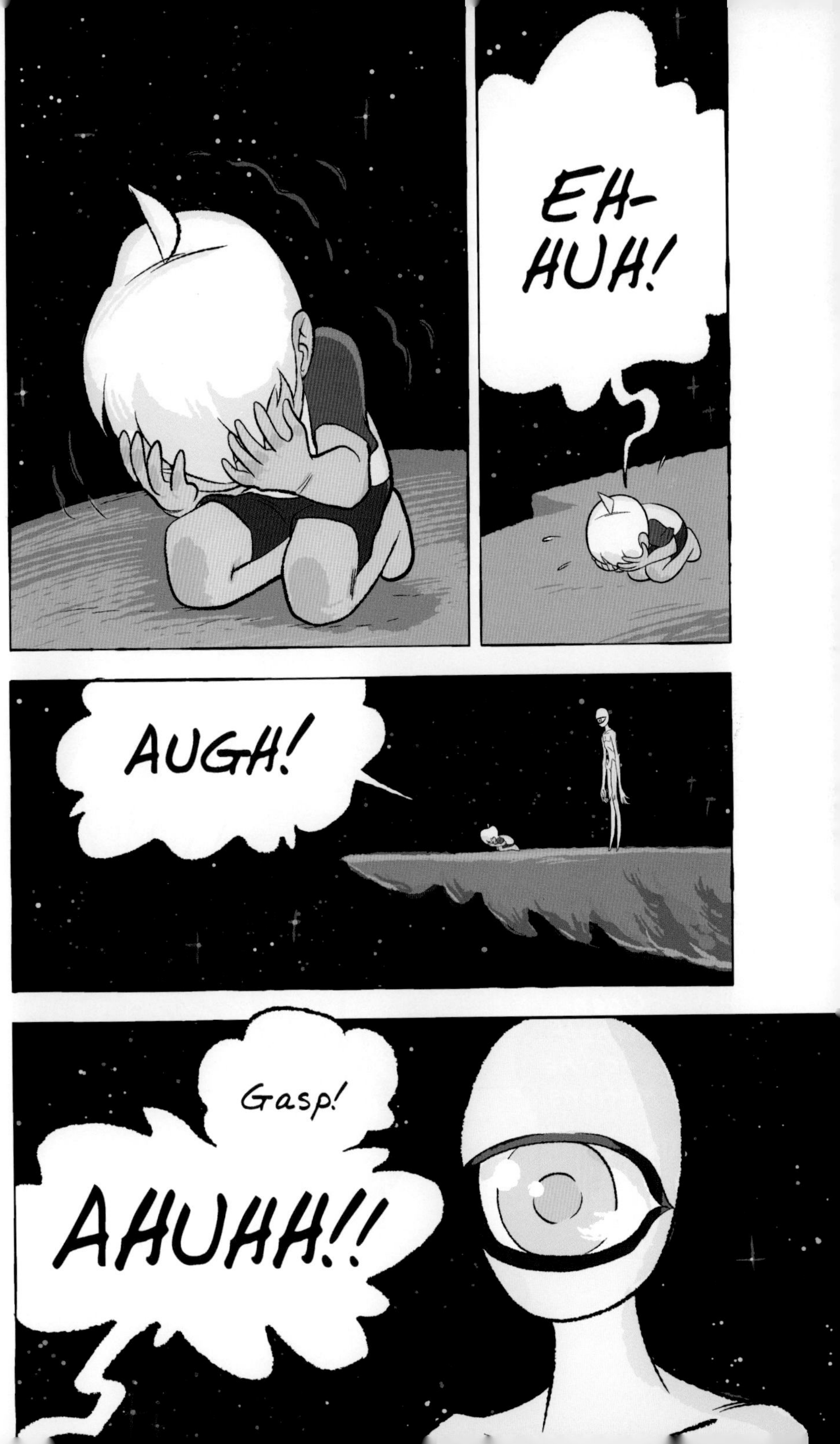
EH-
HUH!
AUGH!
Gasp!
AHUHH!!

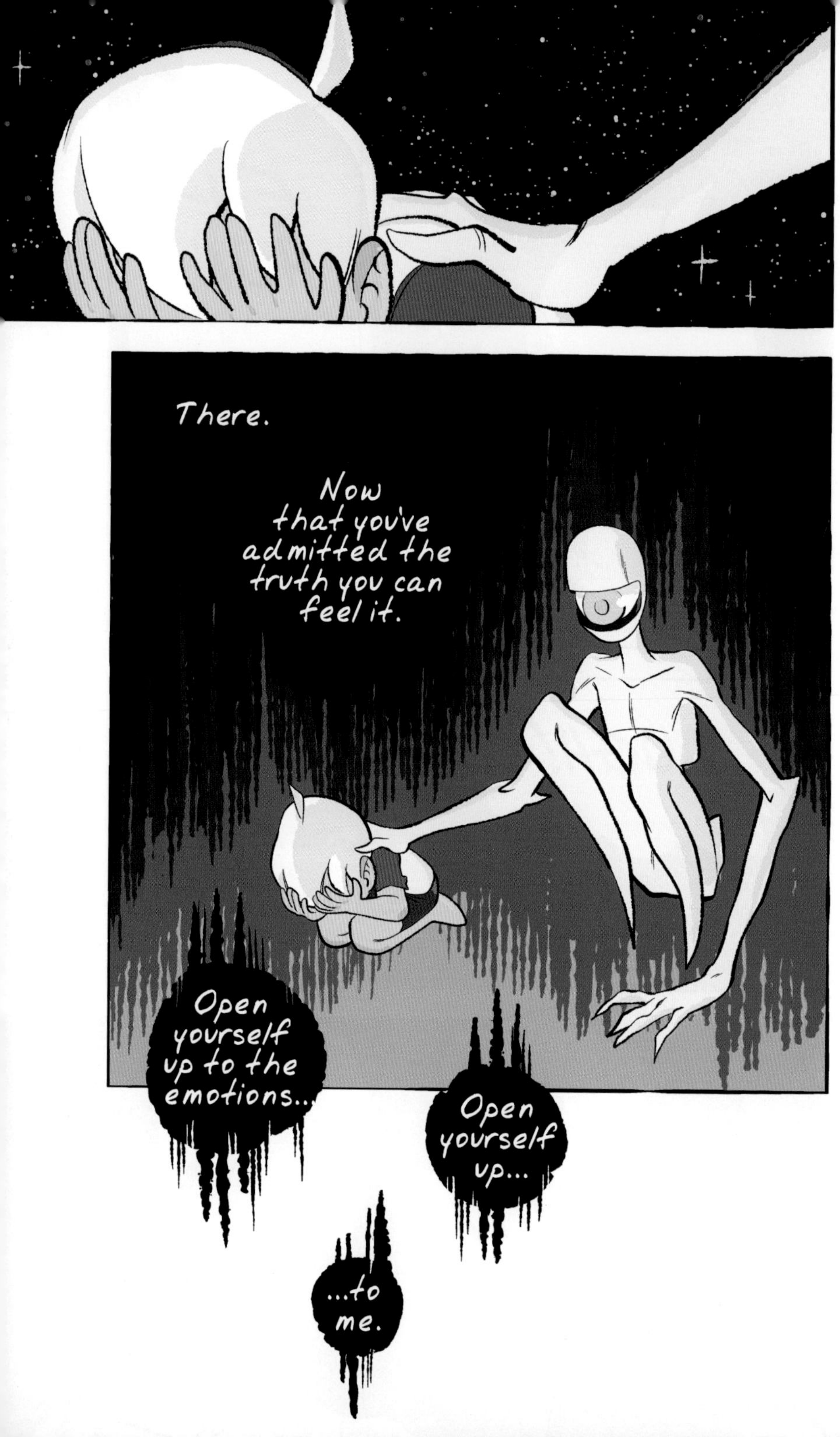
There.
Now that you've admitted the truth you can feel it.
Open yourself up to the emotions...
Open yourself up...
...to me.

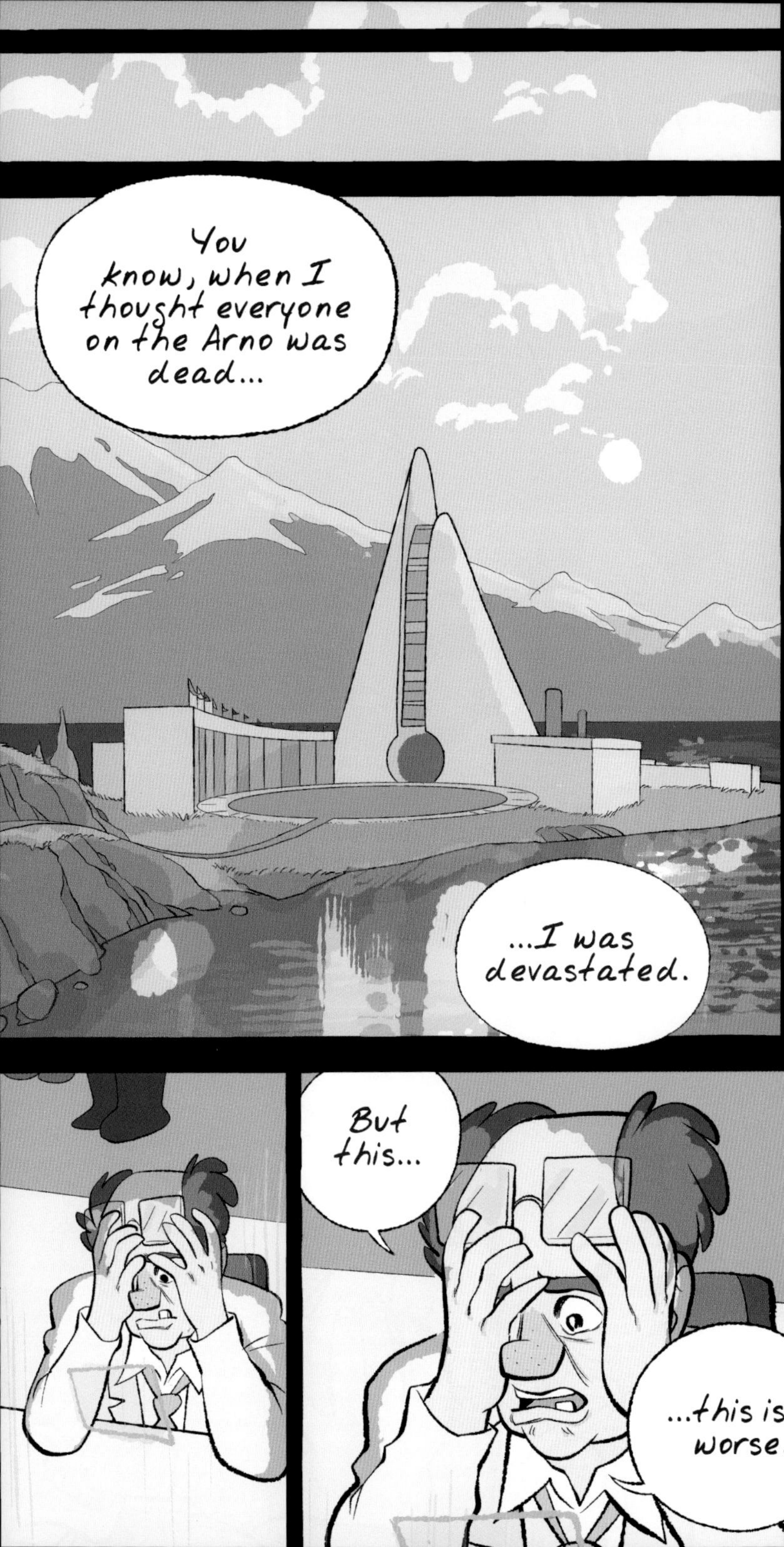
You know, when I thought everyone on the Arno was dead...
...I was devastated.
But this...
...this is worse.

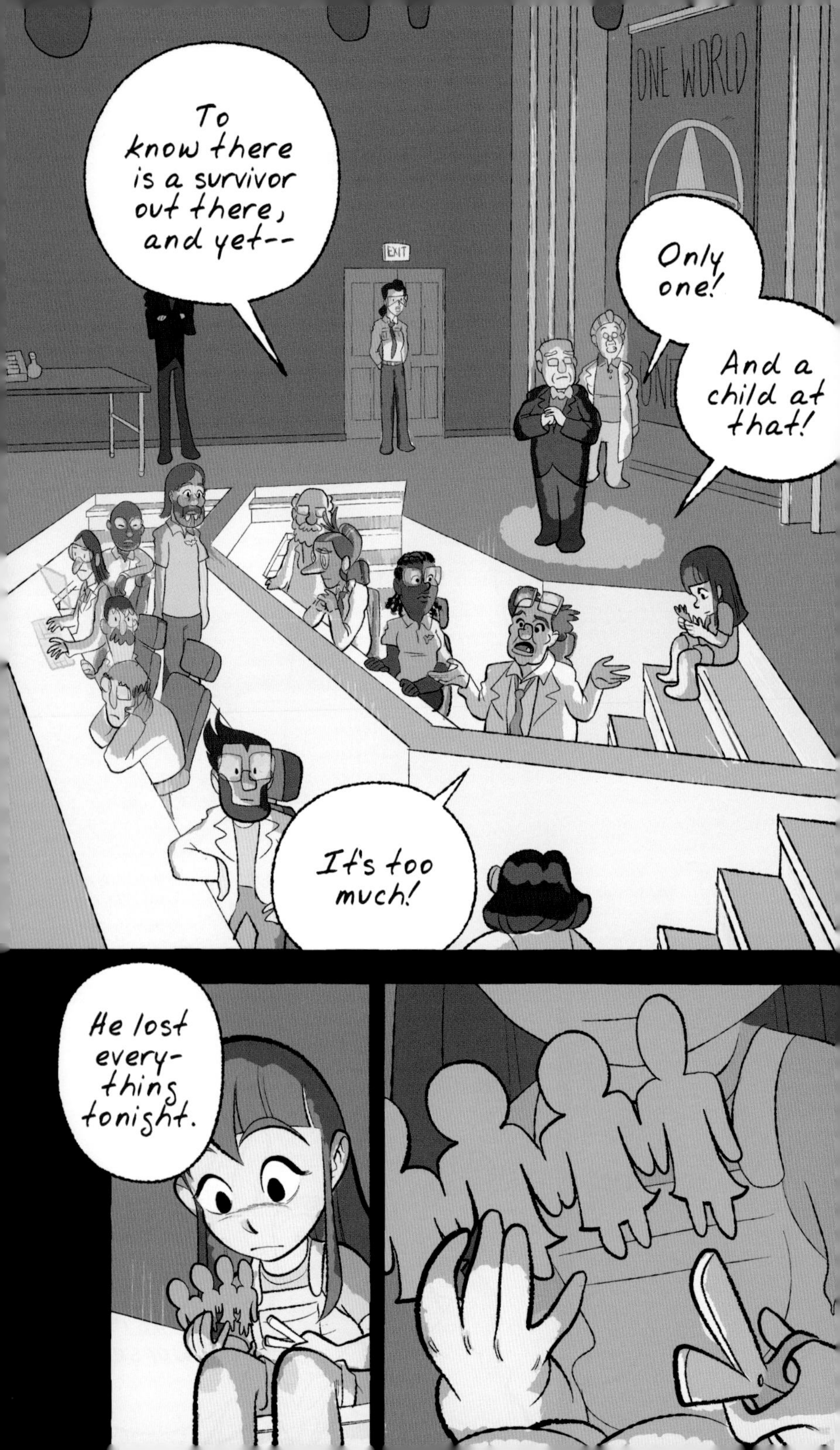
ONE WORLD
EXIT
To know there is a survivor out there, and yet--
Only one!
And a child at that!
It's too much!
He lost every-thing tonight.

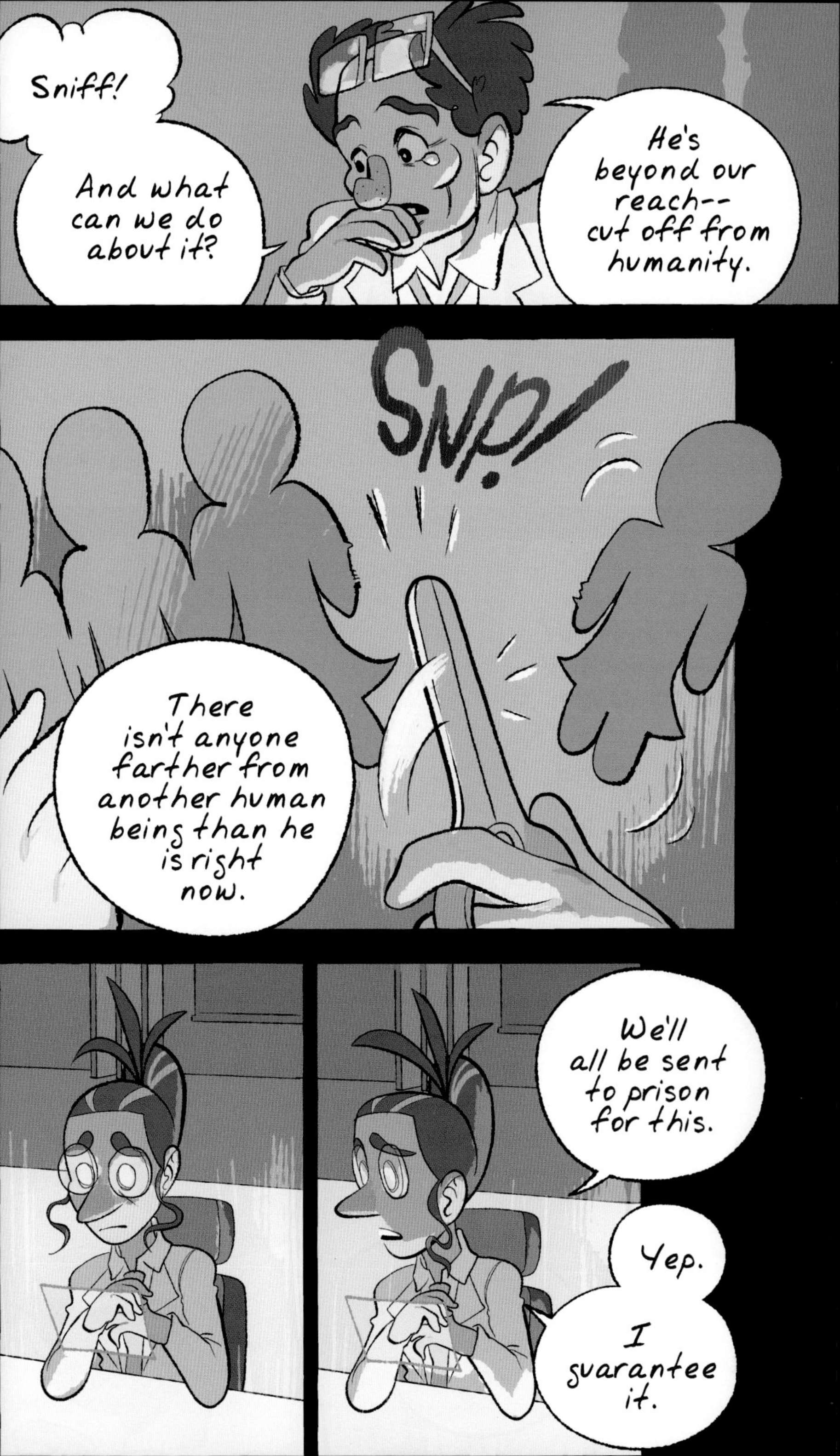
Sniff!
And what can we do about it?
He's beyond our reach-- cut off from humanity.
SNAP!
There isn't anyone farther from another human being than he is right now.
We'll all be sent to prison for this.
Yep.
I guarantee it.

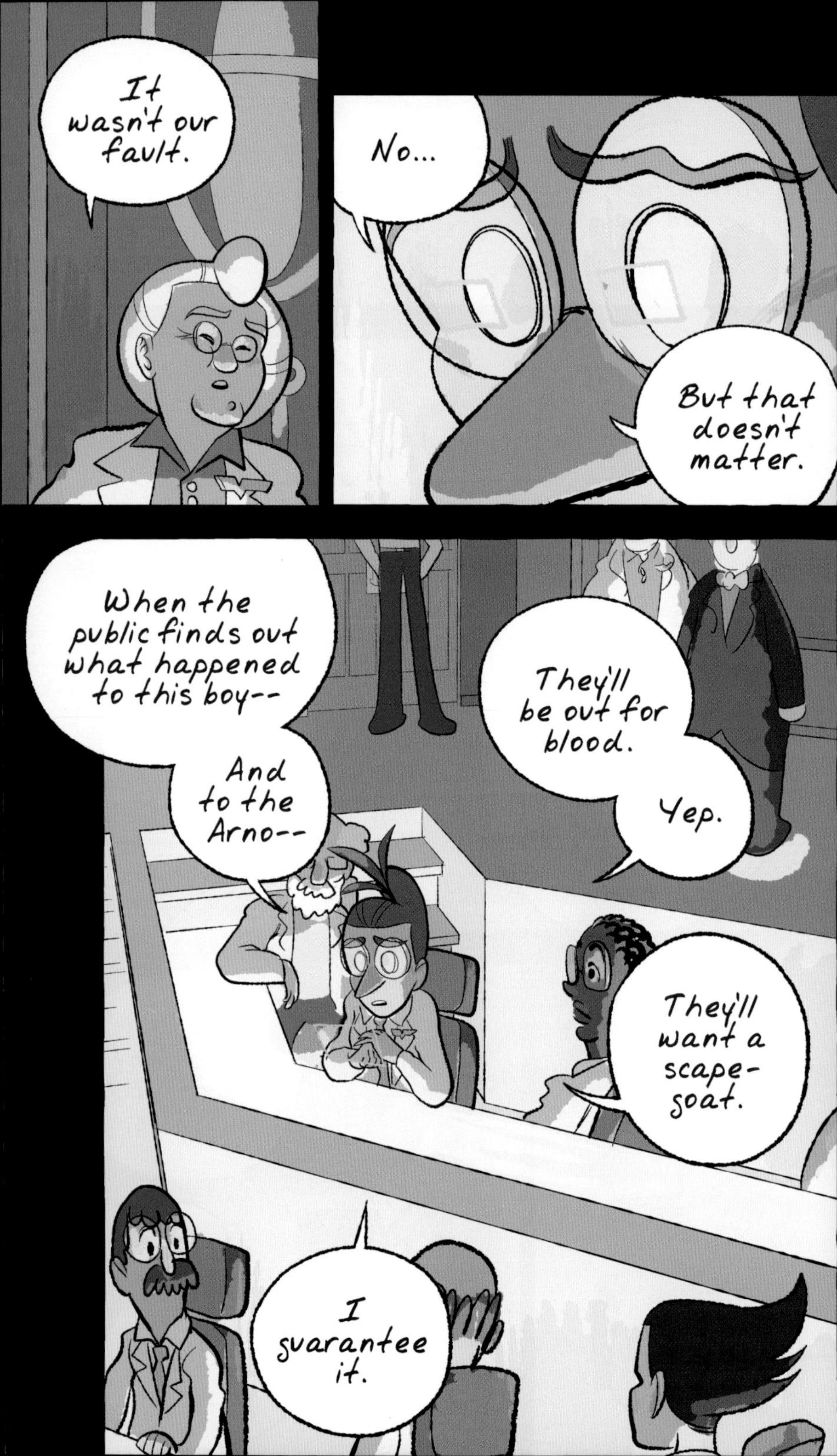
It wasn't our fault.
No...
But that doesn't matter.
When the public finds out what happened to this boy--
And to the Arno--
They'll be out for blood.
Yep.
They'll want a scape-goat.
I guarantee it.

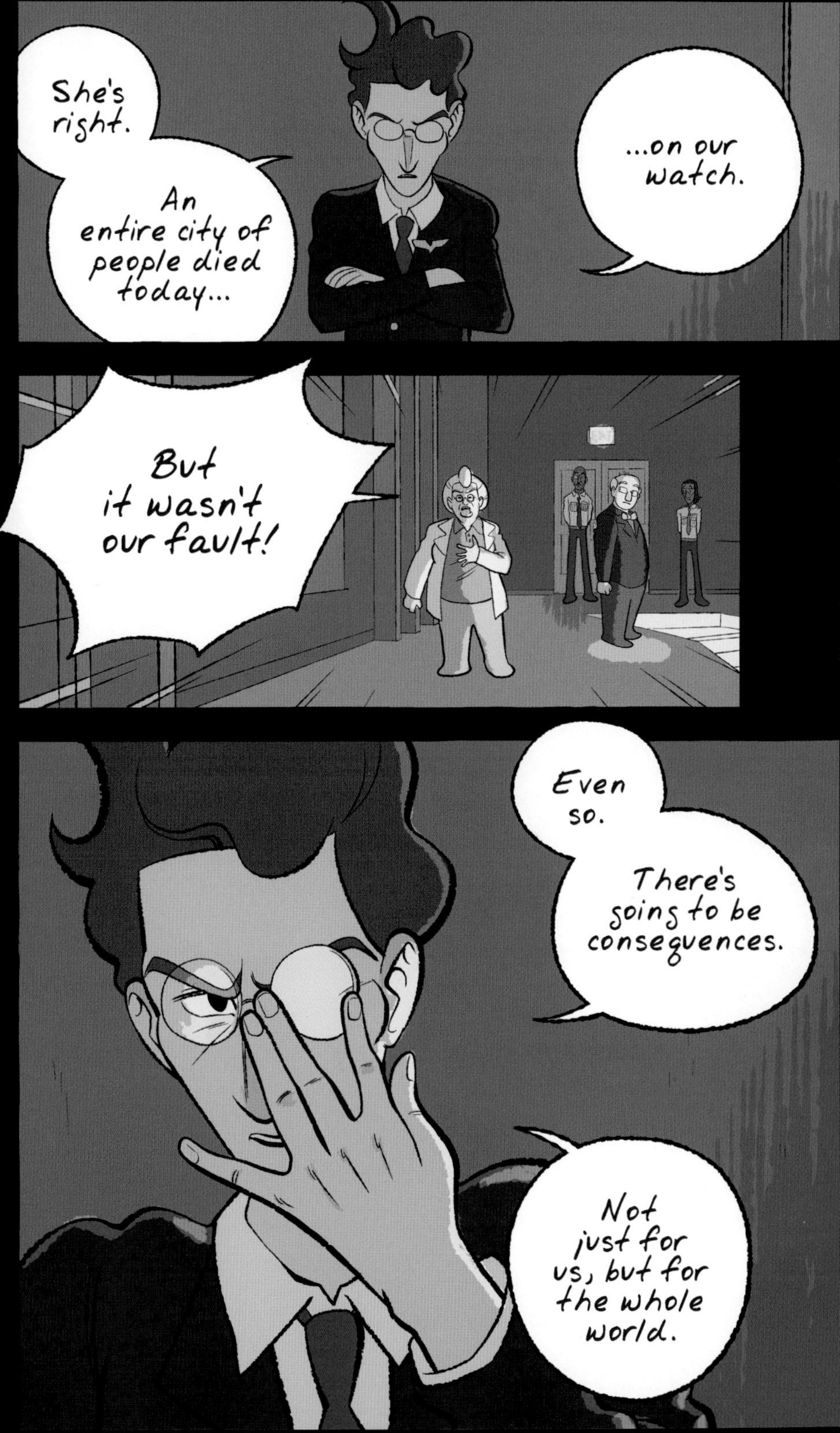
She's right.
An entire city of people died today...
...on our watch.
But it wasn't our fault!
Even so.
There's going to be consequences.
Not just for us, but for the whole world.

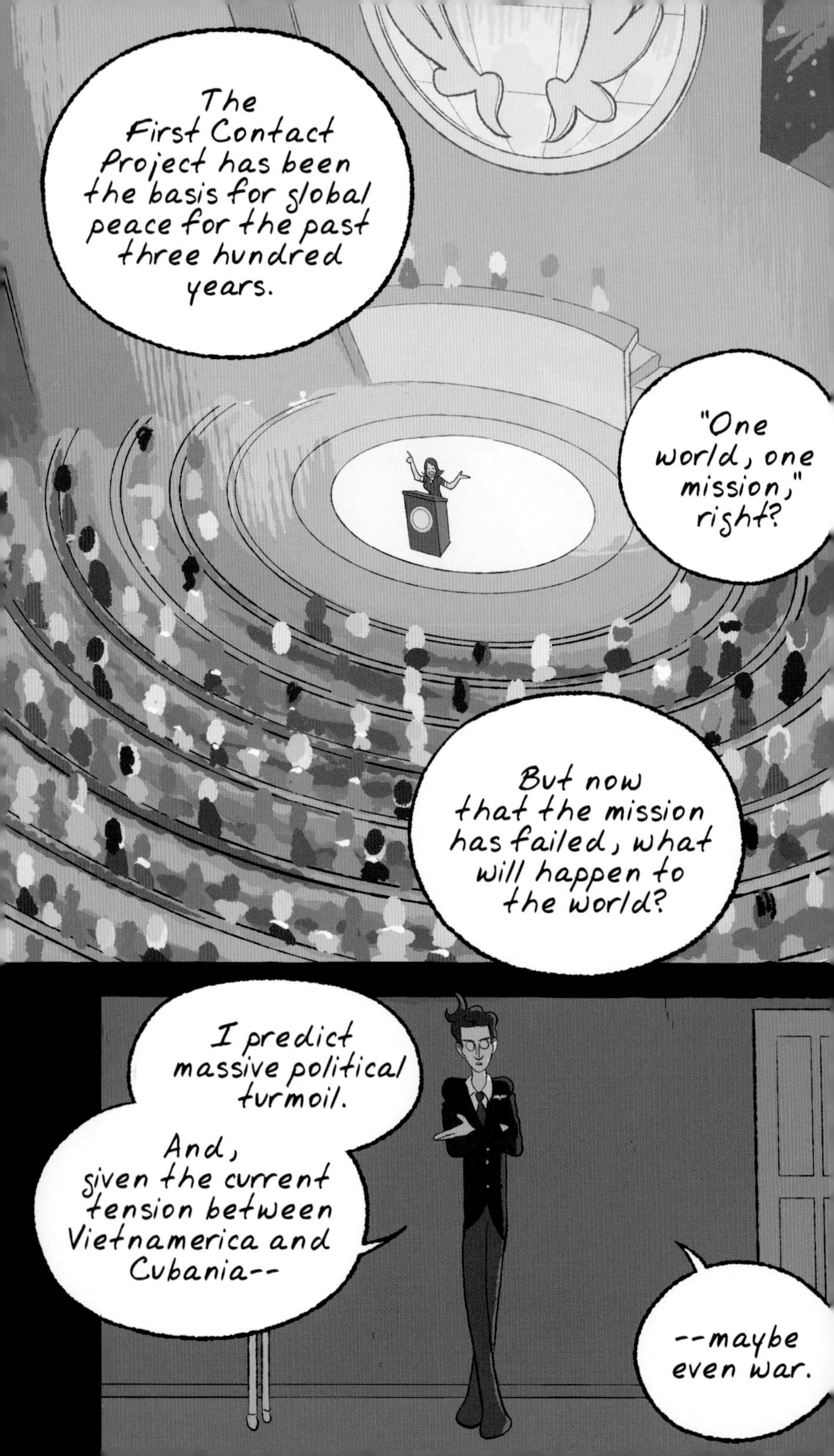
The First Contact Project has been the basis for global peace for the past three hundred years.
"One world, one mission," right?
But now that the mission has failed, what will happen to the world?
I predict massive political turmoil.
And, given the current tension between Vietnamerica and Cubania--
--maybe even war.

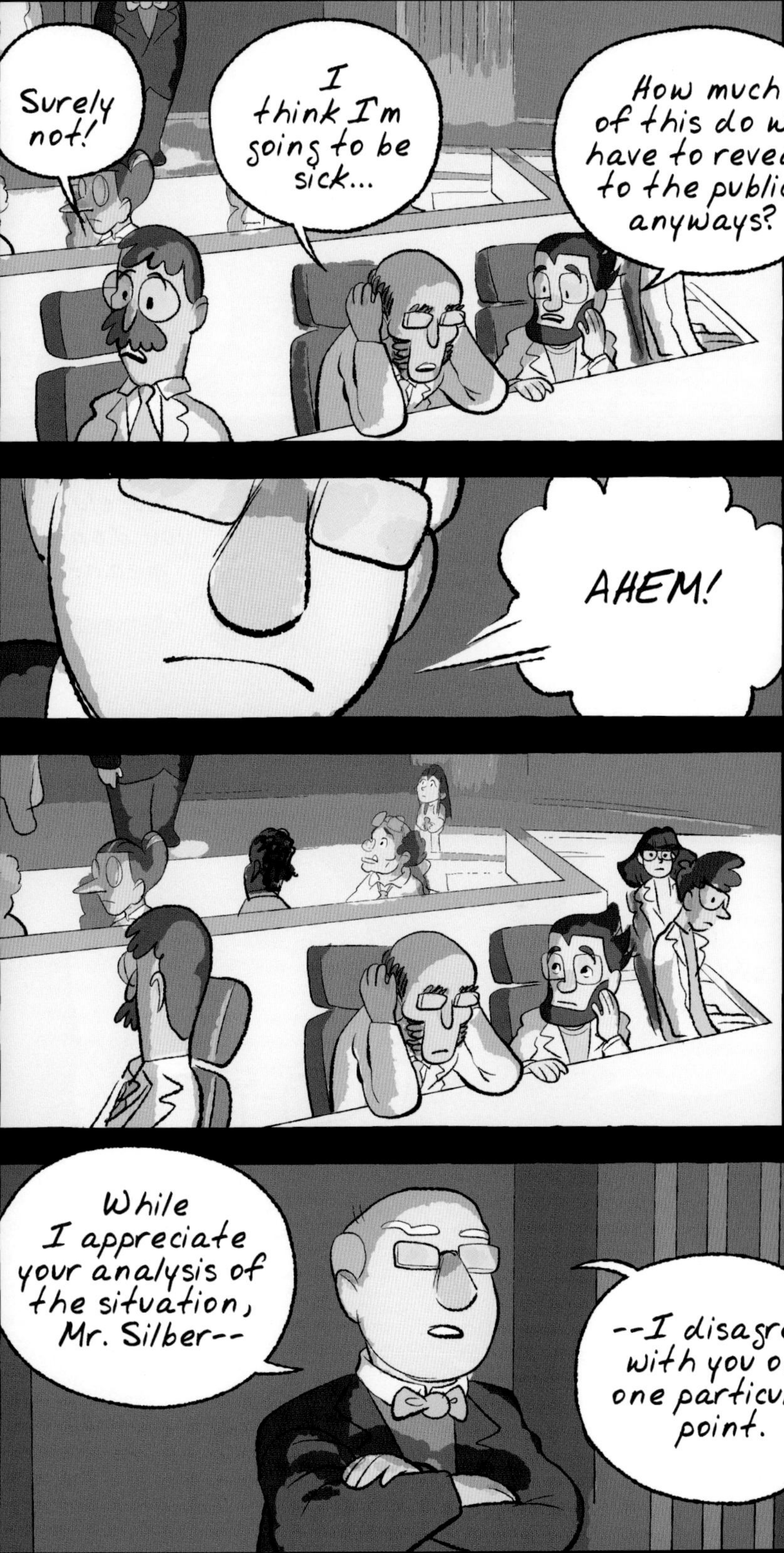
Surely not!
I think I'm going to be sick...
How much of this do we have to reveal to the public, anyways?
AHEM!
While I appreciate your analysis of the situation, Mr. Silber--
--I disagree with you on one particular point.

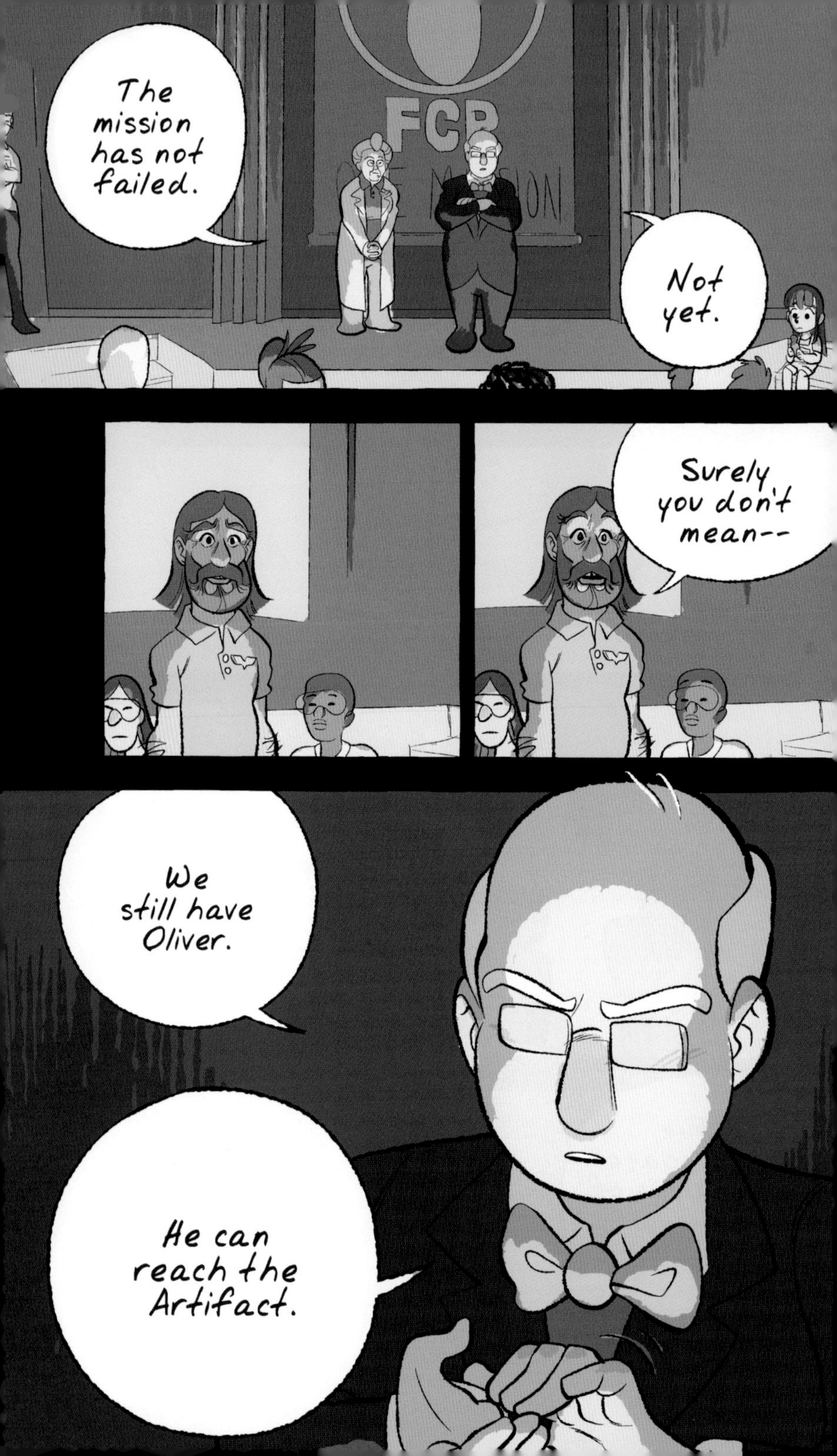
The mission has not failed.
Not yet.
Surely you don't mean--
We still have Oliver.
He can reach the Artifact.

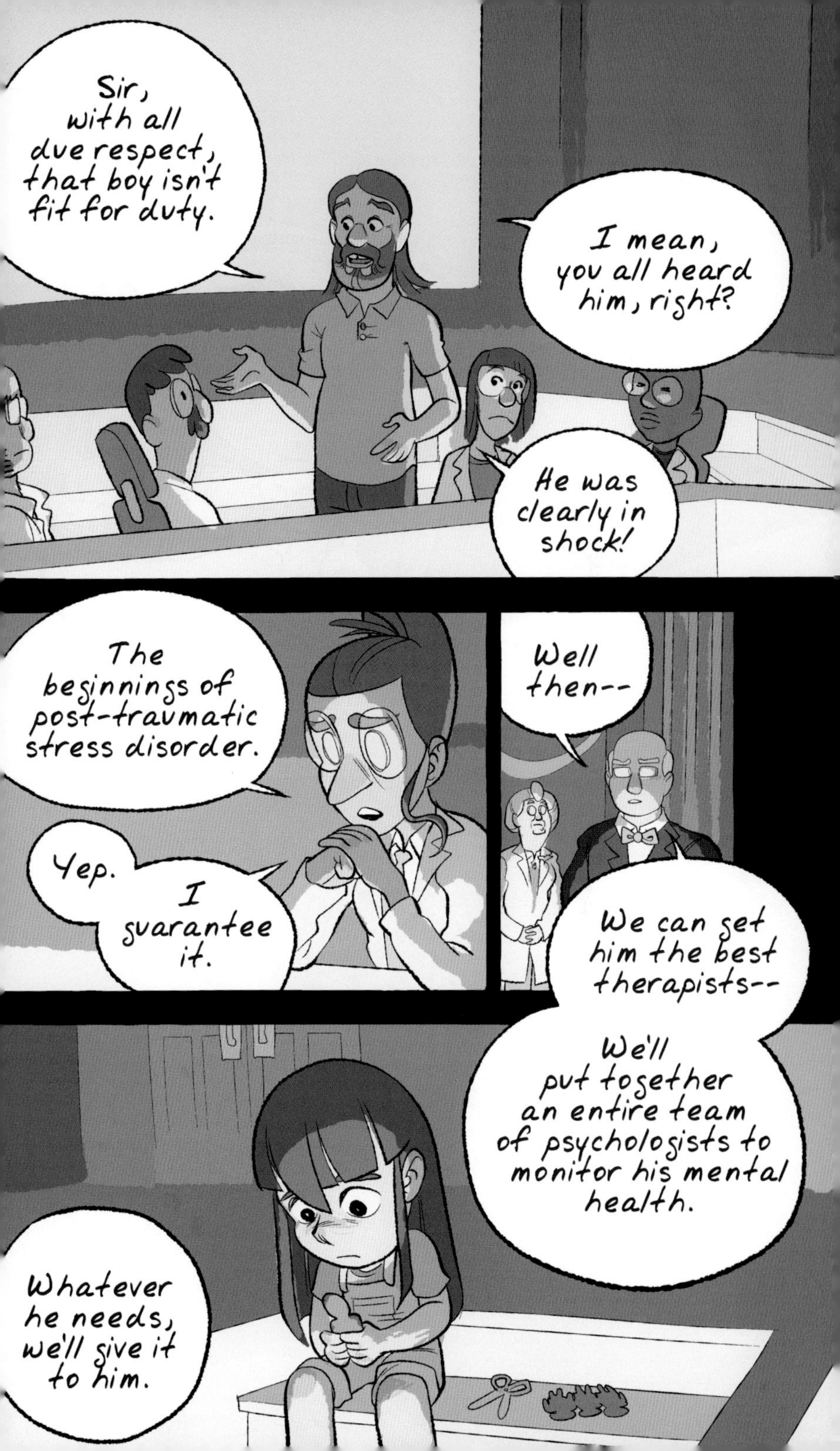
Sir, with all due respect, that boy isn't fit for duty.
I mean, you all heard him, right?
He was clearly in shock!
The beginnings of post-traumatic stress disorder.
Yep.
I guarantee it.
Well then--
We can get him the best therapists--
We'll put together an entire team of psychologists to monitor his mental health.
Whatever he needs, we'll give it to him.

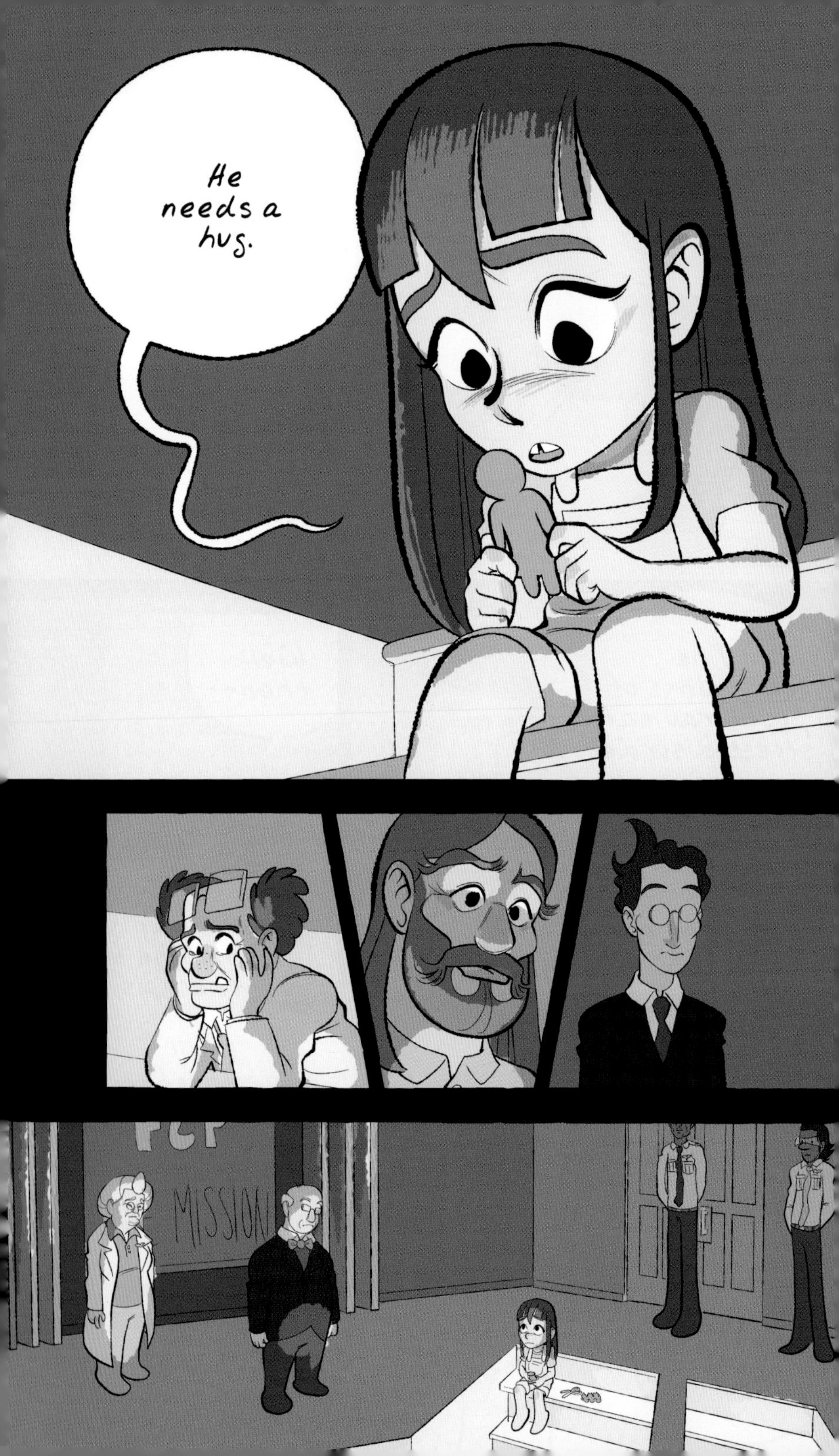
He needs a hug.
MISSION

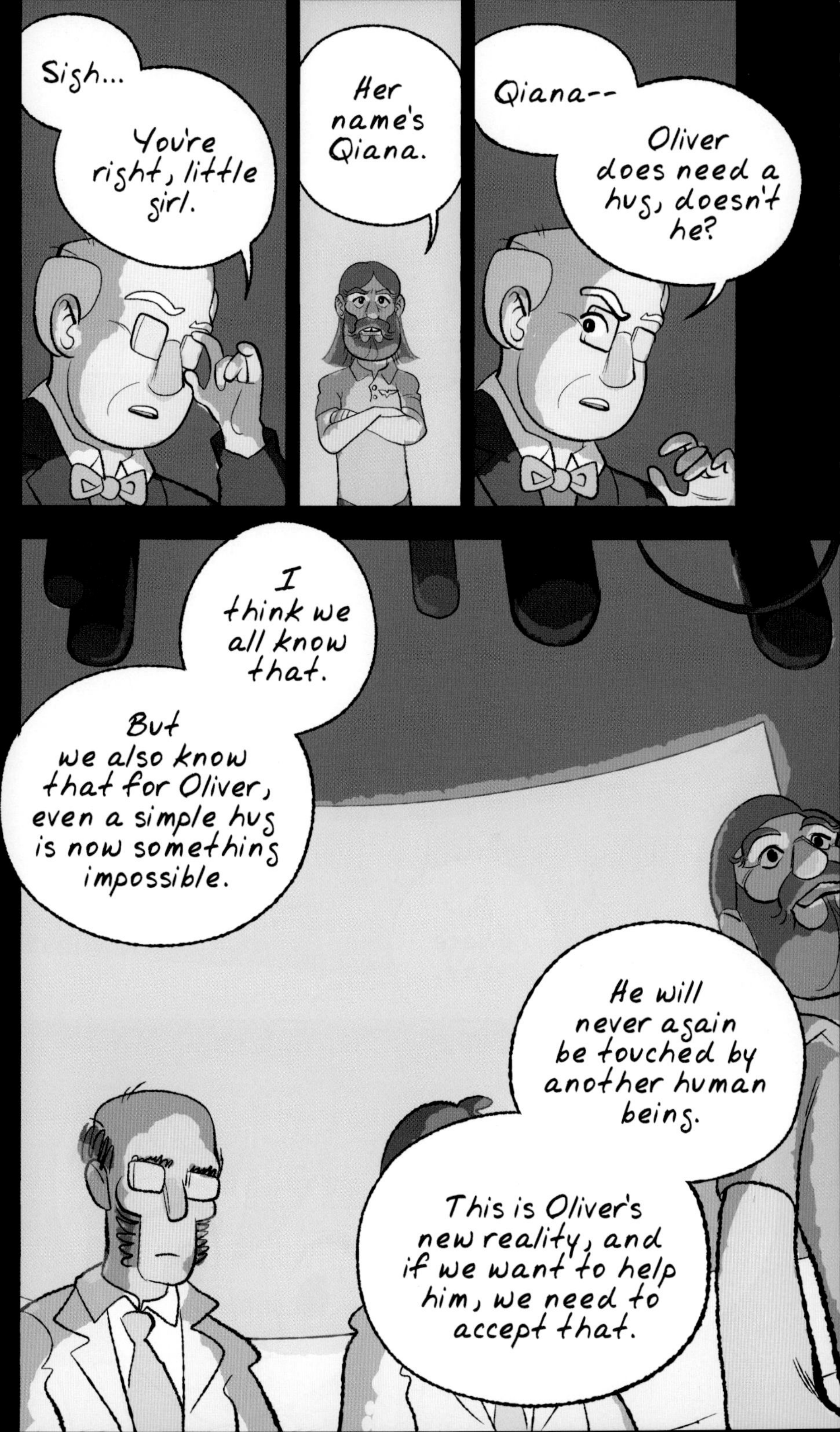
Sigh...
You're right, little girl.
Her name's Qiana.
Qiana--
Oliver does need a hug, doesn't he?
I think we all know that.
But we also know that for Oliver, even a simple hug is now something impossible.
He will never again be touched by another human being.
This is Oliver's new reality, and if we want to help him, we need to accept that.

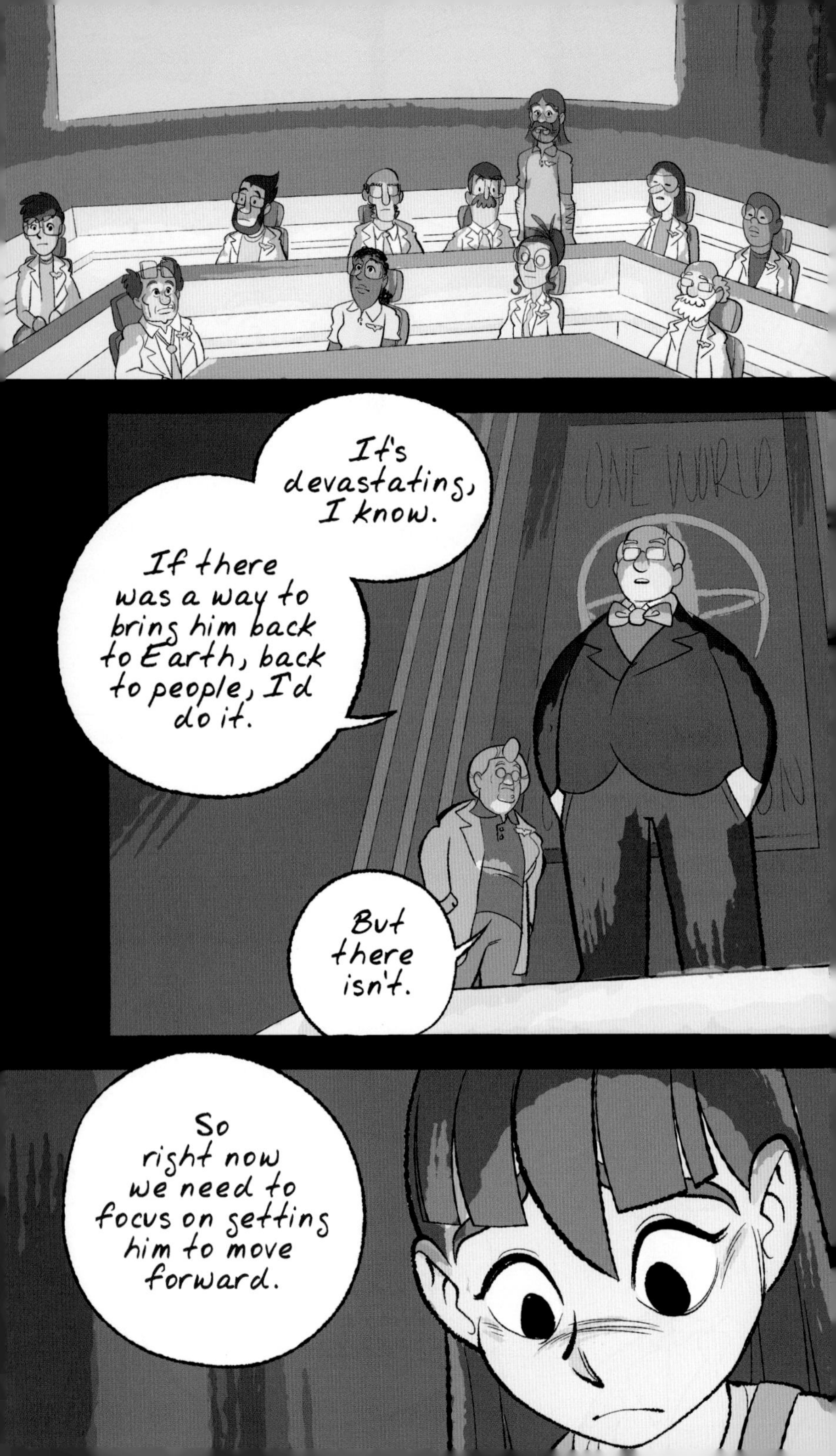

It's devastating, I know.
If there was a way to bring him back to Earth, back to people, I'd do it.
ONE WORLD
But there isn't.
So right now we need to focus on getting him to move forward.

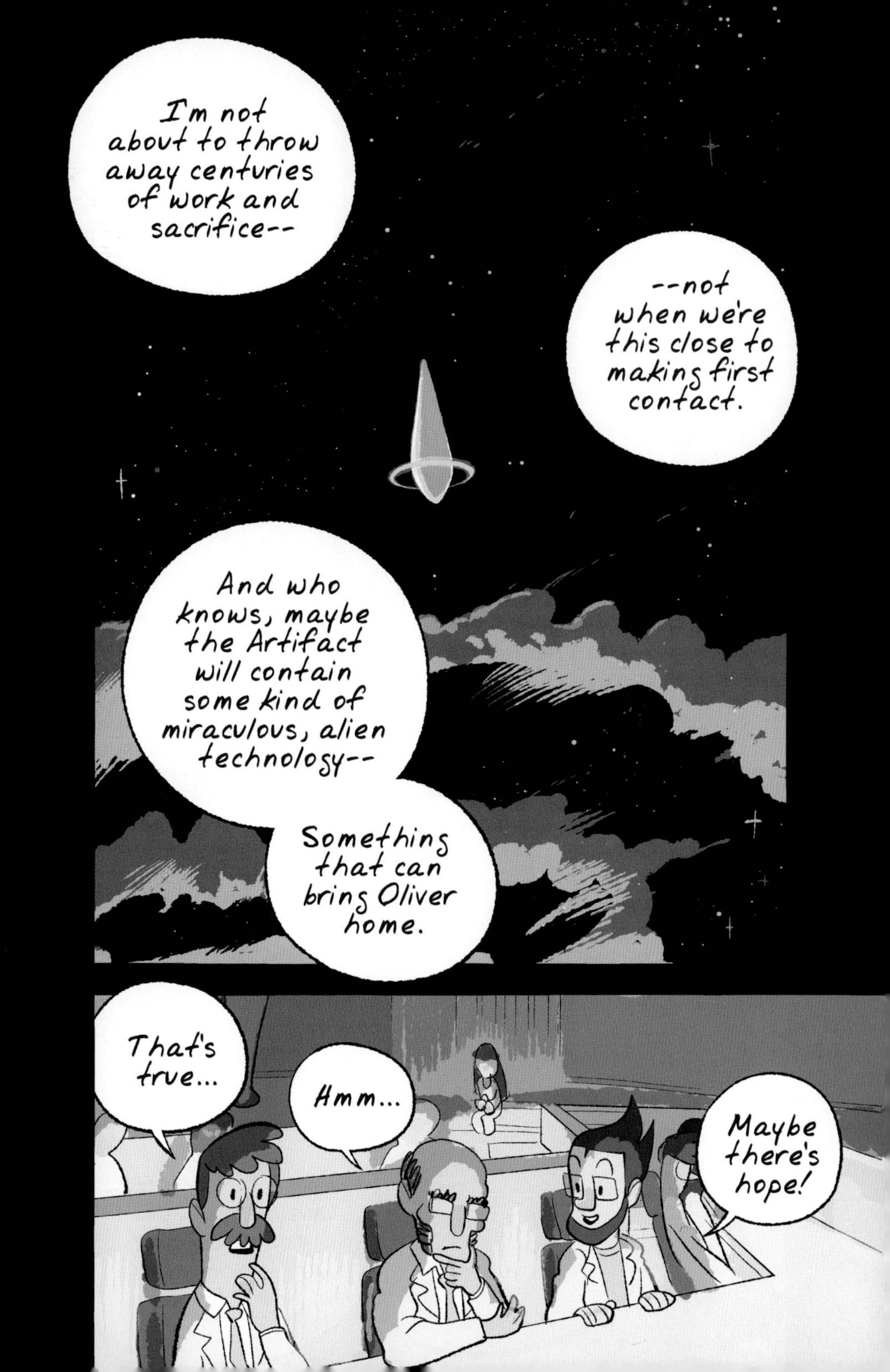
I'm not about to throw away centuries of work and sacrifice--
--not when we're this close to making first contact.
And who knows, maybe the Artifact will contain some kind of miraculous, alien technology--
Something that can bring Oliver home.
That's true...
Hmm...
Maybe there's hope!

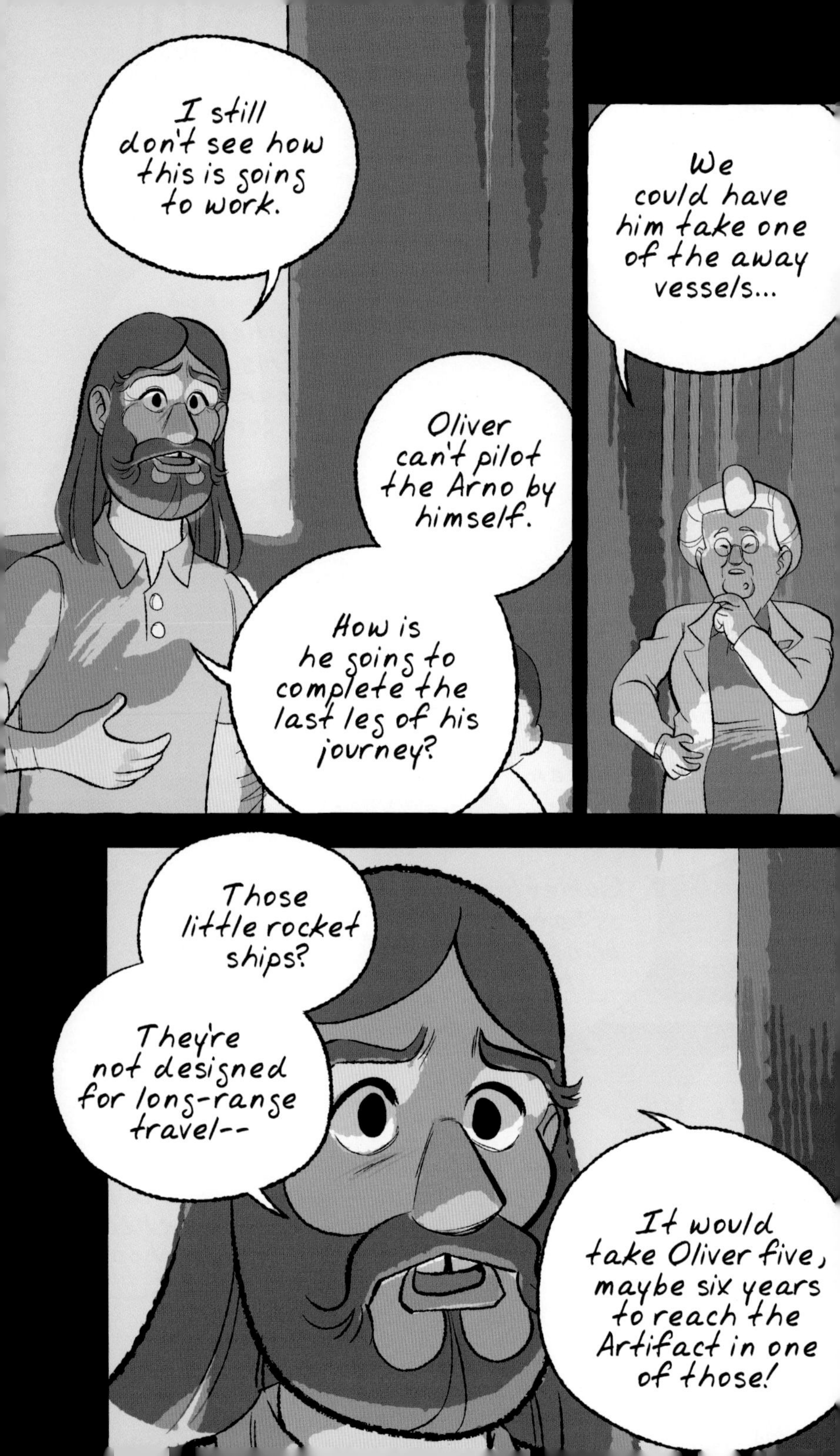
I still don't see how this is going to work.
Oliver can't pilot the Arno by himself.
How is he going to complete the last leg of his journey?
We could have him take one of the away vessels...
Those little rocket ships?
They're not designed for long-range travel--
It would take Oliver five, maybe six years to reach the Artifact in one of those!

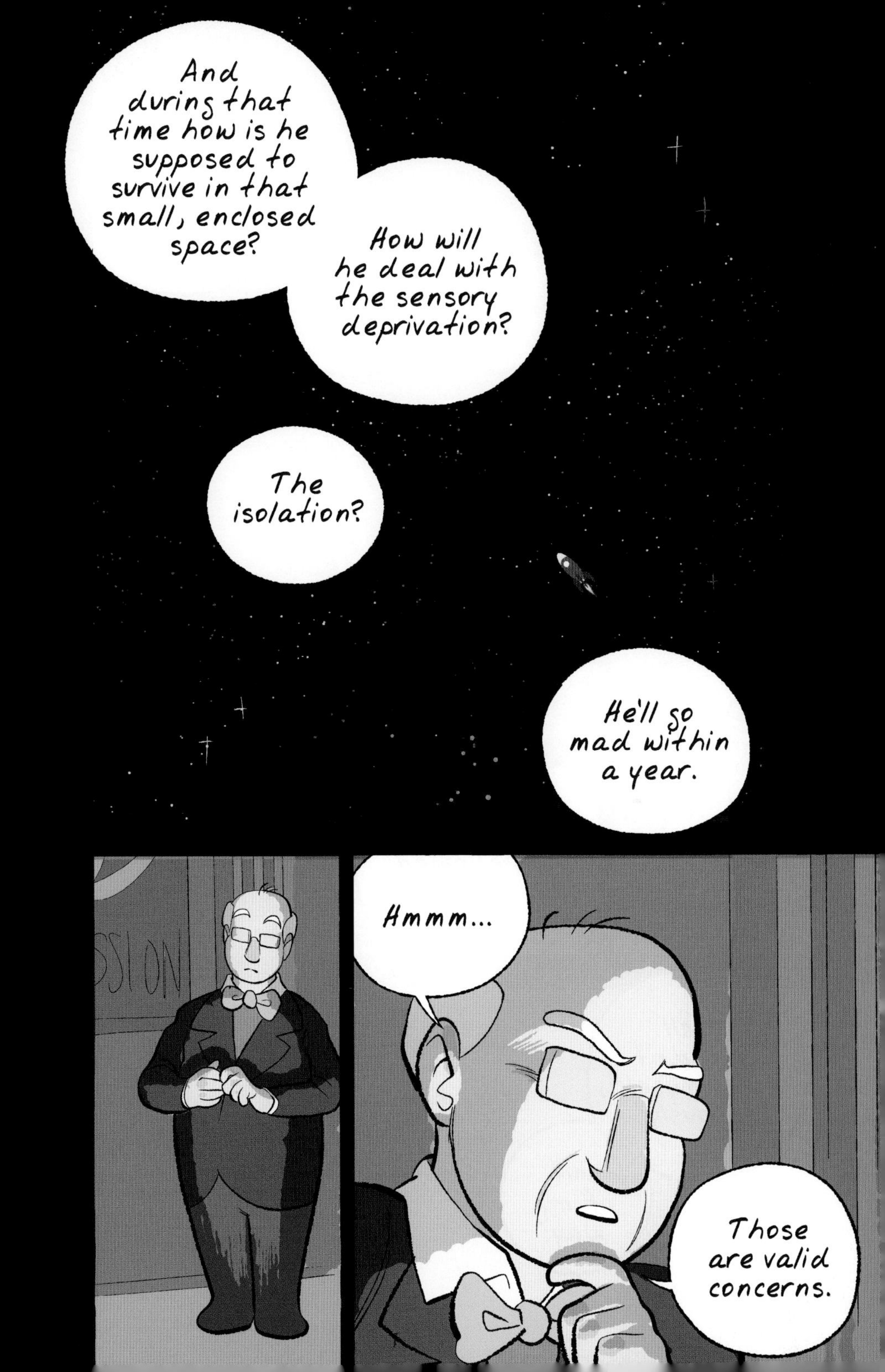
And during that time how is he supposed to survive in that small, enclosed space?
How will he deal with the sensory deprivation?
The isolation?
He'll go mad within a year.
Hmmm...
Those are valid concerns.

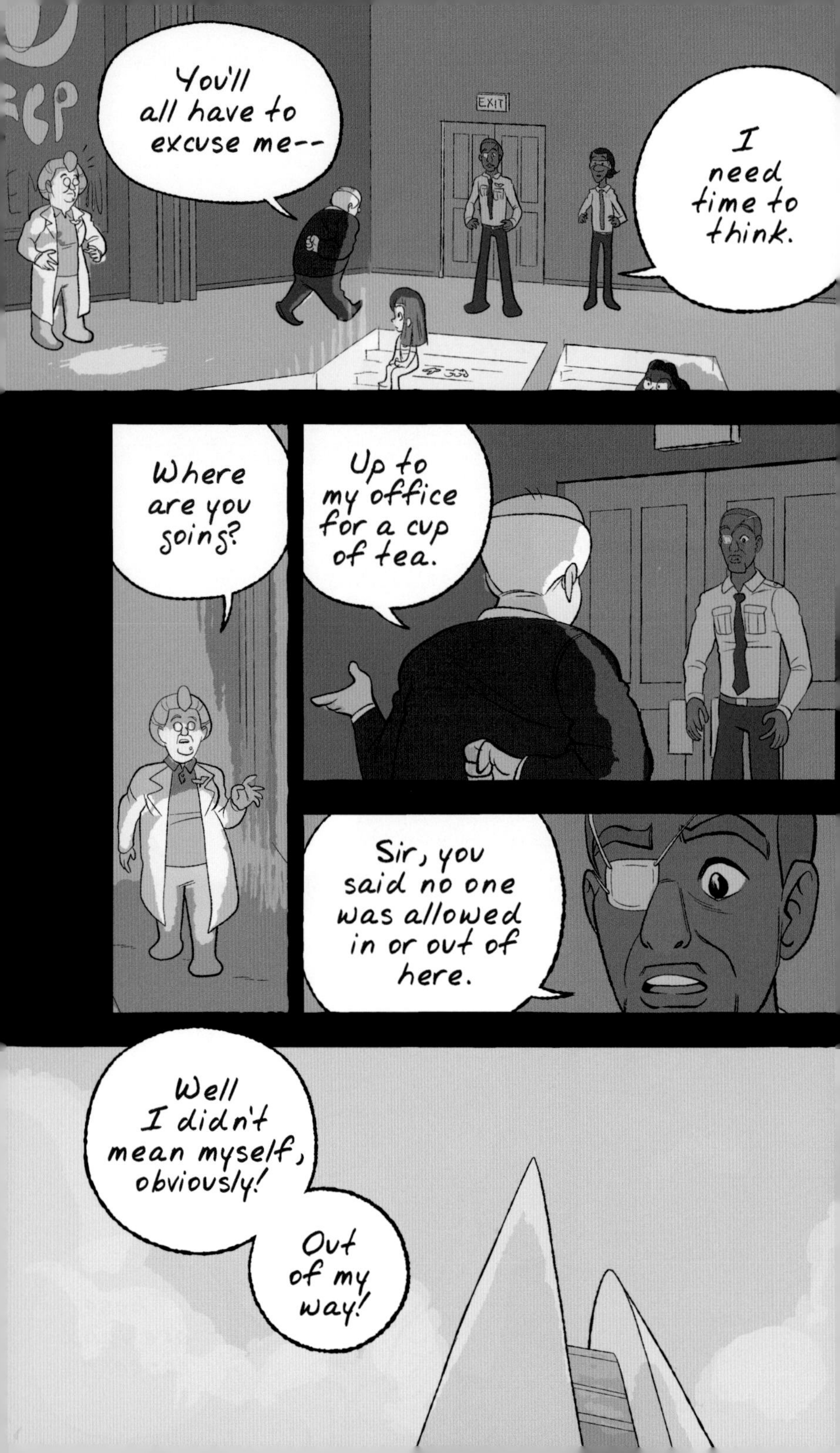
You'll all have to excuse me--
I need time to think.
EXIT
Where are you going?
Up to my office for a cup of tea.
Sir, you said no one was allowed in or out of here.
Well I didn't mean myself, obviously!
Out of my way!

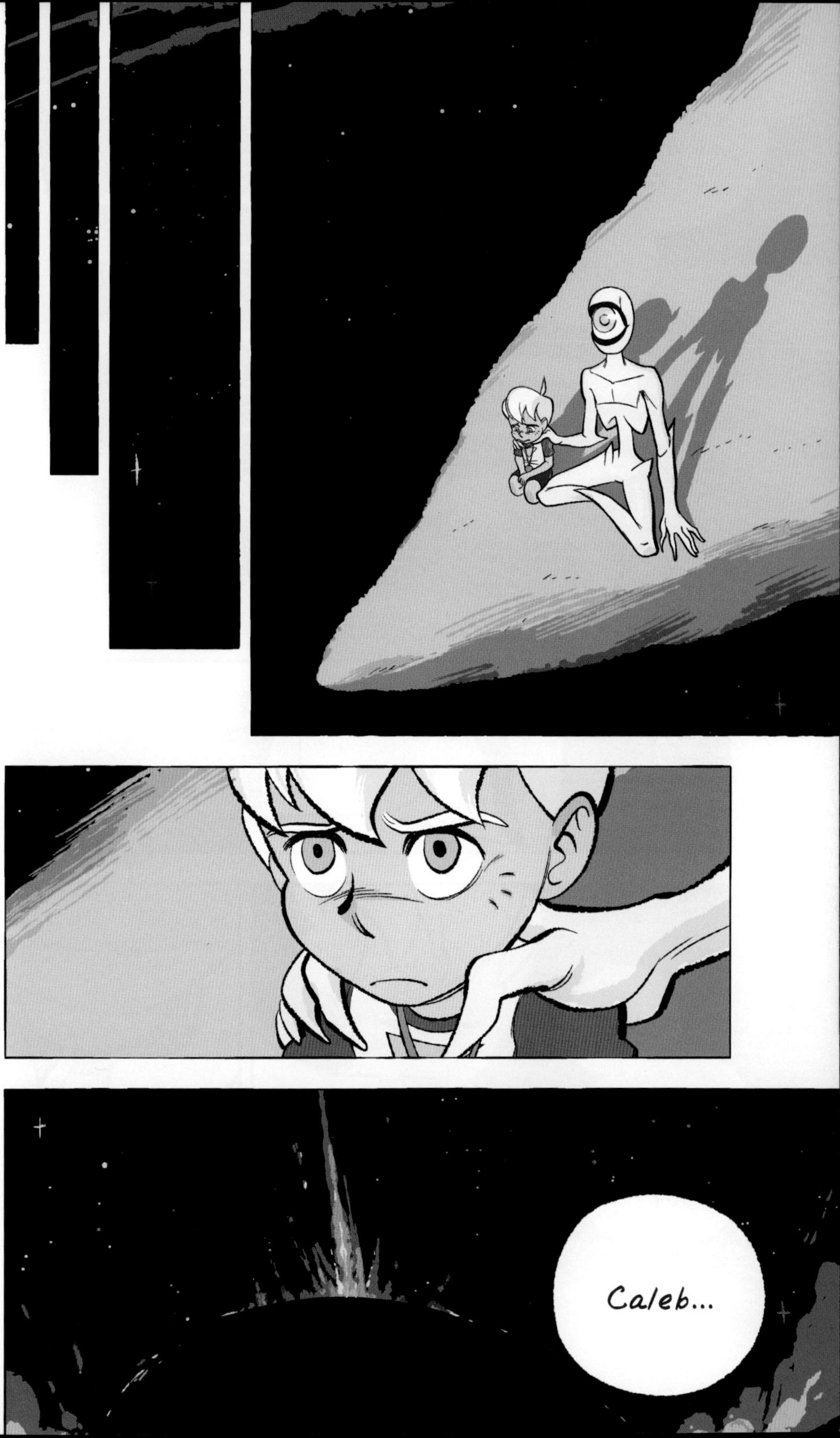
Caleb...

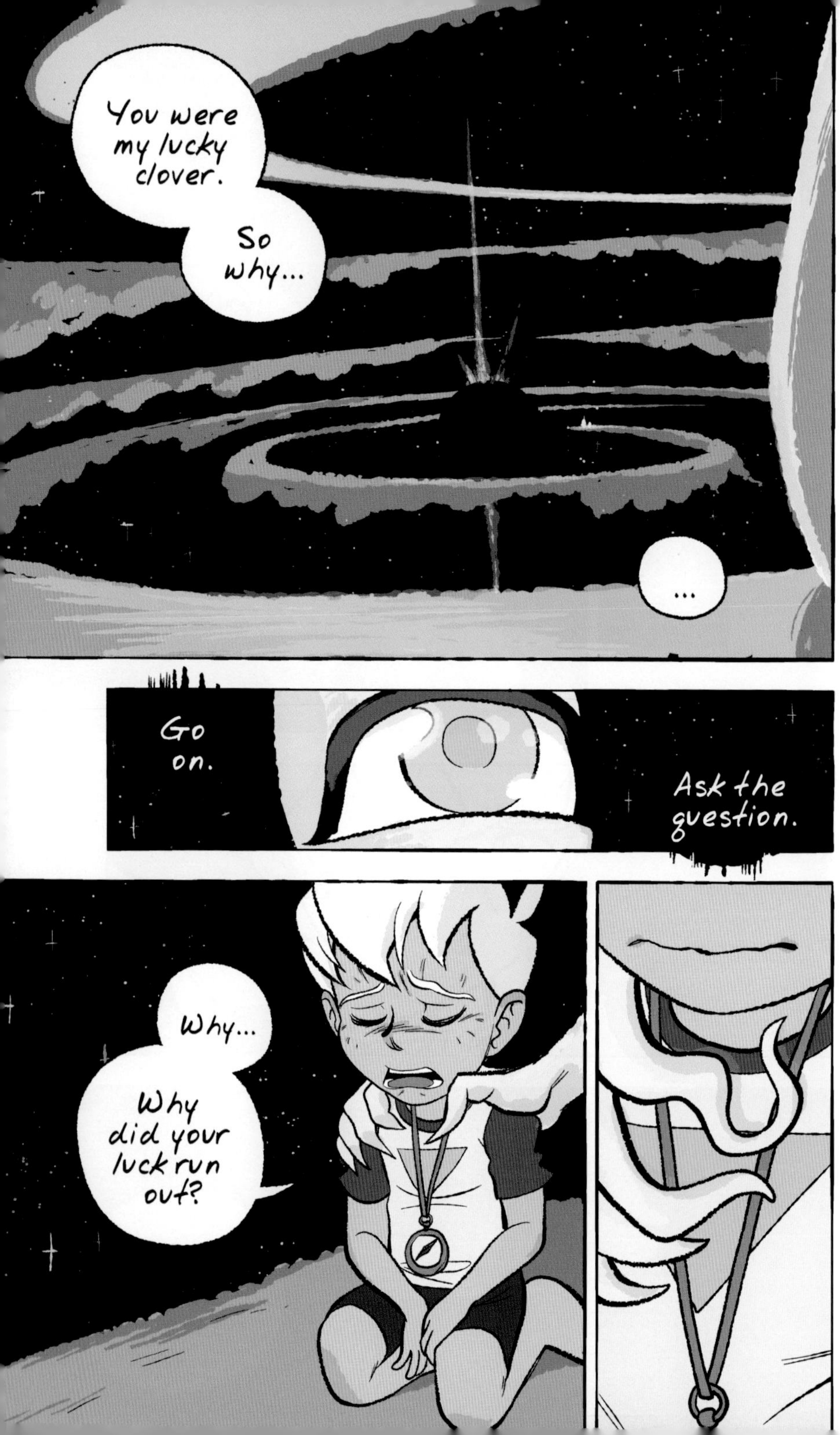
You were my lucky clover.
So why...
...
Go on.
Ask the question.
Why...
Why did your luck run out?

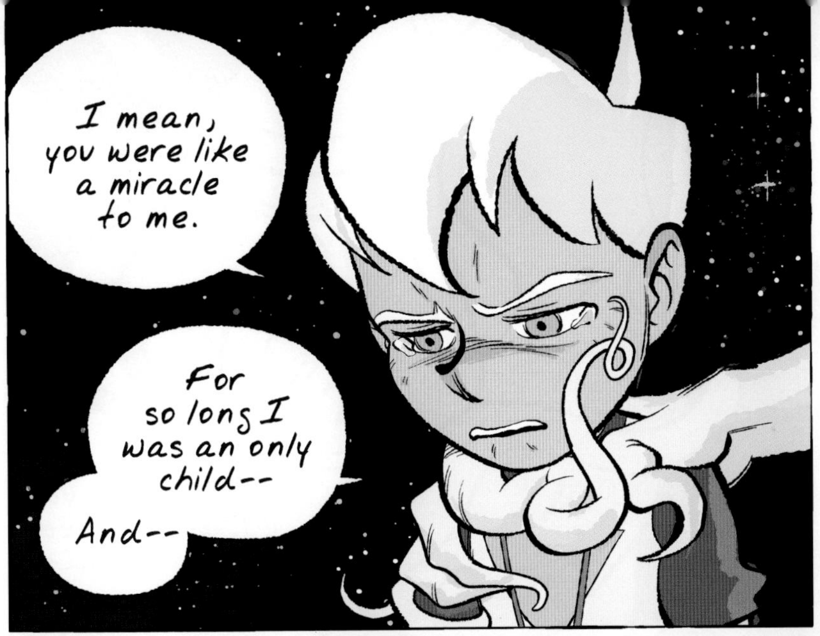
I mean, you were like a miracle to me.
For so long I was an only child--
And--
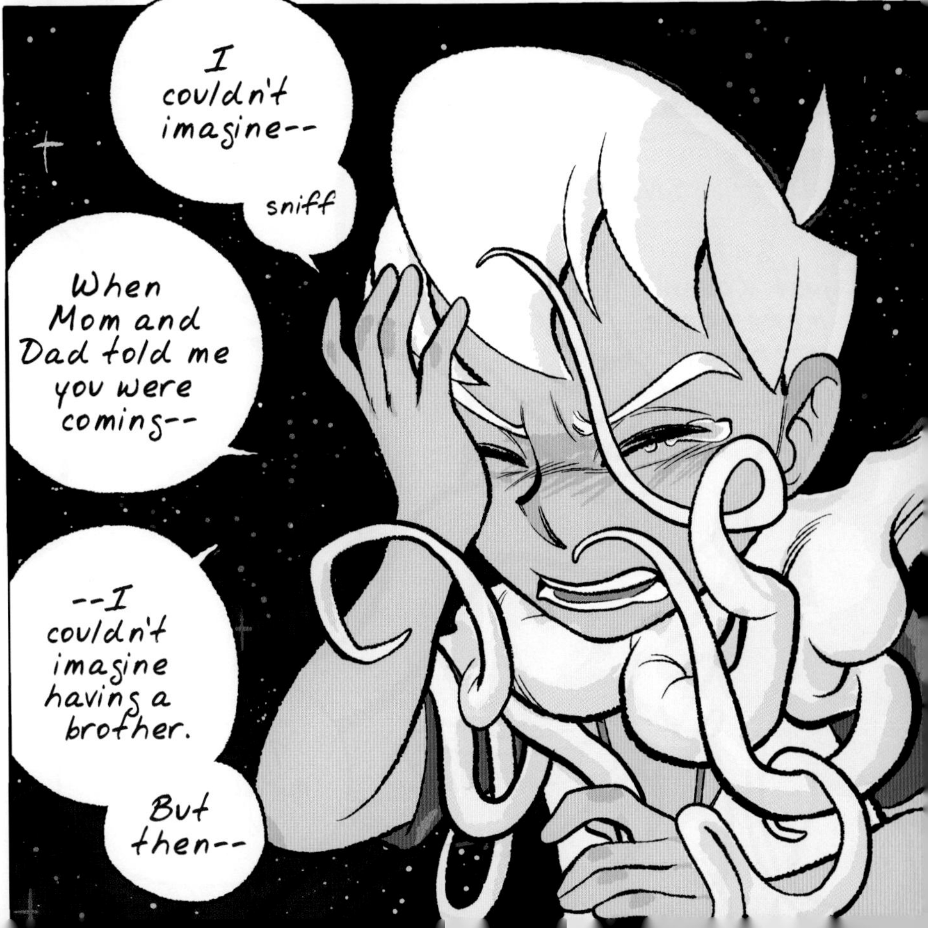
I couldn't imagine--
sniff
When Mom and Dad told me you were coming--
--I couldn't imagine having a brother.
But then--

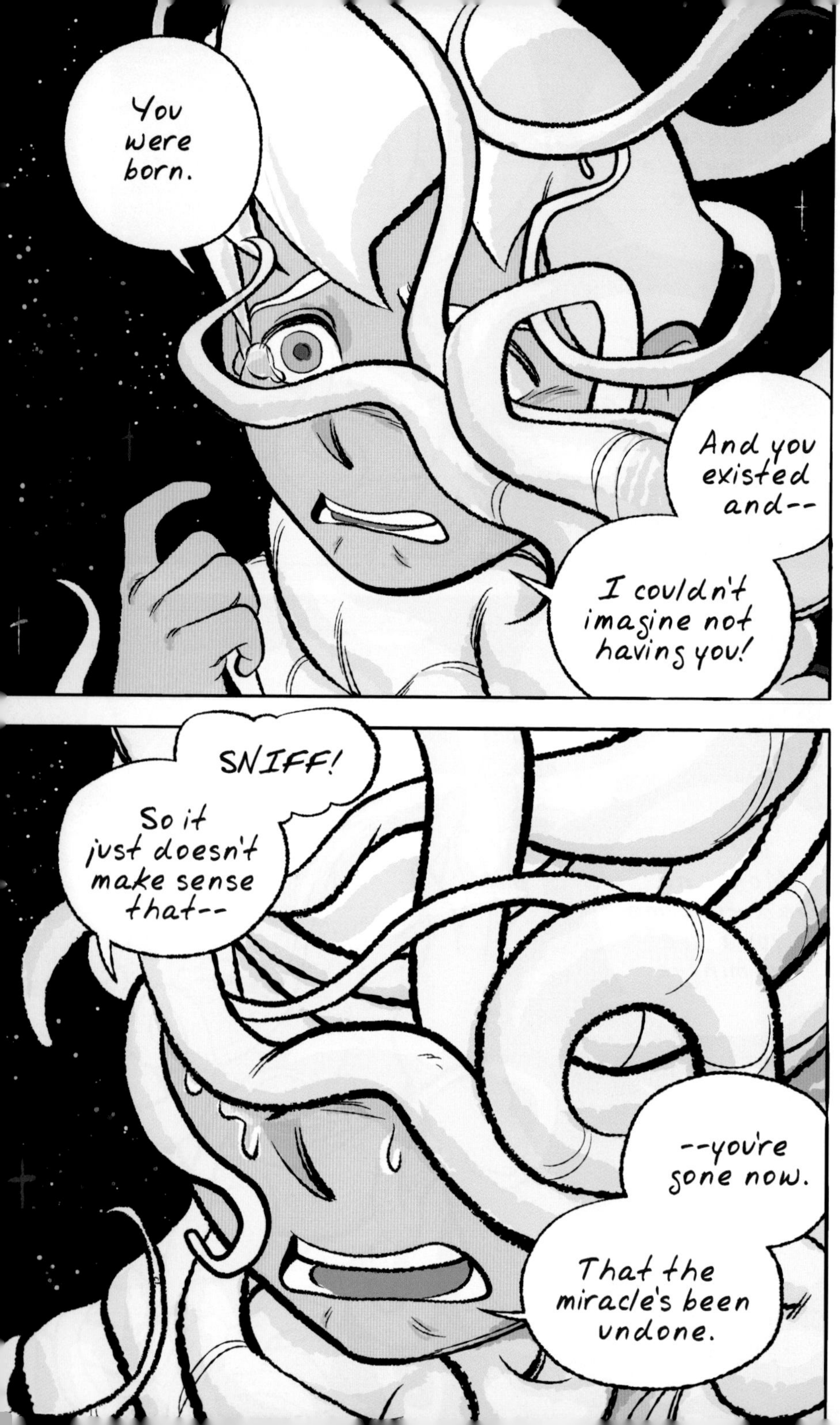
You were born.
And you existed and--
I couldn't imagine not having you!
SNIFF!
So it just doesn't make sense that--
--you're gone now.
That the miracle's been undone.

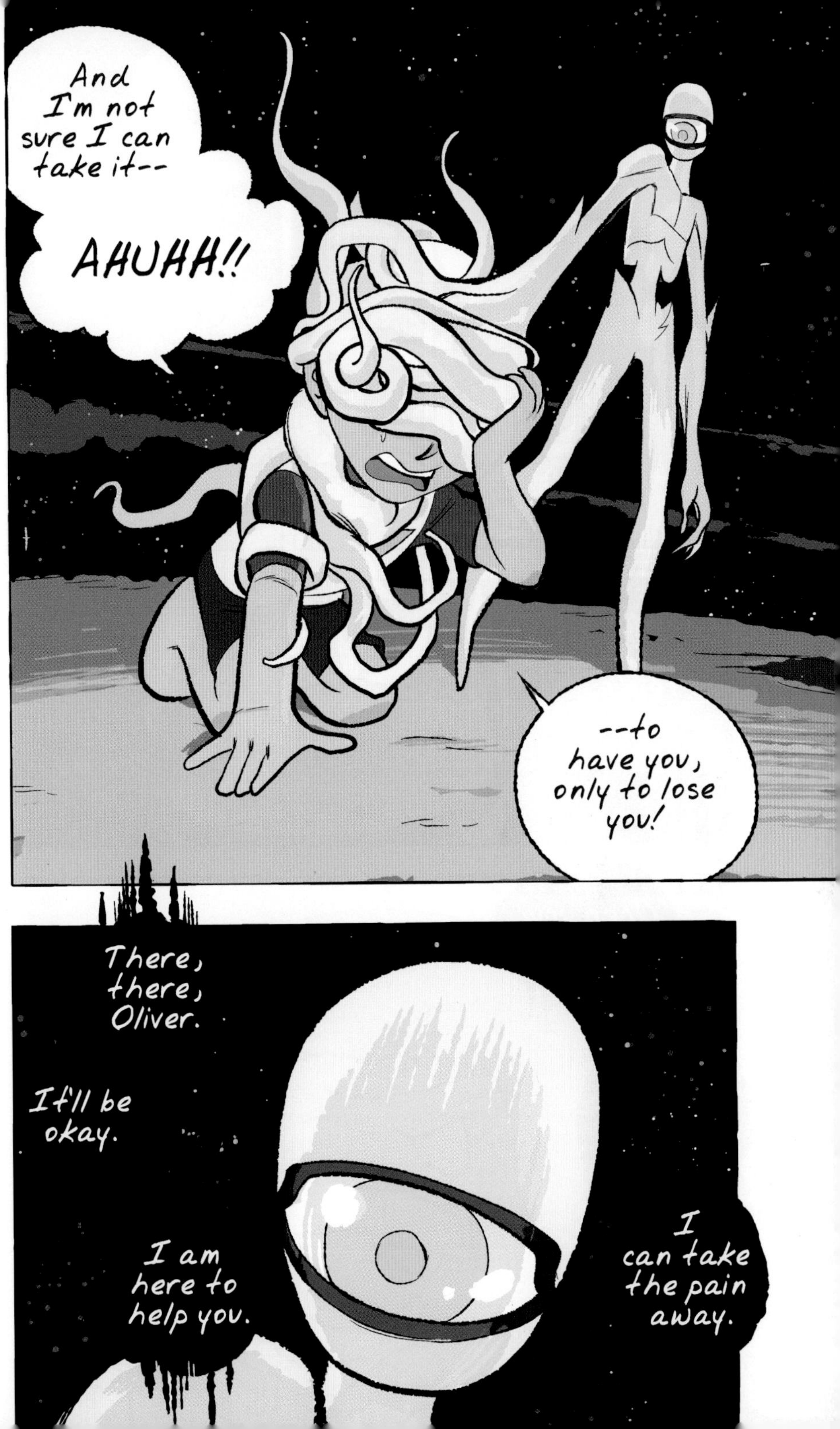
And I'm not sure I can take it--
AHUHH!!
--to have you, only to lose you!
There, there, Oliver.
It'll be okay.
I am here to help you.
I can take the pain away.

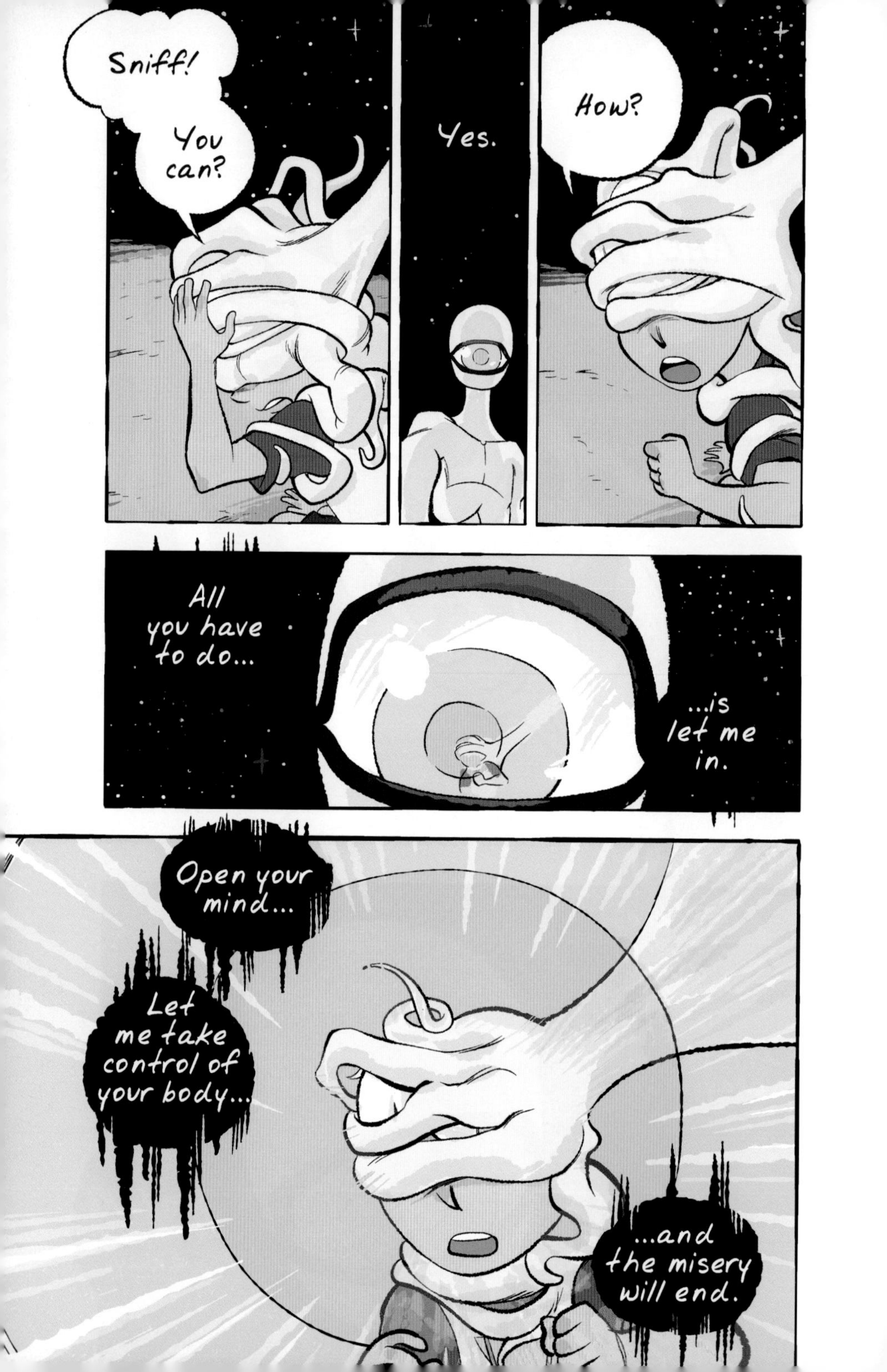
Sniff!
You can?
Yes.
How?
All you have to do...
...is let me in.
Open your mind...
Let me take control of your body...
...and the misery will end.

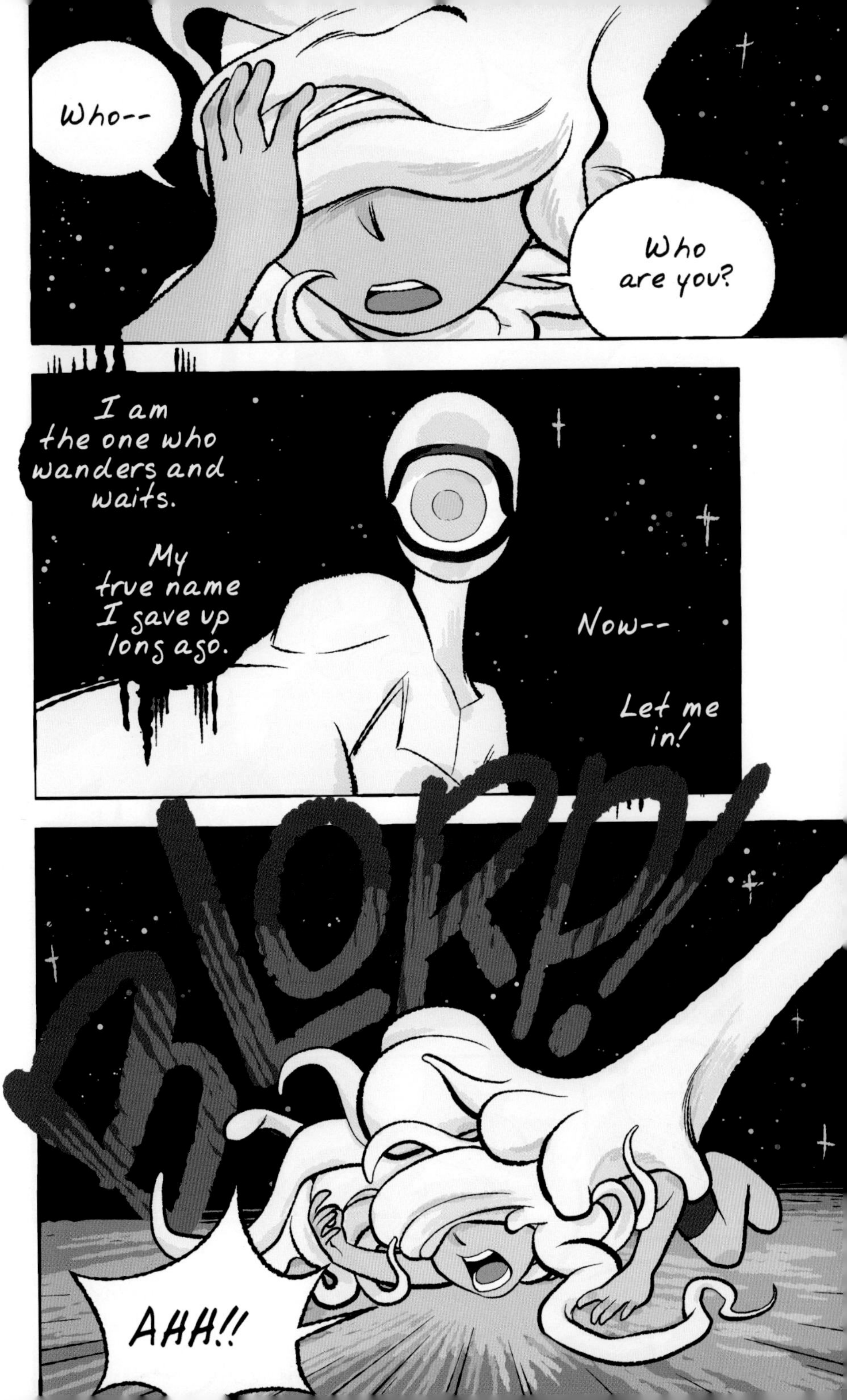
Who--
Who are you?
I am the one who wanders and waits.
My true name I gave up long ago.
Now--
Let me in!
BLORP!
AHH!!

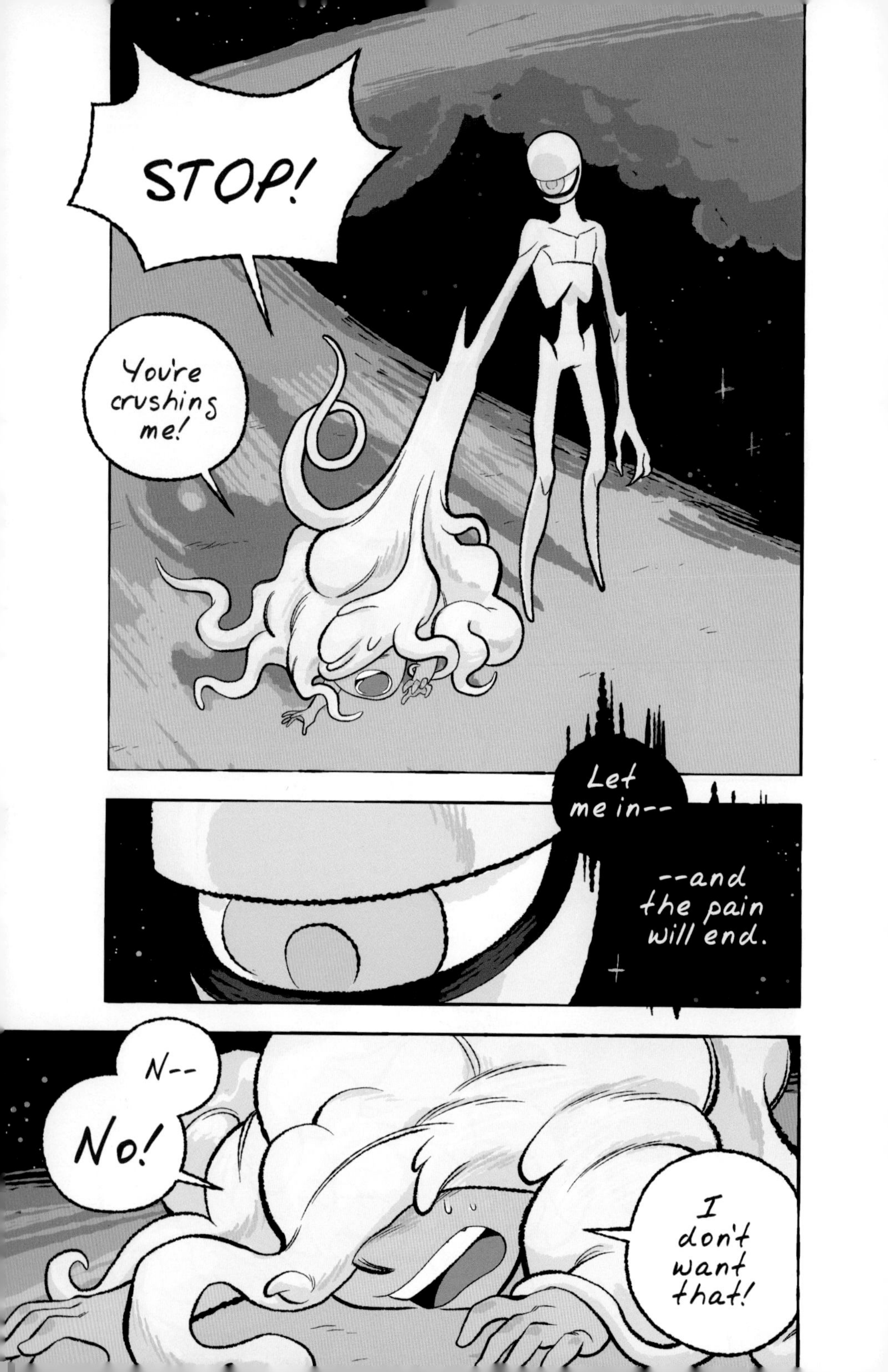
STOP!
You're crushing me!
Let me in--
--and the pain will end.
N--
No!
I don't want that!

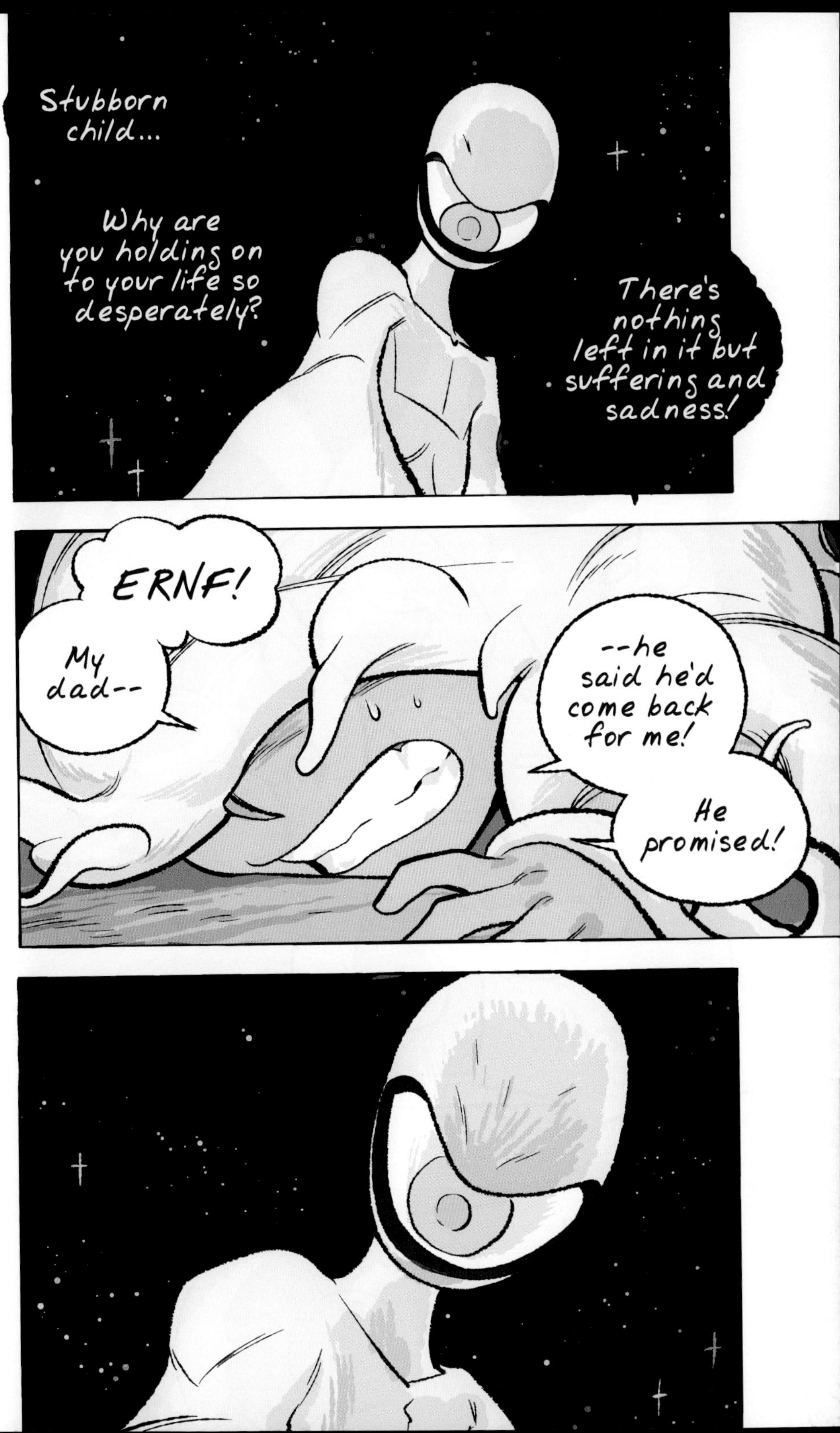
Stubborn child...
Why are you holding on to your life so desperately?
There's nothing left in it but suffering and sadness!
ERNF!
My dad--
--he said he'd come back for me!
He promised!

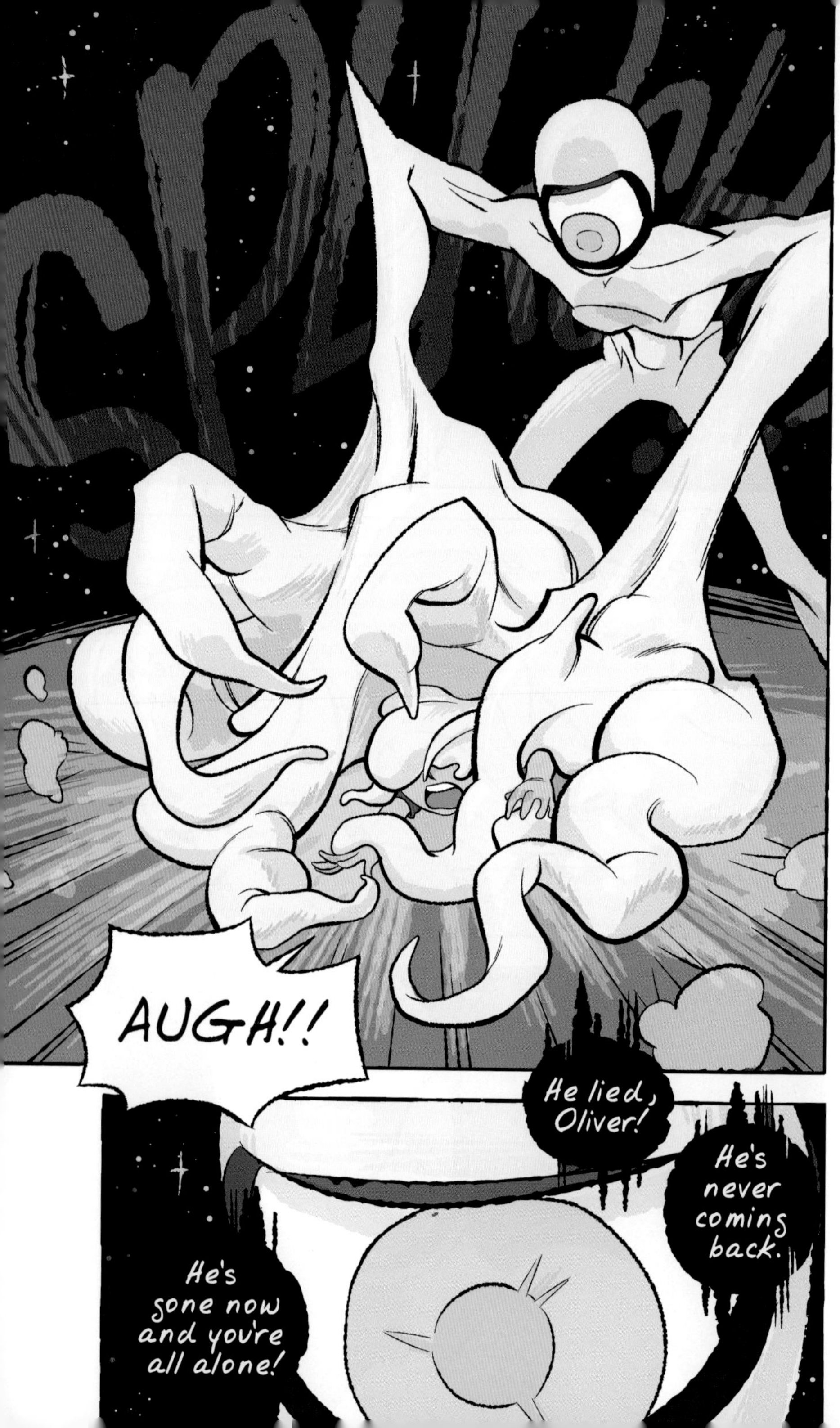
AUGH!!
He lied, Oliver!
He's never coming back.
He's gone now and you're all alone!

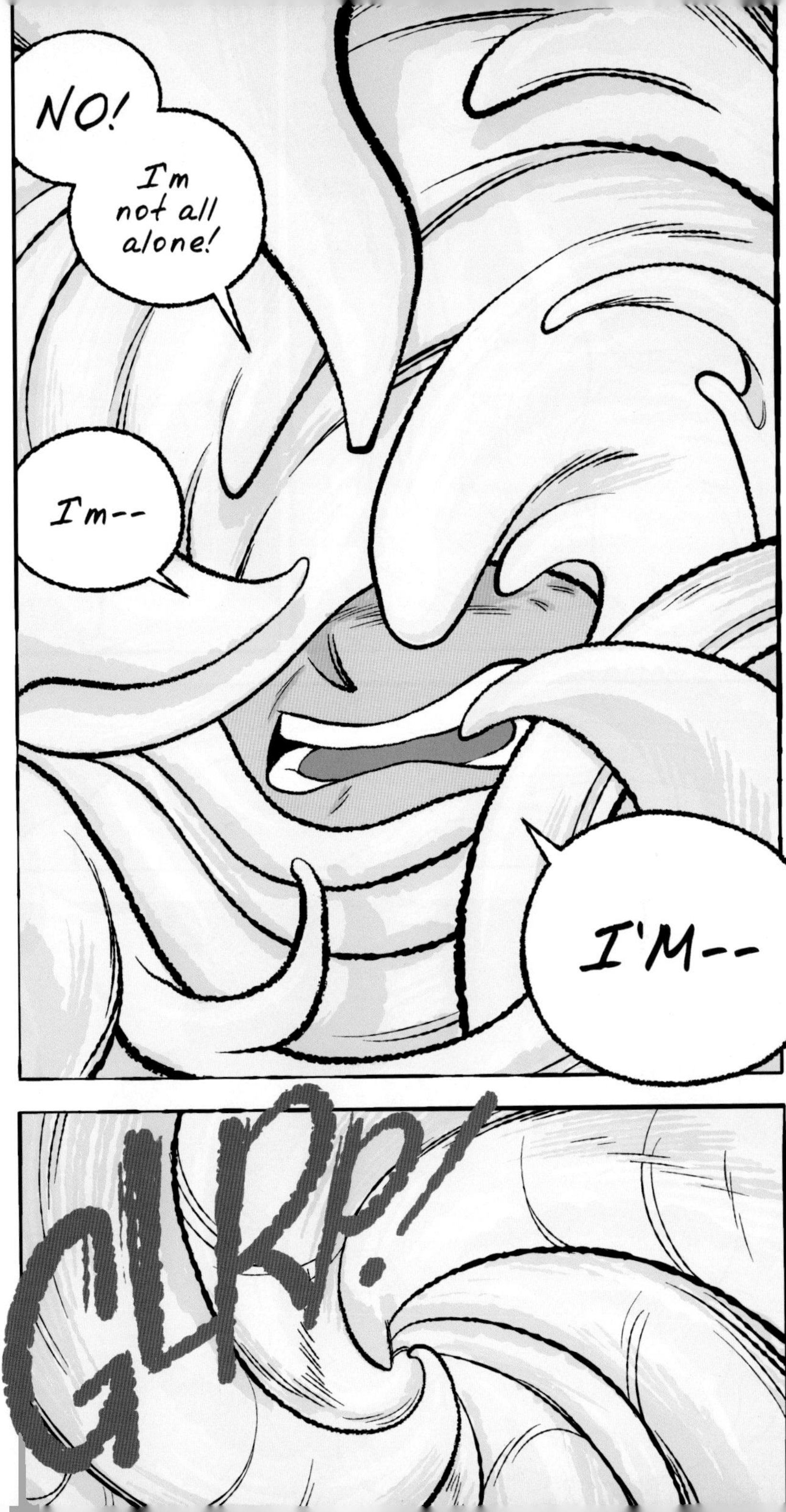
NO!
I'm not all alone!
I'm--
I'M--
GLRP!

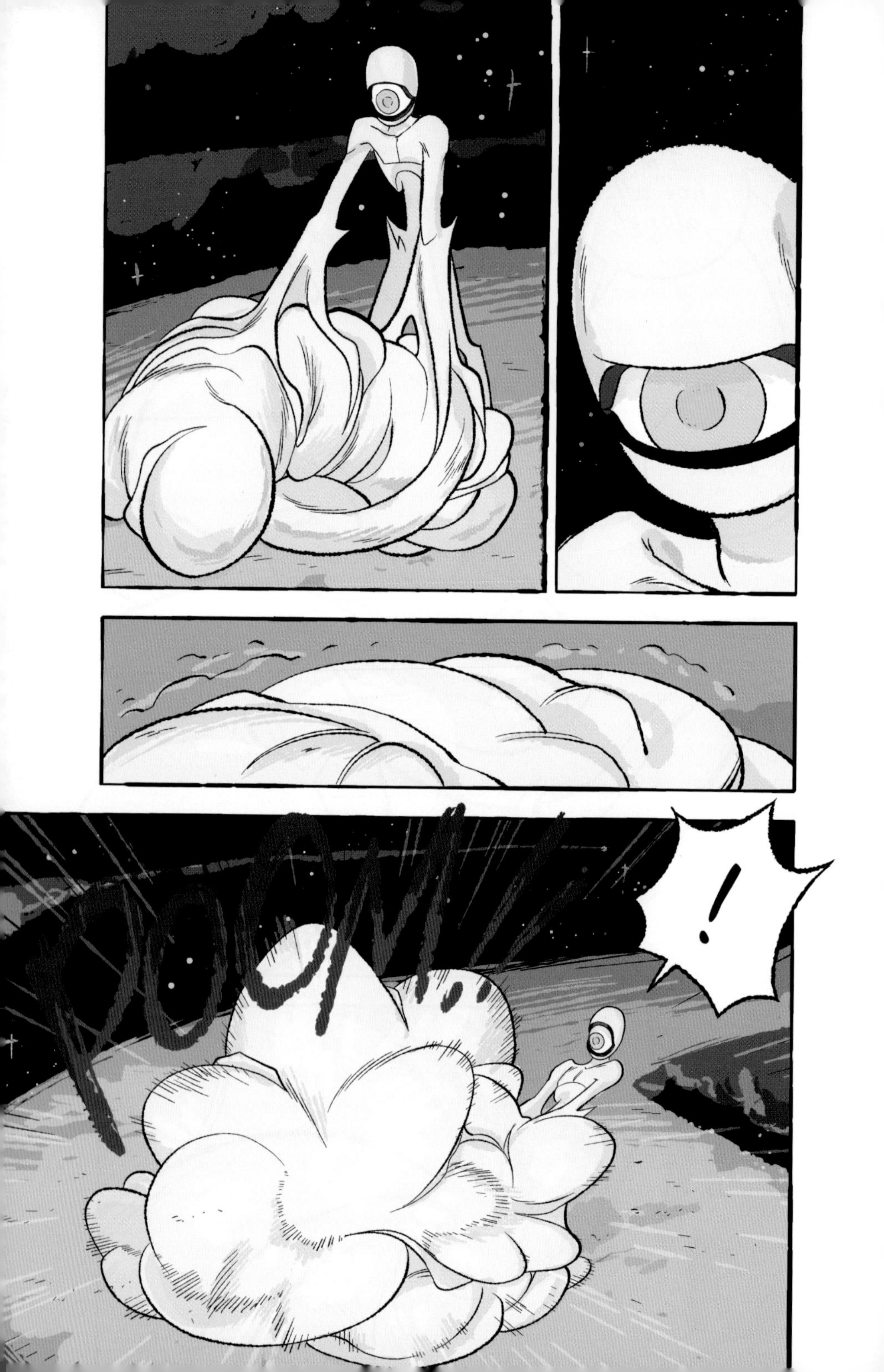
POOM...
!

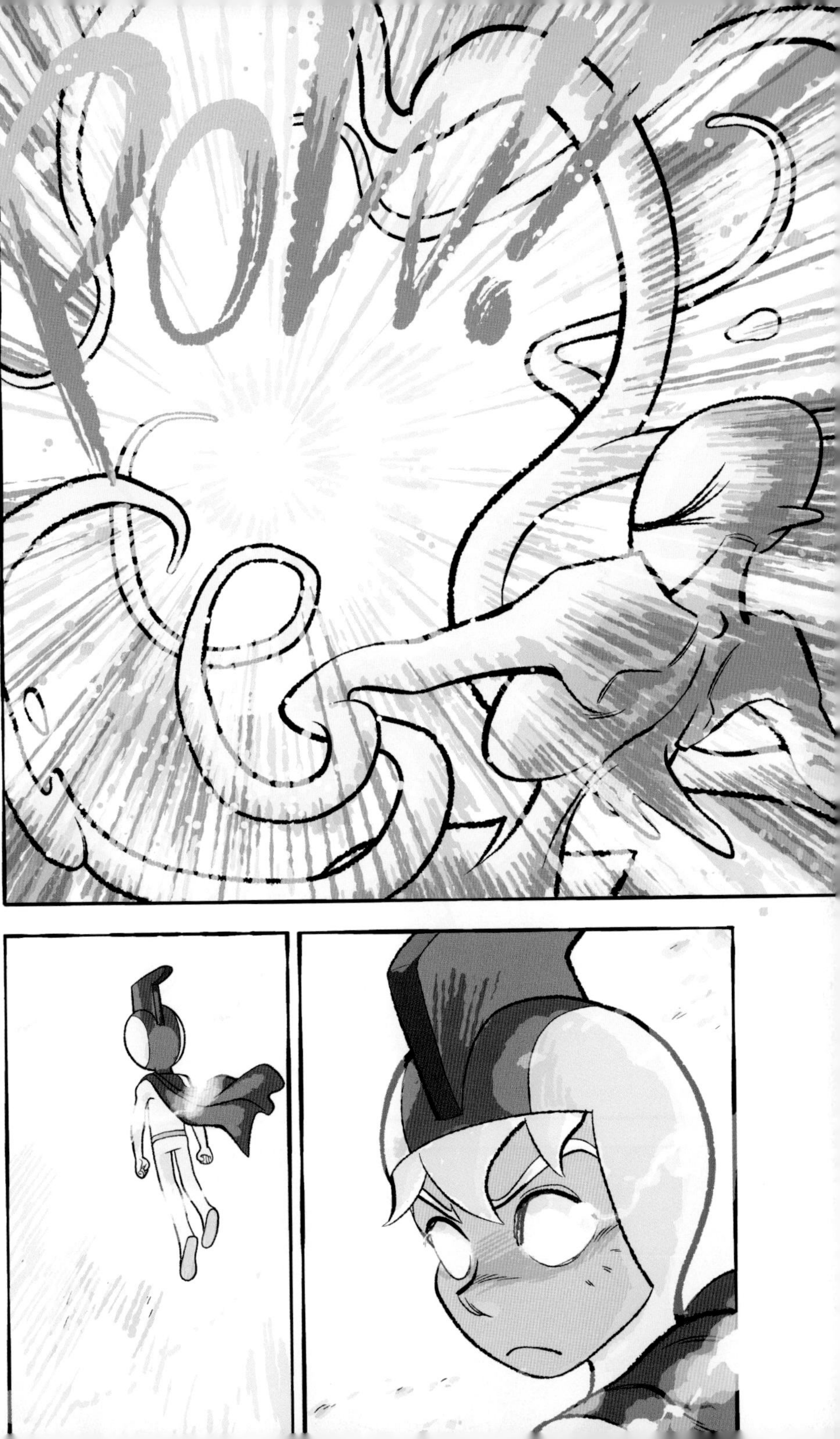
POW!

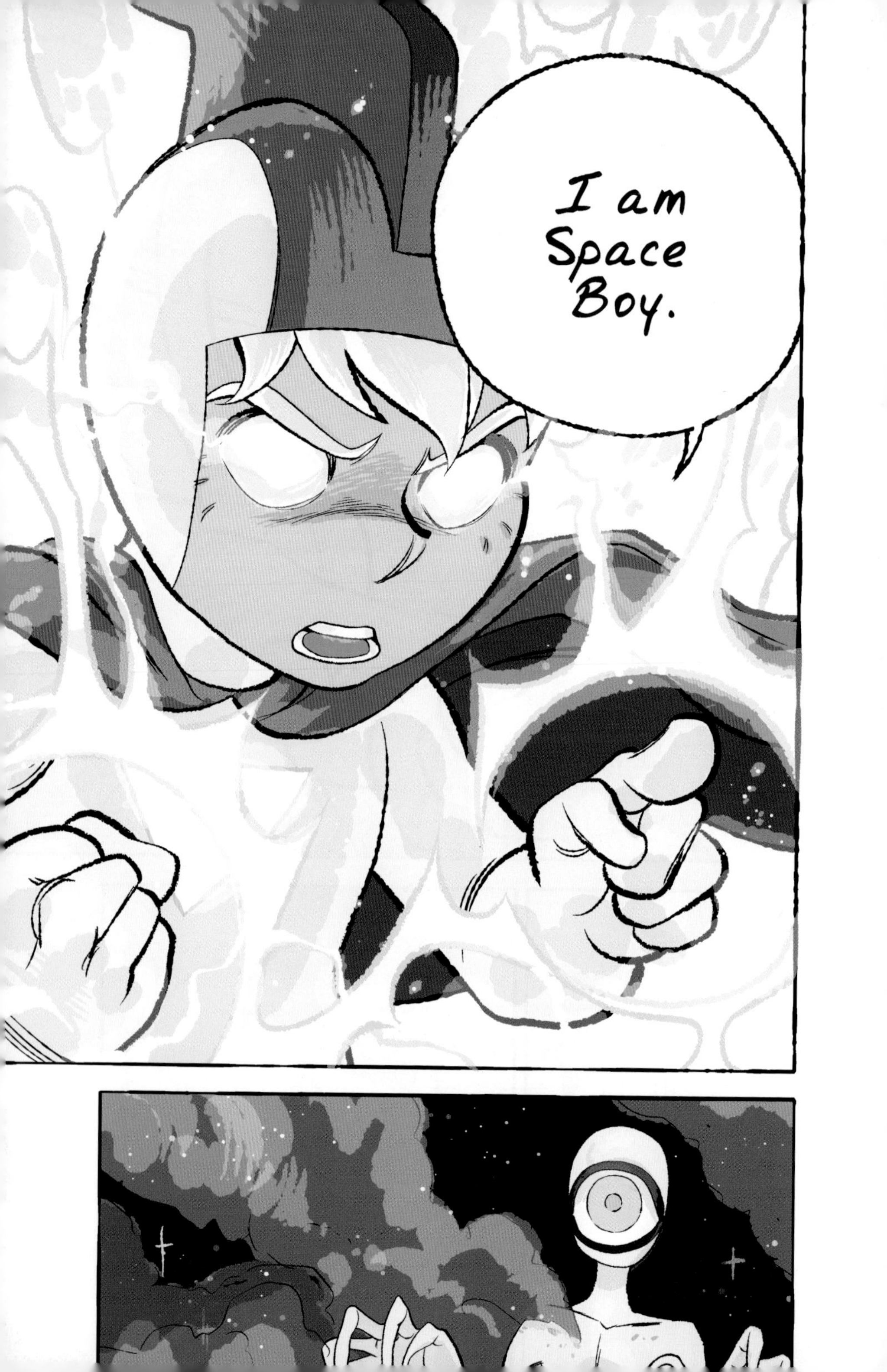
I am Space Boy.

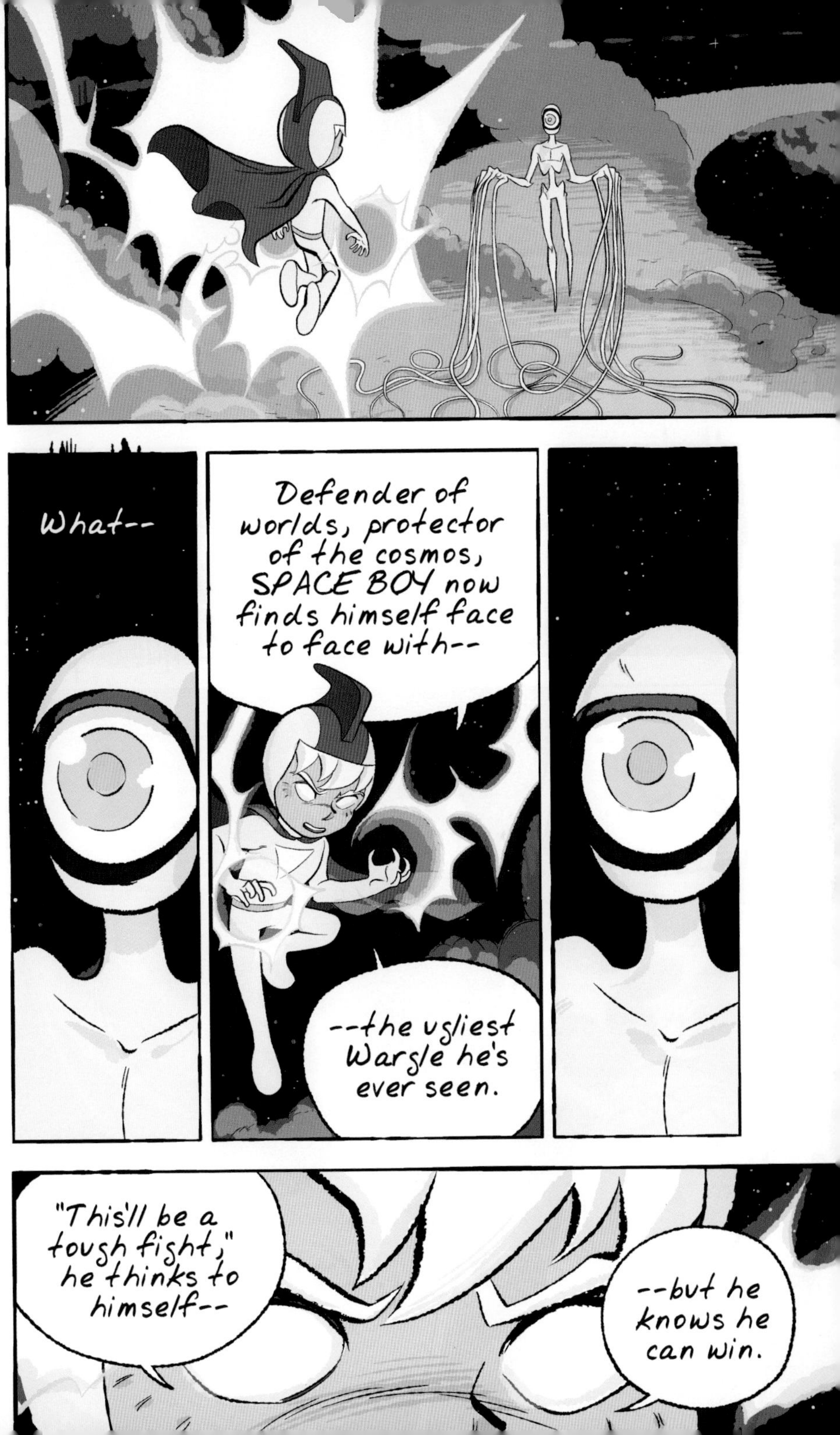
What--
Defender of worlds, protector of the cosmos, SPACE BOY now finds himself face to face with--
--the ugliest Wargle he's ever seen.
"This'll be a tough fight," he thinks to himself--
--but he knows he can win.

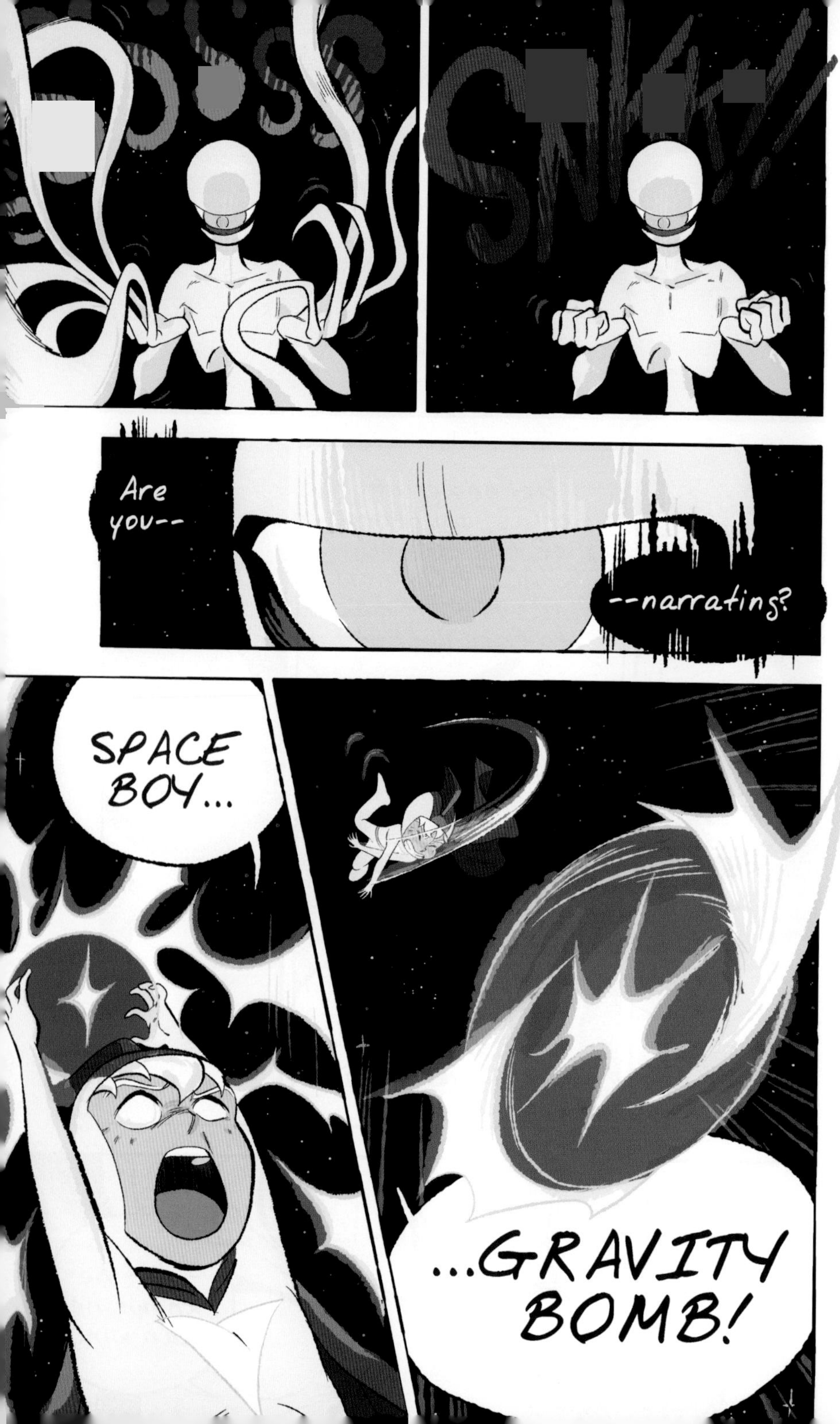
Are you--
--narrating?
SPACE BOY...
...GRAVITY BOMB!

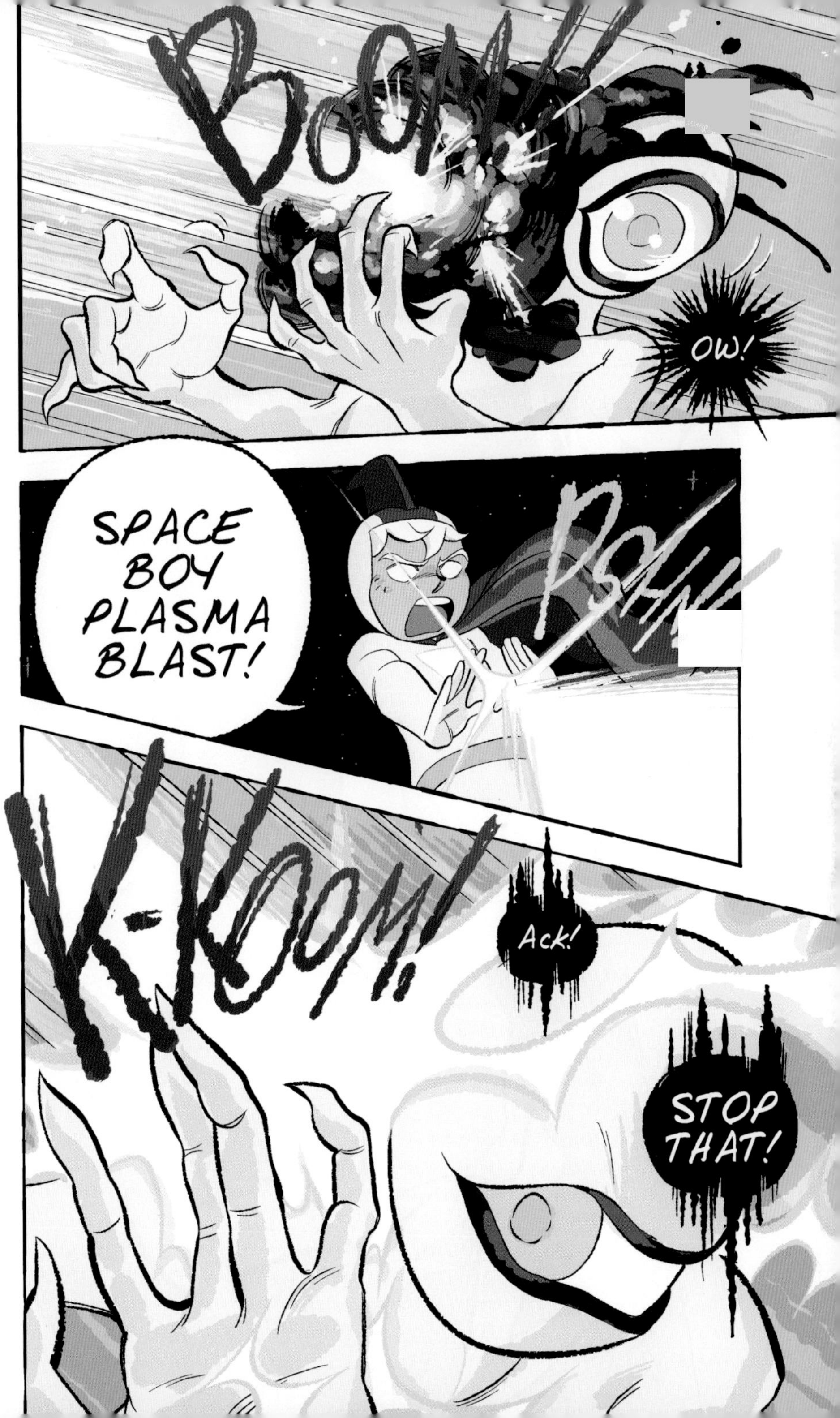
BOOM!
OW!
SPACE BOY PLASMA BLAST!
K-KOOM!
Ack!
STOP THAT!

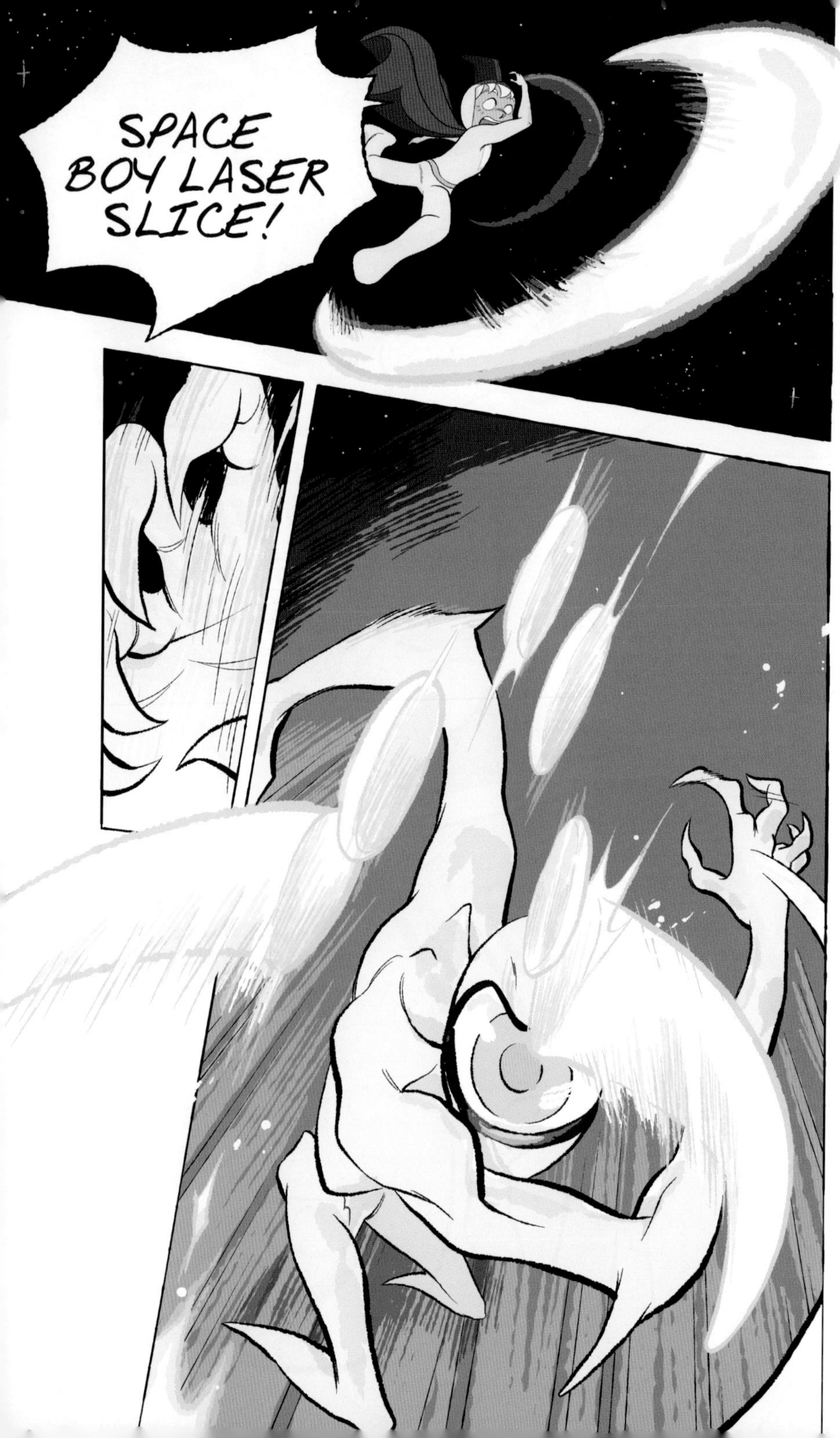
SPACE BOY LASER SLICE!

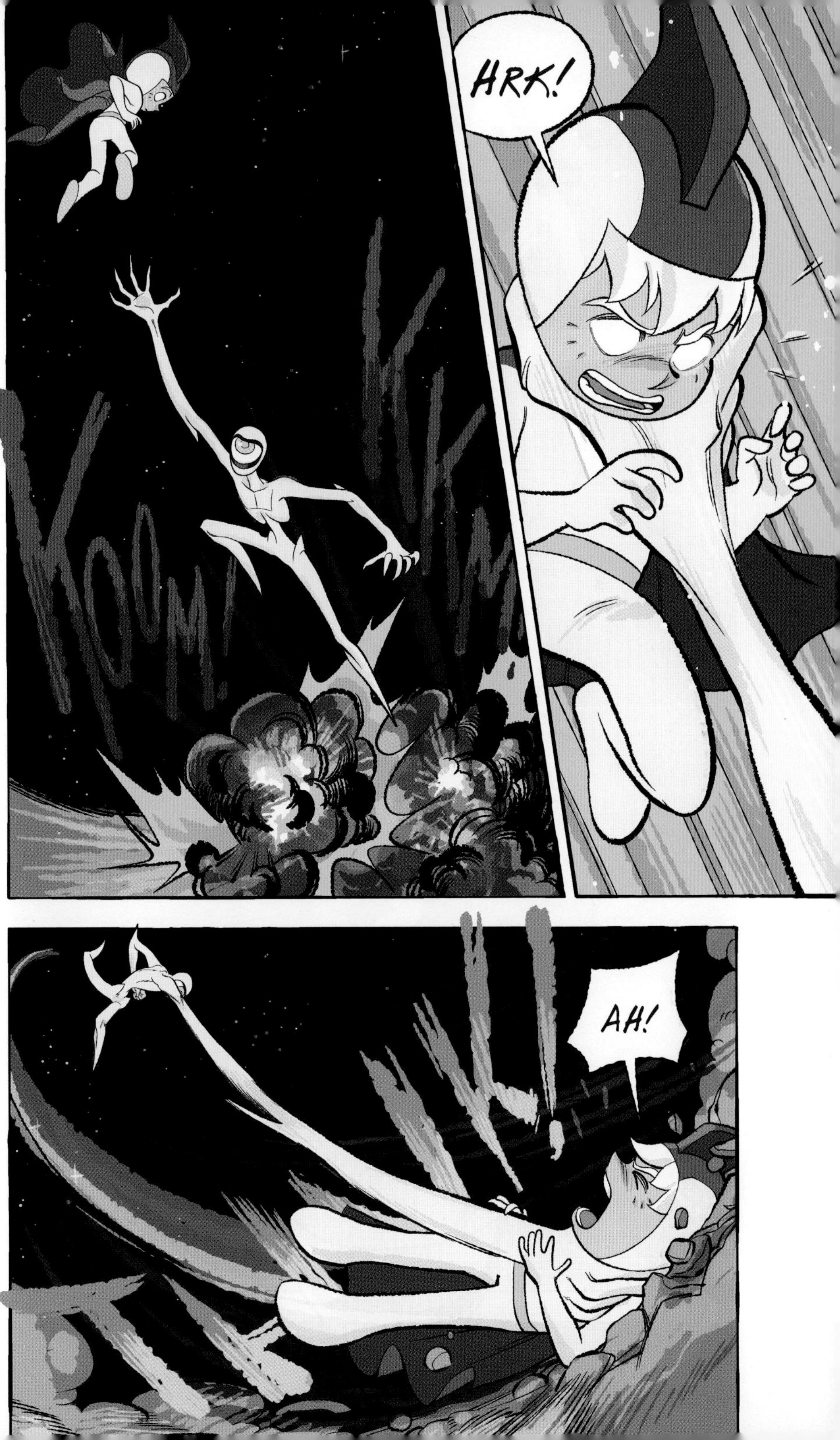
HRK!
AH!

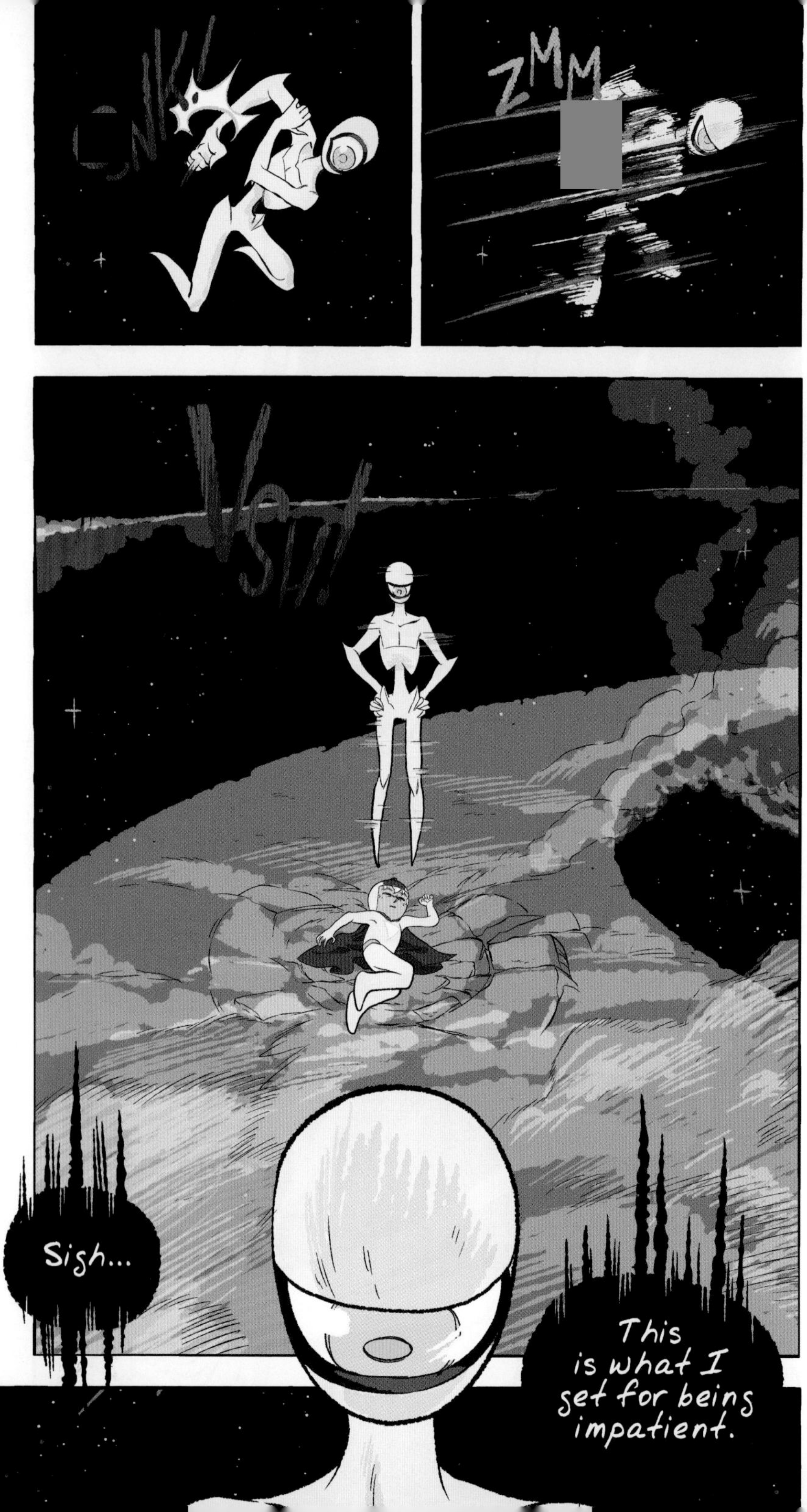
ZMM
Sigh...
This is what I get for being impatient.

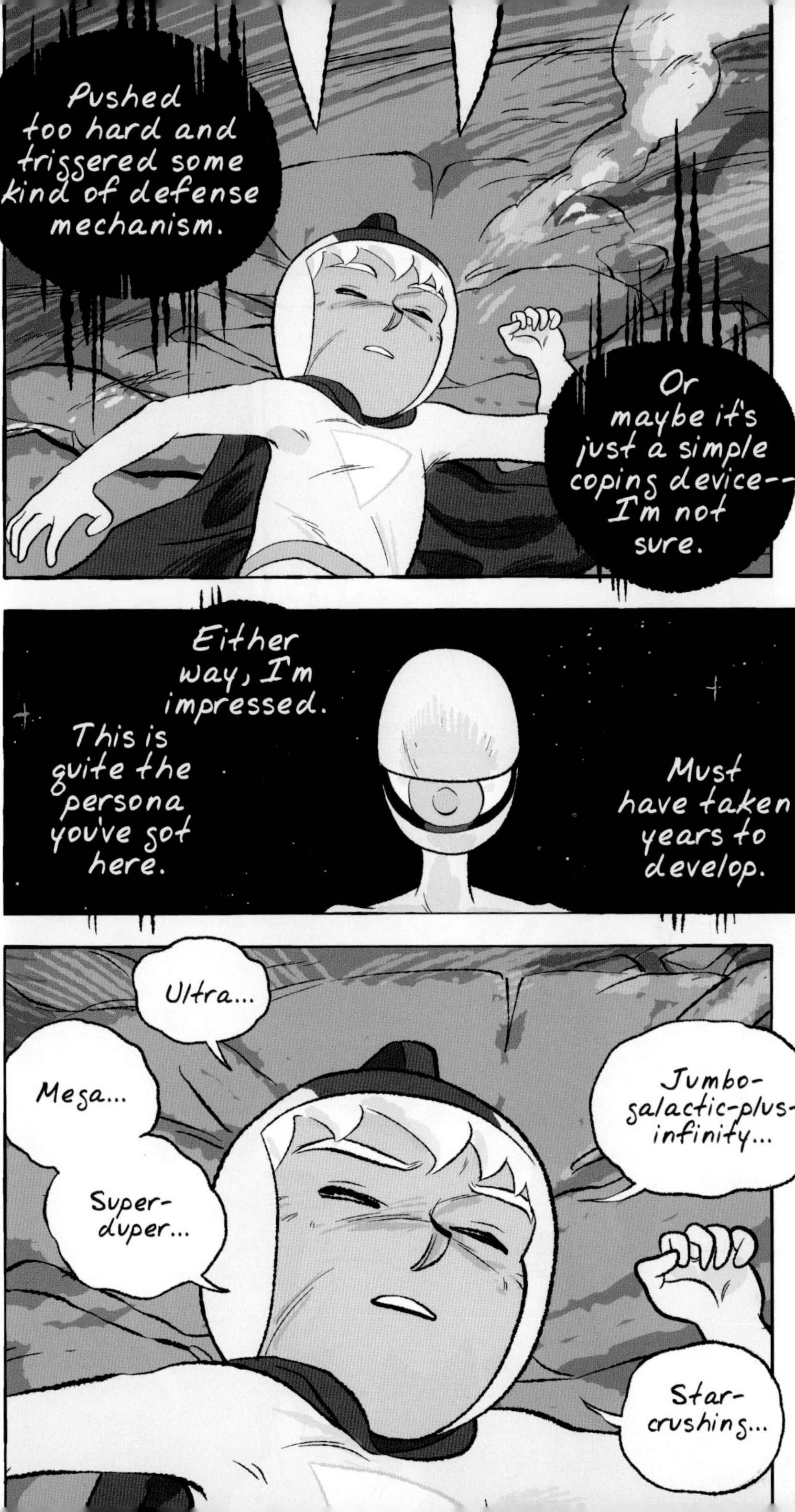
Pushed too hard and triggered some kind of defense mechanism.
Or maybe it's just a simple coping device-- I'm not sure.
Either way, I'm impressed.
This is quite the persona you've got here.
Must have taken years to develop.
Ultra...
Mega...
Super-duper...
Jumbo-galactic-plus-infinity...
Star-crushing...

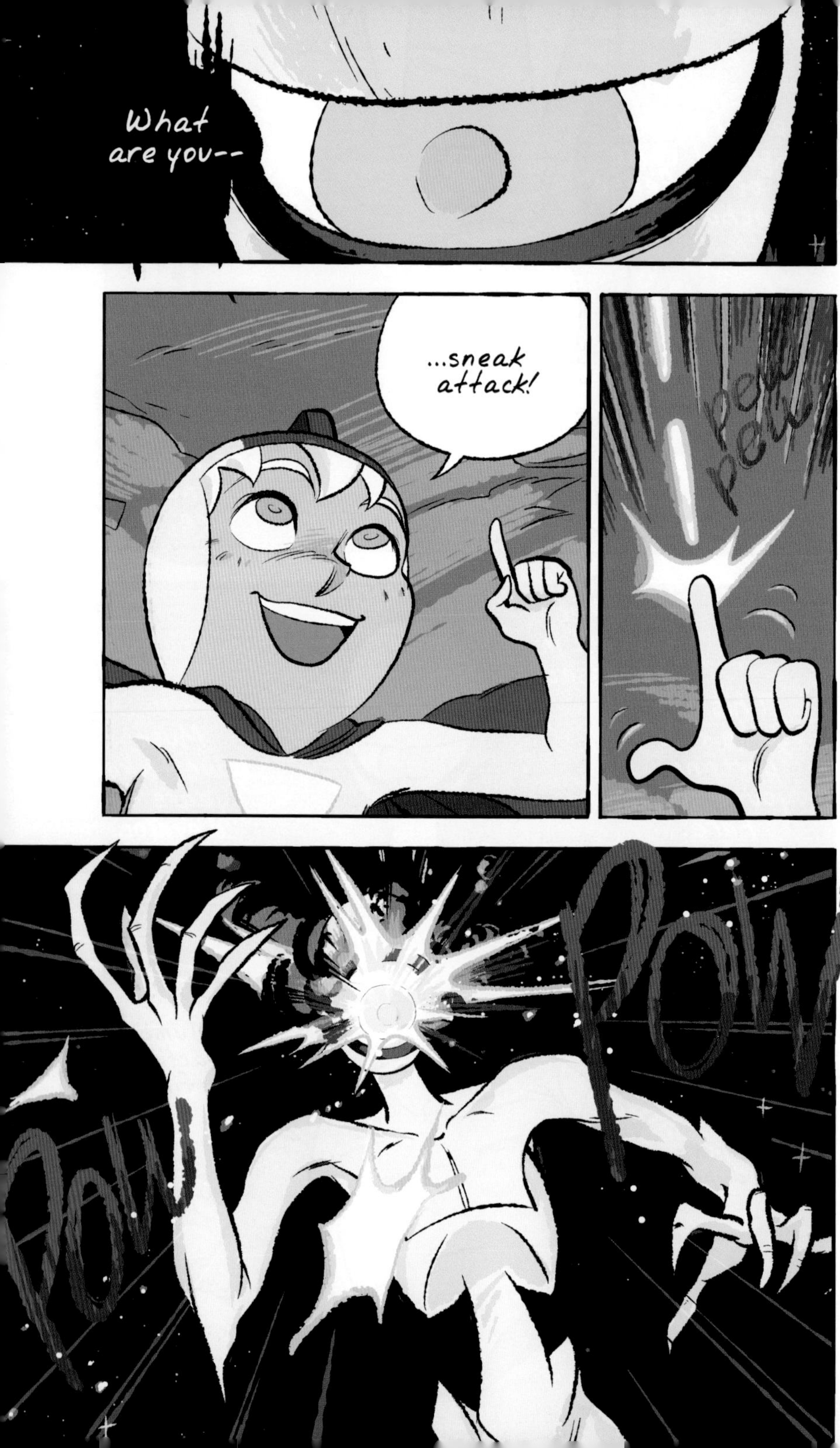
What are you--
...sneak attack!
pew pew pew
POW POW

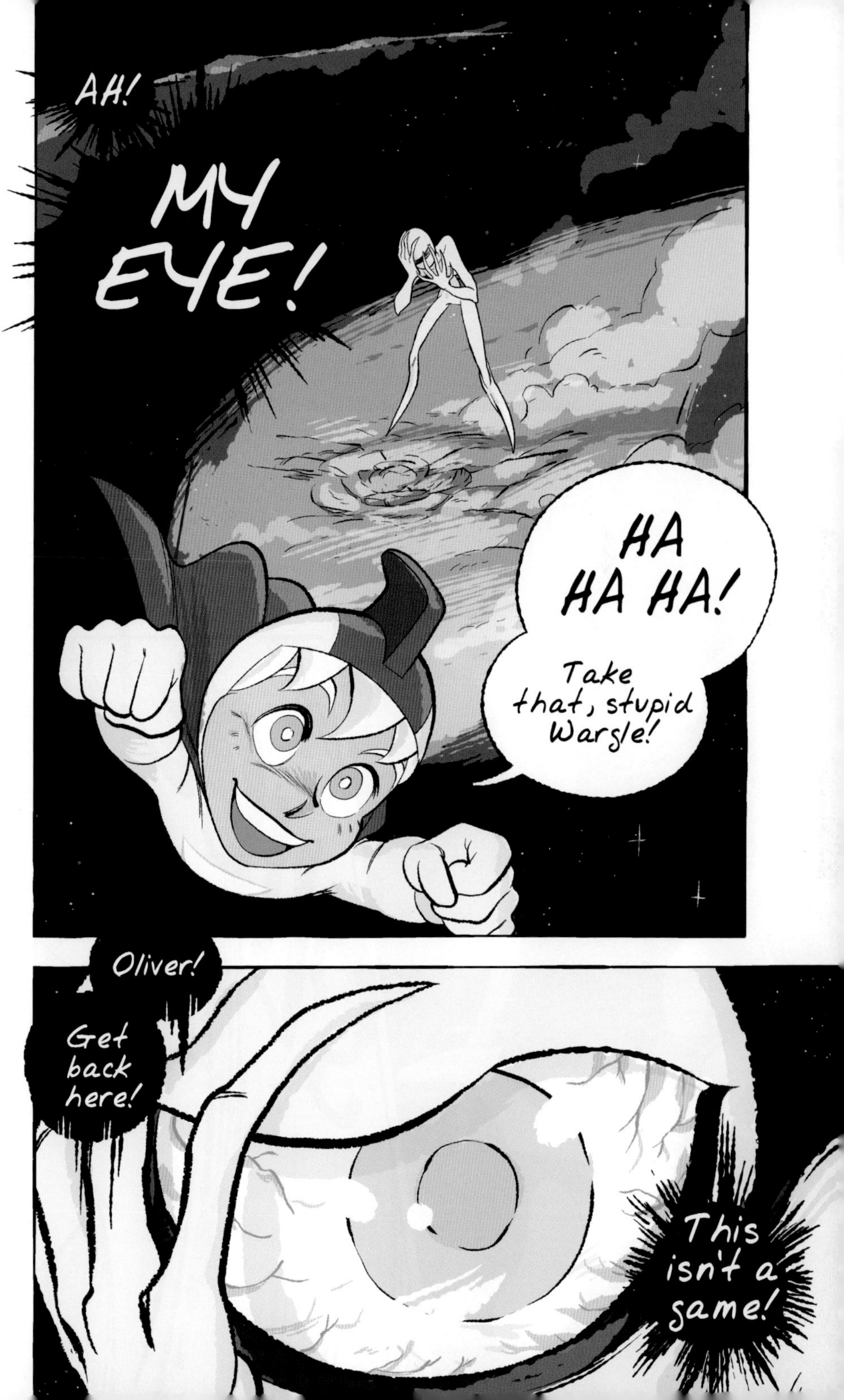
AH!
MY EYE!
HA HA HA!
Take that, stupid Wargle!
Oliver!
Get back here!
This isn't a game!

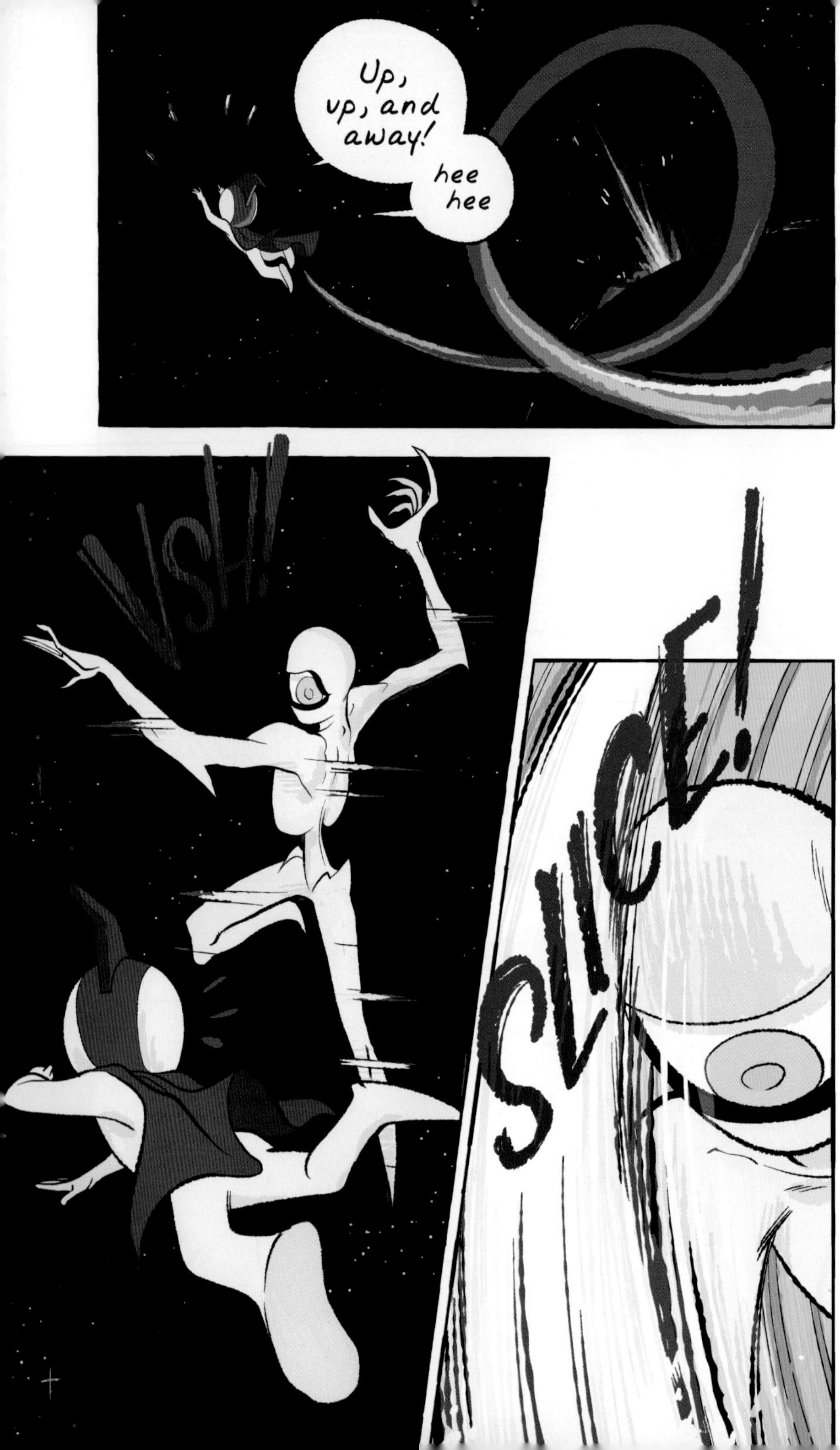

Up, up, and away!
hee hee
WSH!!
SLICE!

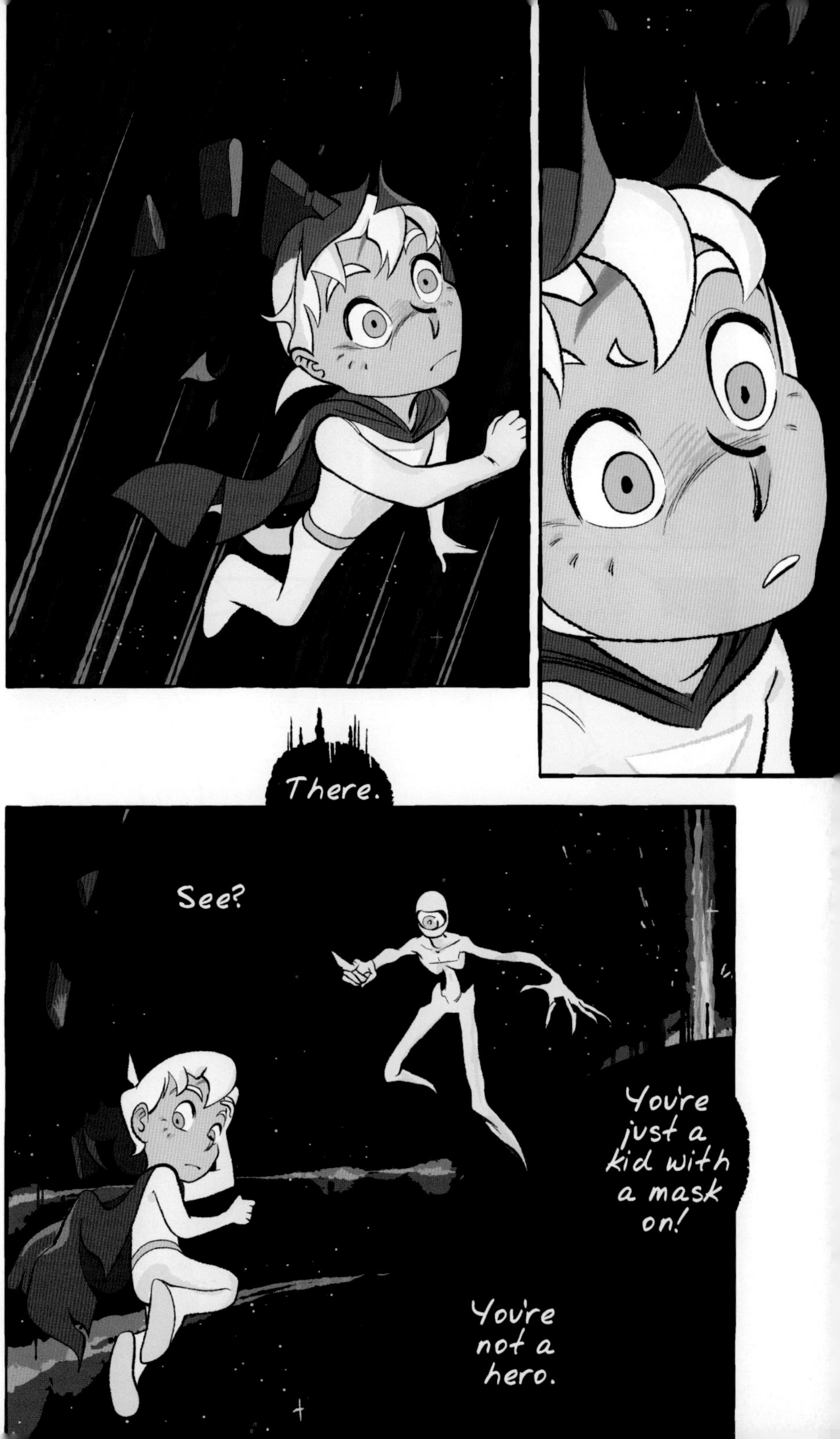
There.
See?
You're just a kid with a mask on!
You're not a hero.

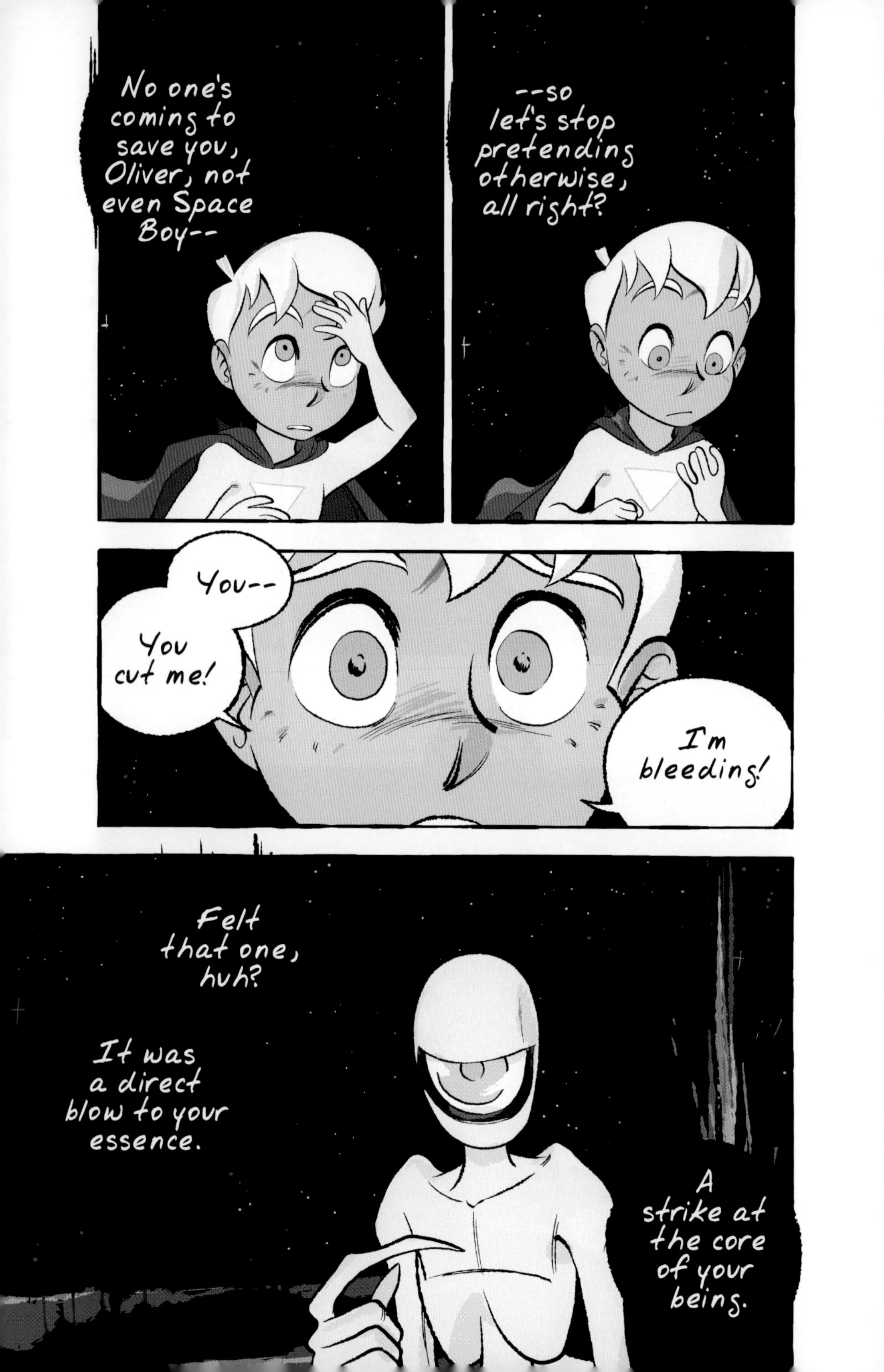
No one's coming to save you, Oliver, not even Space Boy--
--so let's stop pretending otherwise, all right?
You--
You cut me!
I'm bleeding!
Felt that one, huh?
It was a direct blow to your essence.
A strike at the core of your being.

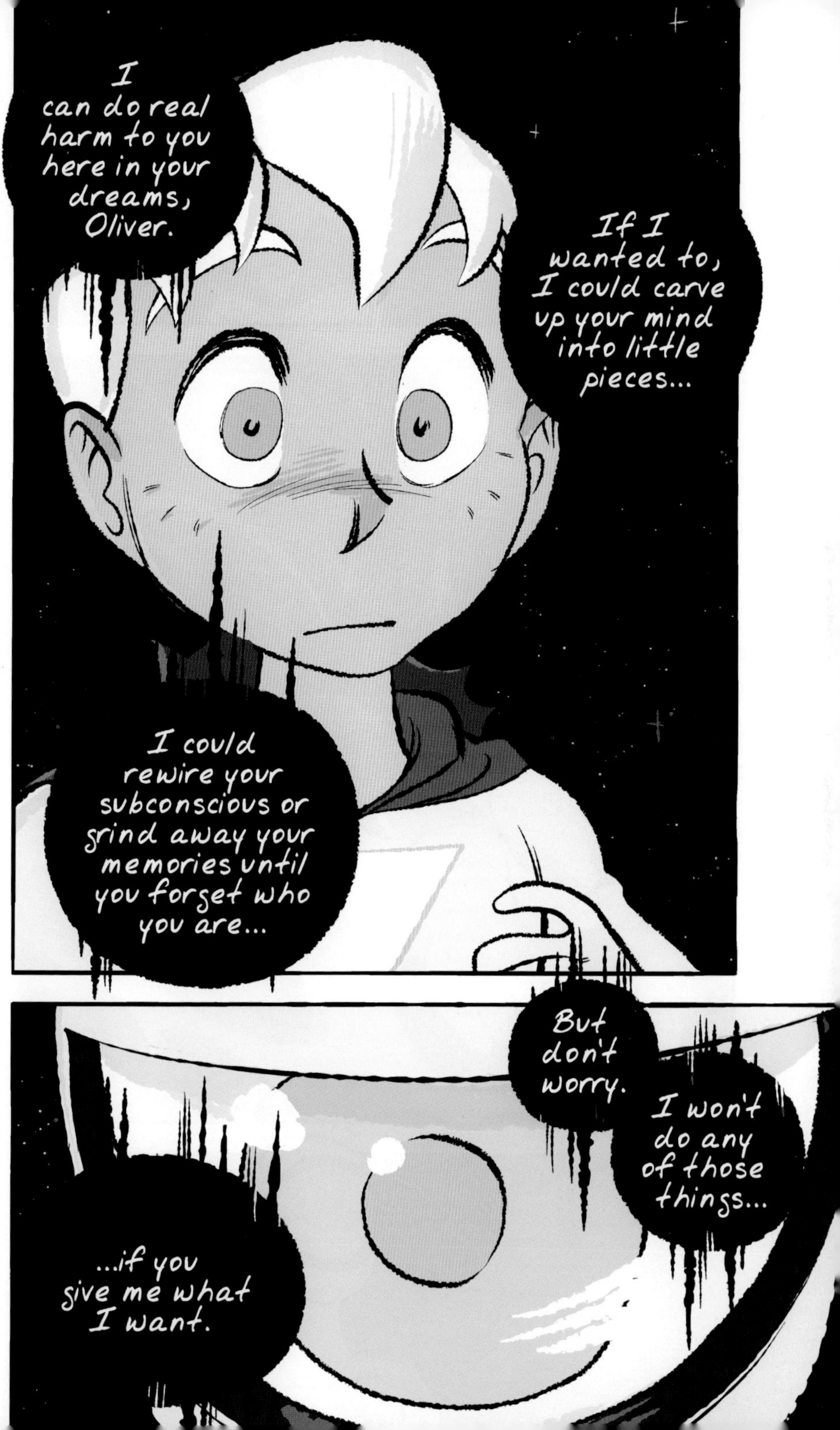
I can do real harm to you here in your dreams, Oliver.
If I wanted to, I could carve up your mind into little pieces...
I could rewire your subconscious or grind away your memories until you forget who you are...
But don't worry.
I won't do any of those things...
...if you give me what I want.

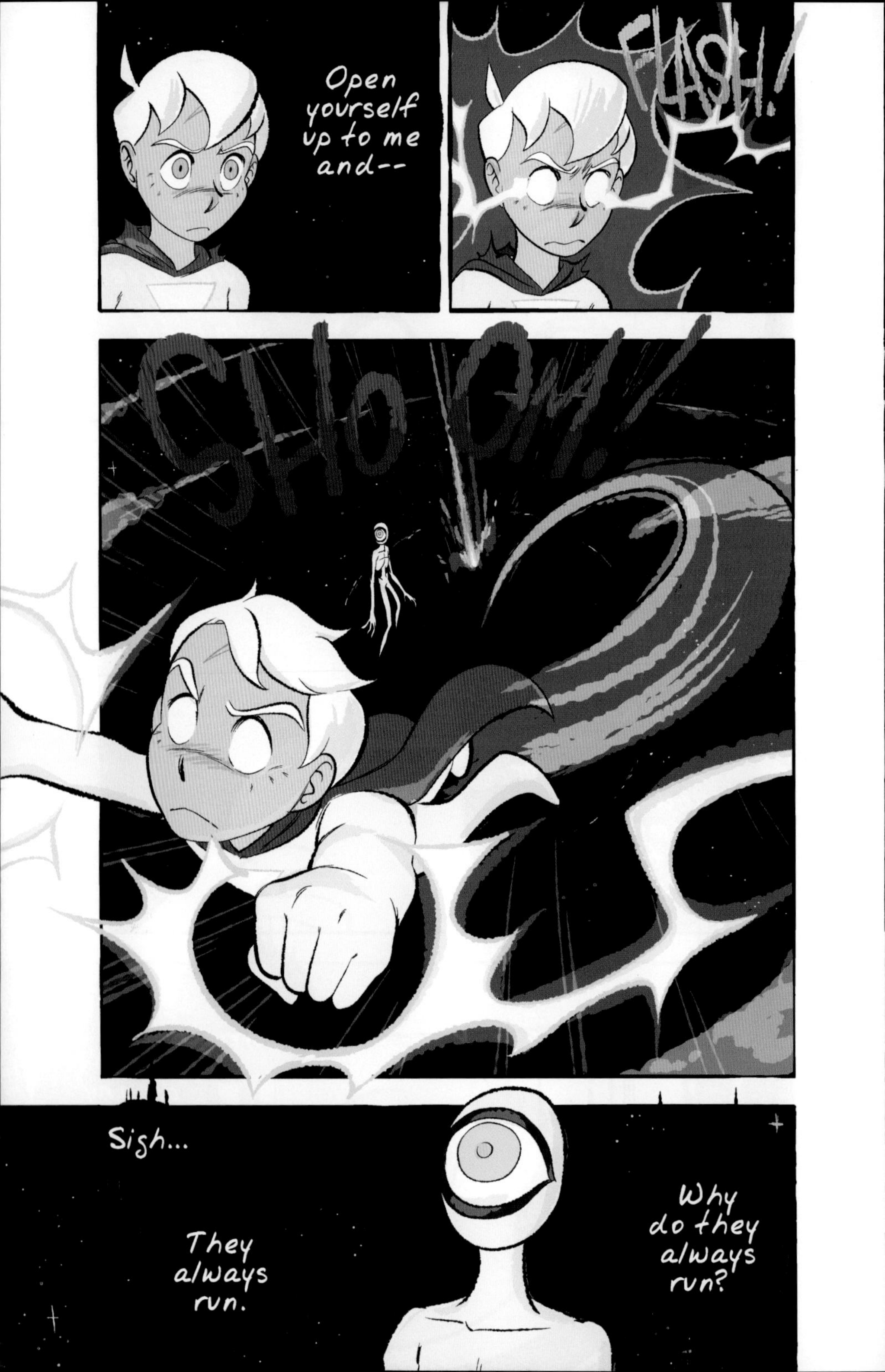
Open yourself up to me and--
FLASH!!
SHOOM!!
Sigh...
They always run.
Why do they always run?

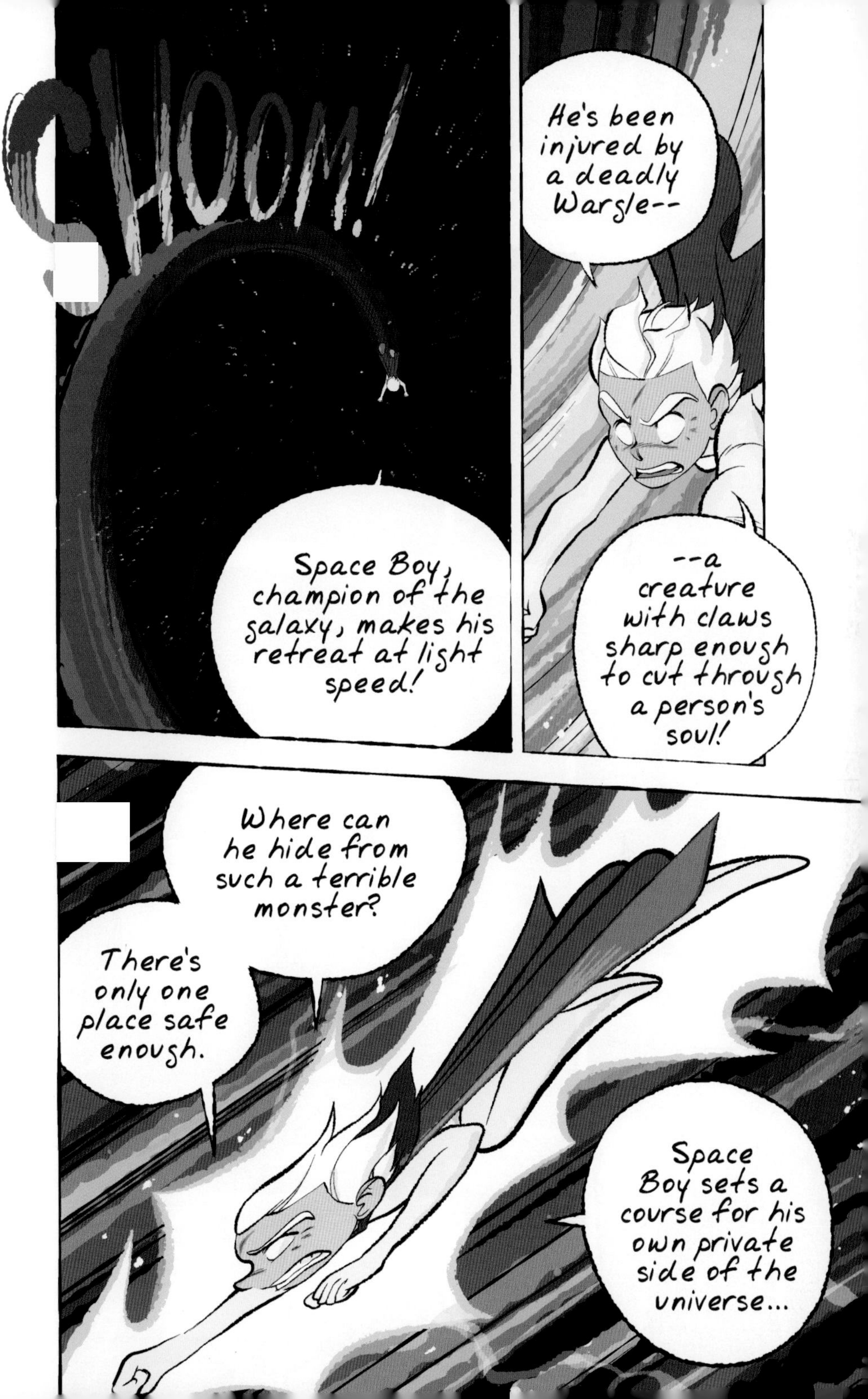
SHOOM!
Space Boy, champion of the galaxy, makes his retreat at light speed!
He's been injured by a deadly Wargle--
--a creature with claws sharp enough to cut through a person's soul!
Where can he hide from such a terrible monster?
There's only one place safe enough.
Space Boy sets a course for his own private side of the universe...

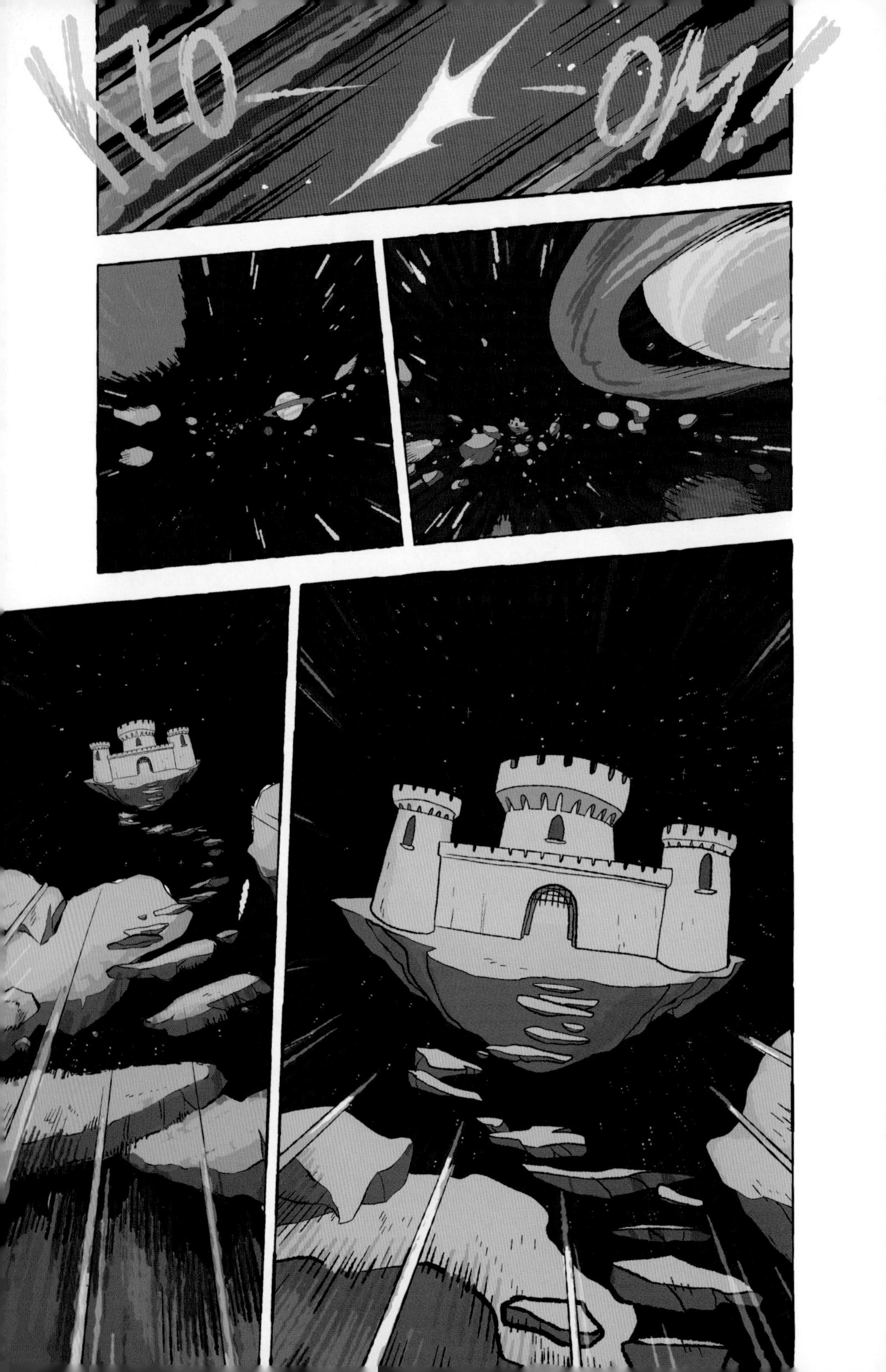
VRO—OM!!

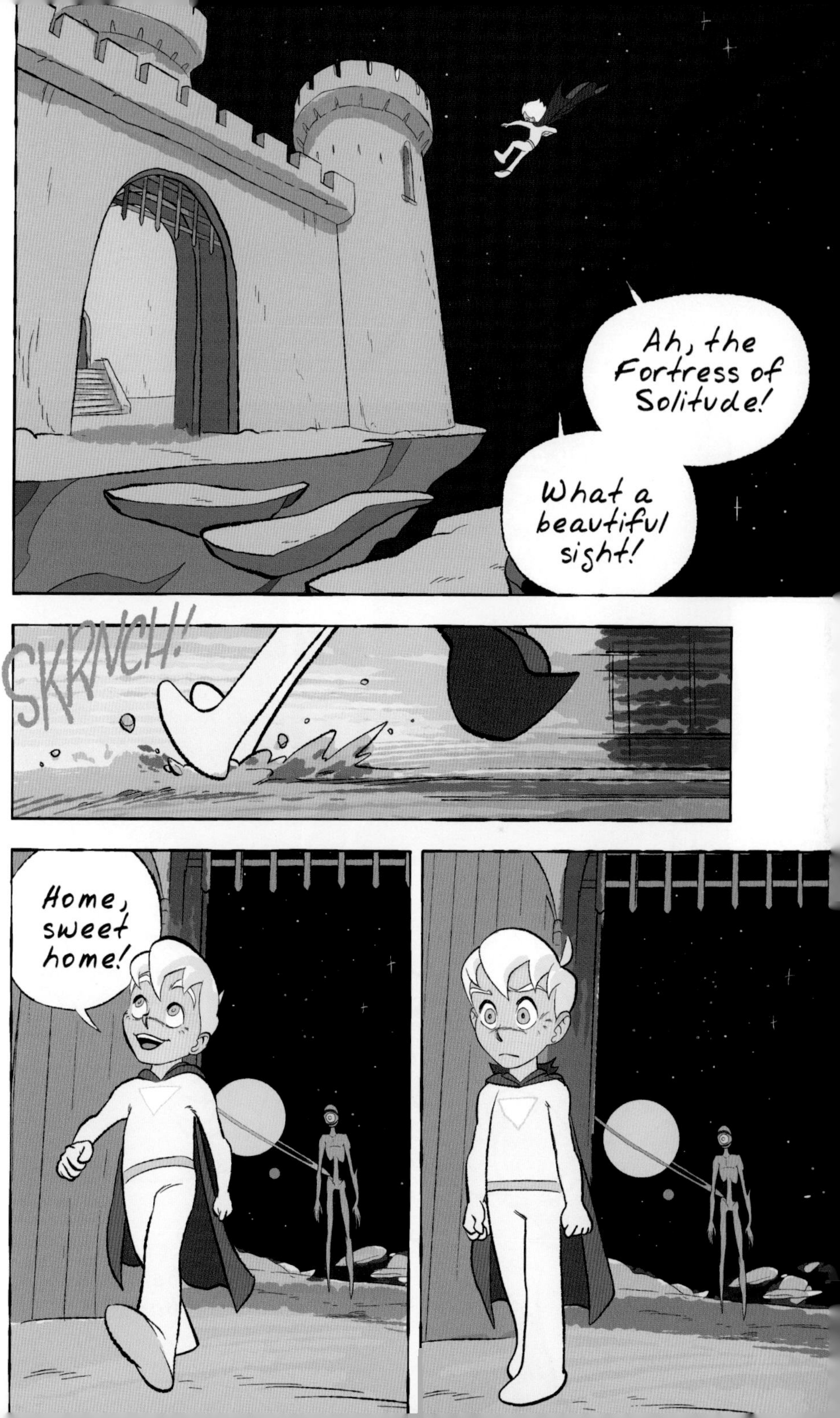
Ah, the Fortress of Solitude!
What a beautiful sight!
SKRNCH!
Home, sweet home!

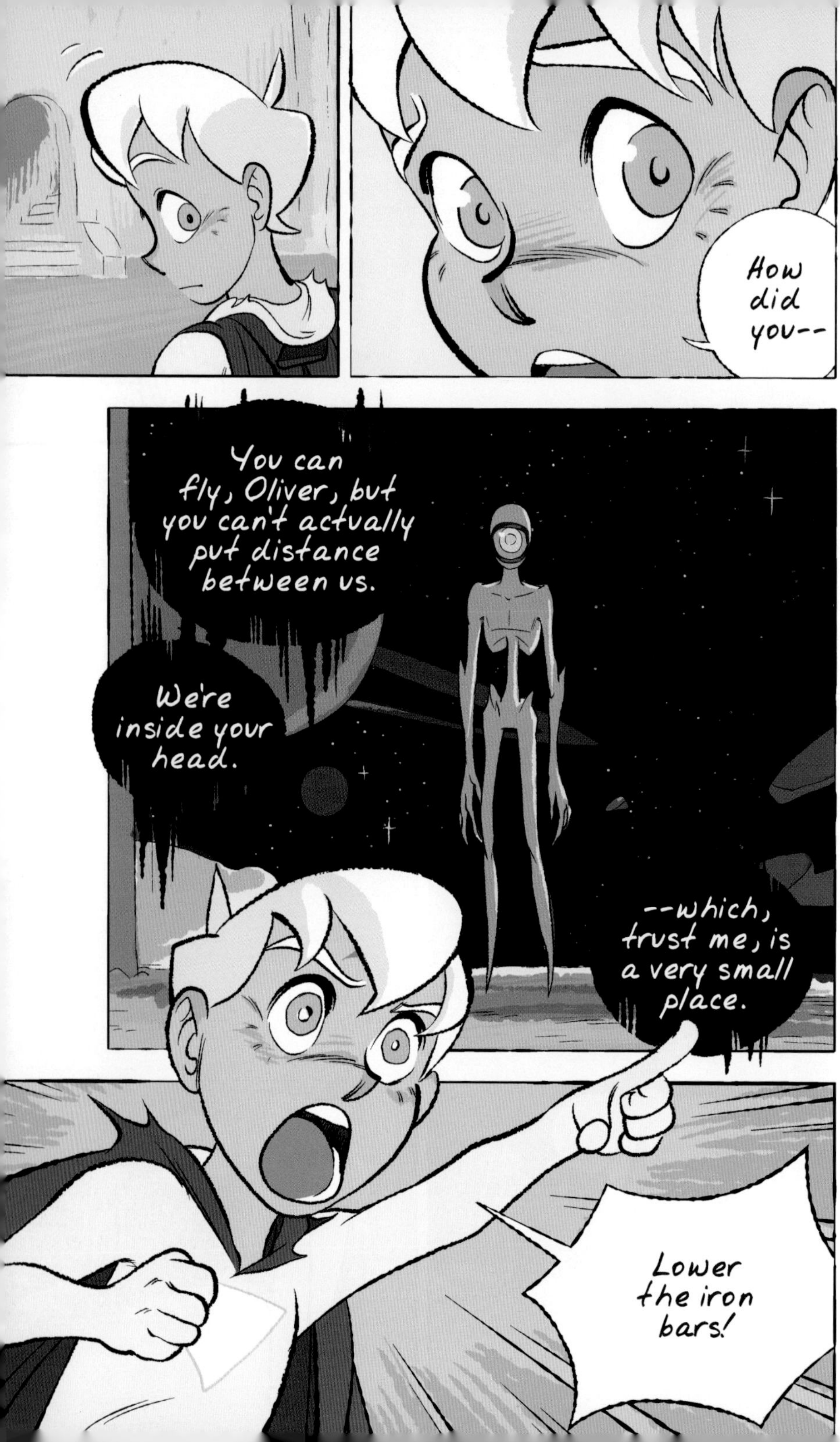
How did you--
You can fly, Oliver, but you can't actually put distance between us.
We're inside your head.
--which, trust me, is a very small place.
Lower the iron bars!

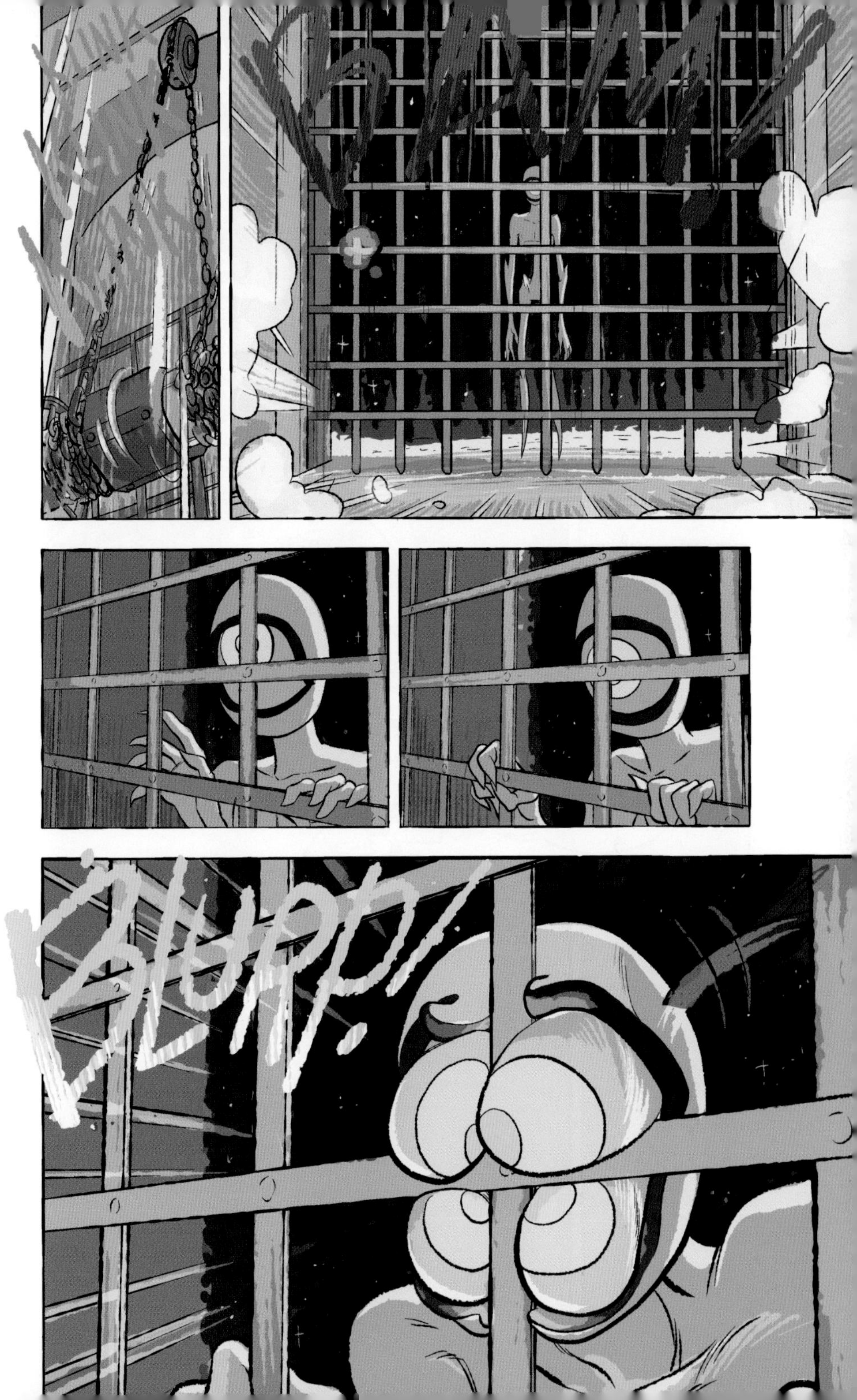
BLUPP!

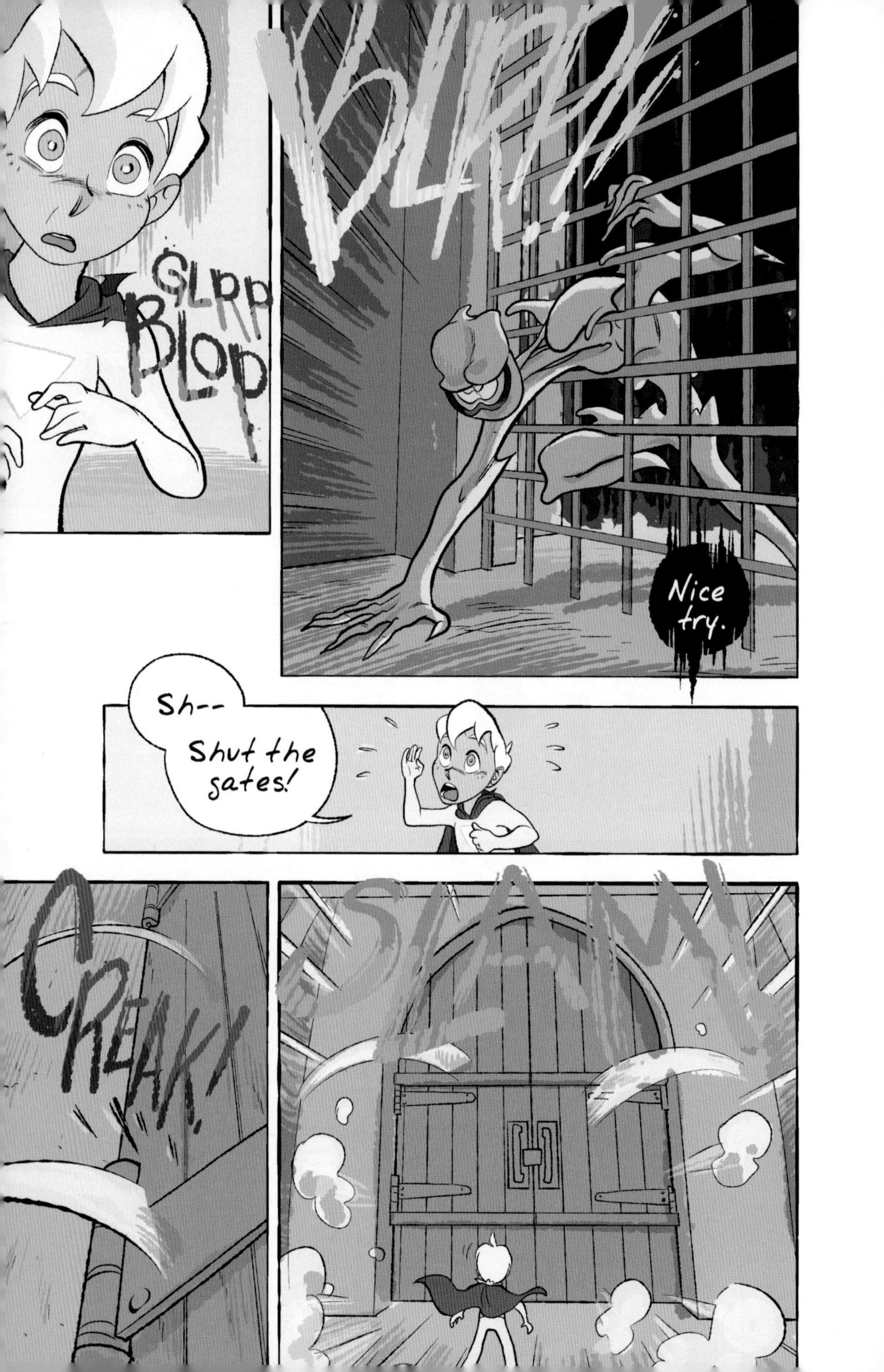
GLRP
BLOP
BLAM!
Nice try.
Sh--
Shut the gates!
CREAK!
SLAM!

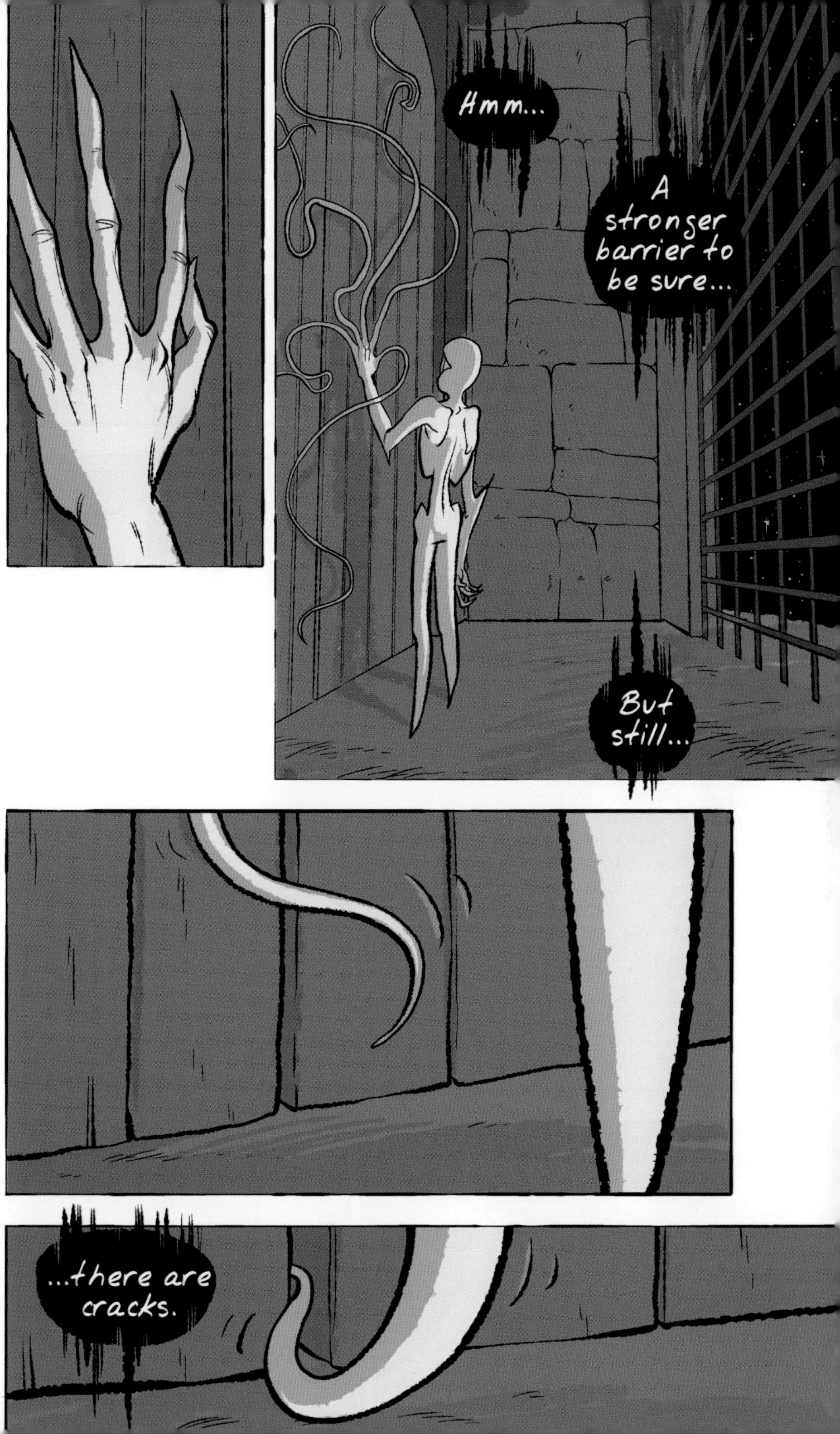
Hmm...
A stronger barrier to be sure...
But still...
...there are cracks.

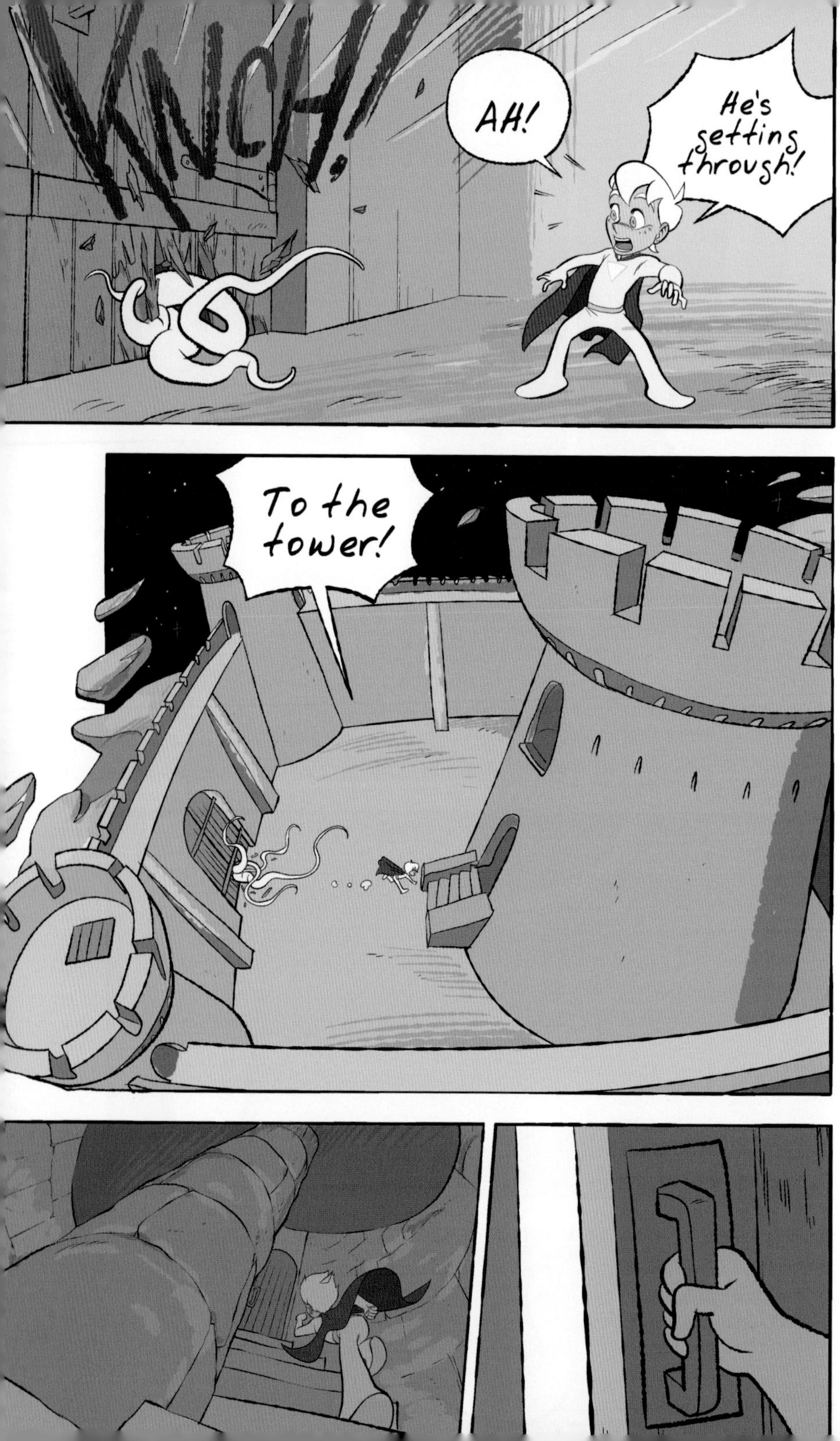
KNCH!
AH!
He's getting through!
To the tower!

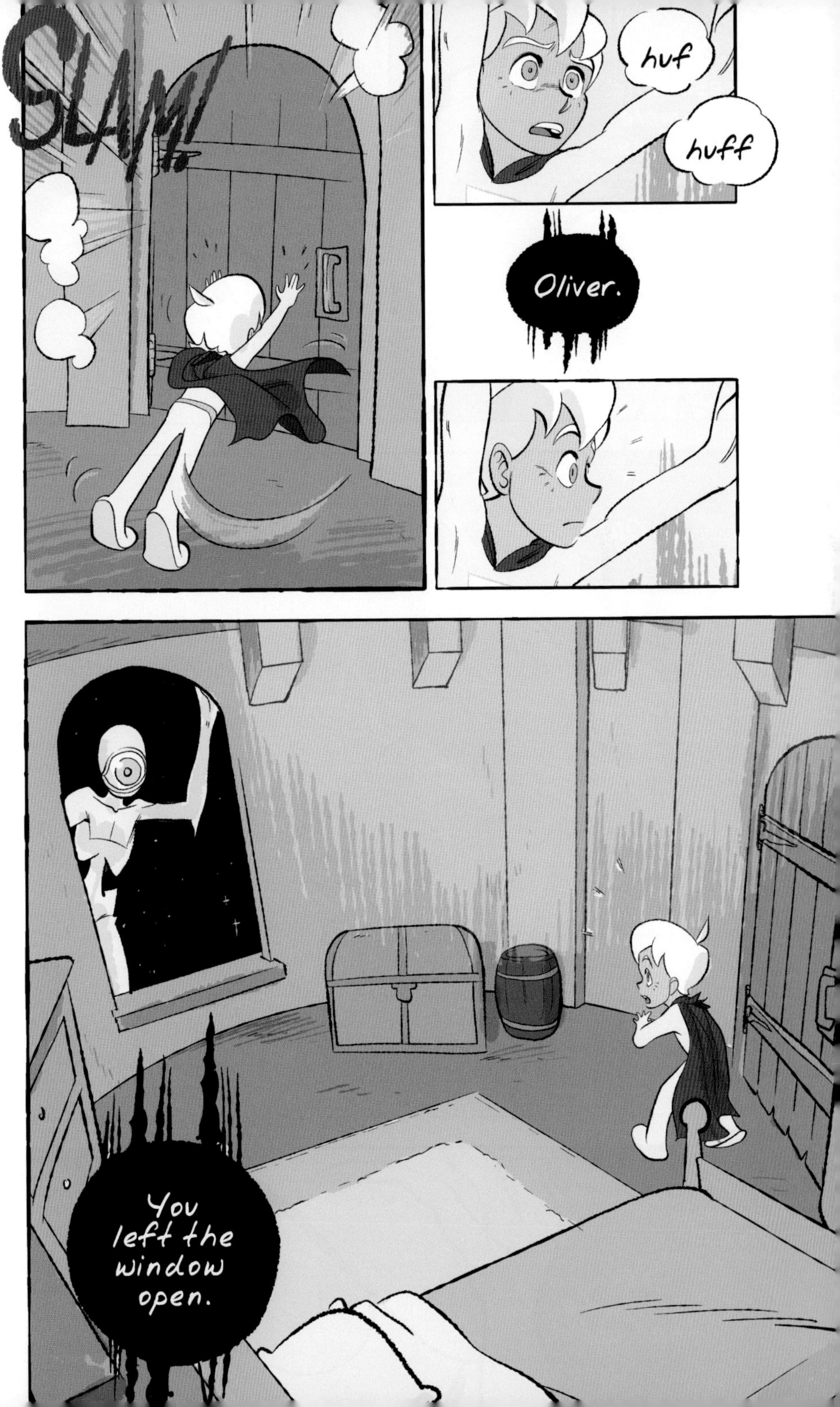
SLAM!
huf
huff
Oliver.
You left the window open.

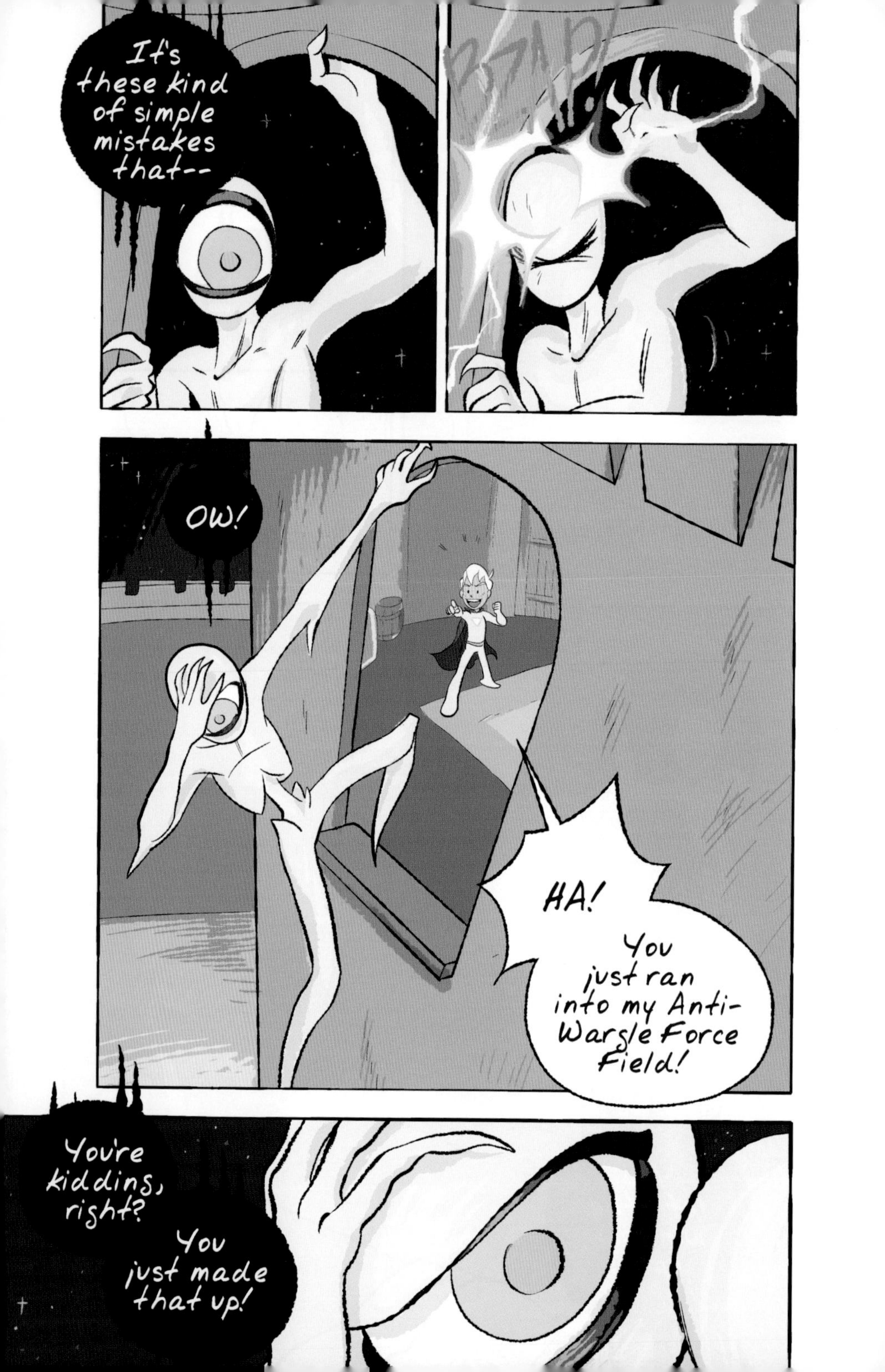
It's these kind of simple mistakes that--
BZAP!
OW!
HA! You just ran into my Anti-Wargle Force Field!
You're kidding, right?
You just made that up!

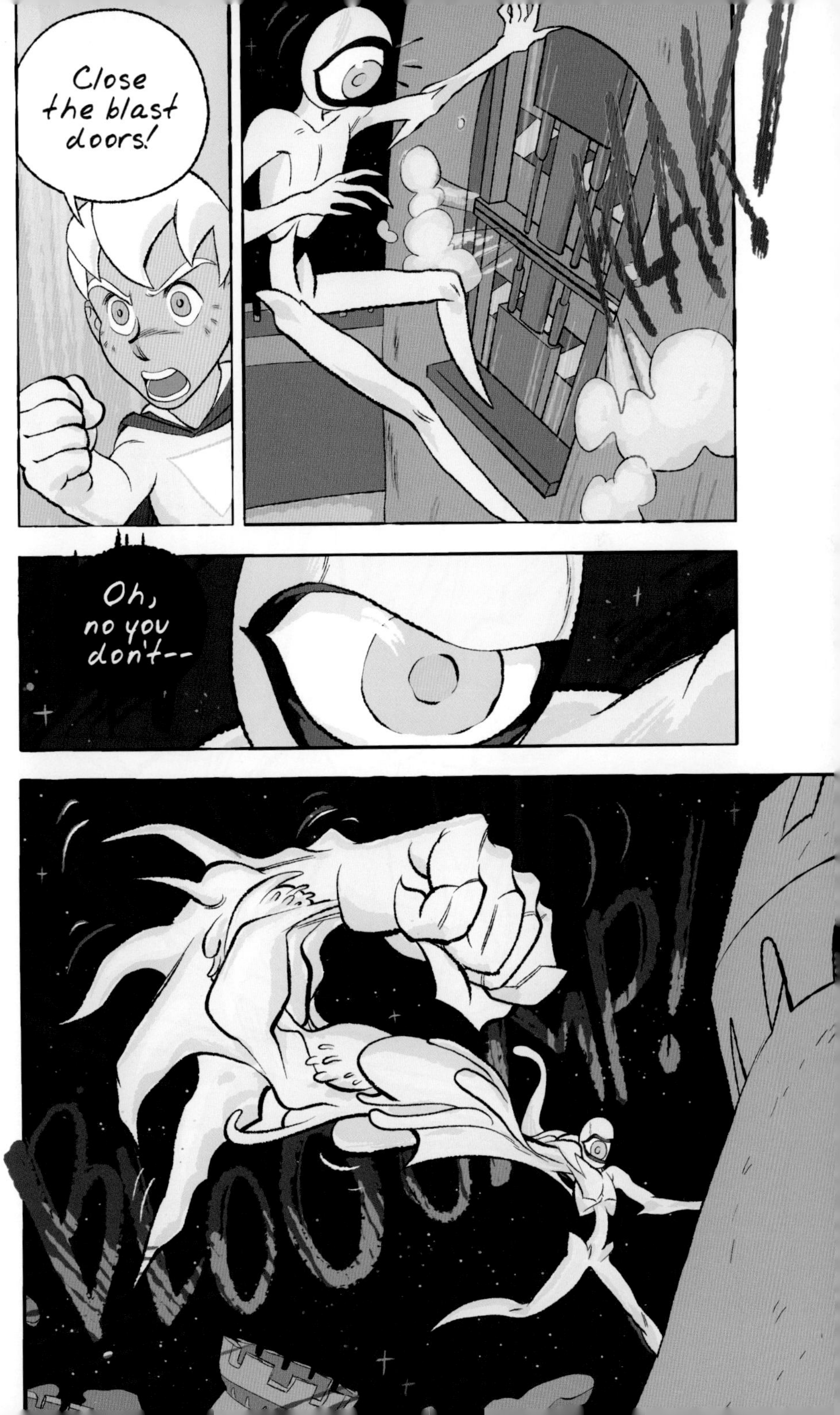
Close the blast doors!
Oh, no you don't--

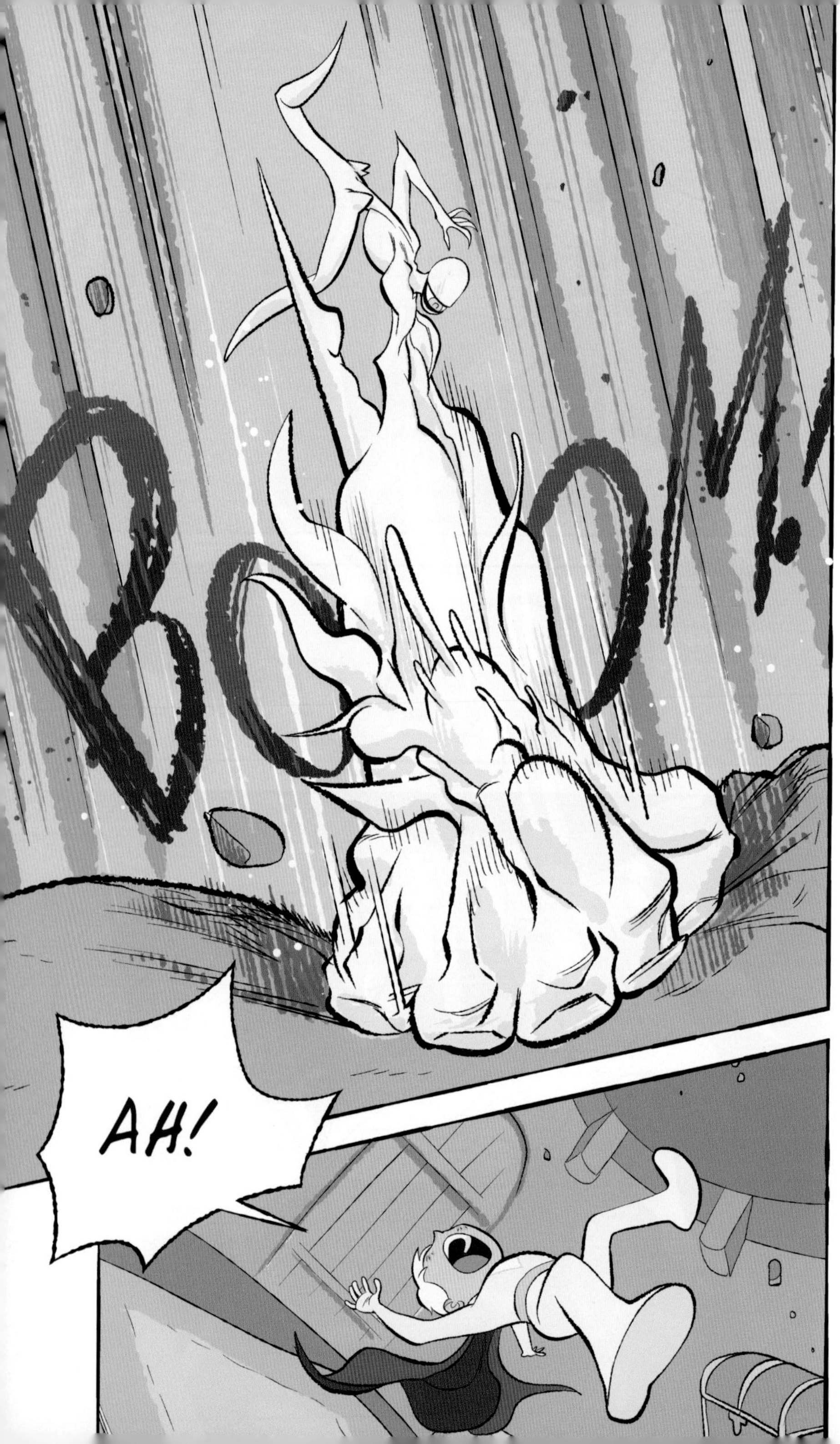
BOOM!
AH!

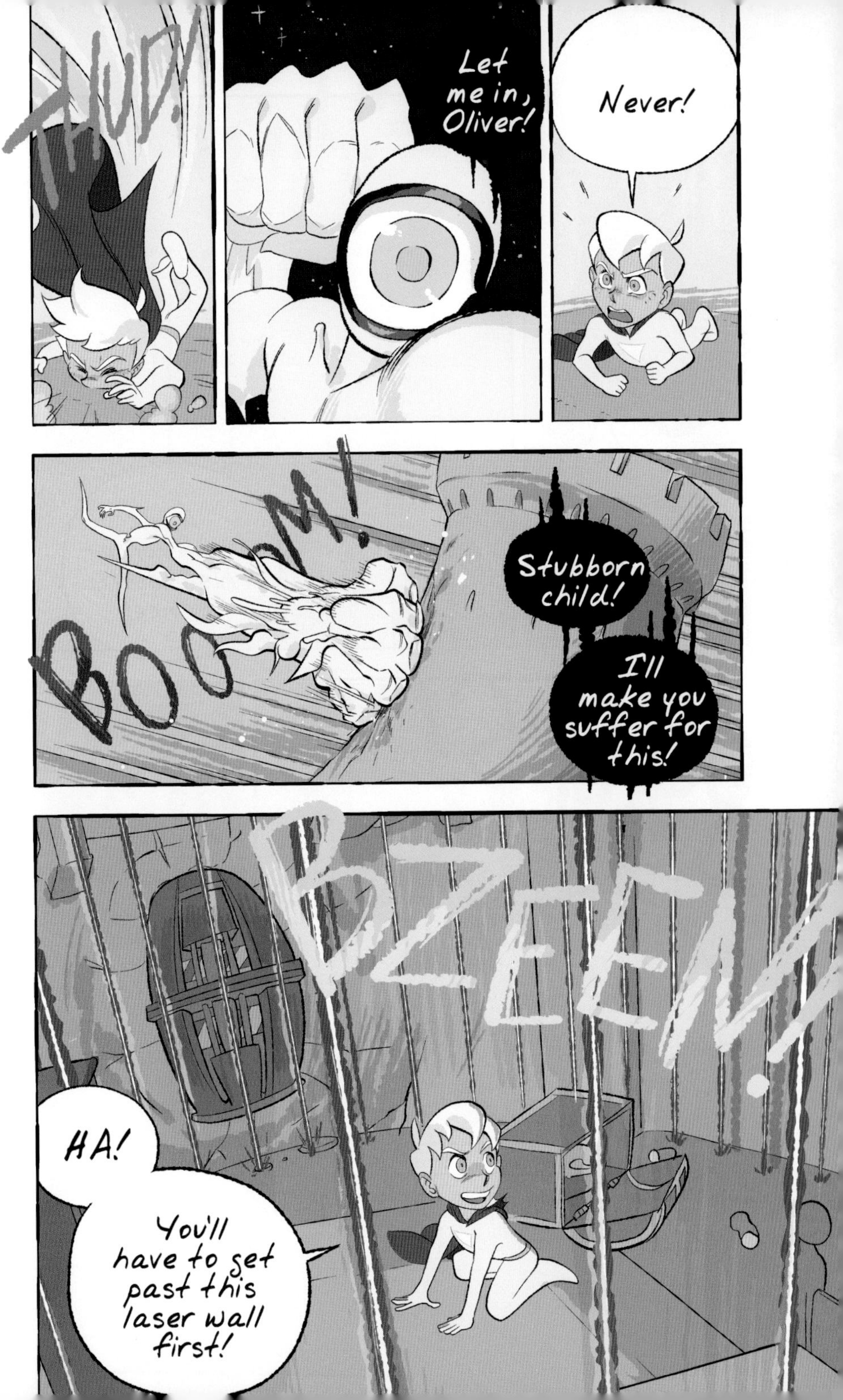
THUD!
Let me in, Oliver!
Never!
BOOOM!
Stubborn child!
I'll make you suffer for this!
BZEEN!
HA!
You'll have to get past this laser wall first!

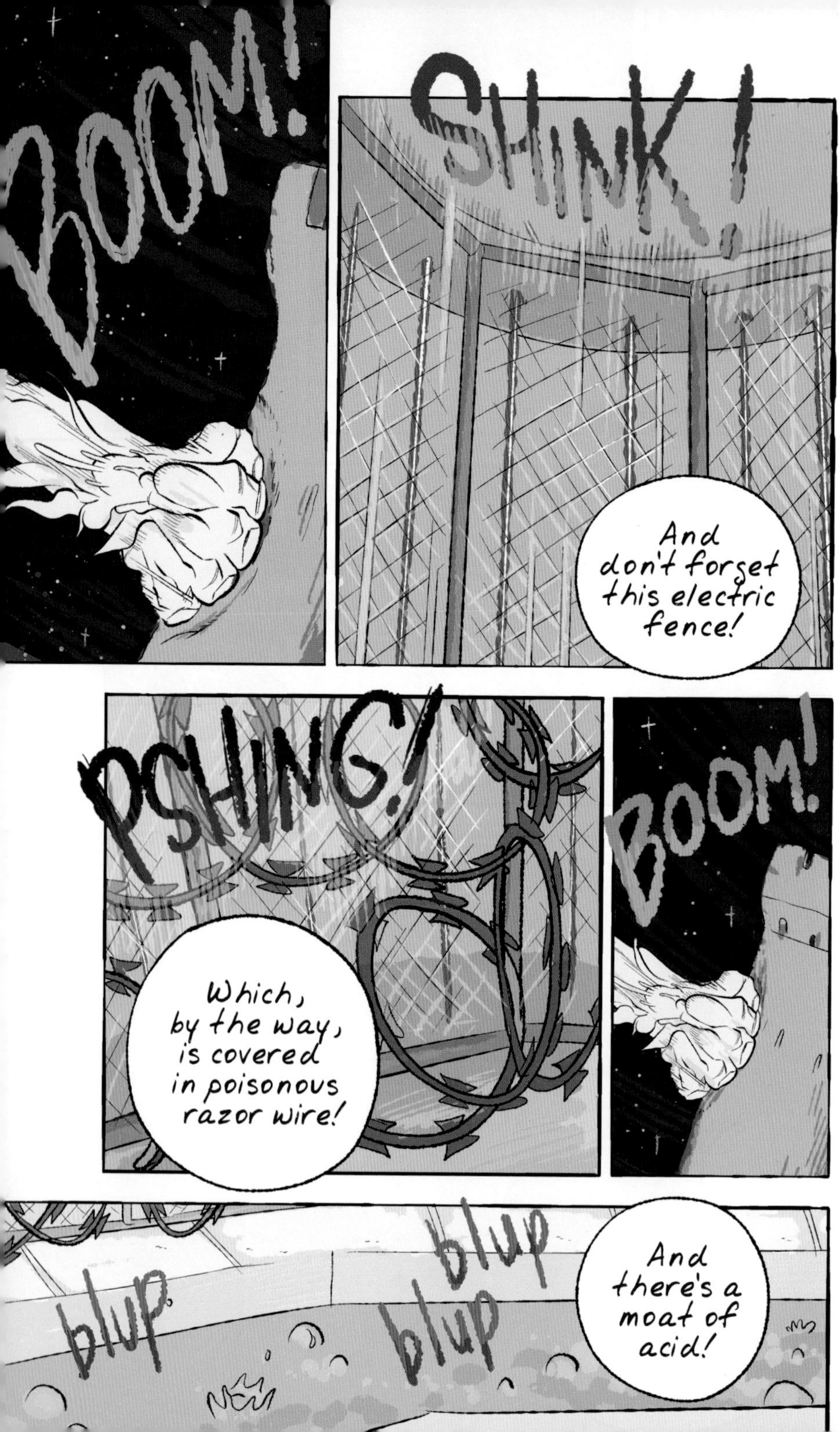
BOOM!
SHINK!
And don't forget this electric fence!
PSHING!
Which, by the way, is covered in poisonous razor wire!
BOOM!
blup
blup
blup
And there's a moat of acid!

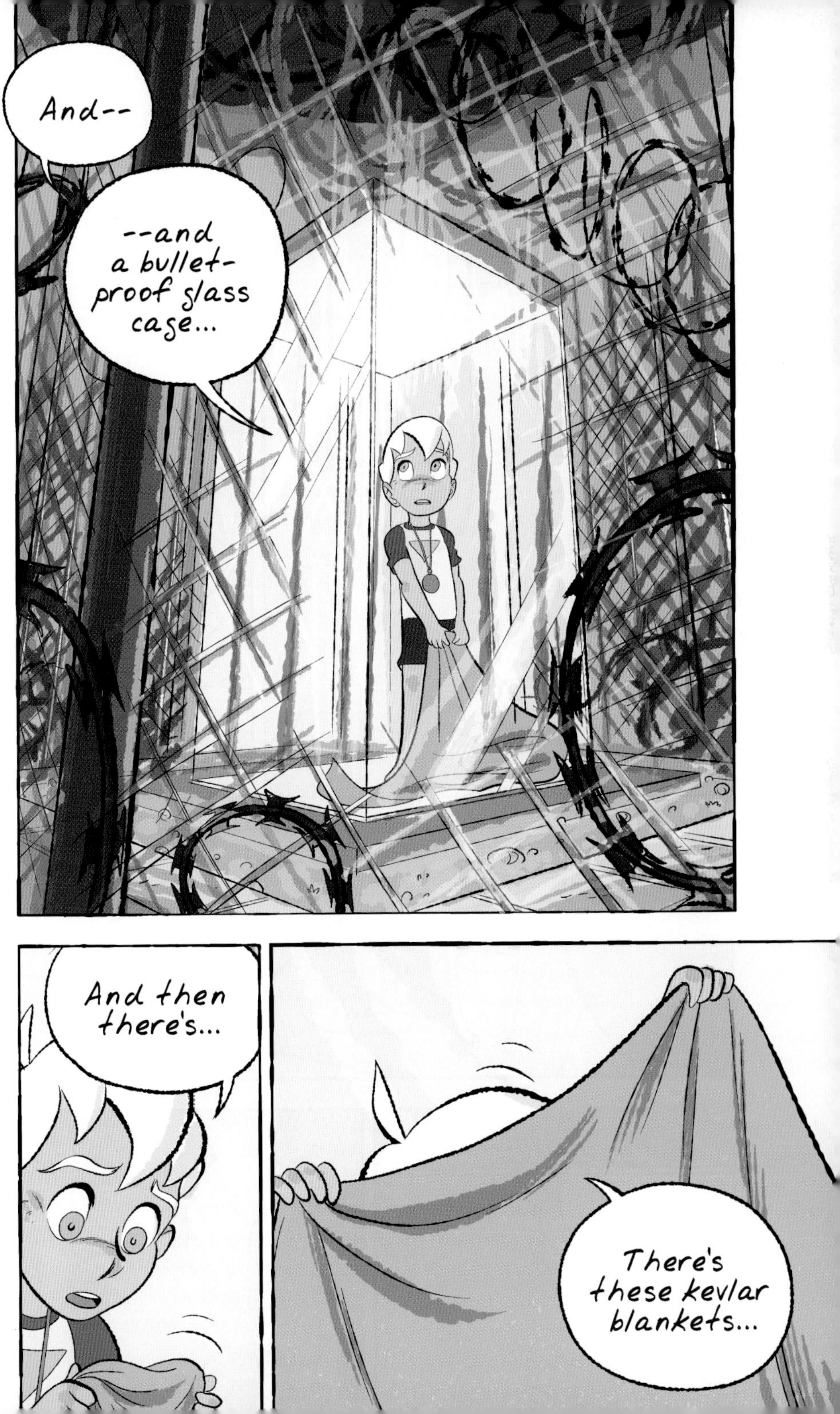
And--
--and a bullet-proof glass case...
And then there's...
There's these kevlar blankets...

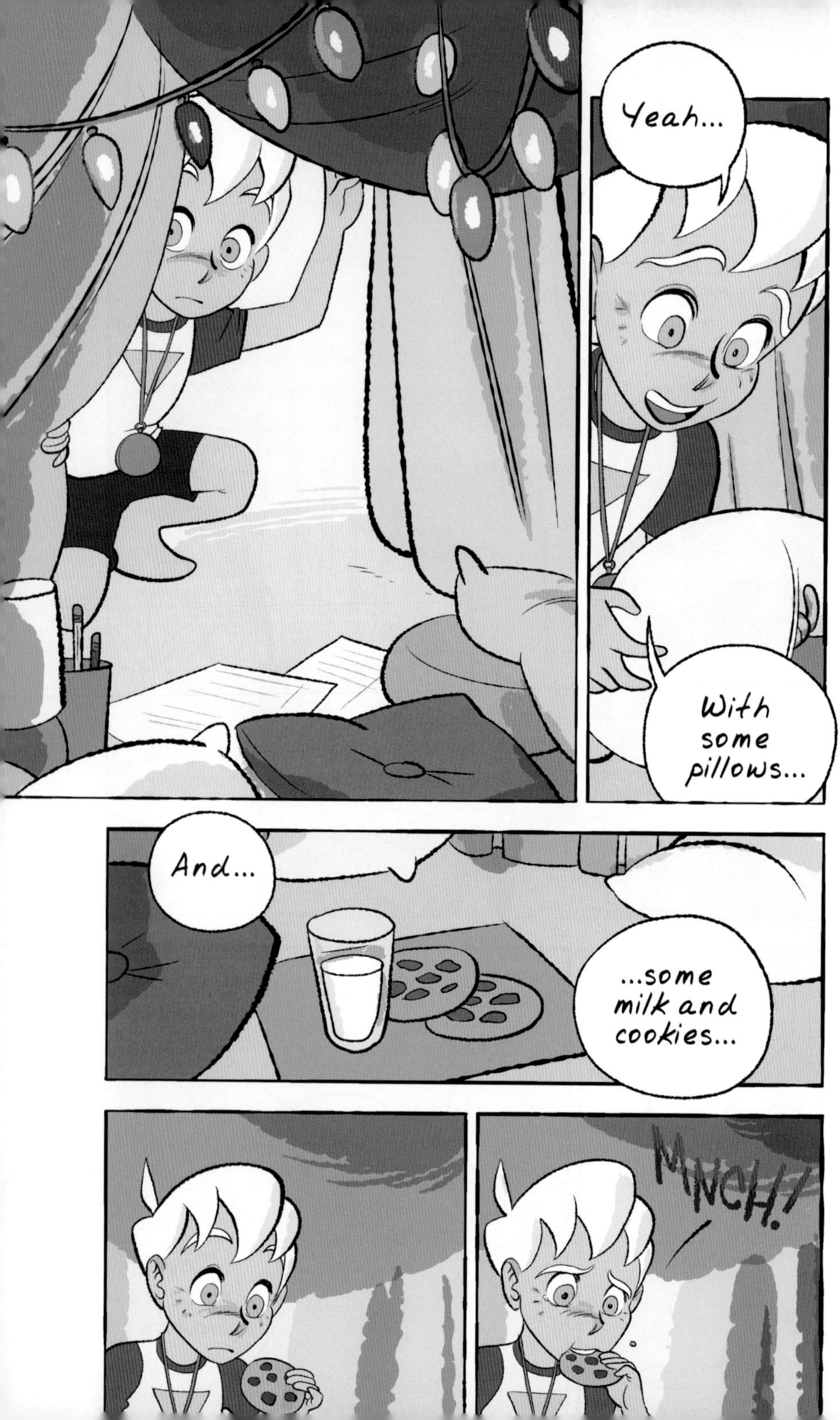
Yeah...
With some pillows...
And...
...some milk and cookies...
MNCH!

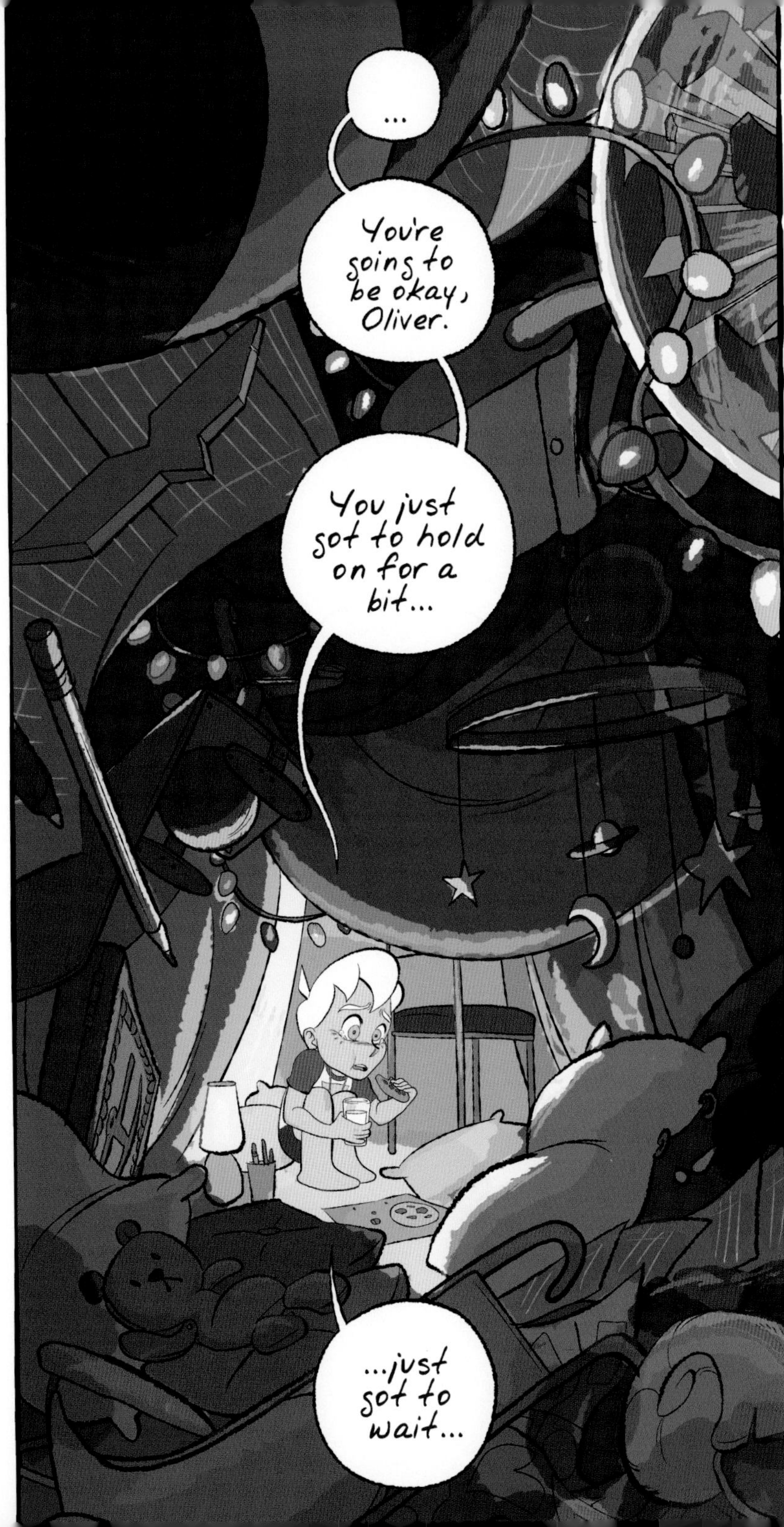
...
You're going to be okay, Oliver.
You just got to hold on for a bit...
...just got to wait...

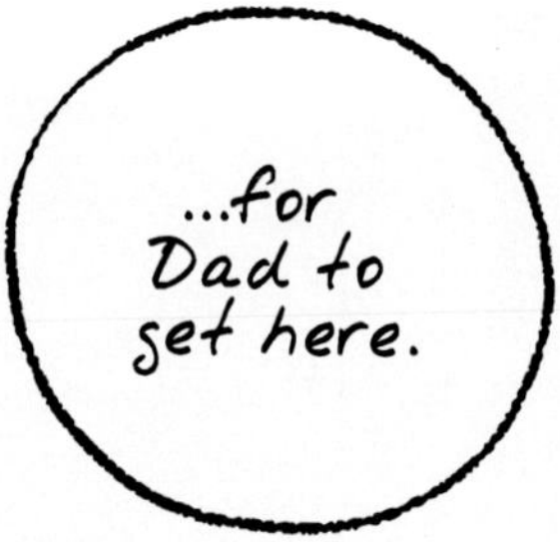
...for Dad to get here.

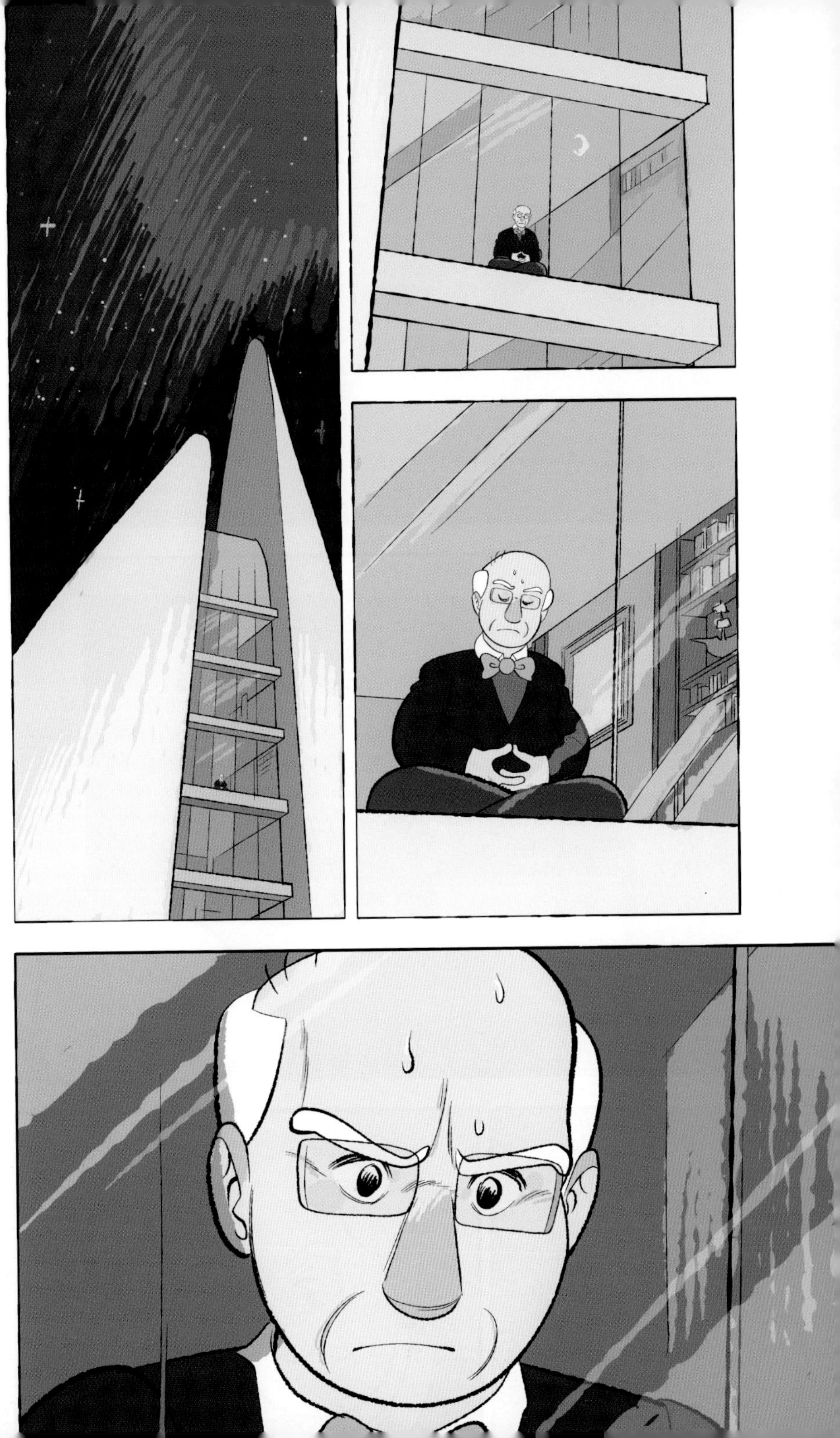

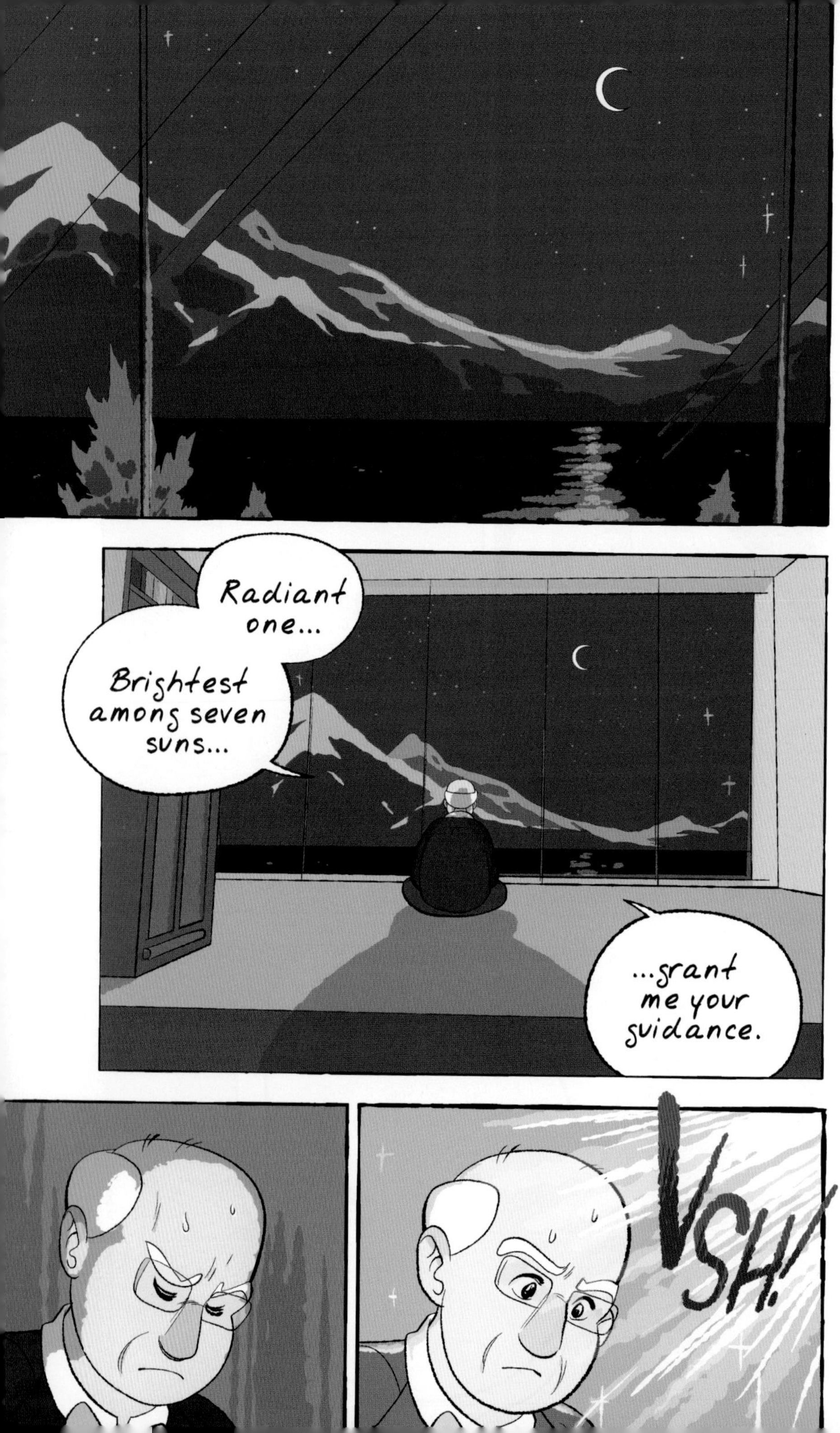
Radiant one...
Brightest among seven suns...
...grant me your guidance.
VSH!

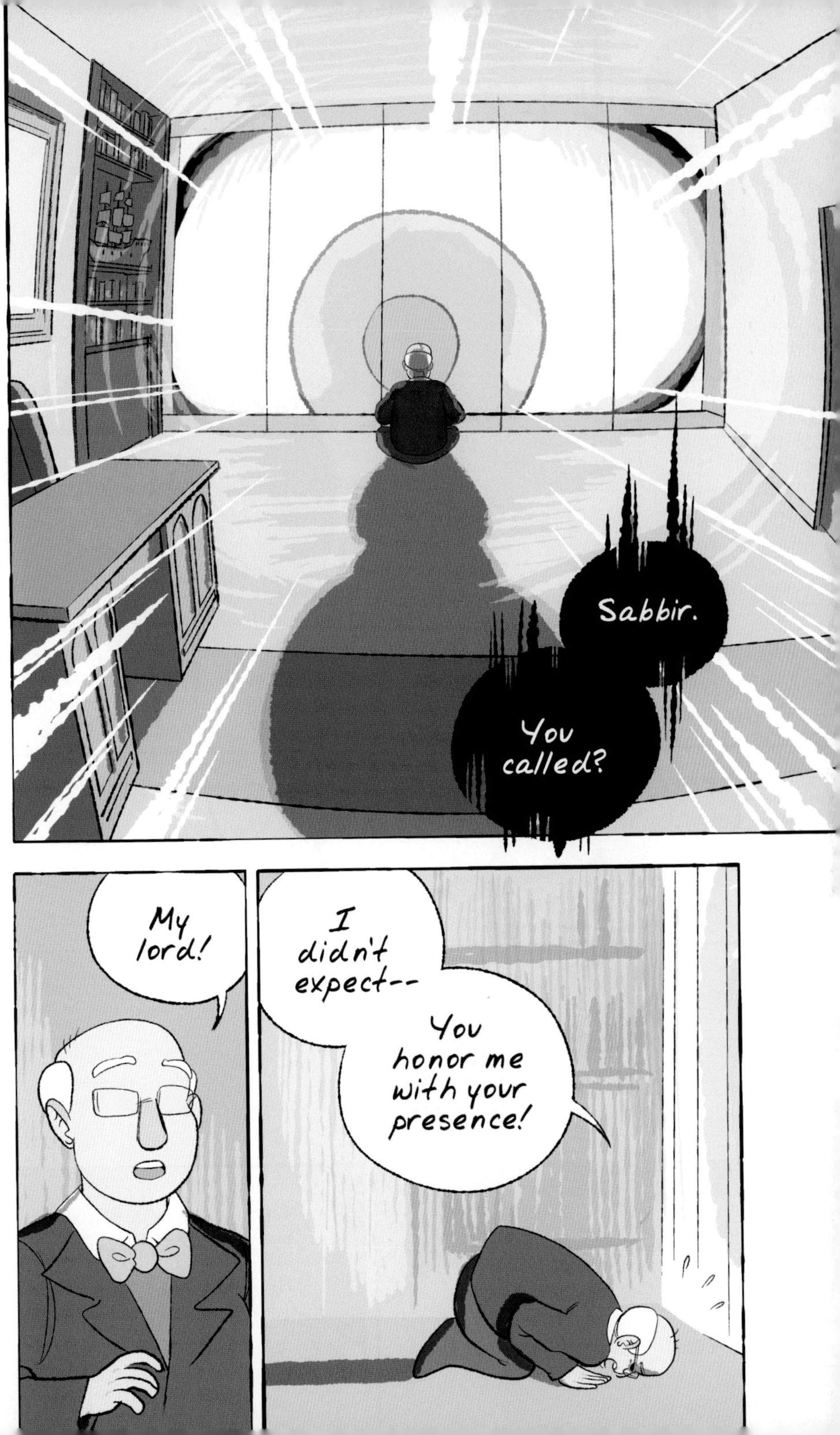
Sabbir.
You called?
My lord!
I didn't expect--
You honor me with your presence!

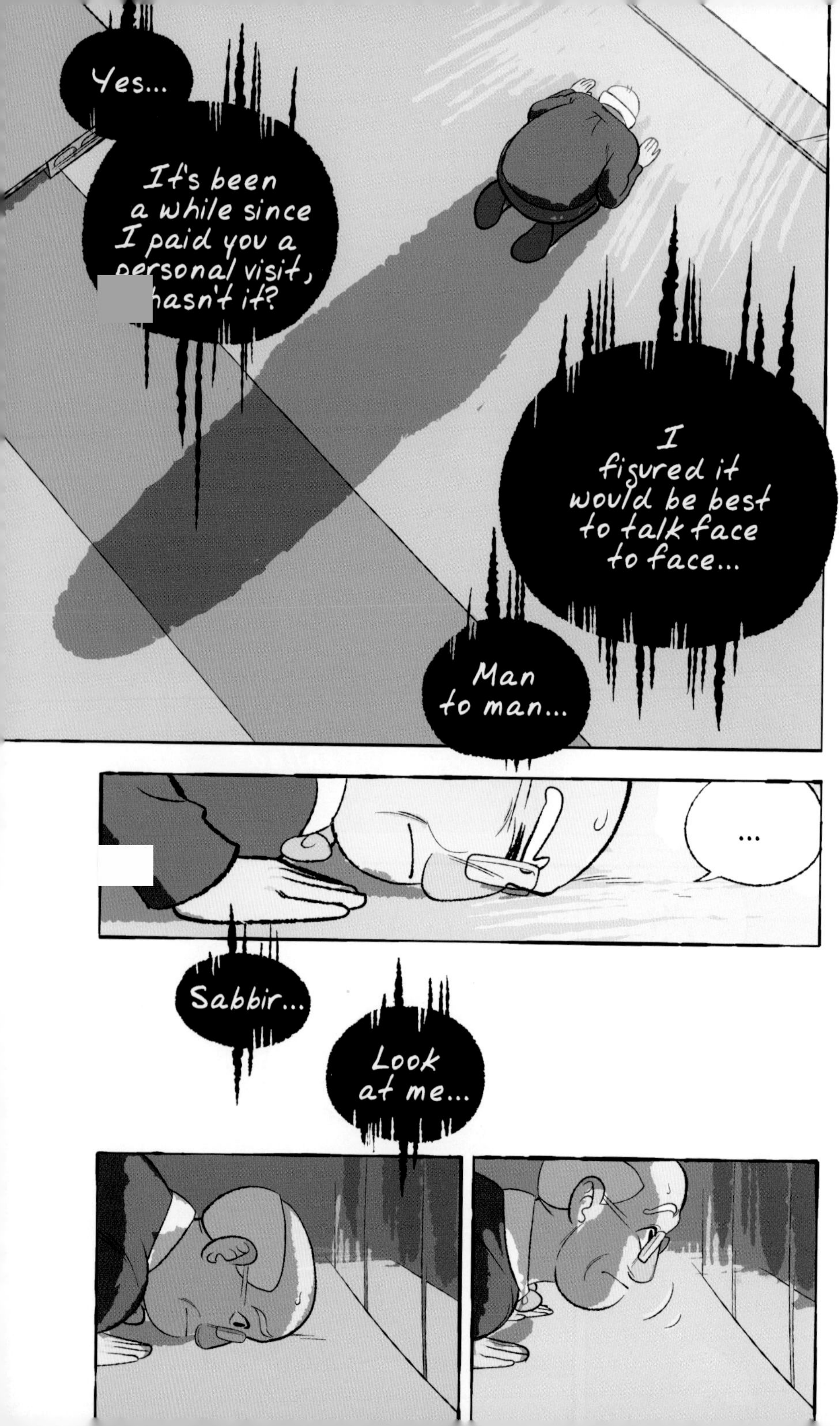

Yes...
It's been a while since I paid you a personal visit, hasn't it?
I figured it would be best to talk face to face...
Man to man...
...
Sabbir...
Look at me...

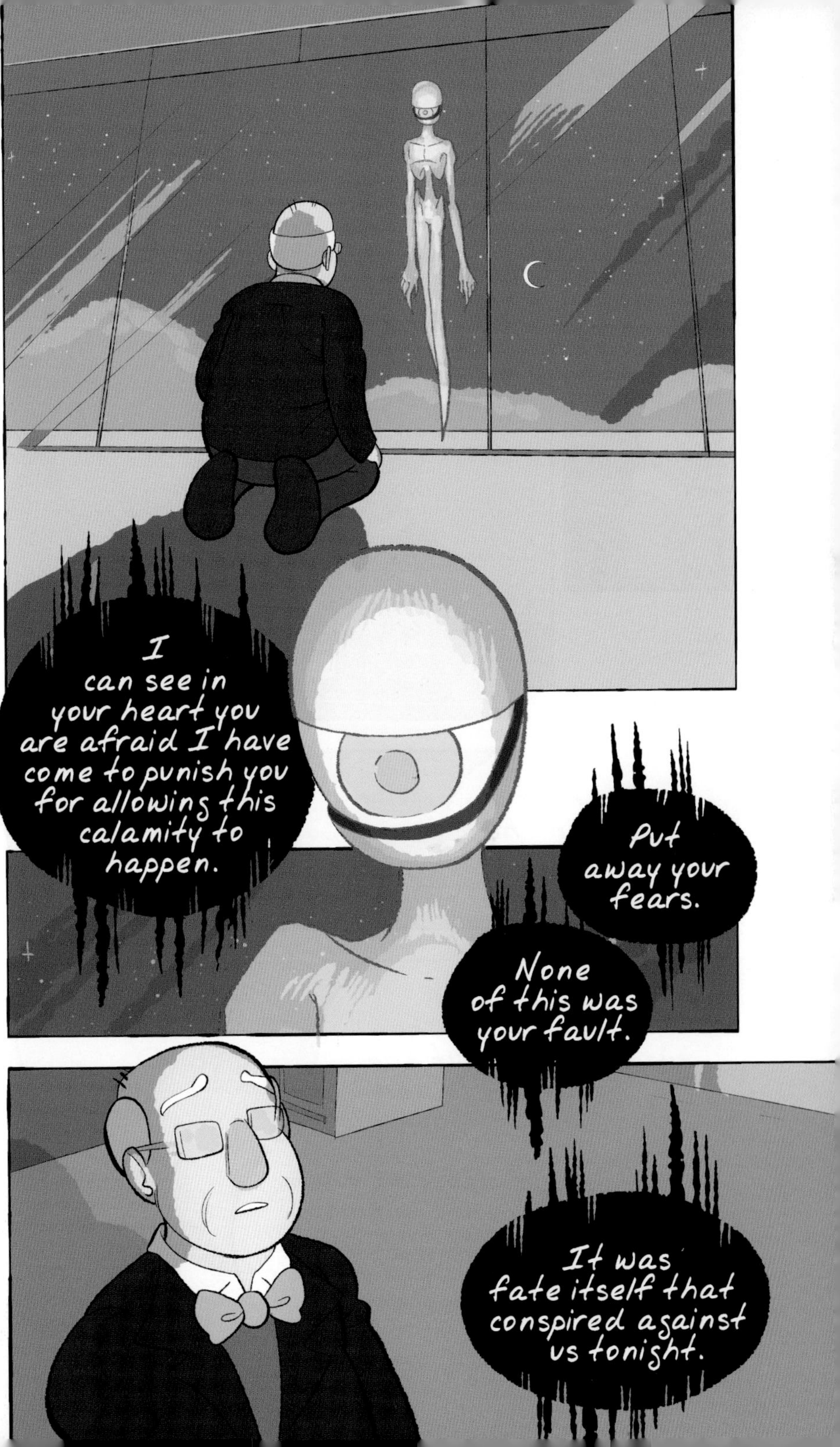
I can see in your heart you are afraid I have come to punish you for allowing this calamity to happen.
Put away your fears.
None of this was your fault.
It was fate itself that conspired against us tonight.

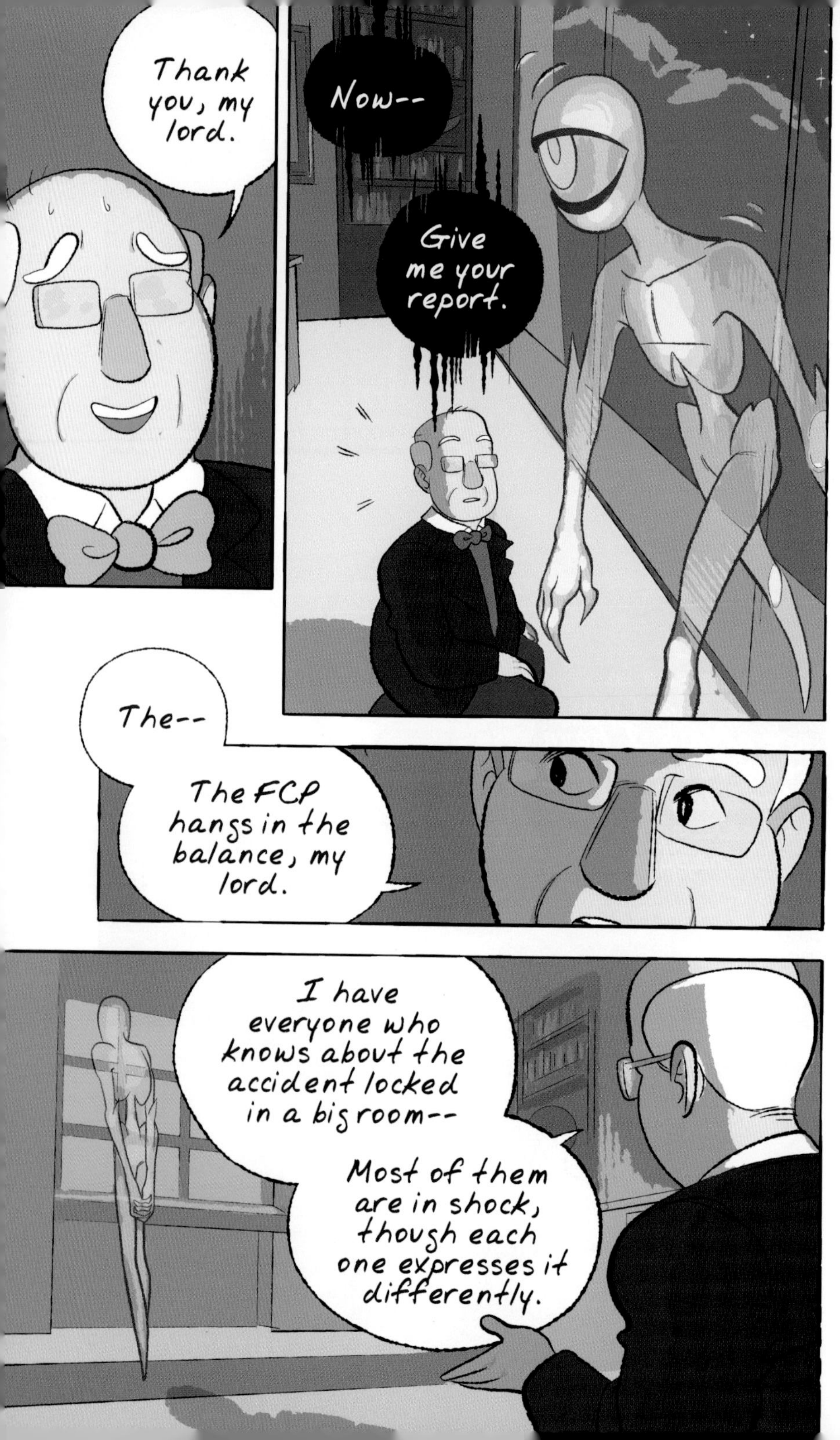
Thank you, my lord.
Now--
Give me your report.
The--
The FCP hangs in the balance, my lord.
I have everyone who knows about the accident locked in a big room--
Most of them are in shock, though each one expresses it differently.

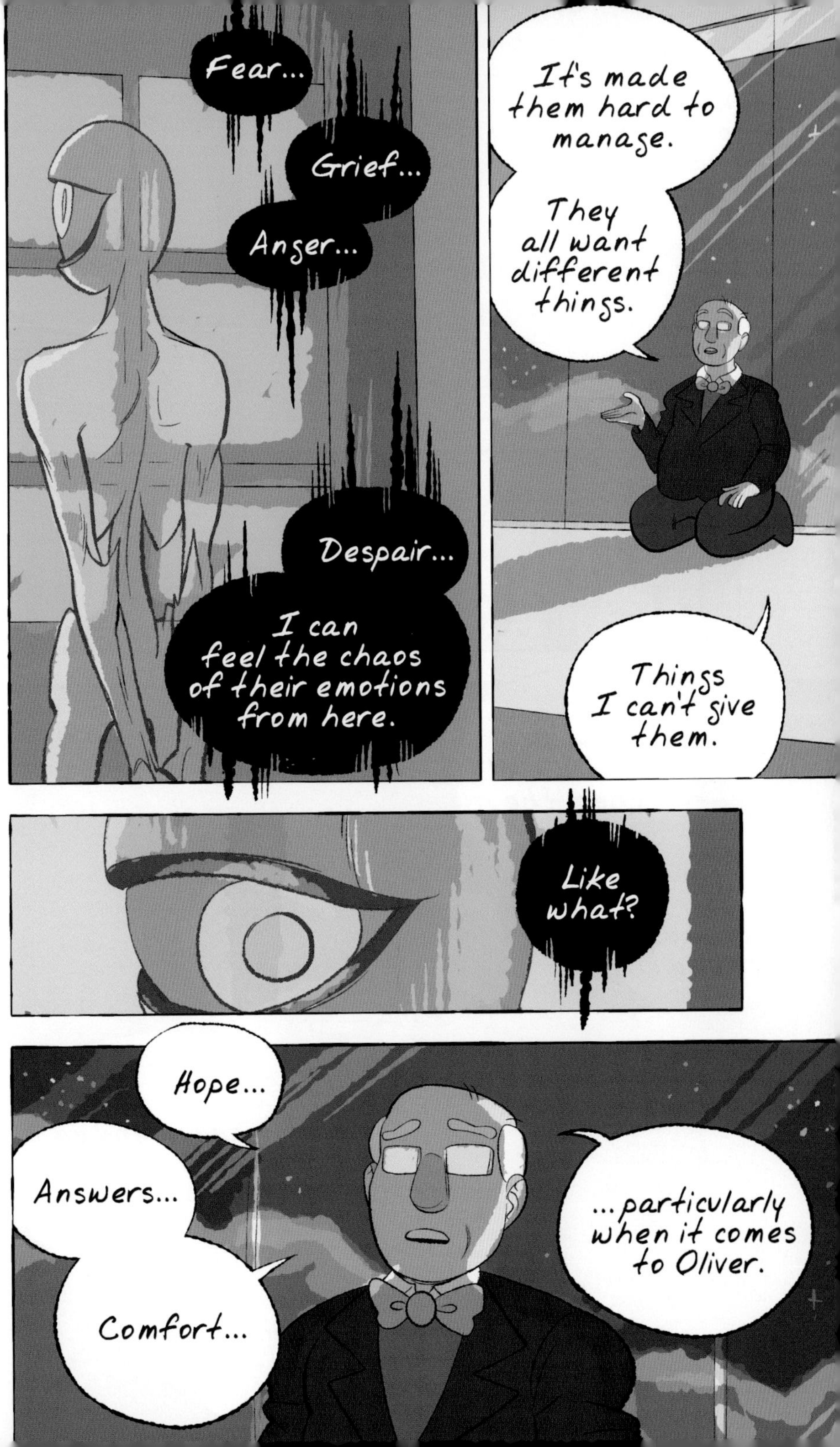
Fear...
Grief...
Anger...
Despair...
I can feel the chaos of their emotions from here.
It's made them hard to manage.
They all want different things.
Things I can't give them.
Like what?
Hope...
Answers...
Comfort...
...particularly when it comes to Oliver.

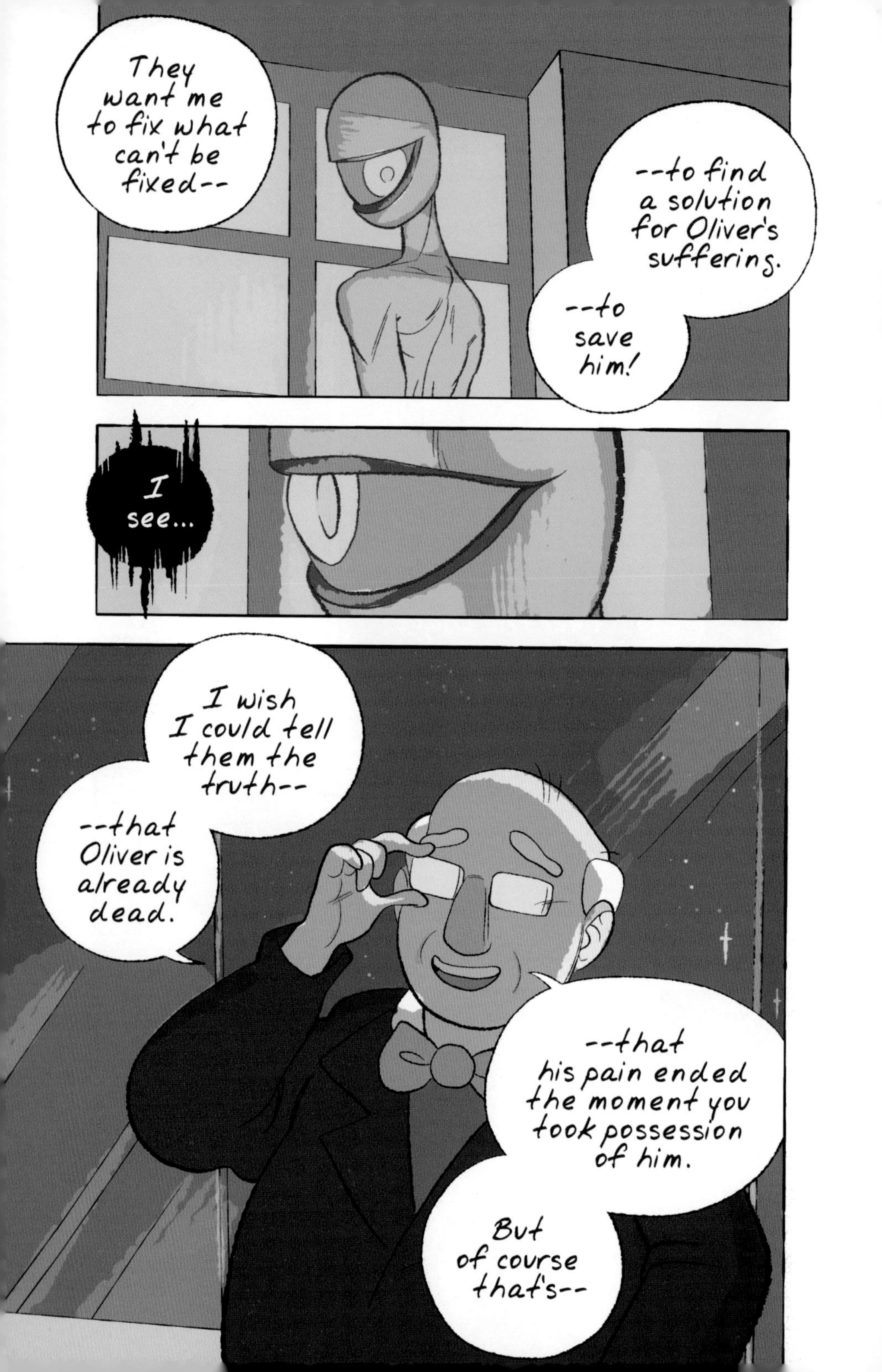
They want me to fix what can't be fixed--
--to find a solution for Oliver's sufferings.
--to save him!
I see...
I wish I could tell them the truth--
--that Oliver is already dead.
--that his pain ended the moment you took possession of him.
But of course that's--

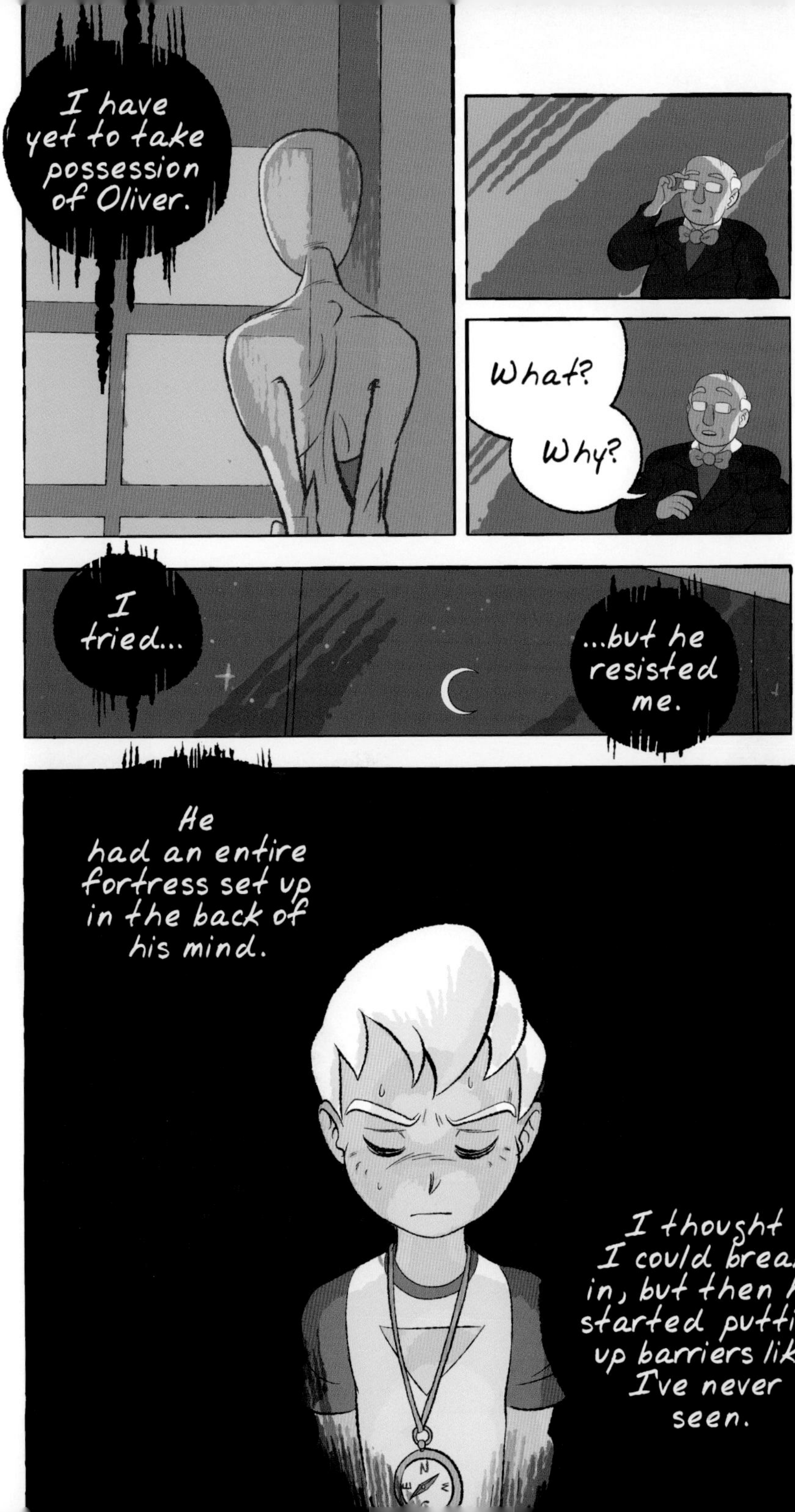
I have yet to take possession of Oliver.
What?
Why?
I tried...
...but he resisted me.
He had an entire fortress set up in the back of his mind.
I thought I could break in, but then he started putting up barriers like I've never seen.

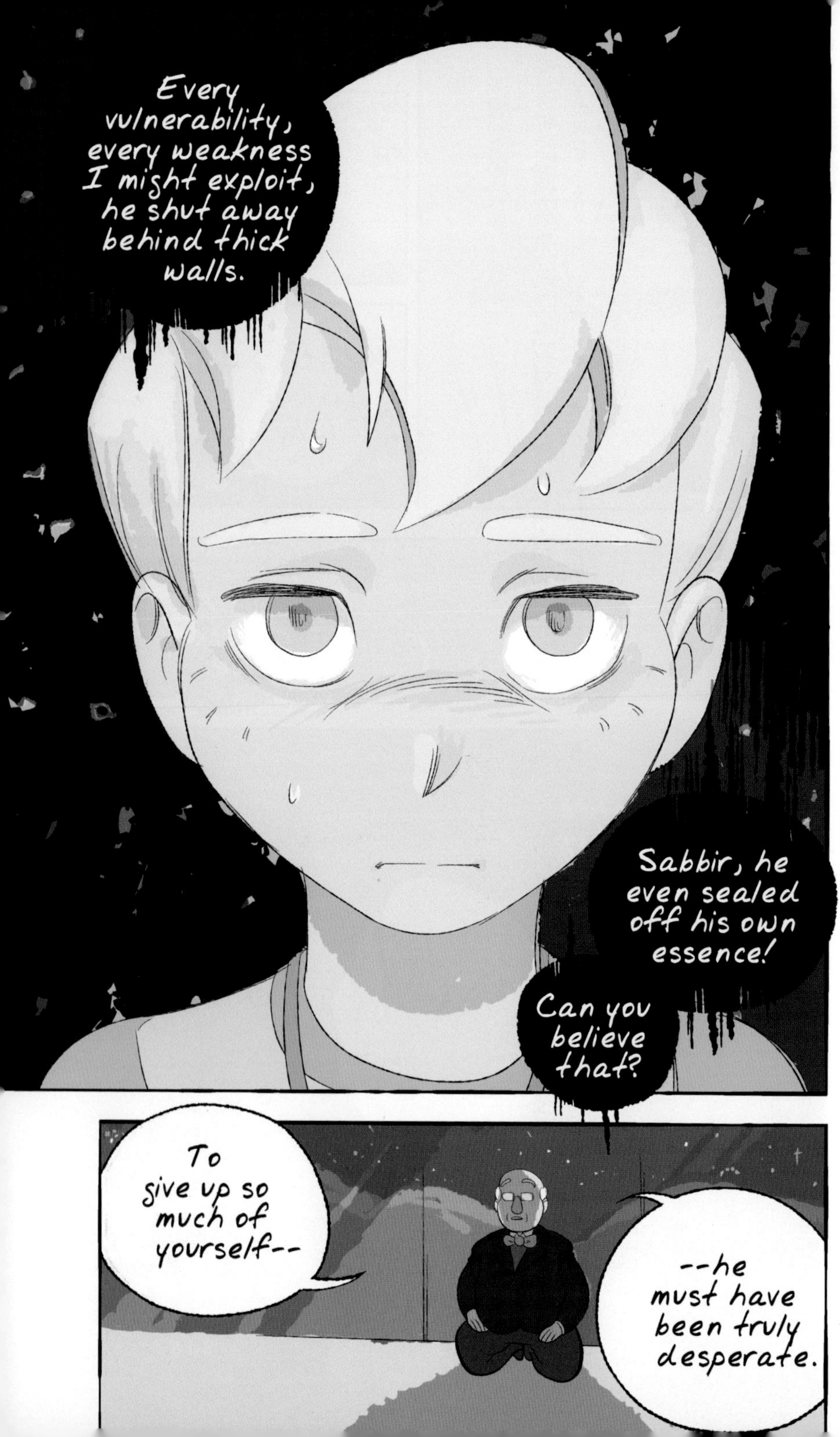

Every vulnerability, every weakness I might exploit, he shut away behind thick walls.
Sabbir, he even sealed off his own essence!
Can you believe that?
To give up so much of yourself--
--he must have been truly desperate.

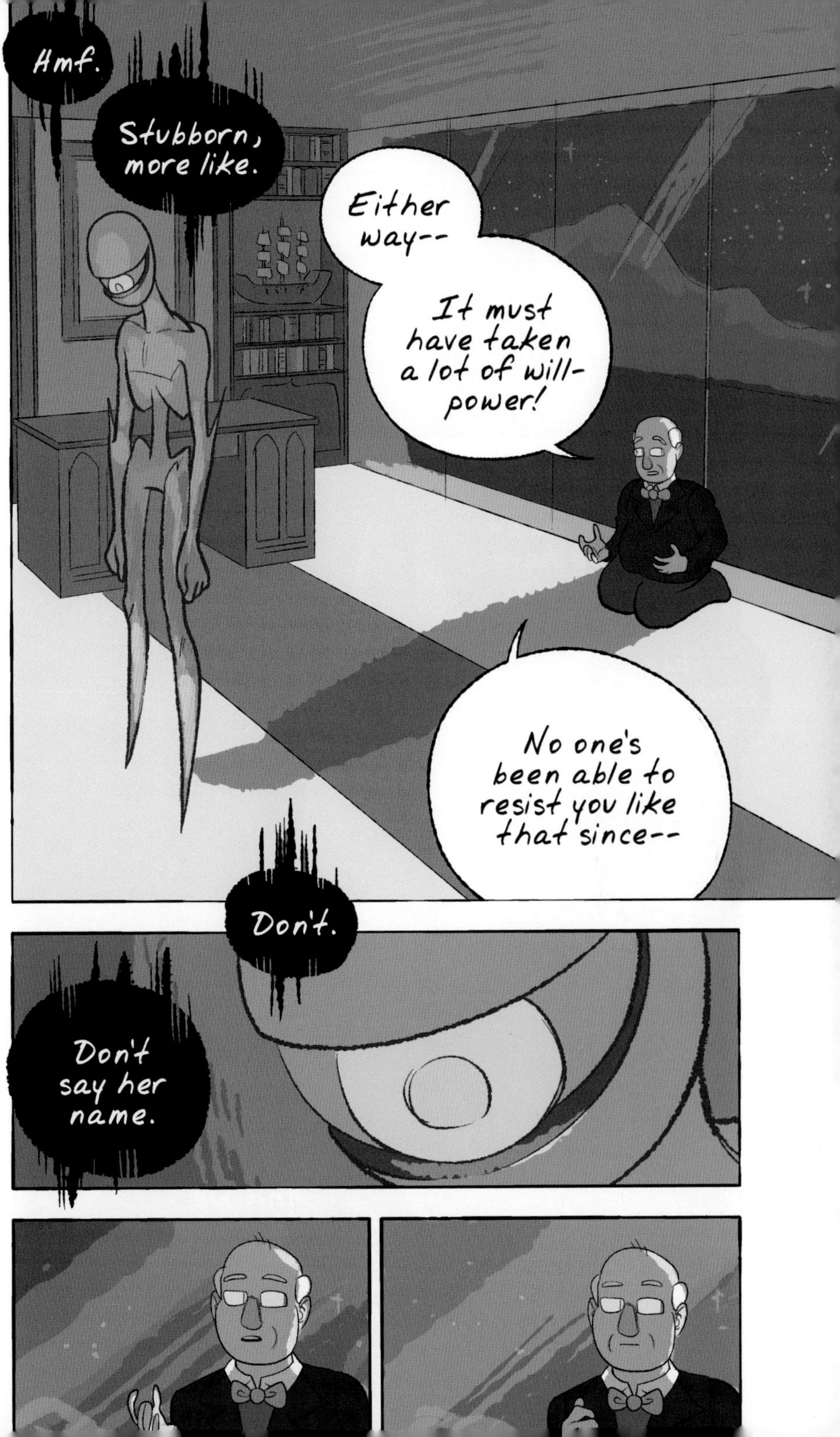
Hmf.
Stubborn, more like.
Either way--
It must have taken a lot of will-power!
No one's been able to resist you like that since--
Don't.
Don't say her name.

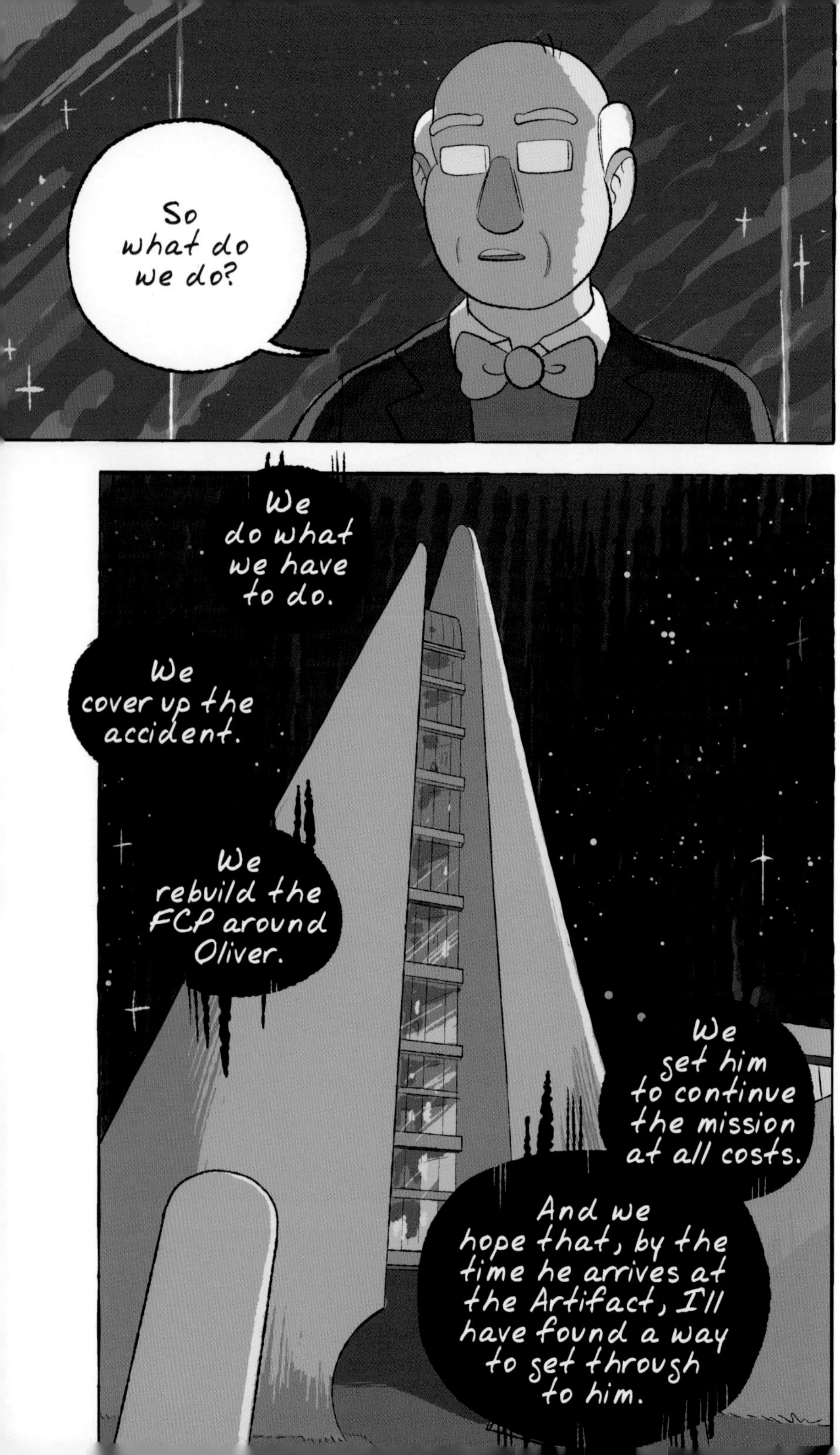
So what do we do?
We do what we have to do.
We cover up the accident.
We rebuild the FCP around Oliver.
We set him to continue the mission at all costs.
And we hope that, by the time he arrives at the Artifact, I'll have found a way to get through to him.

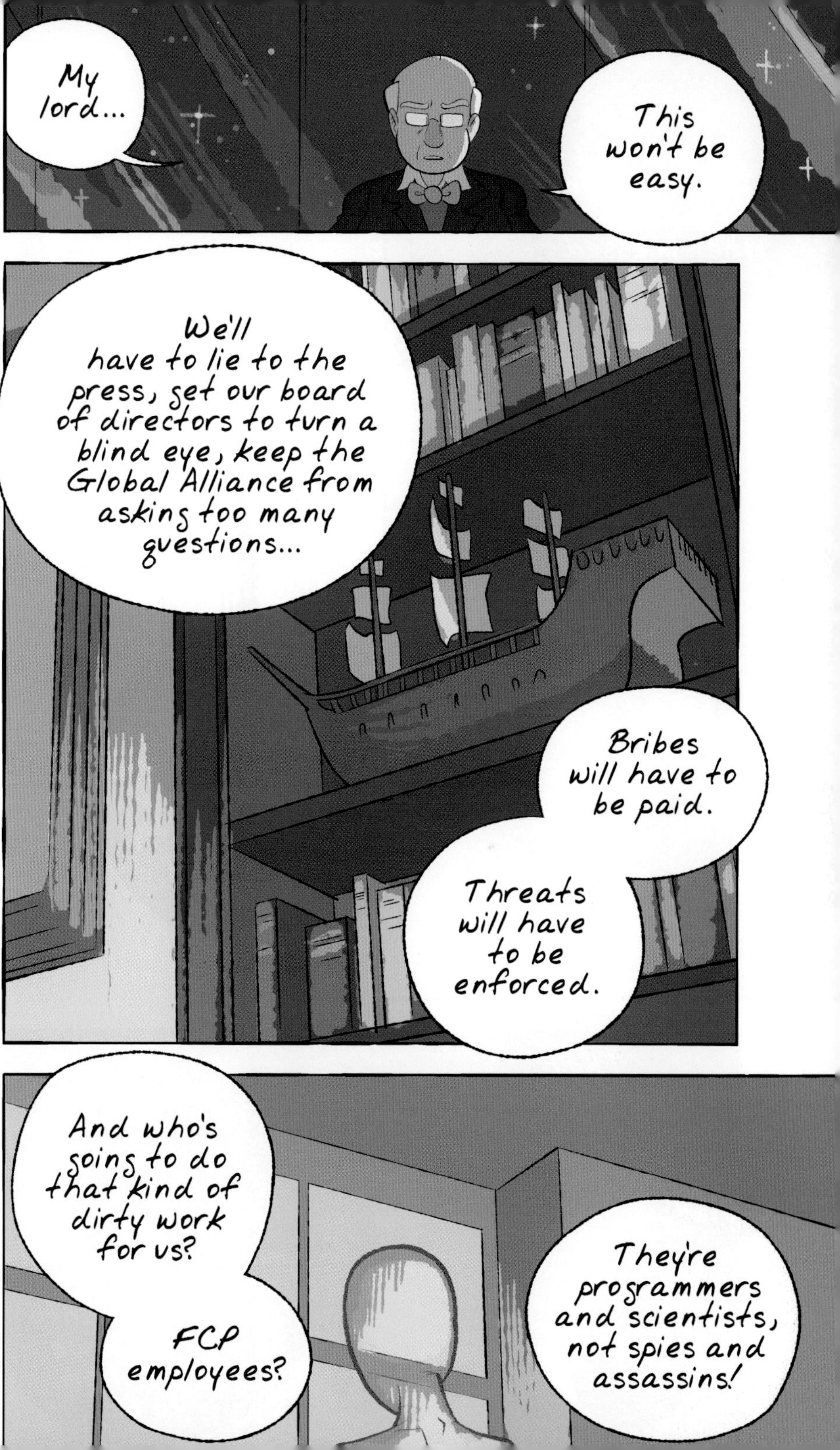
My lord...
This won't be easy.
We'll have to lie to the press, get our board of directors to turn a blind eye, keep the Global Alliance from asking too many questions...
Bribes will have to be paid.
Threats will have to be enforced.
And who's going to do that kind of dirty work for us?
FCP employees?
They're programmers and scientists, not spies and assassins!

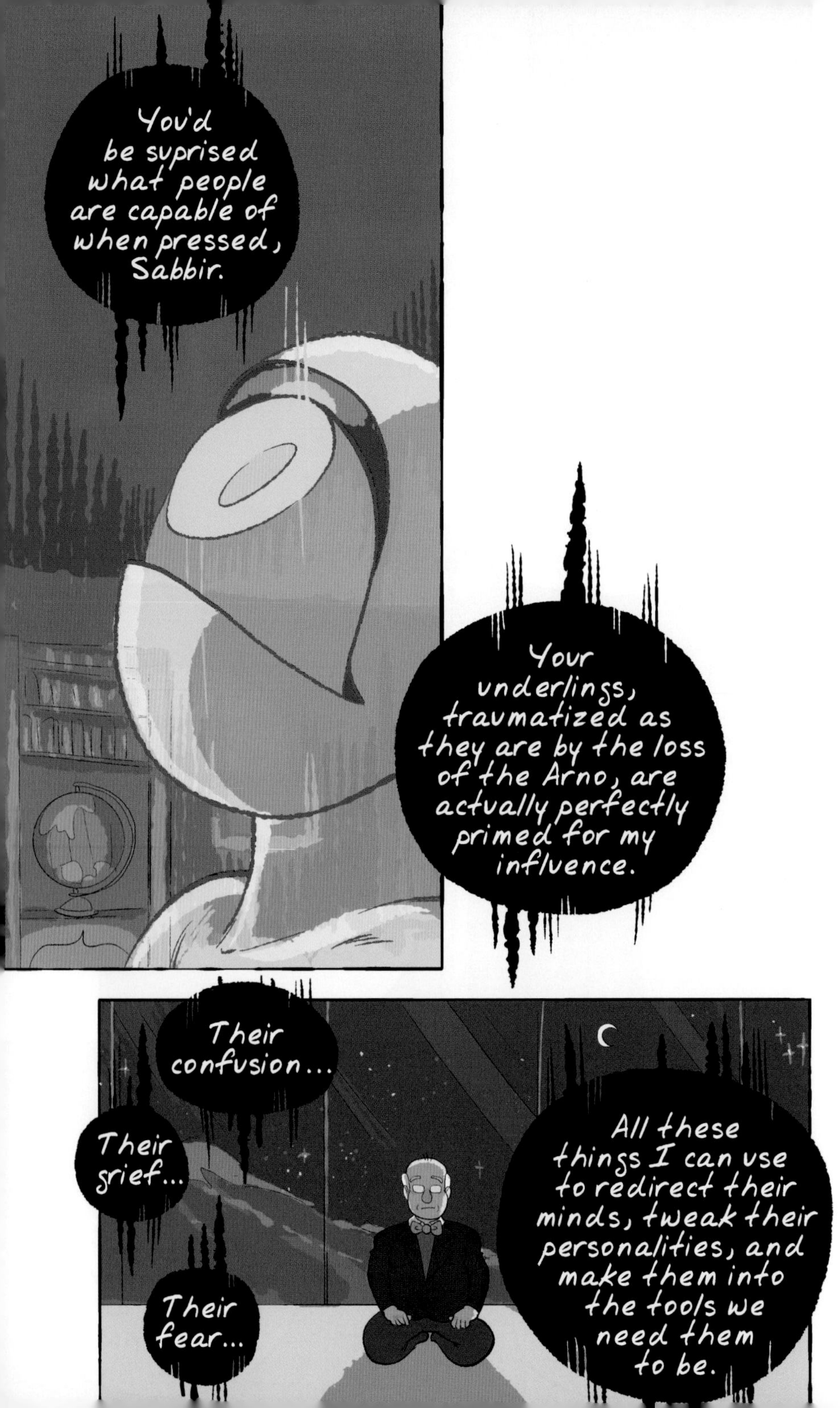
You'd be suprised what people are capable of when pressed, Sabbir.
Your underlings, traumatized as they are by the loss of the Arno, are actually perfectly primed for my influence.
Their confusion...
Their grief...
Their fear...
All these things I can use to redirect their minds, tweak their personalities, and make them into the tools we need them to be.

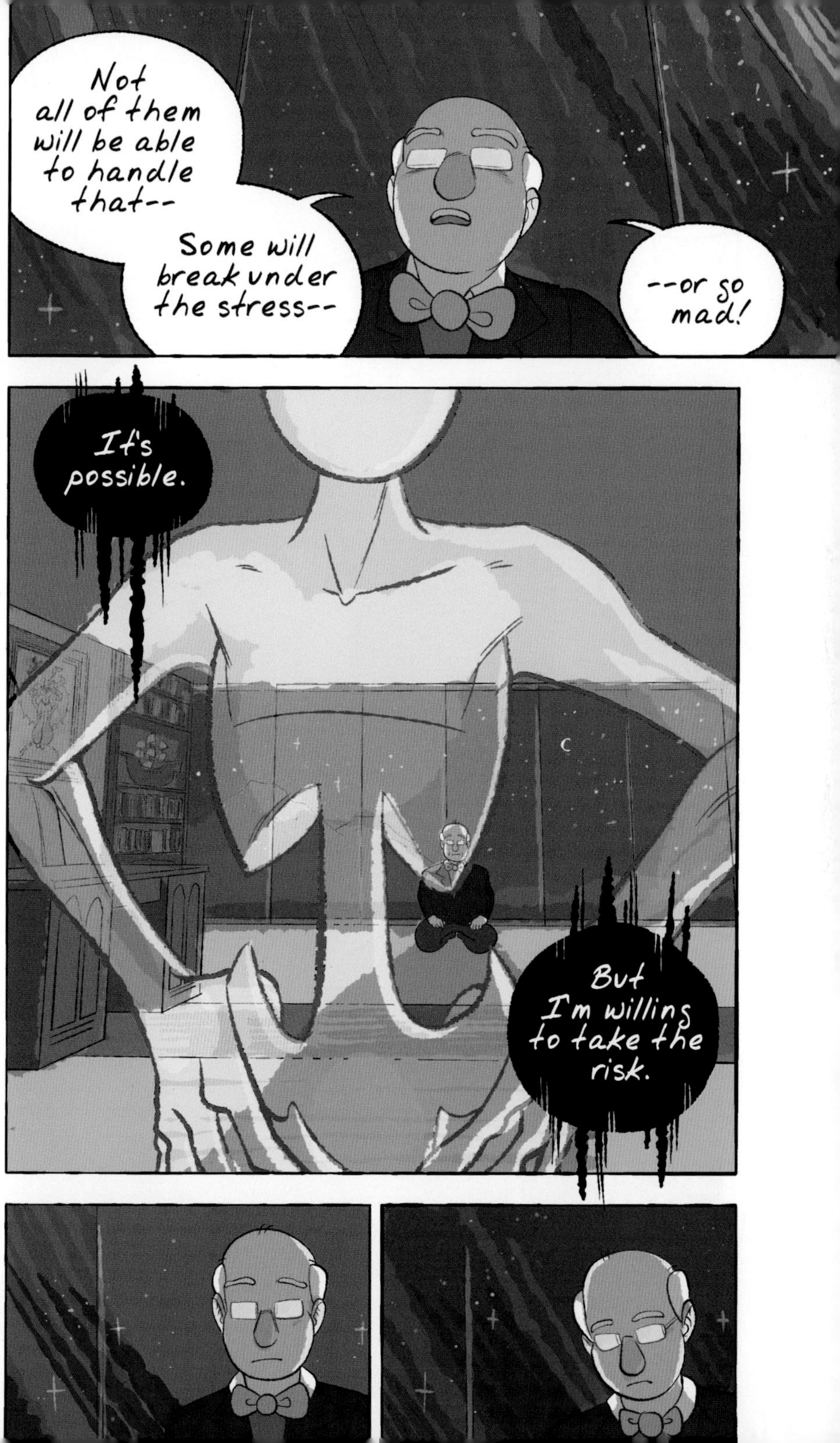
Not all of them will be able to handle that--
Some will break under the stress--
--or go mad!
It's possible.
But I'm willing to take the risk.

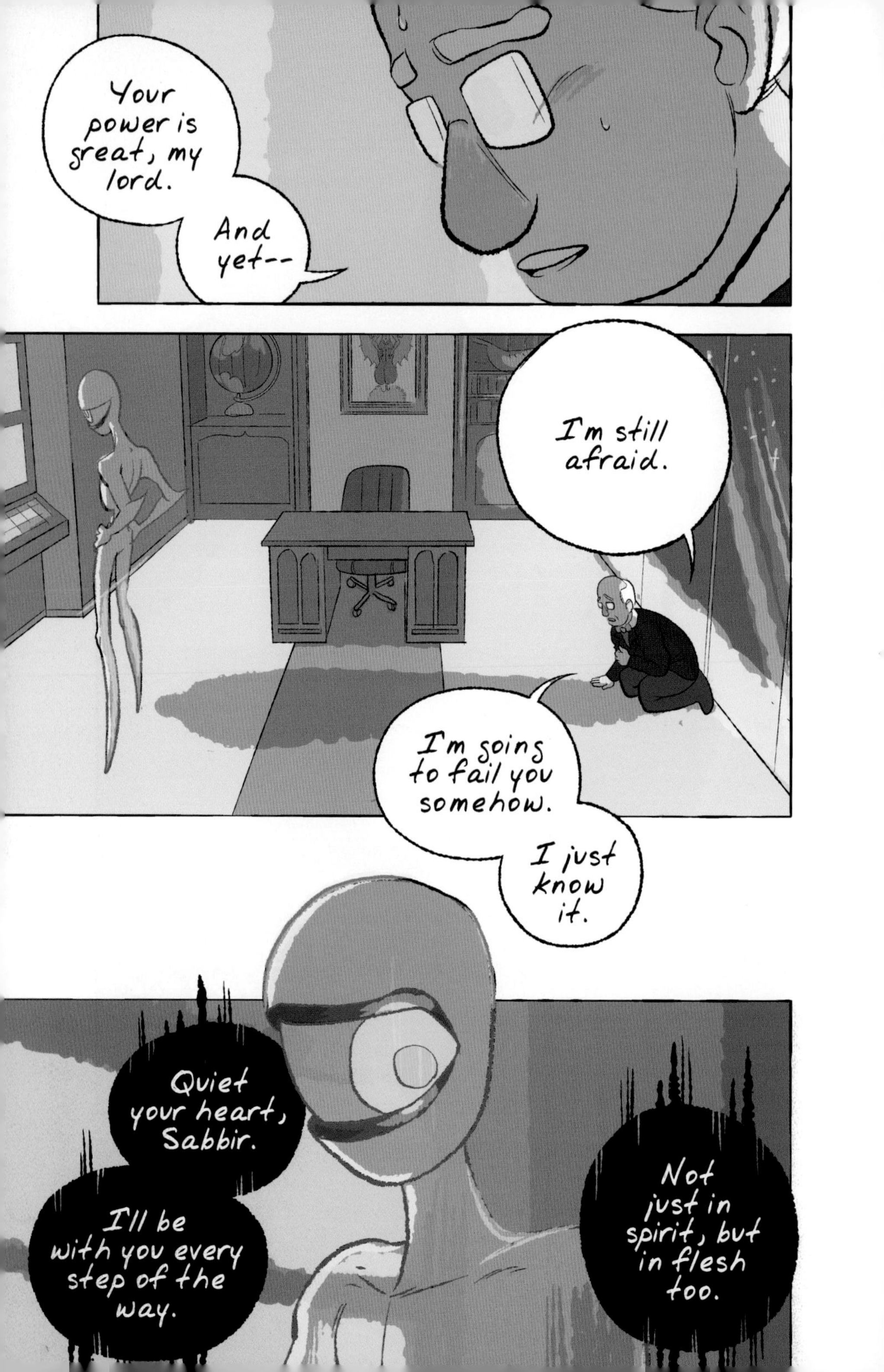
Your power is great, my lord.
And yet--
I'm still afraid.
I'm going to fail you somehow.
I just know it.
Quiet your heart, Sabbir.
I'll be with you every step of the way.
Not just in spirit, but in flesh too.

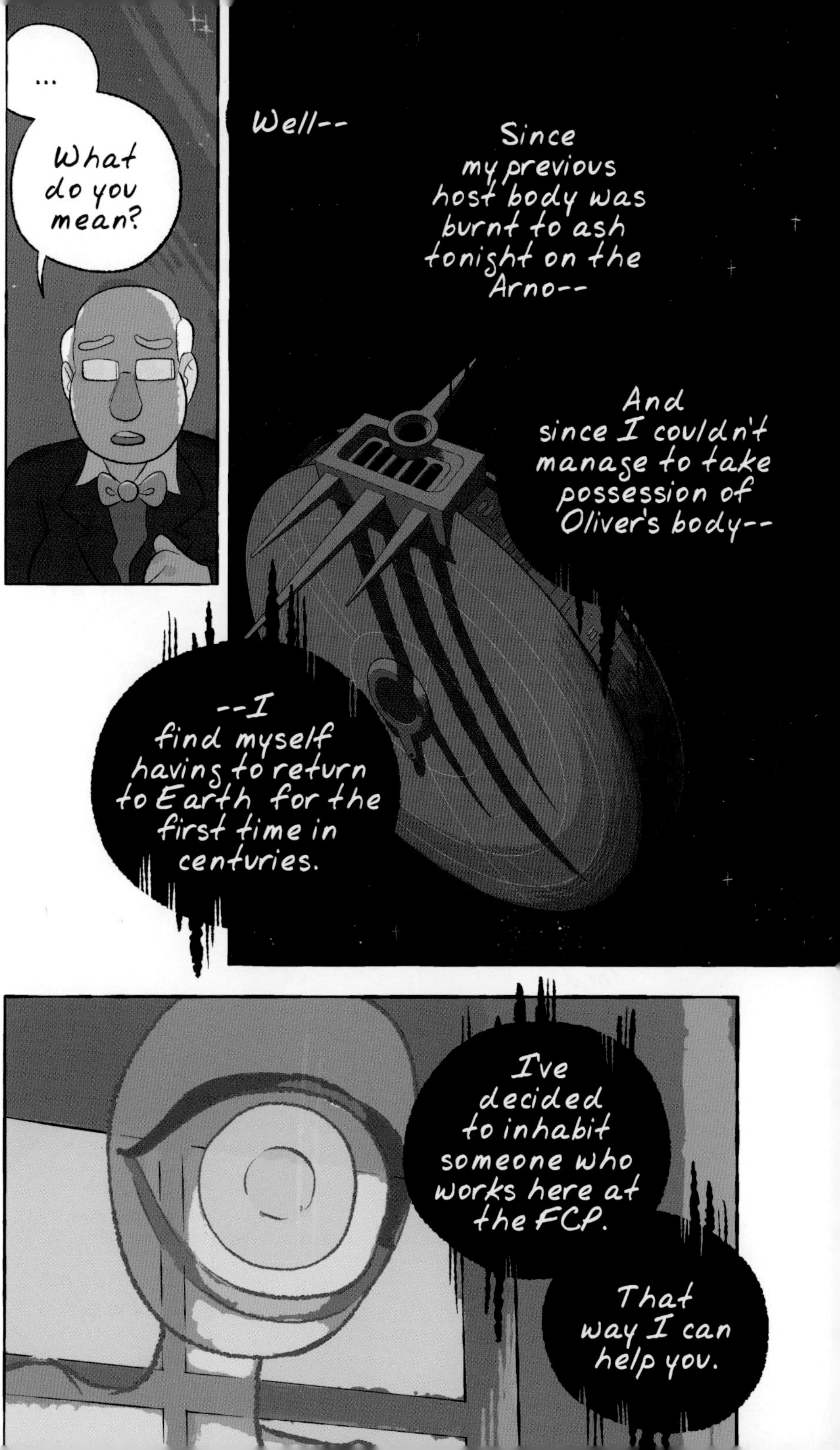
...
What do you mean?
Well--
Since my previous host body was burnt to ash tonight on the Arno--
And since I couldn't manage to take possession of Oliver's body--
--I find myself having to return to Earth for the first time in centuries.
I've decided to inhabit someone who works here at the FCP.
That way I can help you.

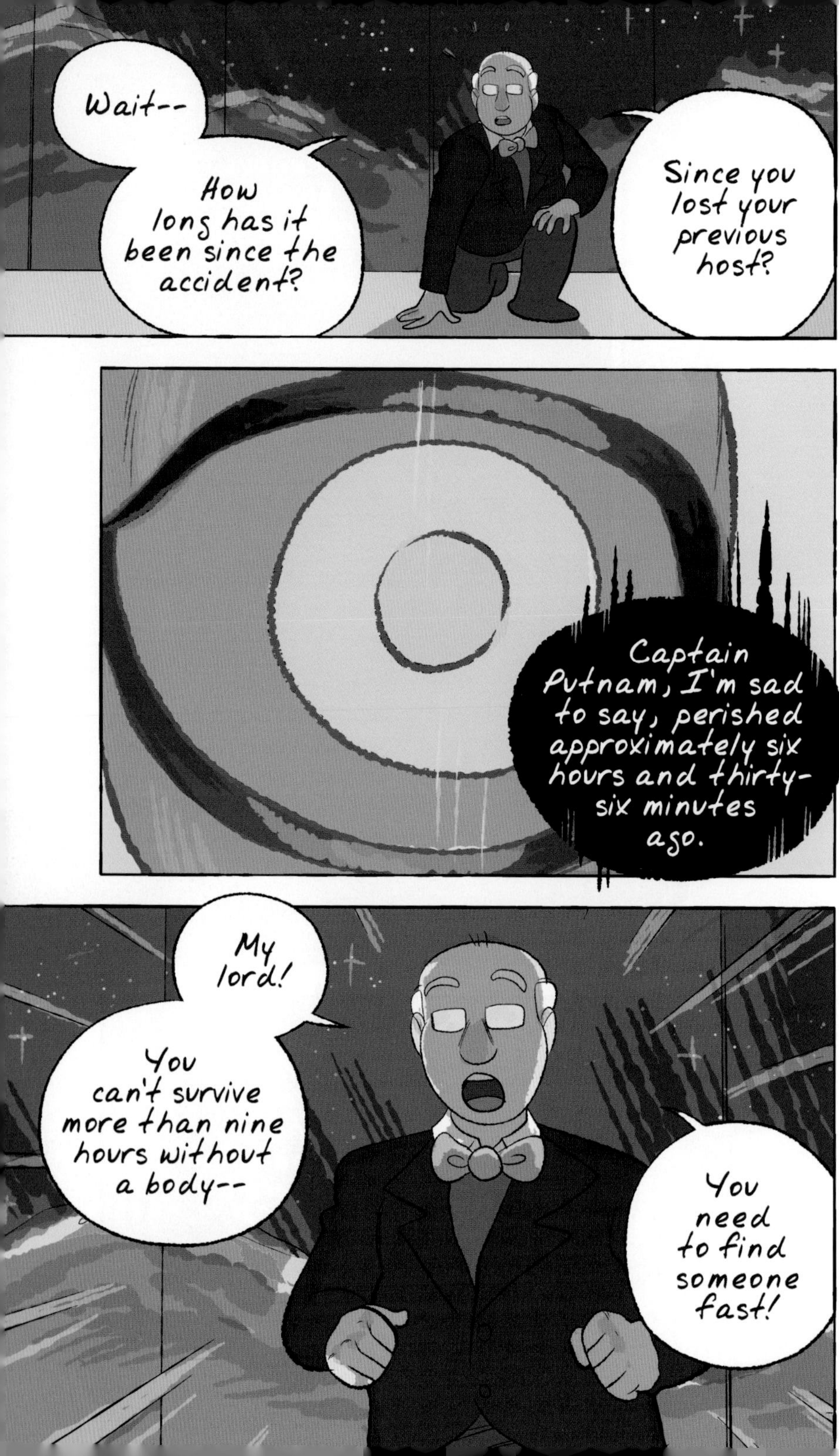
Wait--
How long has it been since the accident?
Since you lost your previous host?
Captain Putnam, I'm sad to say, perished approximately six hours and thirty-six minutes ago.
My lord!
You can't survive more than nine hours without a body--
You need to find someone fast!

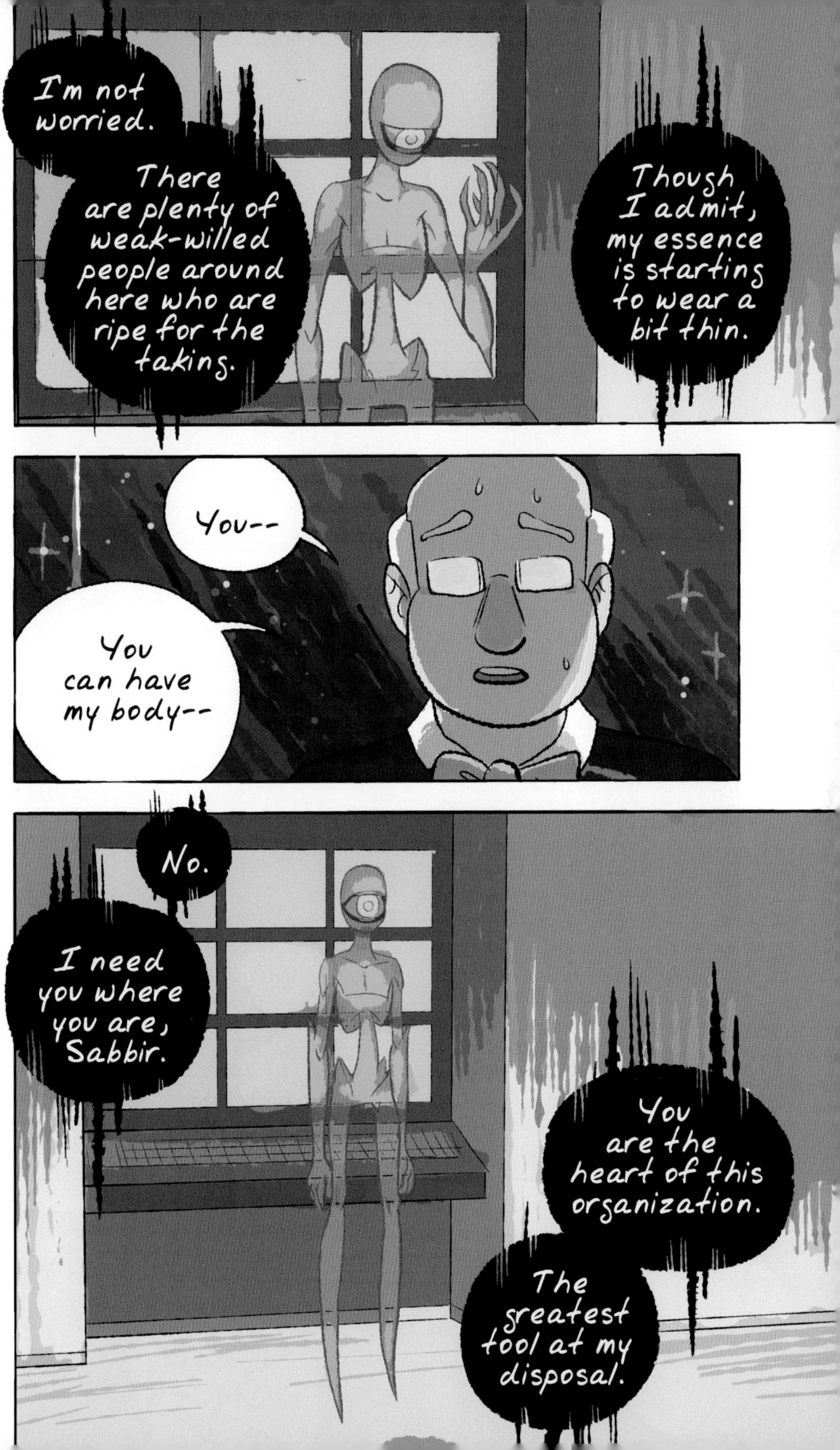
I'm not worried.
There are plenty of weak-willed people around here who are ripe for the taking.
Though I admit, my essence is starting to wear a bit thin.
You--
You can have my body--
No.
I need you where you are, Sabbir.
You are the heart of this organization.
The greatest tool at my disposal.

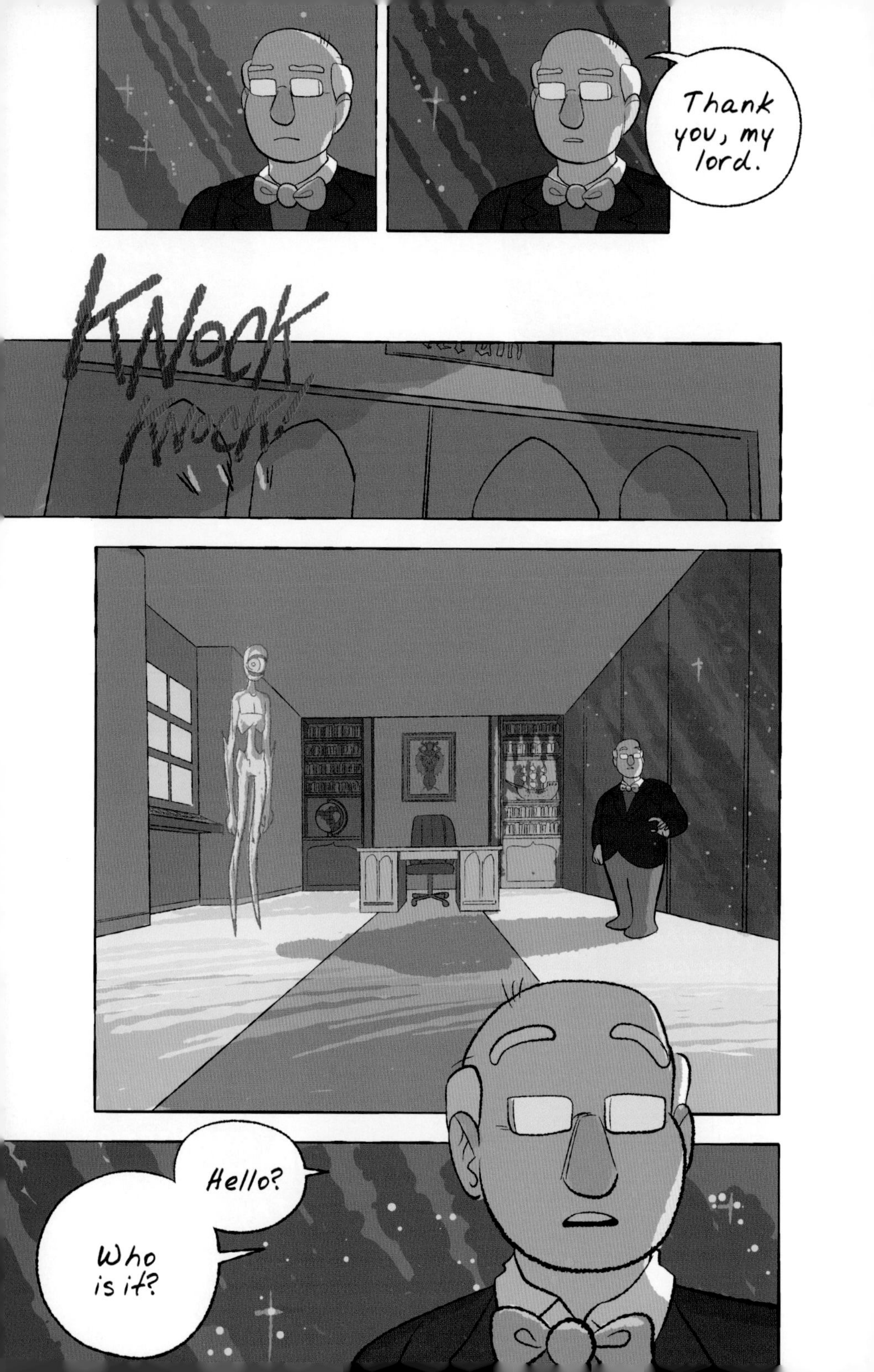
Thank you, my lord.
KNOCK
KNOCK
Hello?
Who is it?

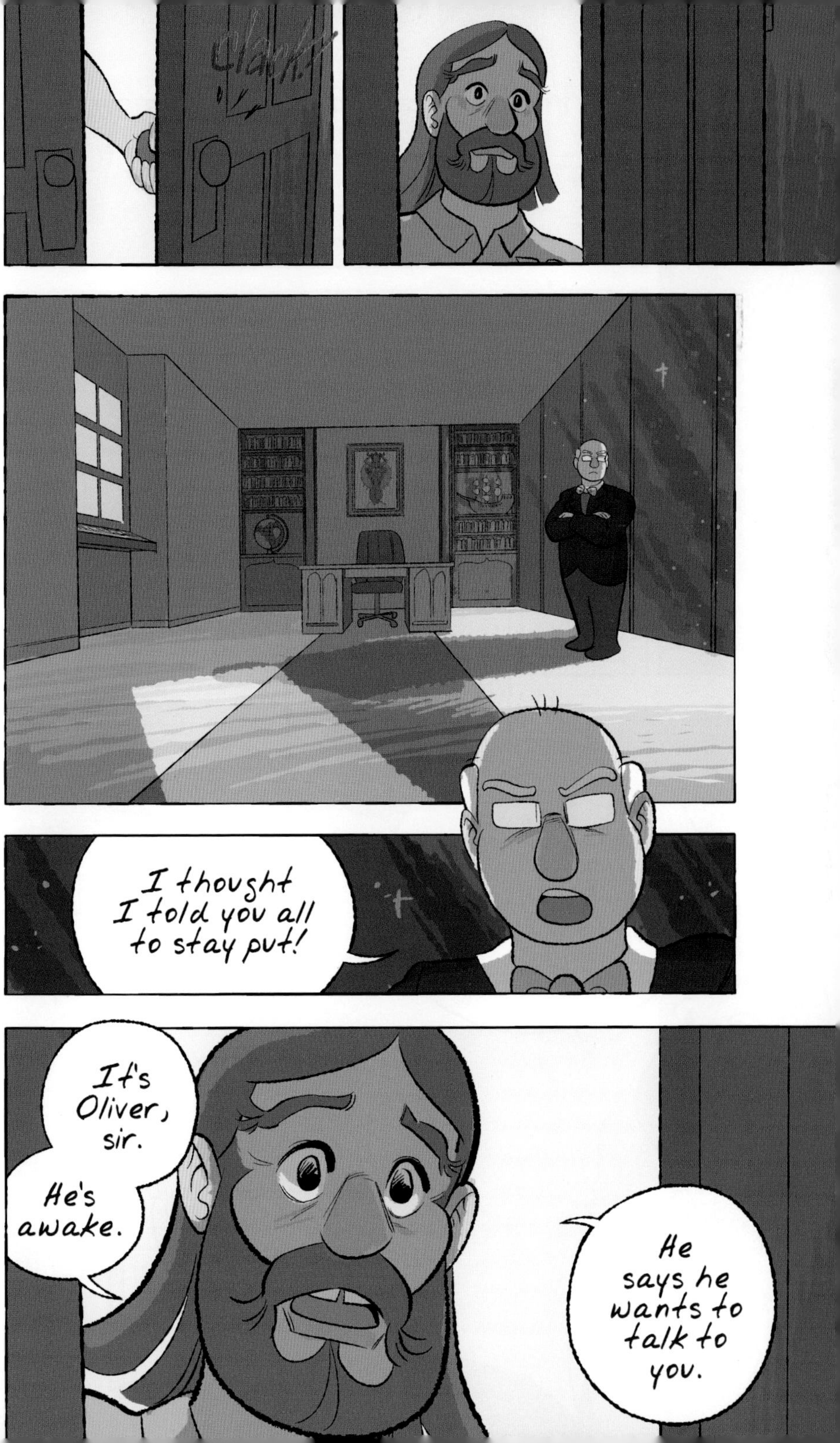
Clack!
I thought I told you all to stay put!
It's Oliver, sir.
He's awake.
He says he wants to talk to you.

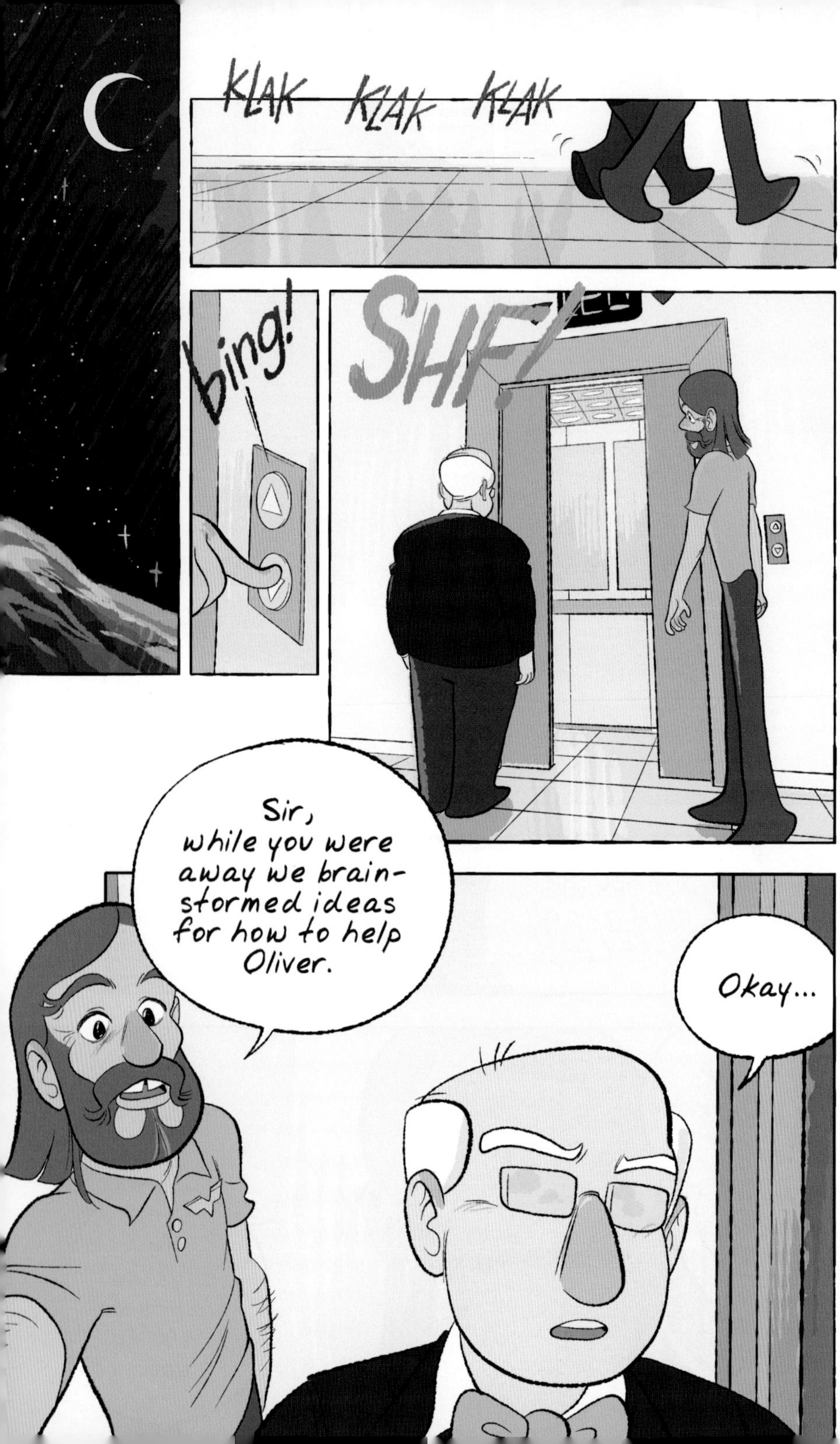
KLAK KLAK KLAK
bing!
SHF!
Sir, while you were away we brain-stormed ideas for how to help Oliver.
Okay...

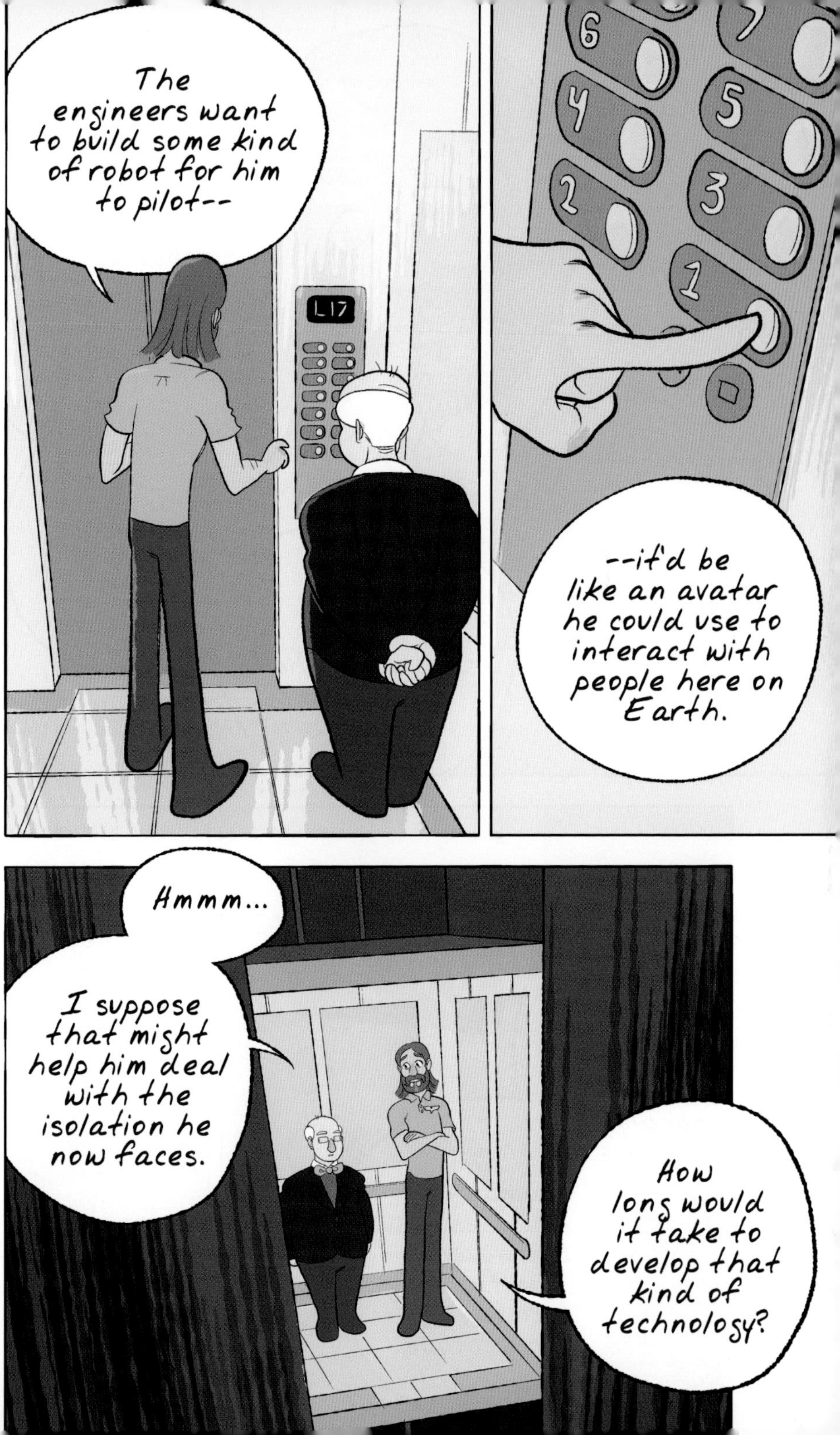
The engineers want to build some kind of robot for him to pilot--
L17
6
7
4
5
2
3
1
--it'd be like an avatar he could use to interact with people here on Earth.
Hmmm...
I suppose that might help him deal with the isolation he now faces.
How long would it take to develop that kind of technology?

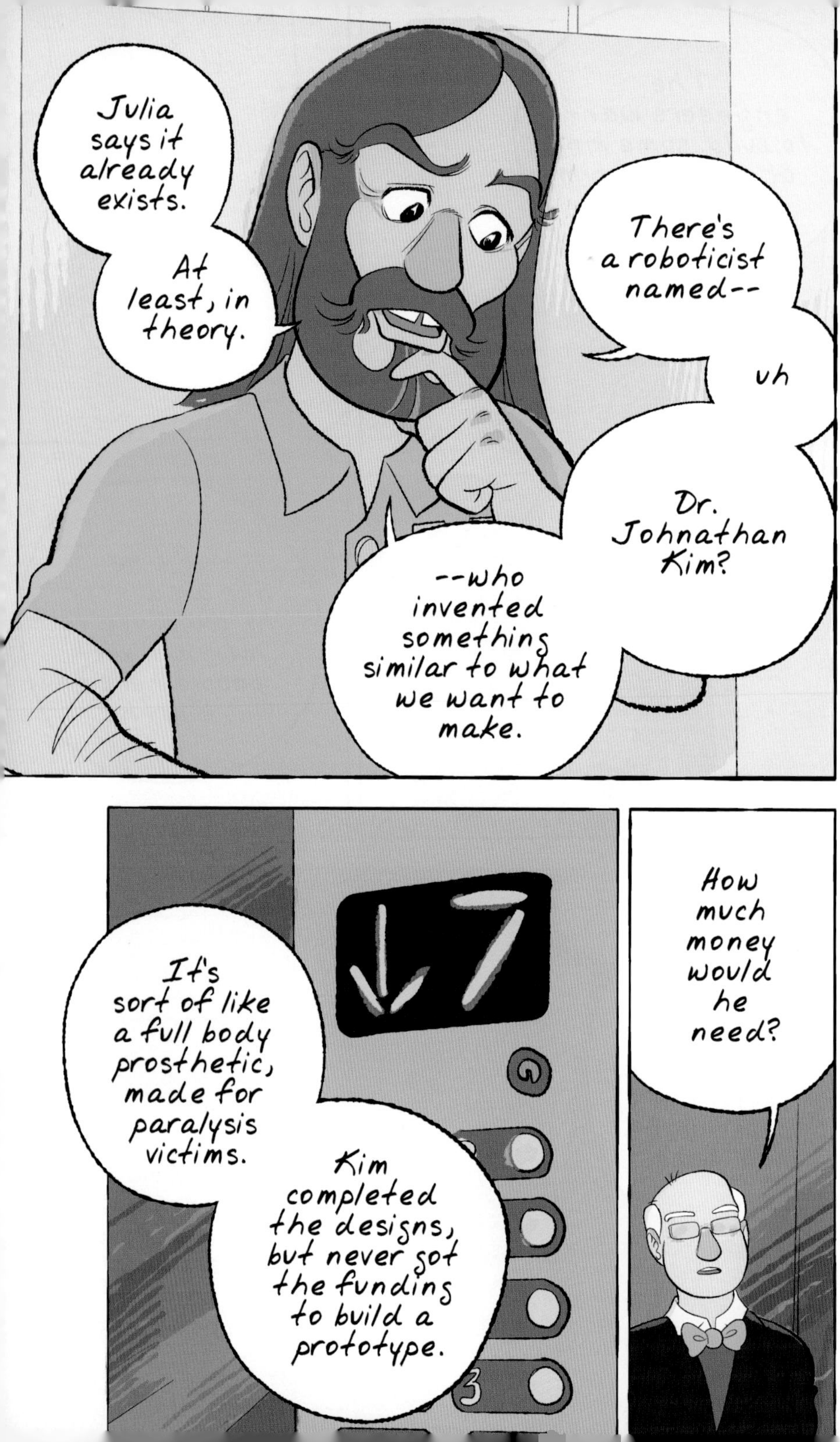
Julia says it already exists.
At least, in theory.
There's a roboticist named--
uh
Dr. Johnathan Kim?
--who invented something similar to what we want to make.
It's sort of like a full body prosthetic, made for paralysis victims.
Kim completed the designs, but never got the funding to build a prototype.
How much money would he need?

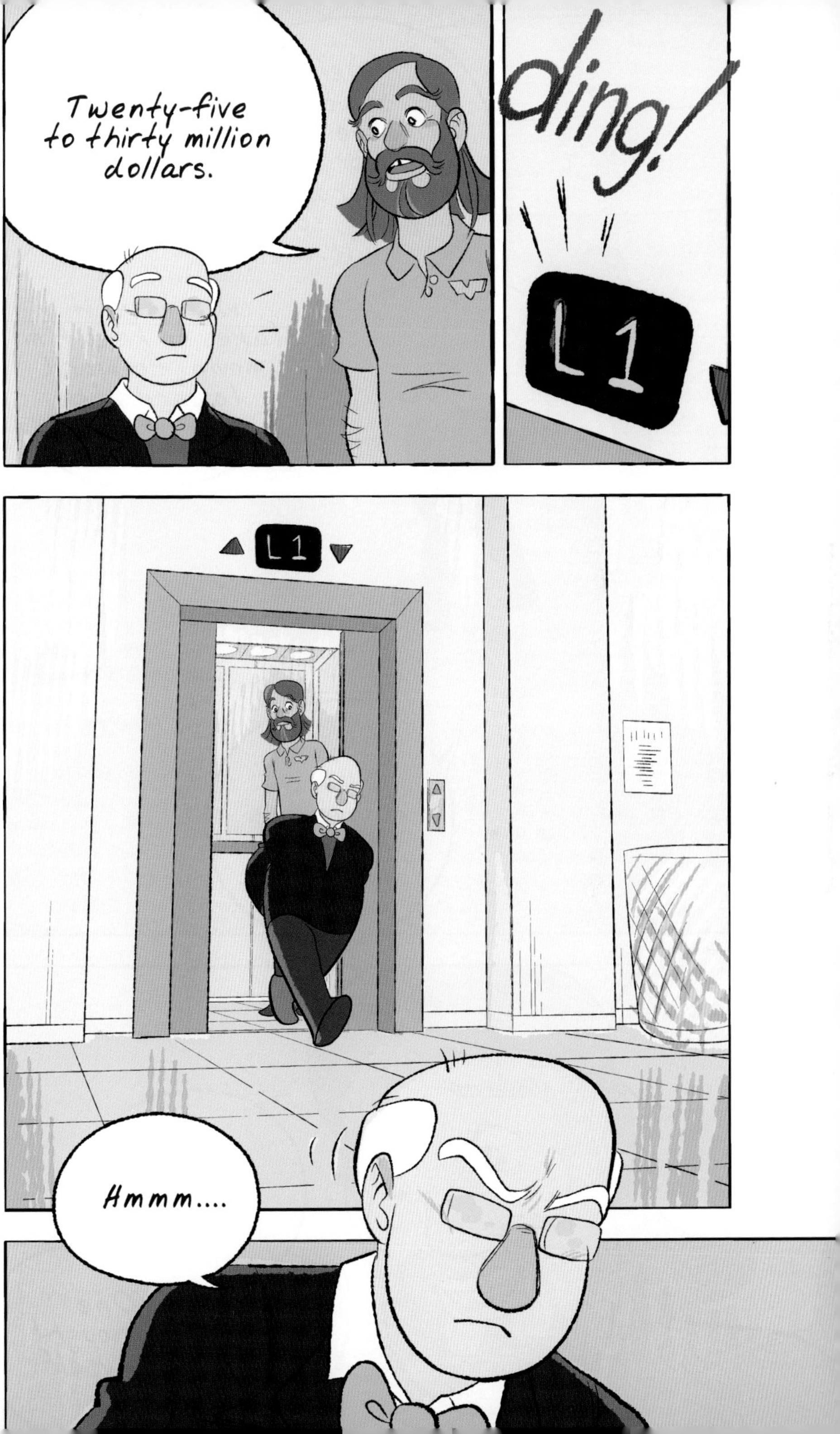
Twenty-five to thirty million dollars.
ding!
L1
L1
Hmmm....

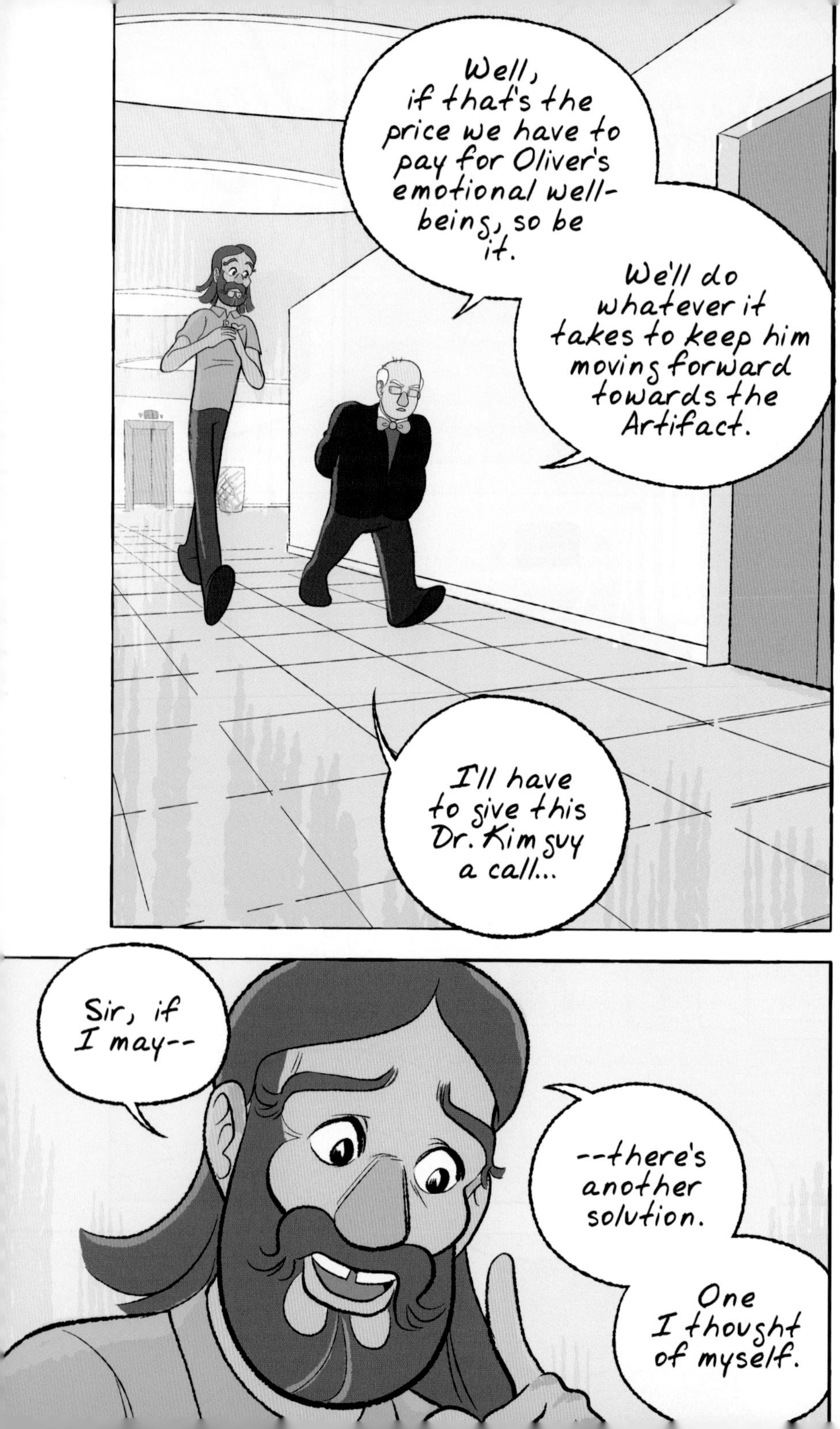
Well, if that's the price we have to pay for Oliver's emotional well-being, so be it.
We'll do whatever it takes to keep him moving forward towards the Artifact.
I'll have to give this Dr. Kim guy a call...
Sir, if I may--
--there's another solution.
One I thought of myself.

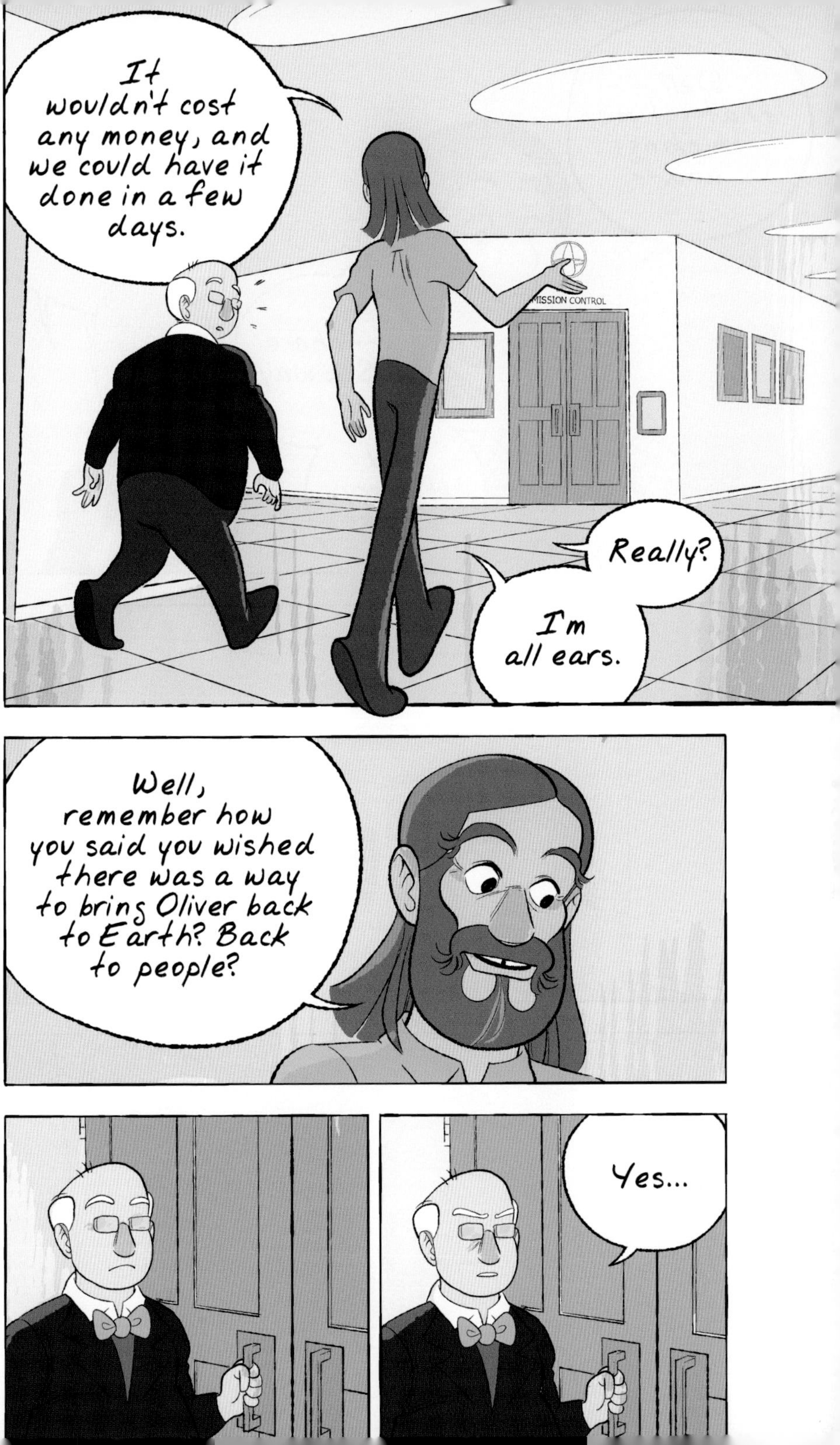
It wouldn't cost any money, and we could have it done in a few days.
MISSION CONTROL
Really?
I'm all ears.
Well, remember how you said you wished there was a way to bring Oliver back to Earth? Back to people?
Yes...

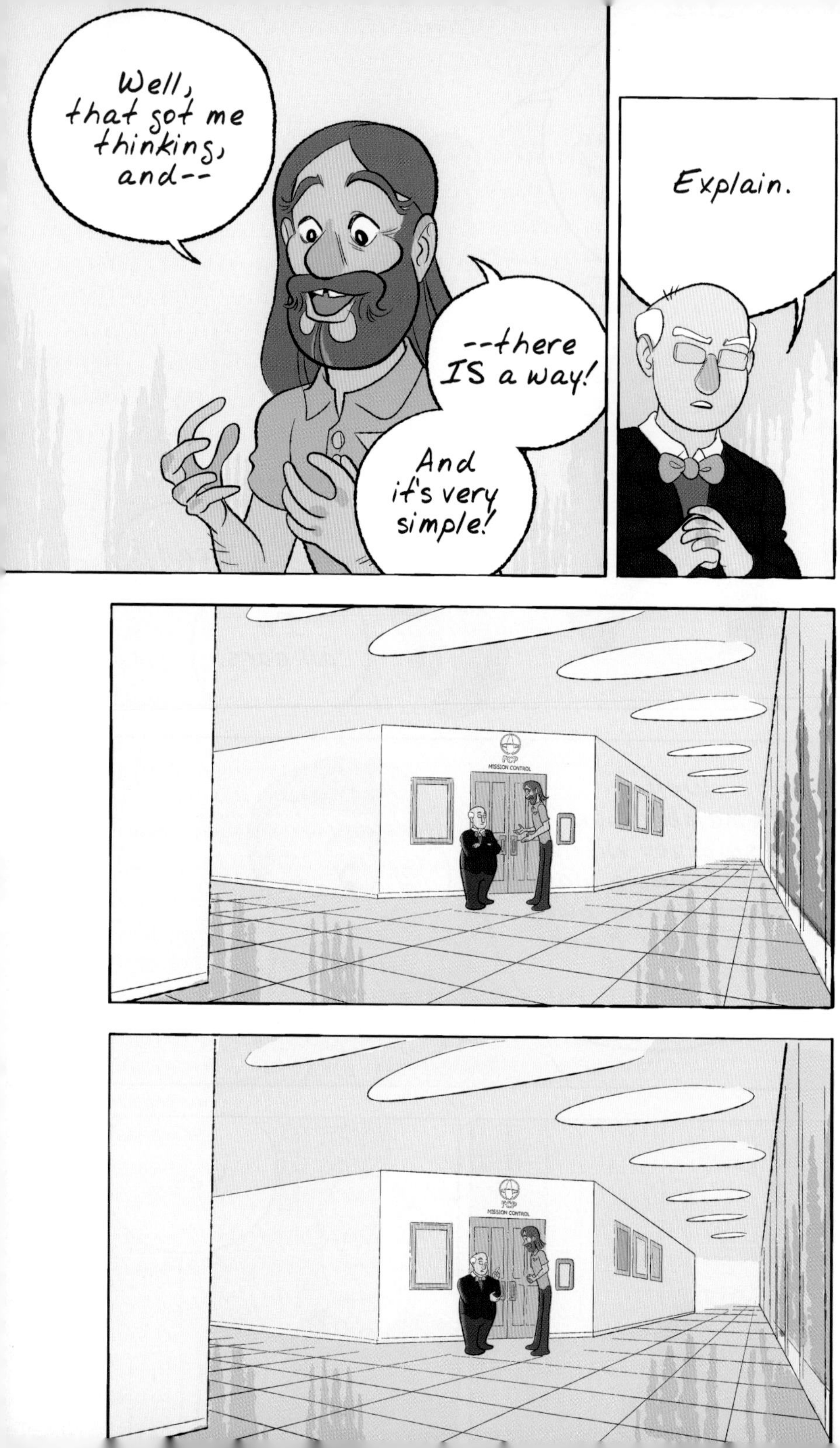
Well, that got me thinking, and--
--there IS a way!
And it's very simple!
Explain.
FCP
MISSION CONTROL
FCP
MISSION CONTROL

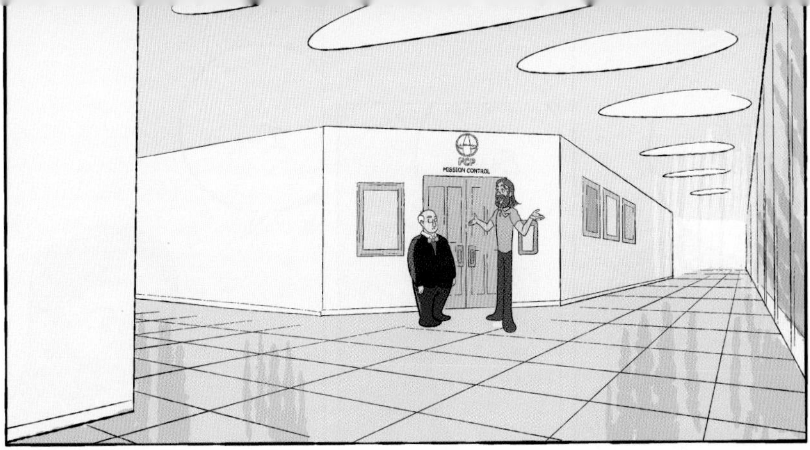
FCP
MISSION CONTROL

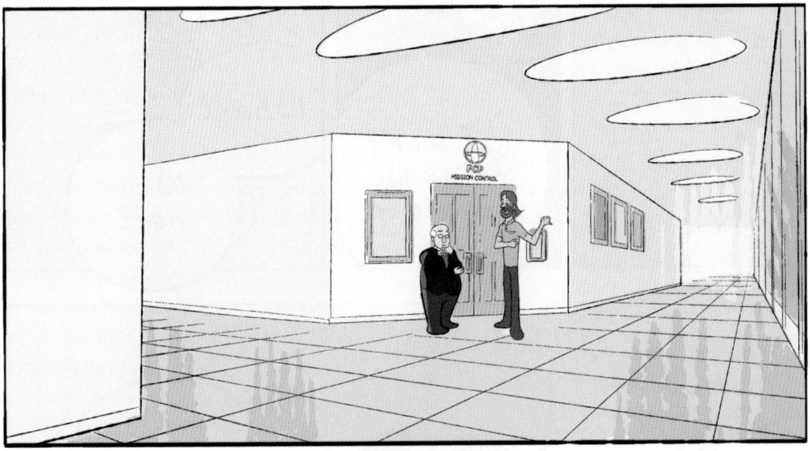
FCP
MISSION CONTROL

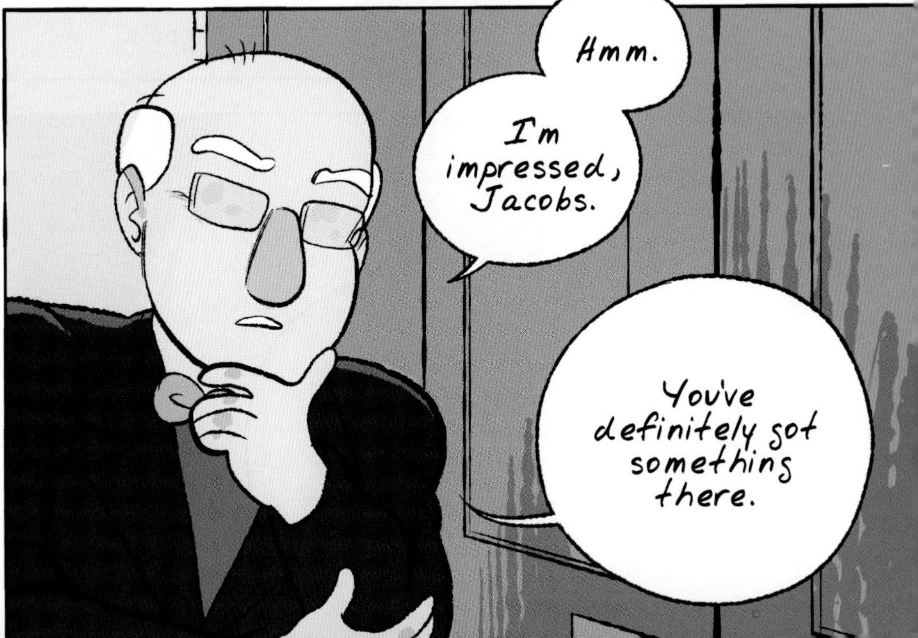
Hmm.
I'm impressed, Jacobs.
You've definitely got something there.

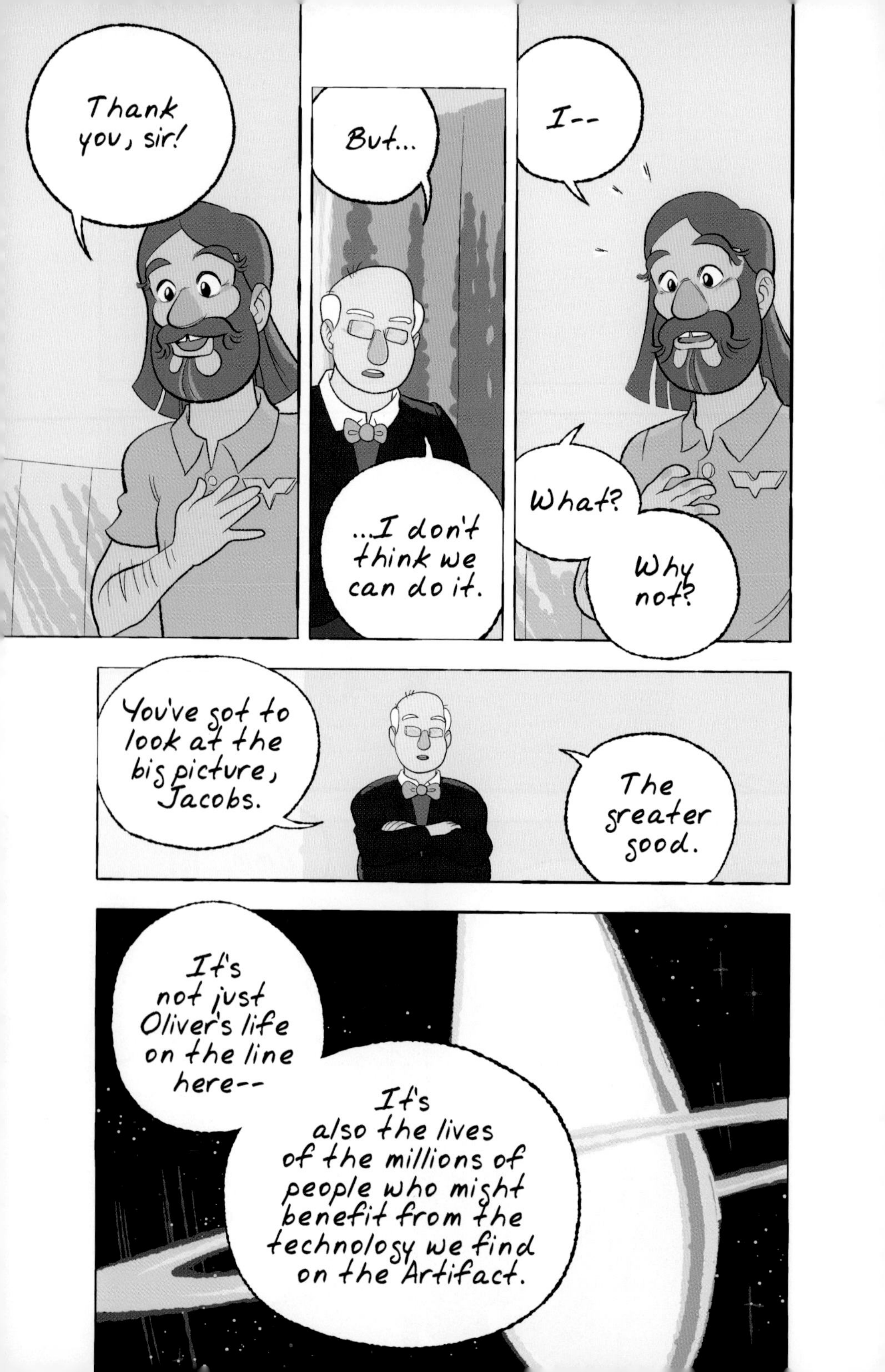
Thank you, sir!
But...
I--
...I don't think we can do it.
What?
Why not?
You've got to look at the big picture, Jacobs.
The greater good.
It's not just Oliver's life on the line here--
It's also the lives of the millions of people who might benefit from the technology we find on the Artifact.

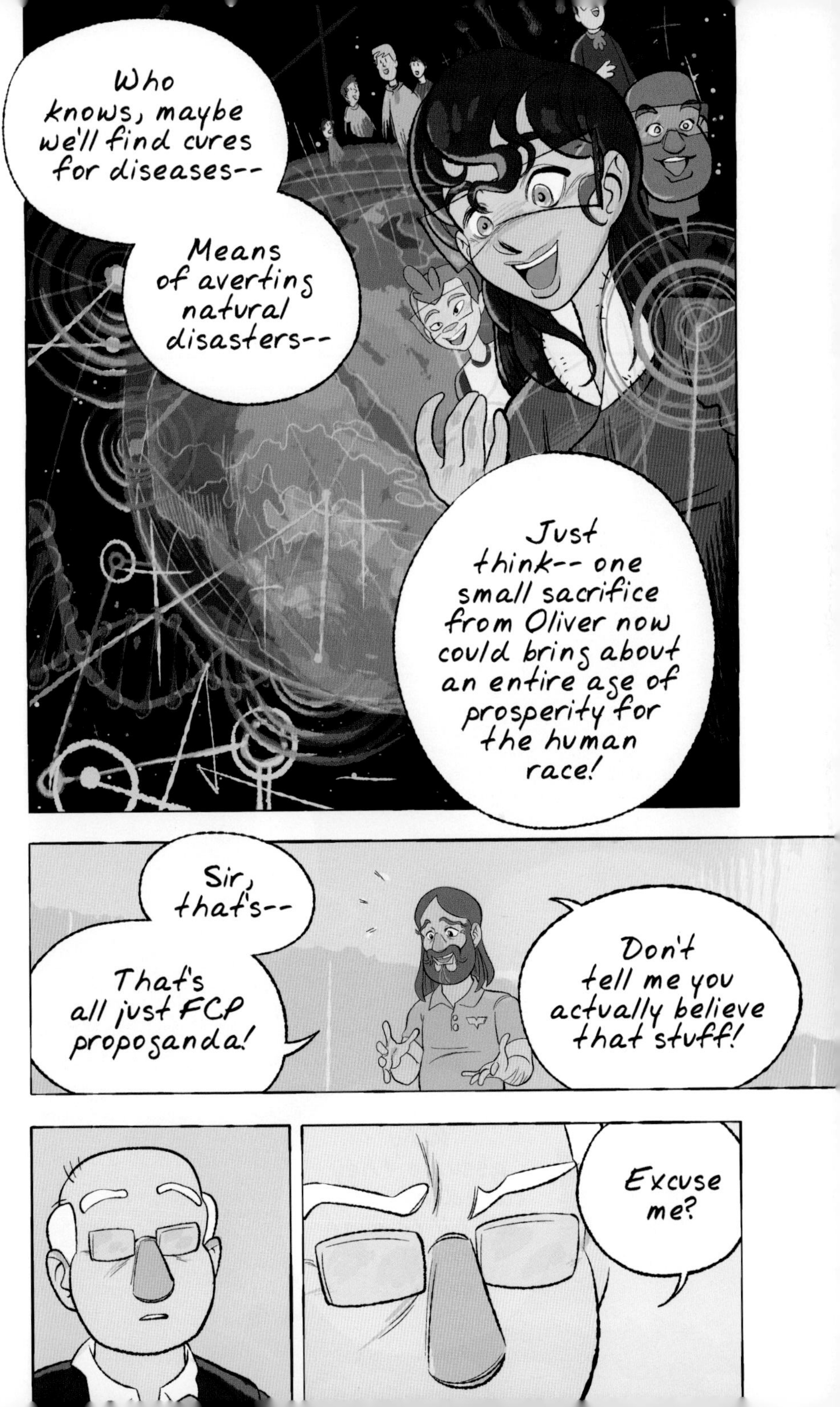
Who knows, maybe we'll find cures for diseases--
Means of averting natural disasters--
Just think-- one small sacrifice from Oliver now could bring about an entire age of prosperity for the human race!
Sir, that's--
That's all just FCP propoganda!
Don't tell me you actually believe that stuff!
Excuse me?

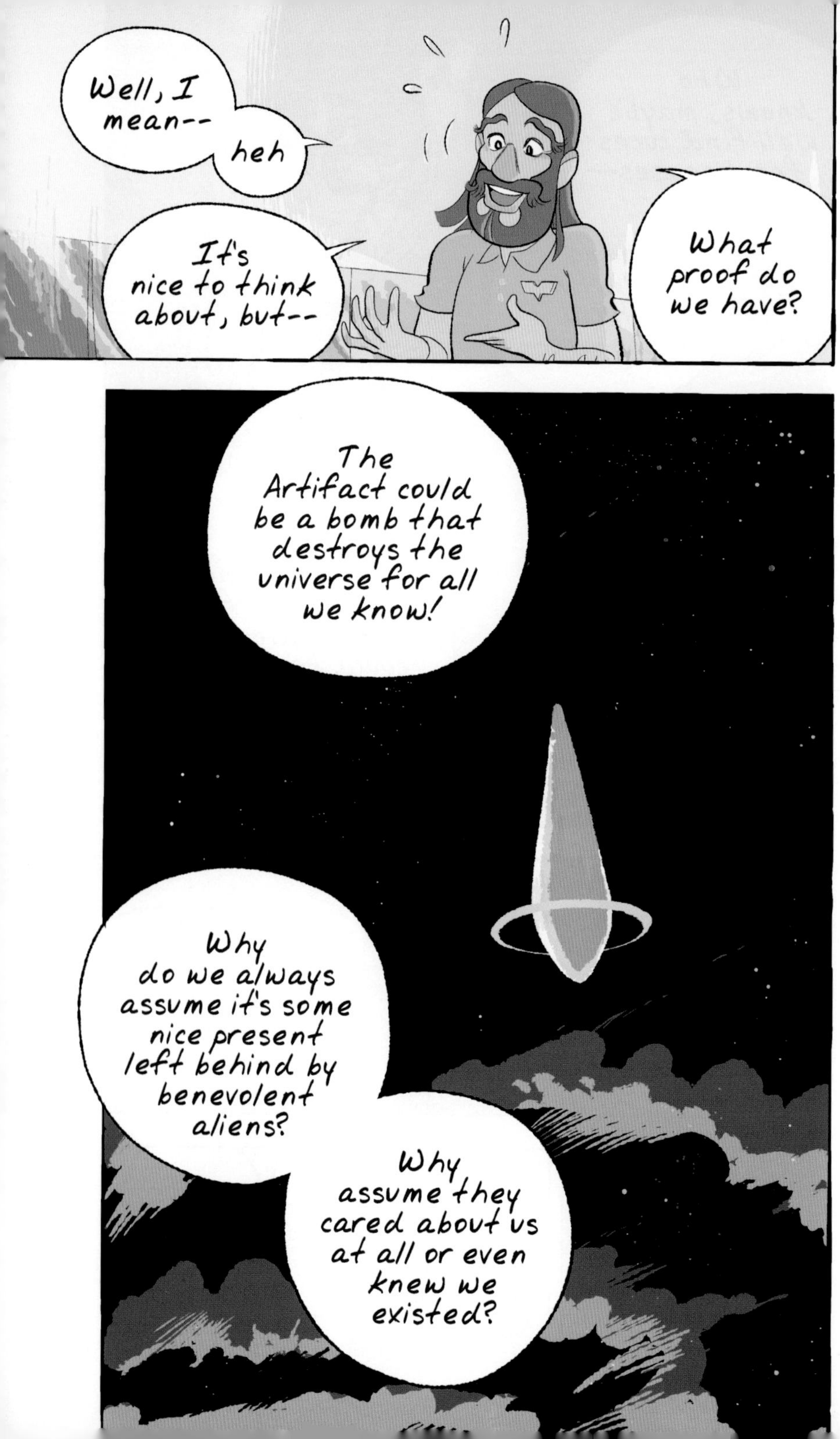
Well, I mean--
heh
It's nice to think about, but--
What proof do we have?
The Artifact could be a bomb that destroys the universe for all we know!
Why do we always assume it's some nice present left behind by benevolent aliens?
Why assume they cared about us at all or even knew we existed?

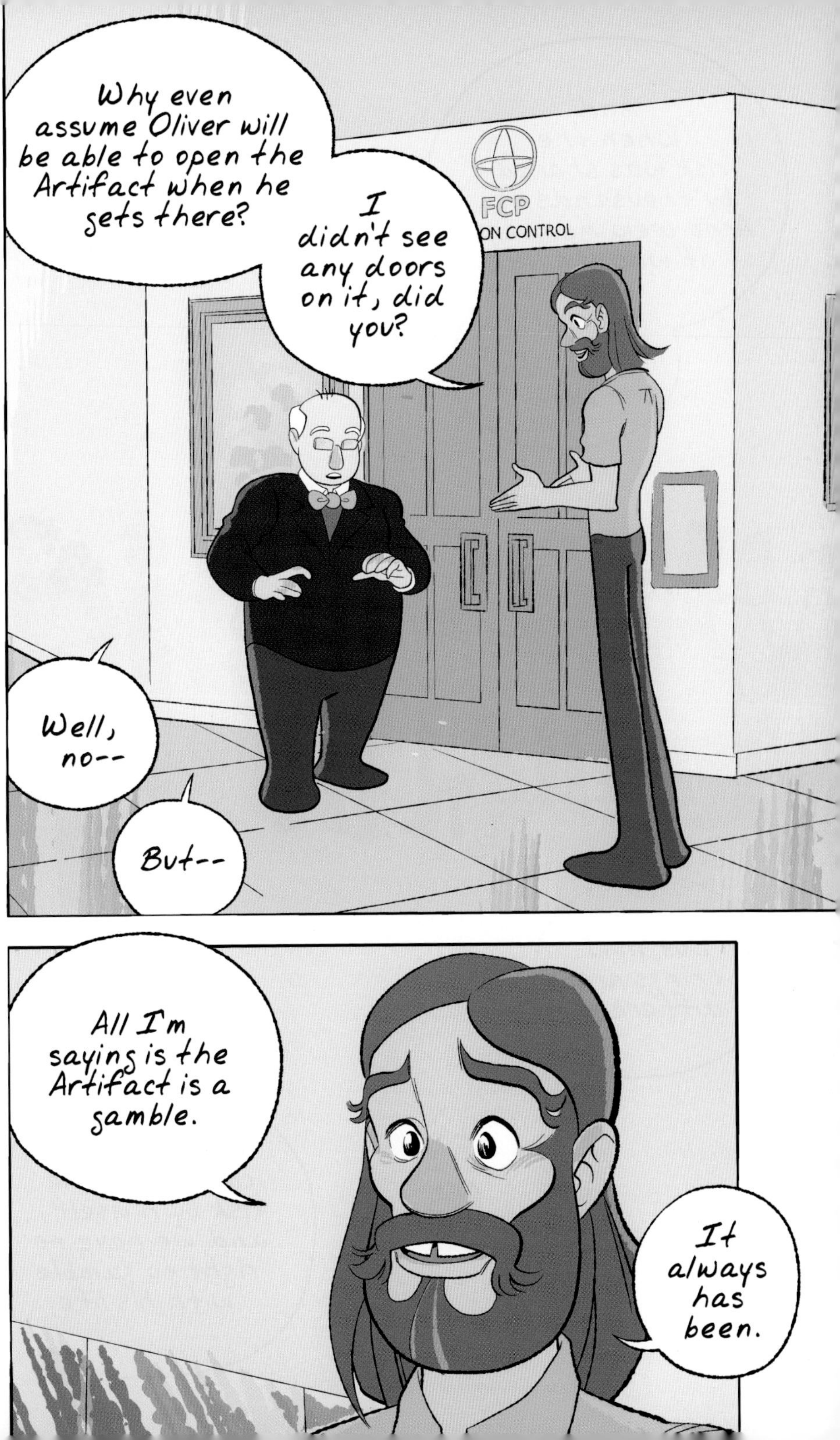
Why even assume Oliver will be able to open the Artifact when he gets there?
I didn't see any doors on it, did you?
FCP
ON CONTROL
Well, no--
But--
All I'm saying is the Artifact is a gamble.
It always has been.

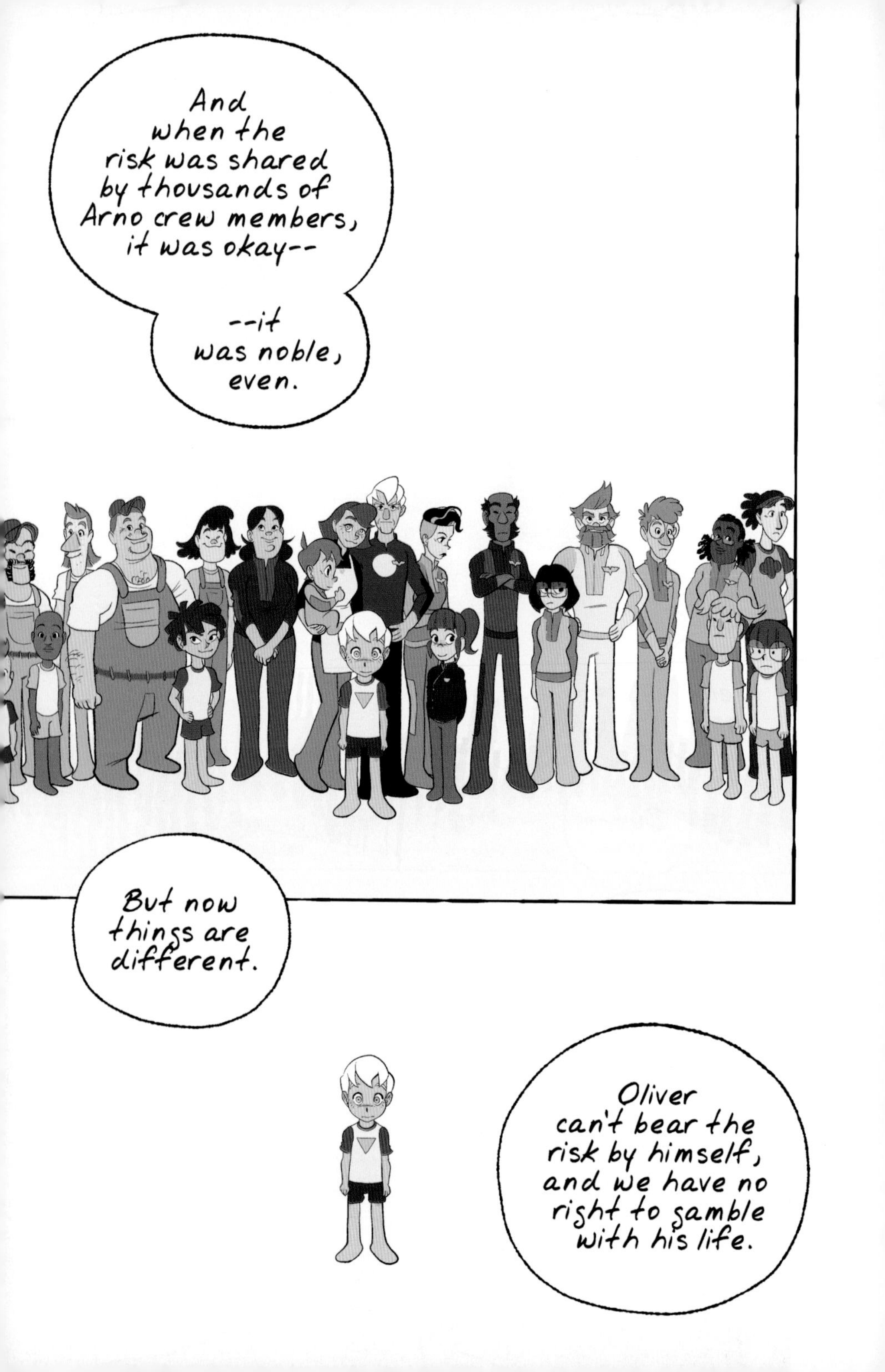
And when the risk was shared by thousands of Arno crew members, it was okay--
--it was noble, even.
But now things are different.
Oliver can't bear the risk by himself, and we have no right to gamble with his life.

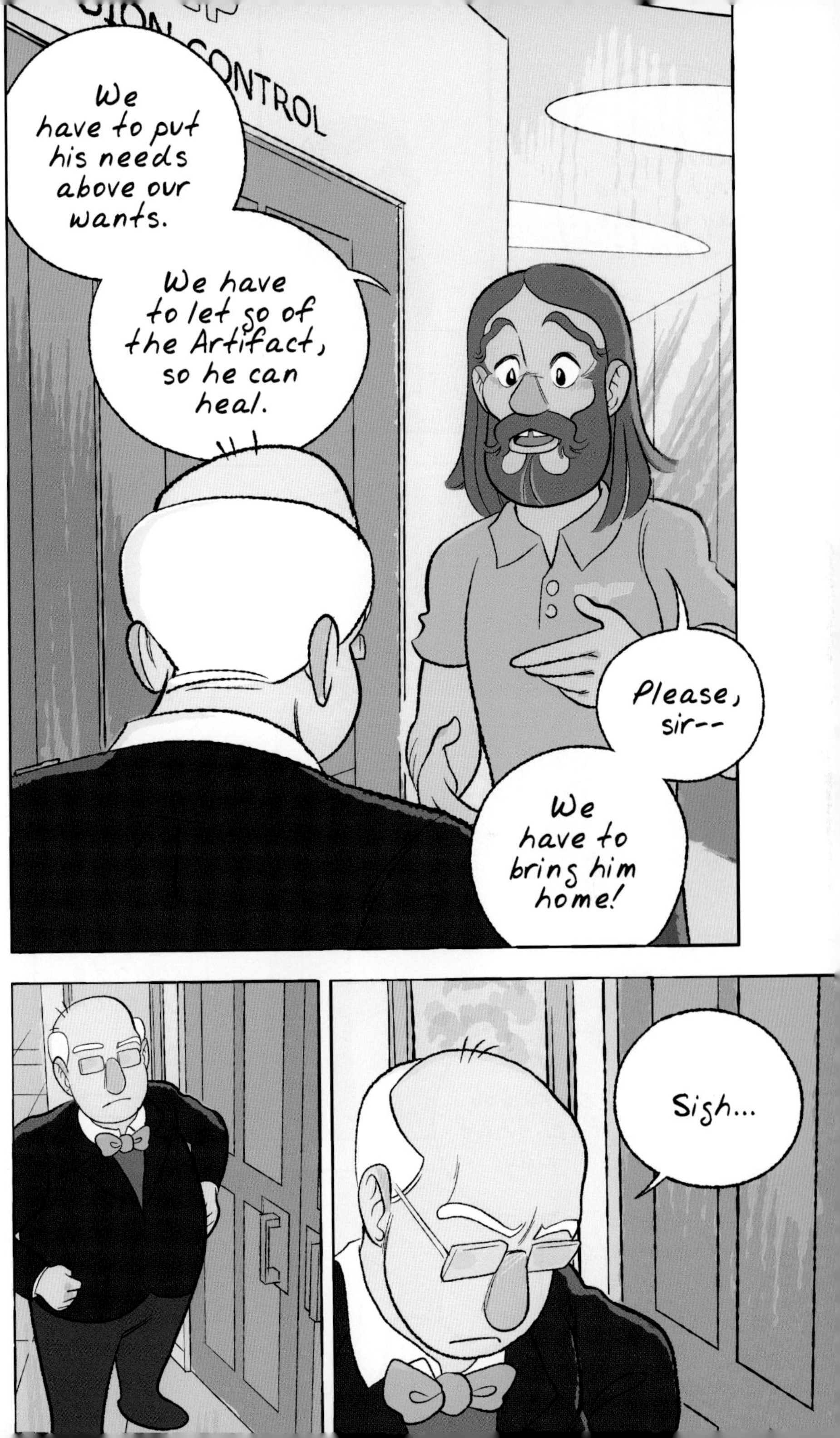

ION CONTROL
We have to put his needs above our wants.
We have to let go of the Artifact, so he can heal.
Please, sir--
We have to bring him home!
Sigh...

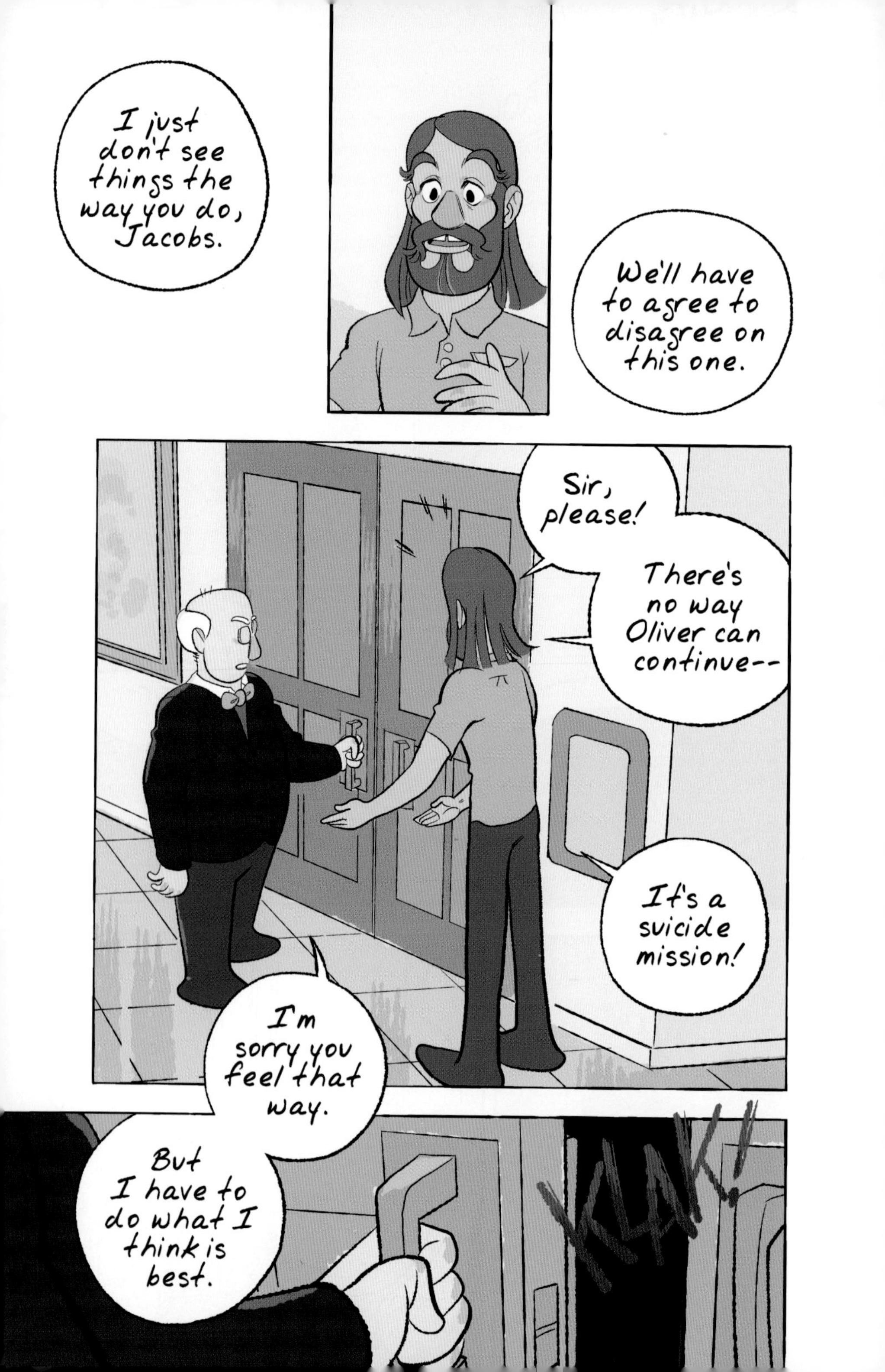
I just don't see things the way you do, Jacobs.
We'll have to agree to disagree on this one.
Sir, please!
There's no way Oliver can continue--
It's a suicide mission!
I'm sorry you feel that way.
But I have to do what I think is best.
KLAK!

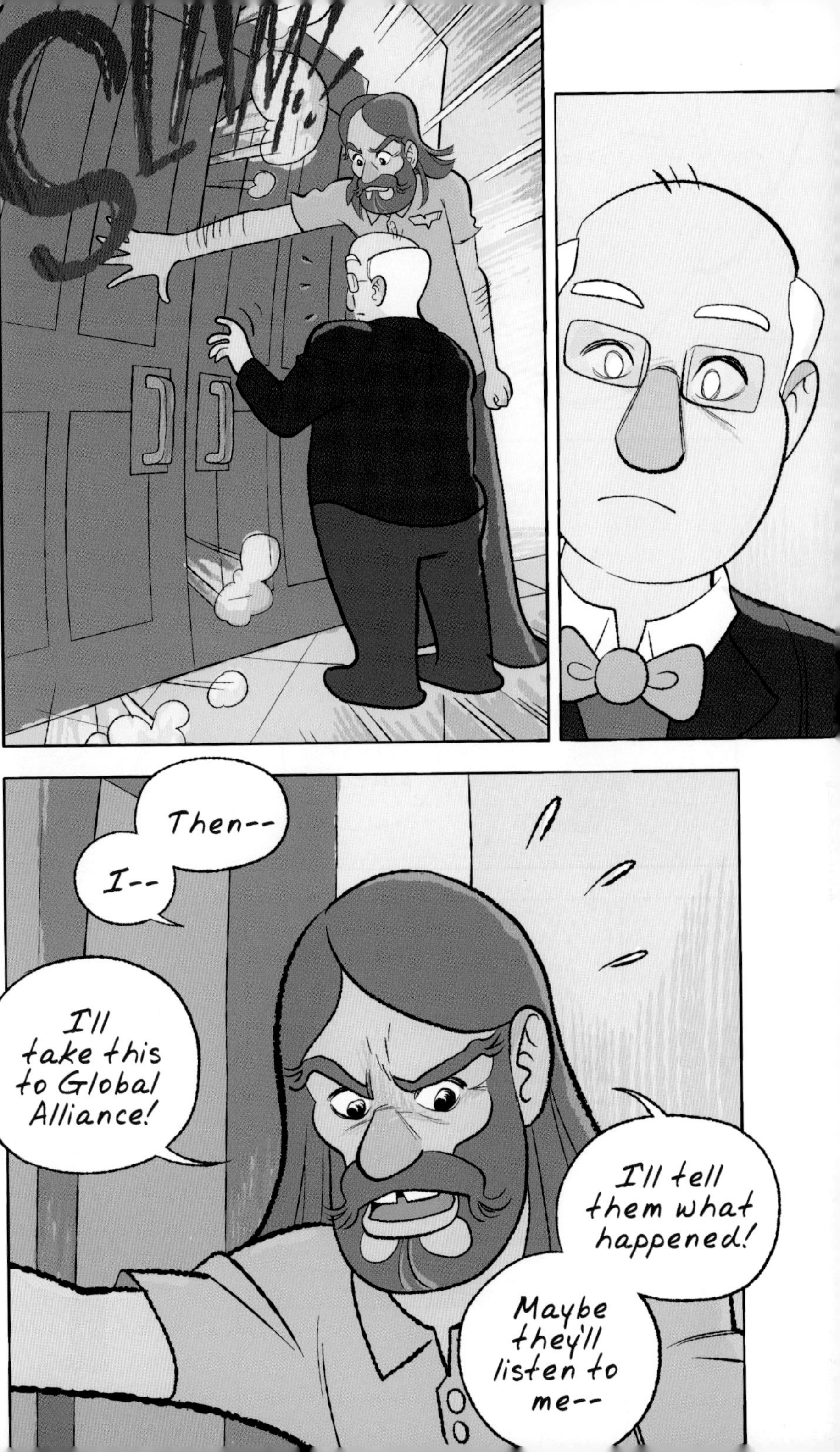
SLAM!
Then--
I--
I'll take this to Global Alliance!
I'll tell them what happened!
Maybe they'll listen to me--

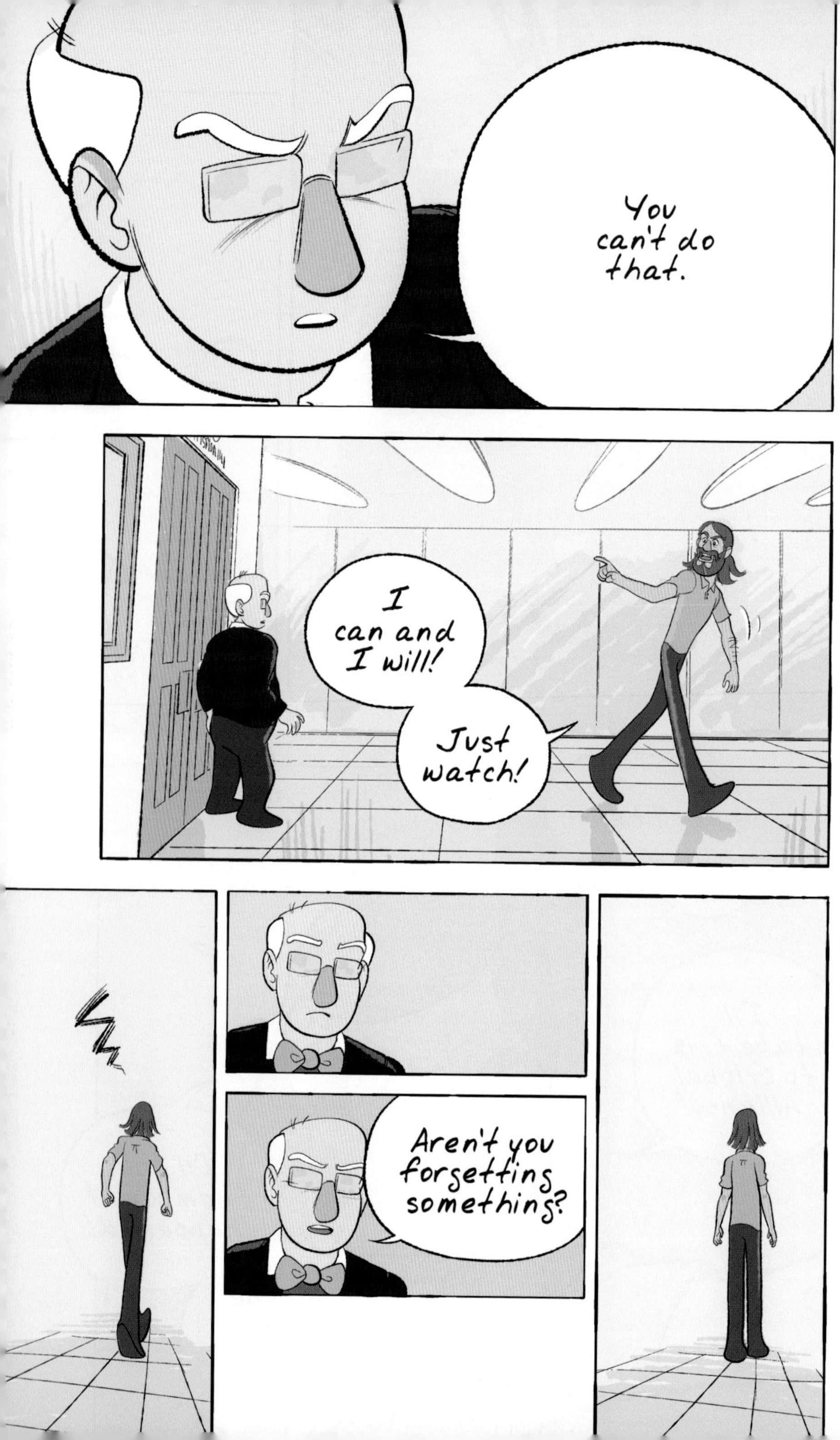
You can't do that.
I can and I will!
Just watch!
Aren't you forgetting something?

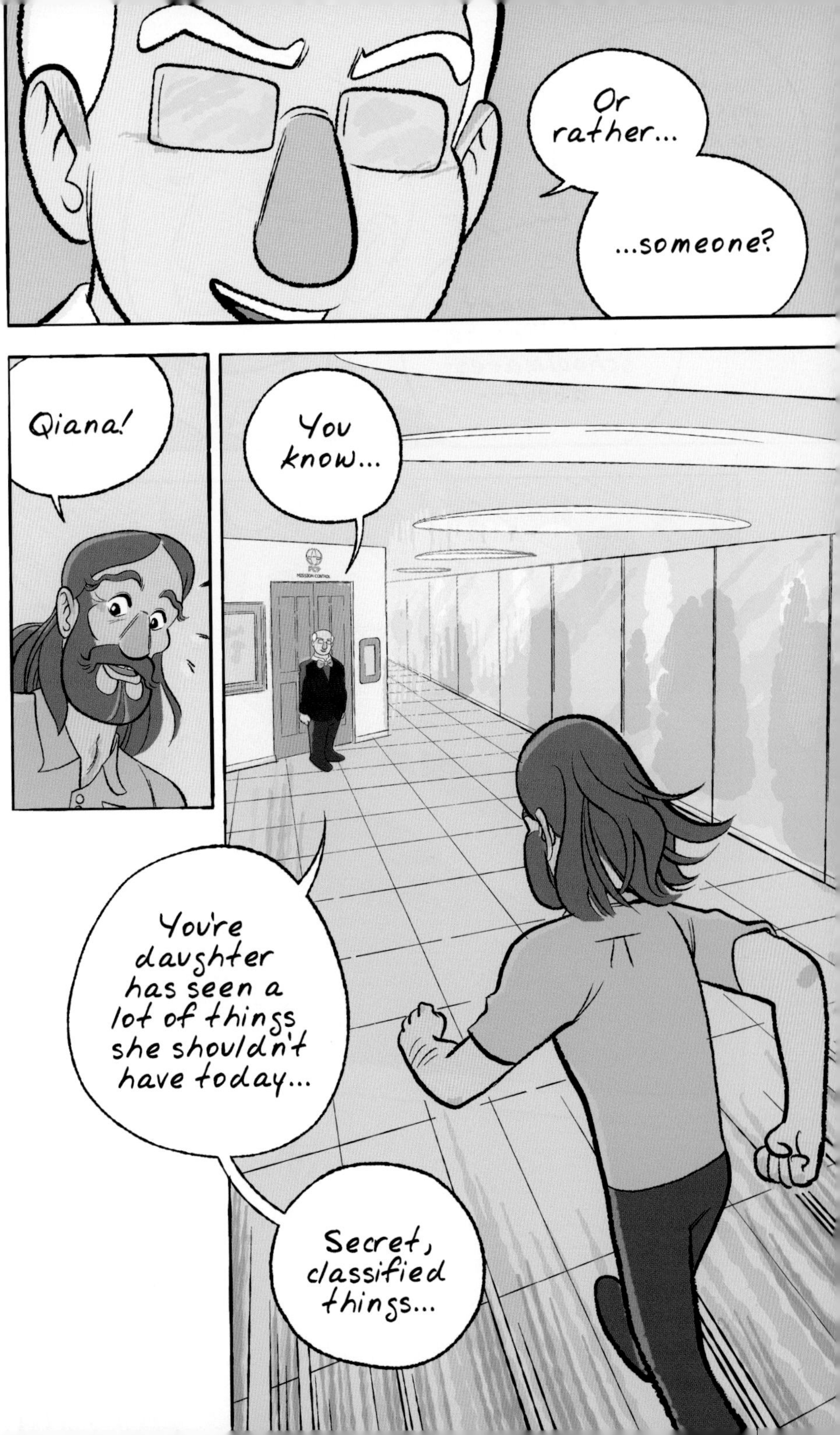
Or rather...
...someone?
Qiana!
You know...
You're daughter has seen a lot of things she shouldn't have today...
Secret, classified things...

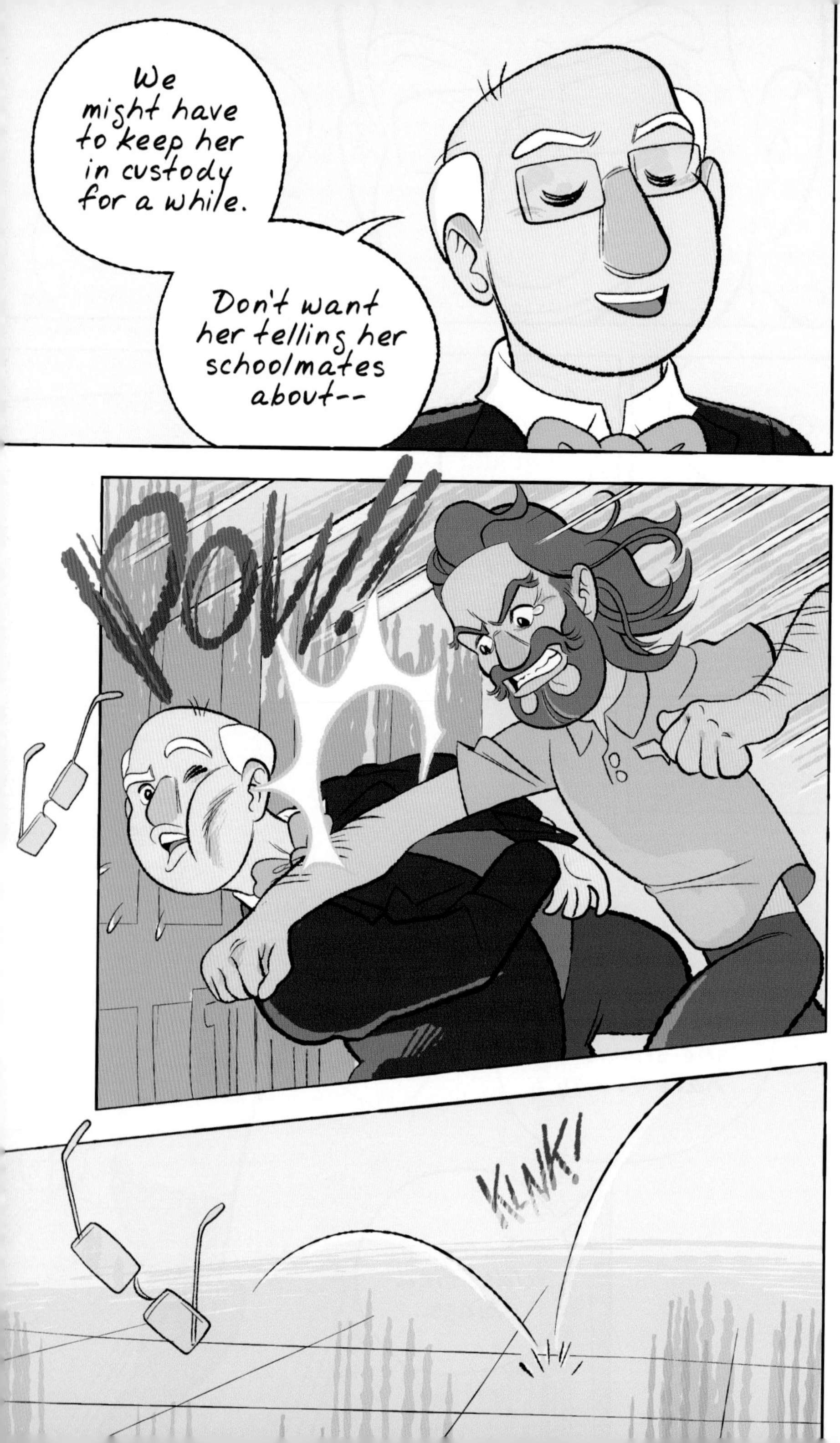
We might have to keep her in custody for a while.
Don't want her telling her schoolmates about--
POW!!
KLINK!

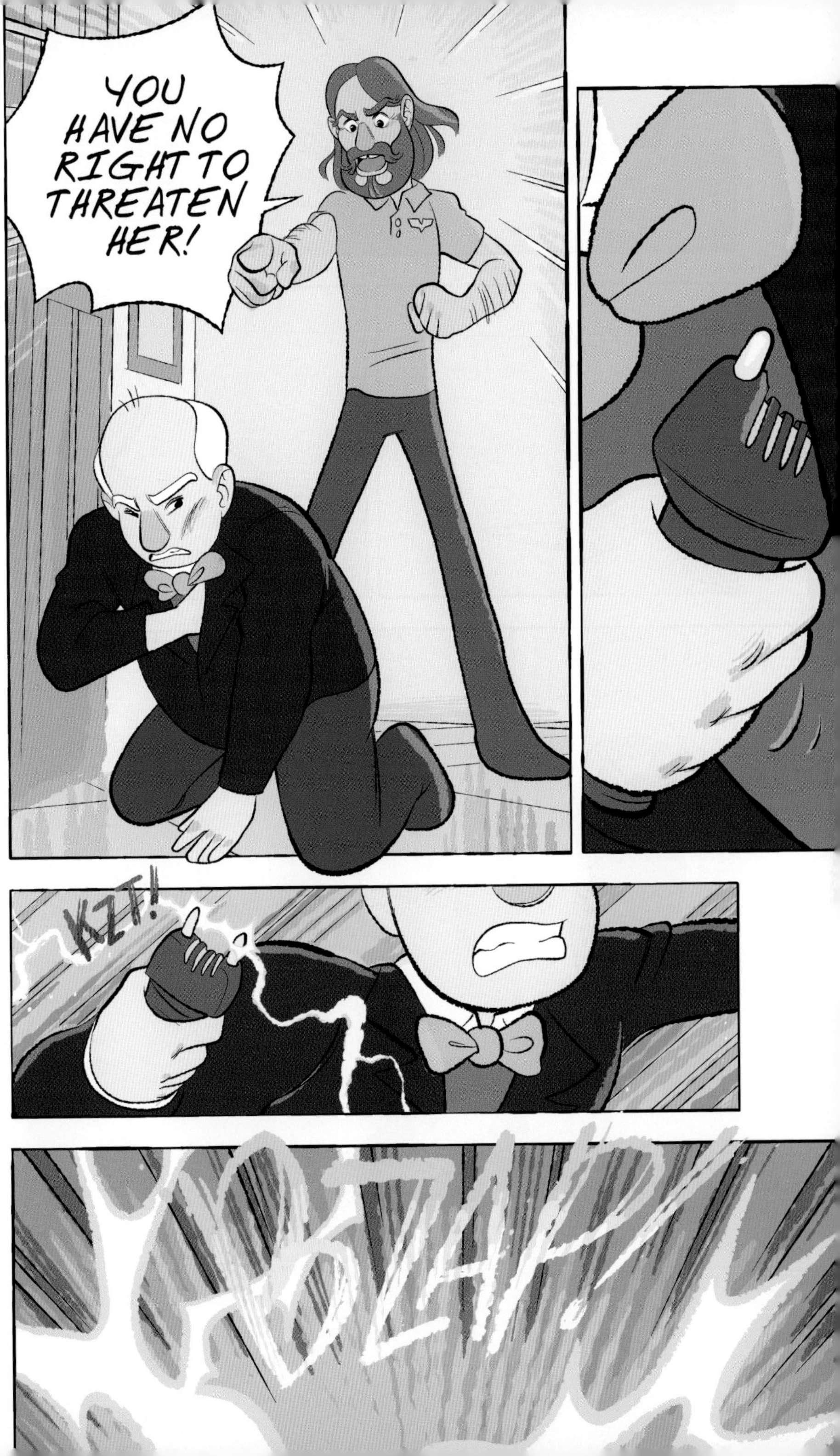
YOU HAVE NO RIGHT TO THREATEN HER!
KZT!
BZZAP!

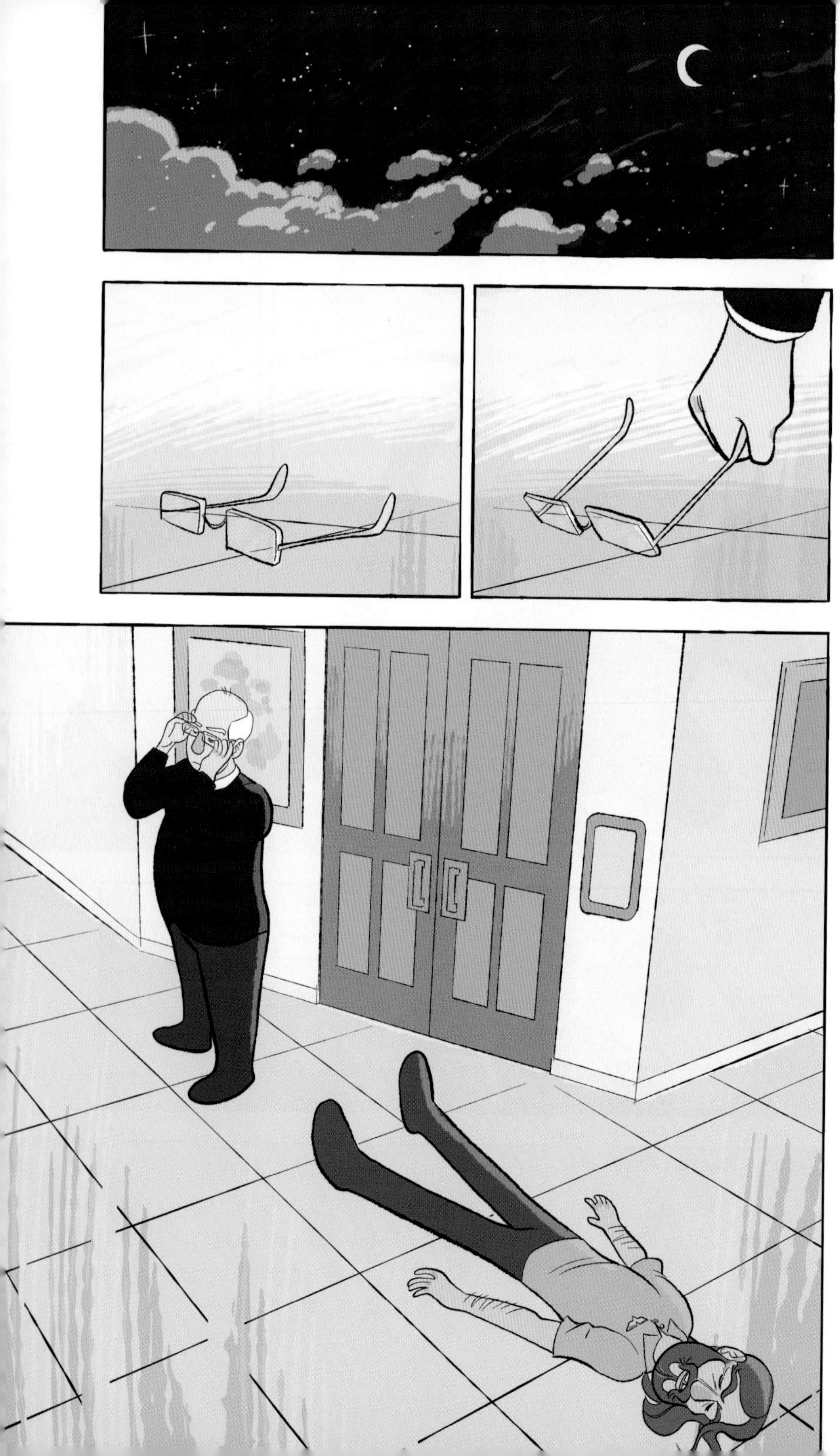

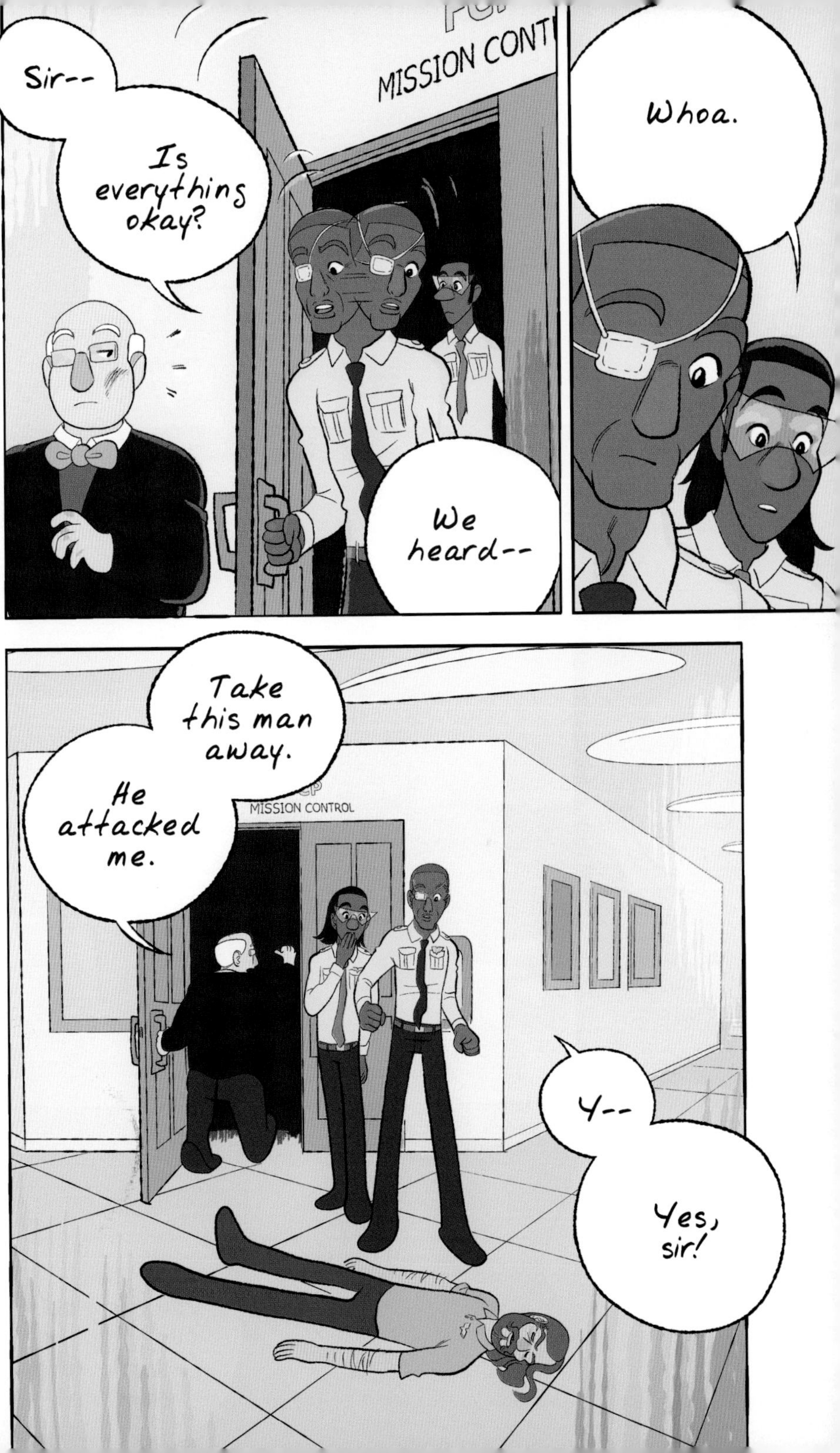
MISSION CONT
Sir--
Is everything okay?
We heard--
Whoa.
Take this man away.
MISSION CONTROL
He attacked me.
Y--
Yes, sir!

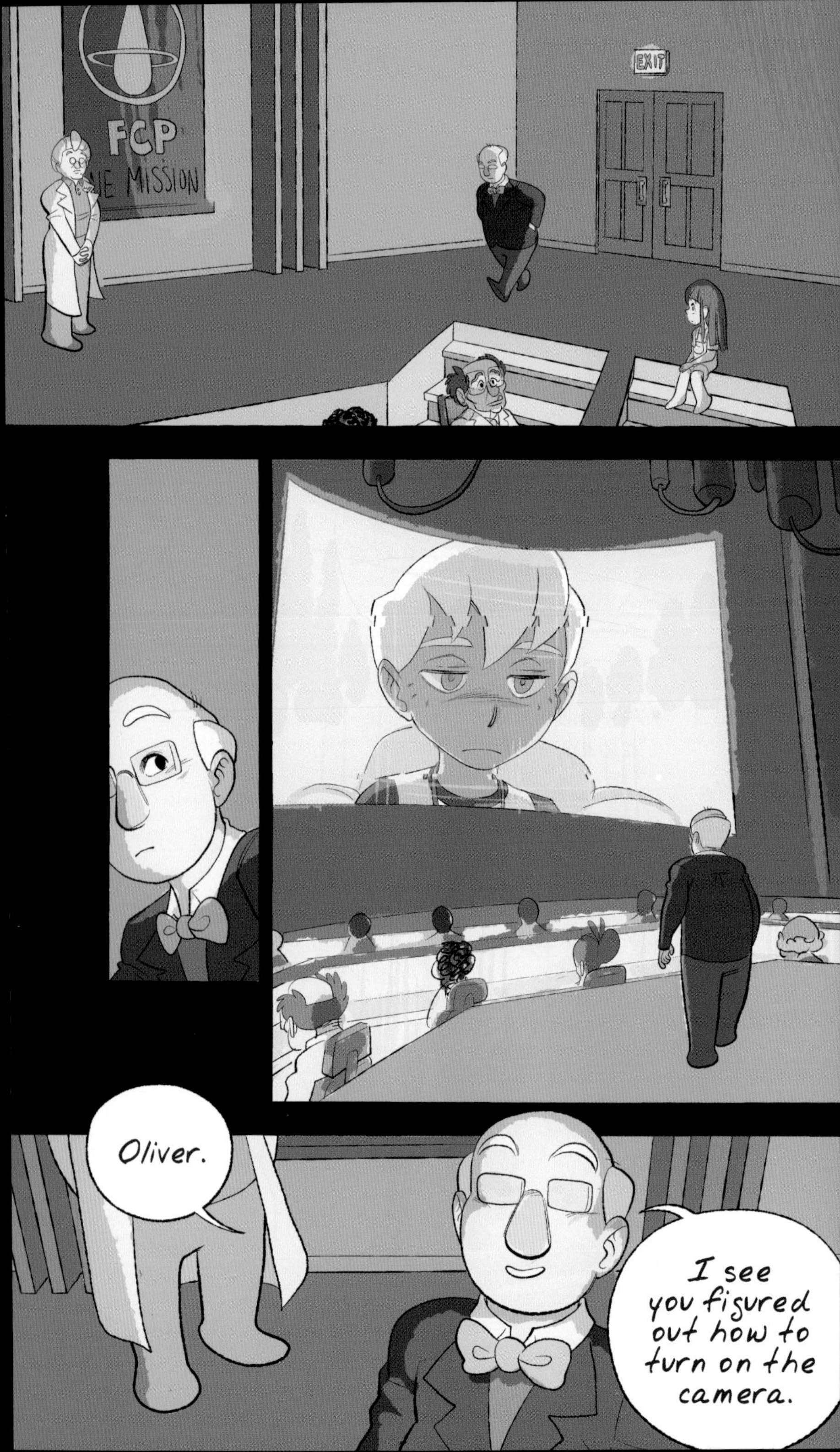
FCP
NE MISSION
EXIT
Oliver.
I see you figured out how to turn on the camera.

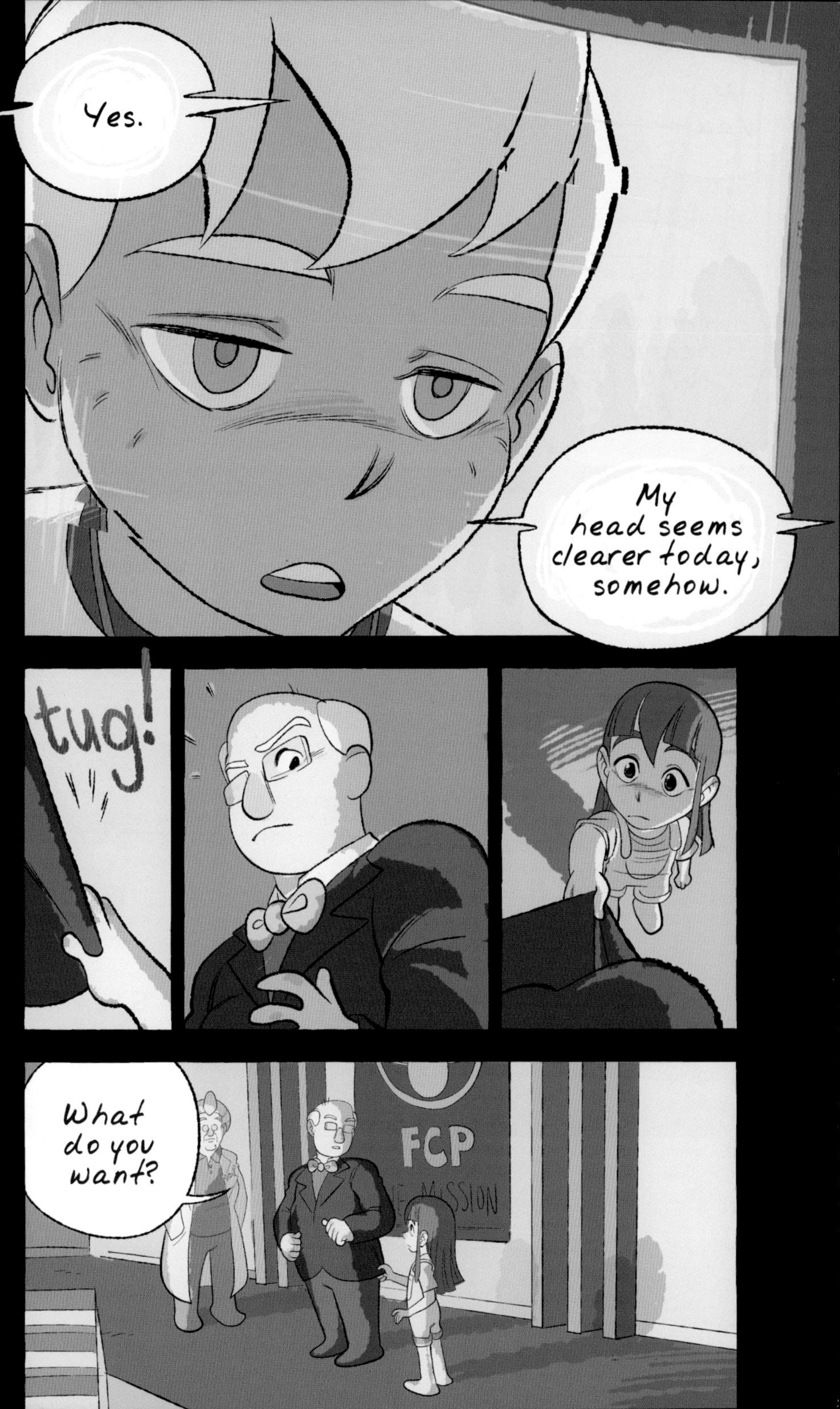

Yes.
My head seems clearer today, somehow.
tug!
What do you want?
FCP

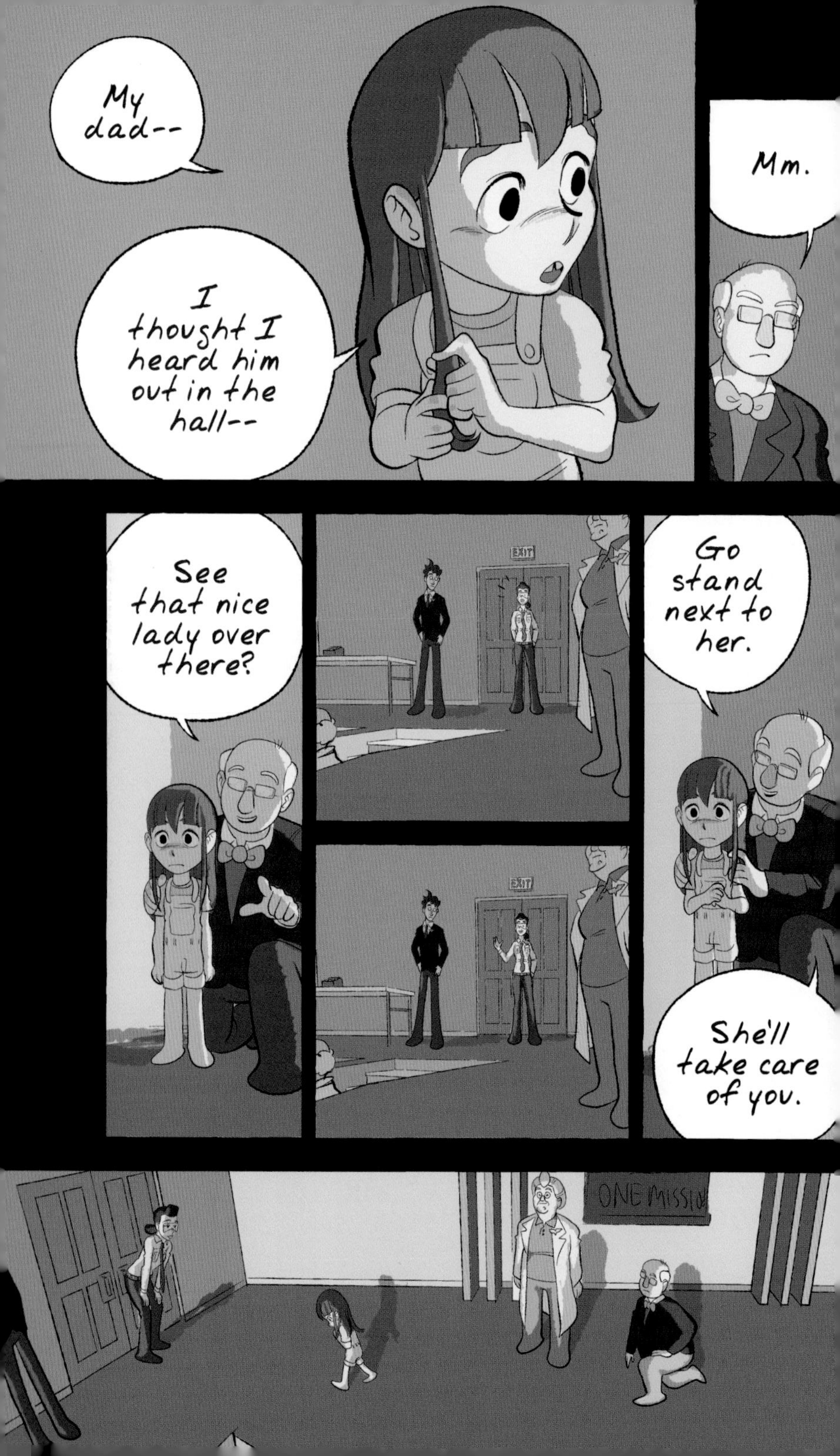
My dad--
I thought I heard him out in the hall--
Mm.
See that nice lady over there?
EXIT
EXIT
Go stand next to her.
She'll take care of you.
ONE MISSIO

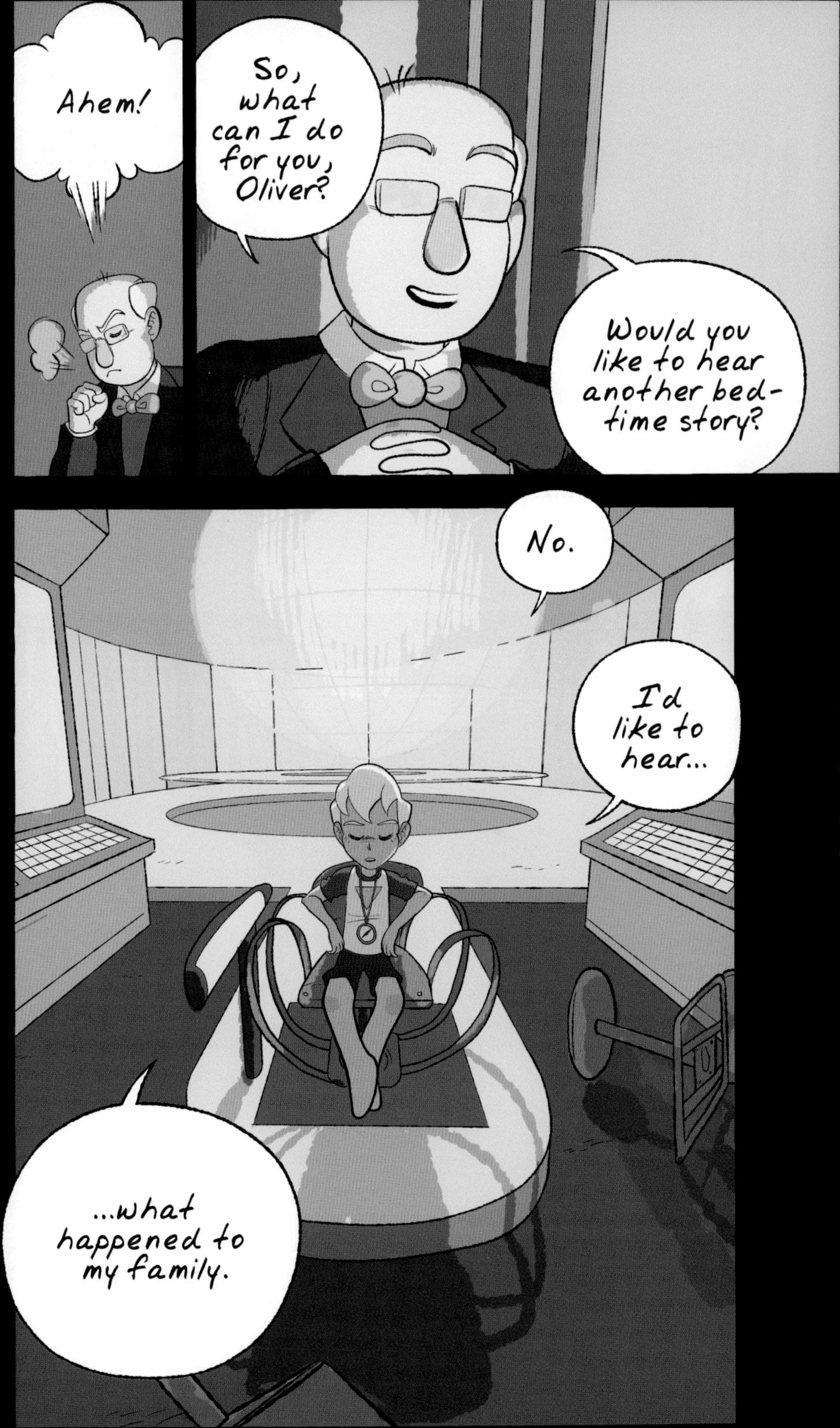
Ahem!
So, what can I do for you, Oliver?
Would you like to hear another bed-time story?
No.
I'd like to hear...
...what happened to my family.

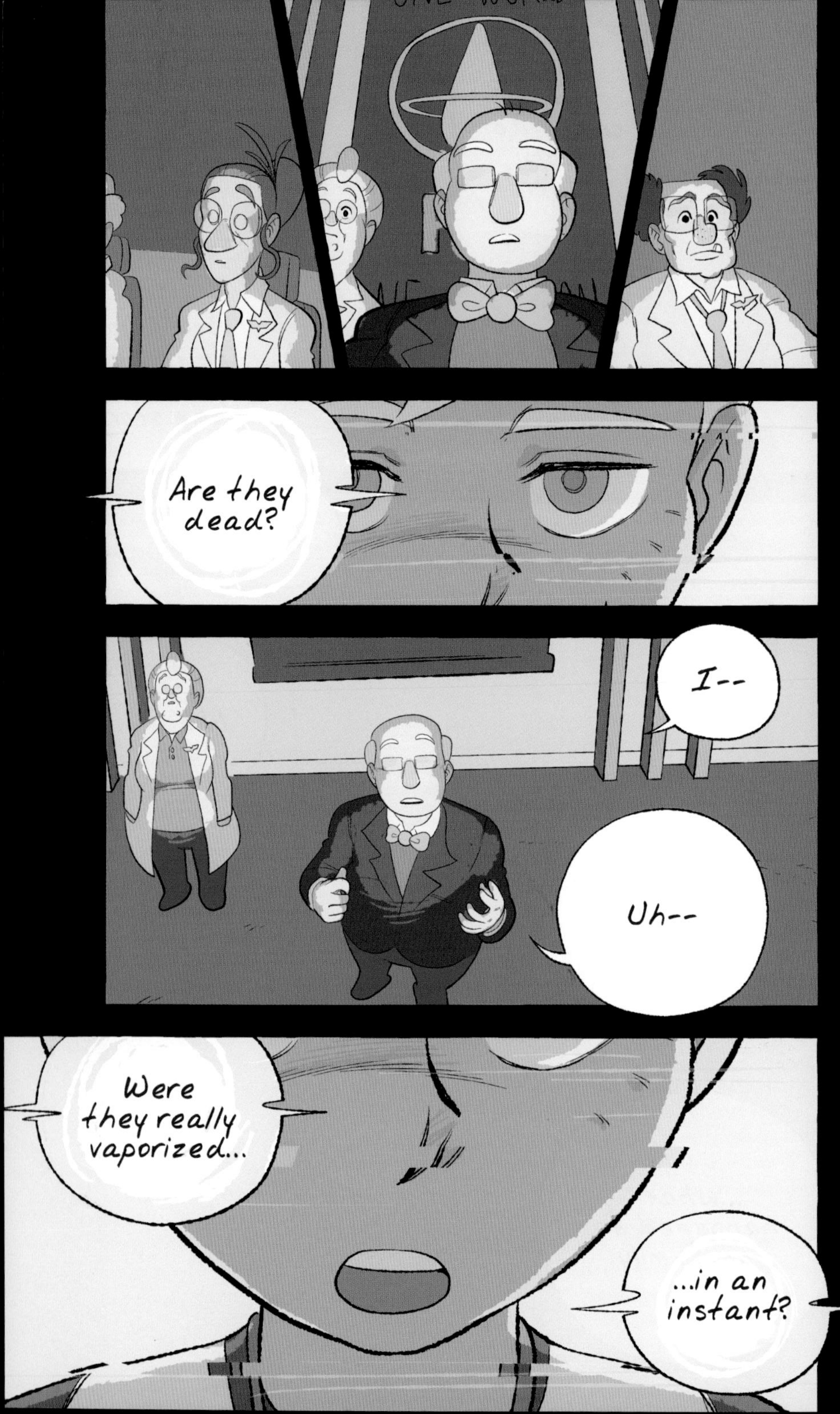
Are they dead?
I--
Uh--
Were they really vaporized...
...in an instant?

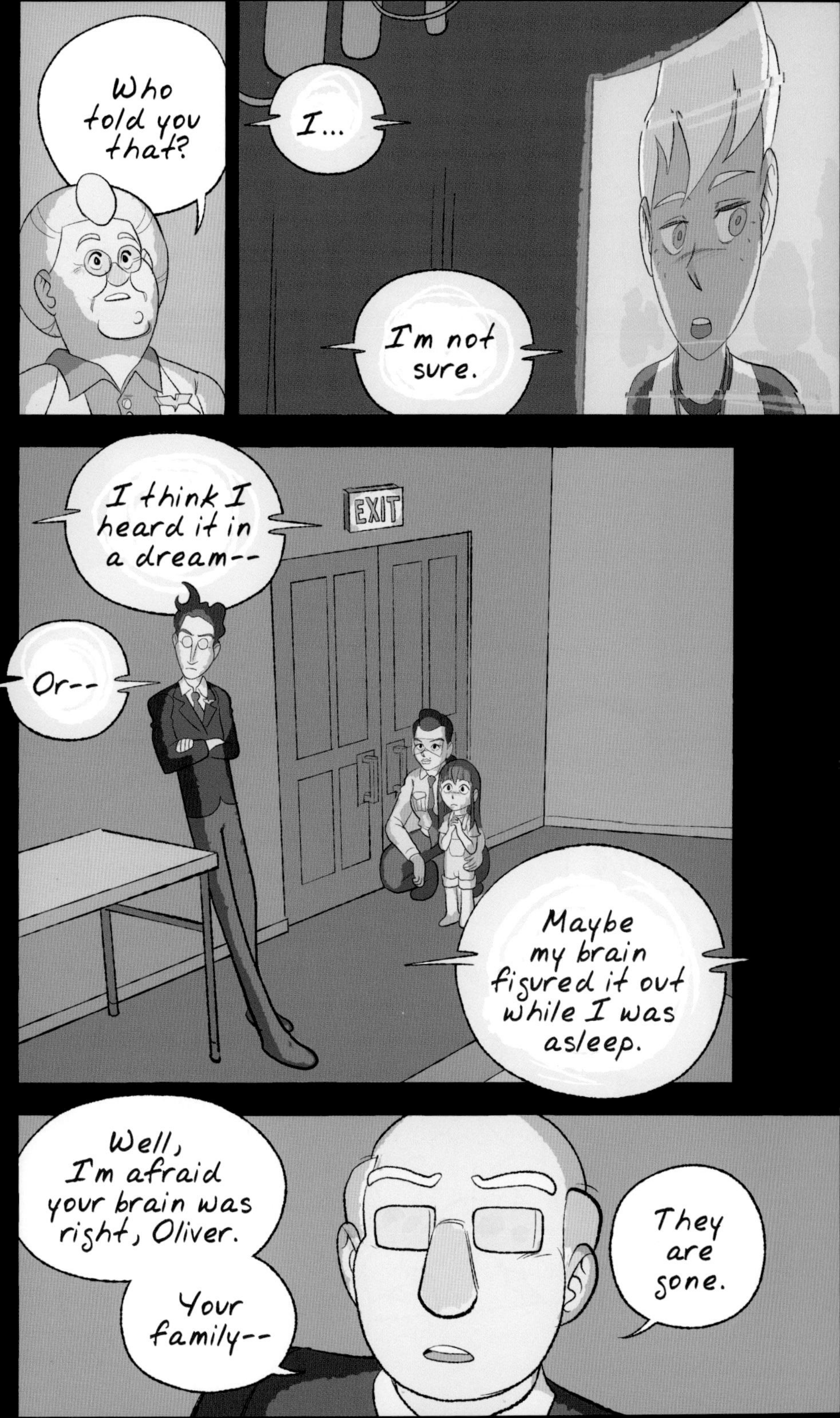
Who told you that?
I...
I'm not sure.
I think I heard it in a dream--
EXIT
Or--
Maybe my brain figured it out while I was asleep.
Well, I'm afraid your brain was right, Oliver.
Your family--
They are gone.

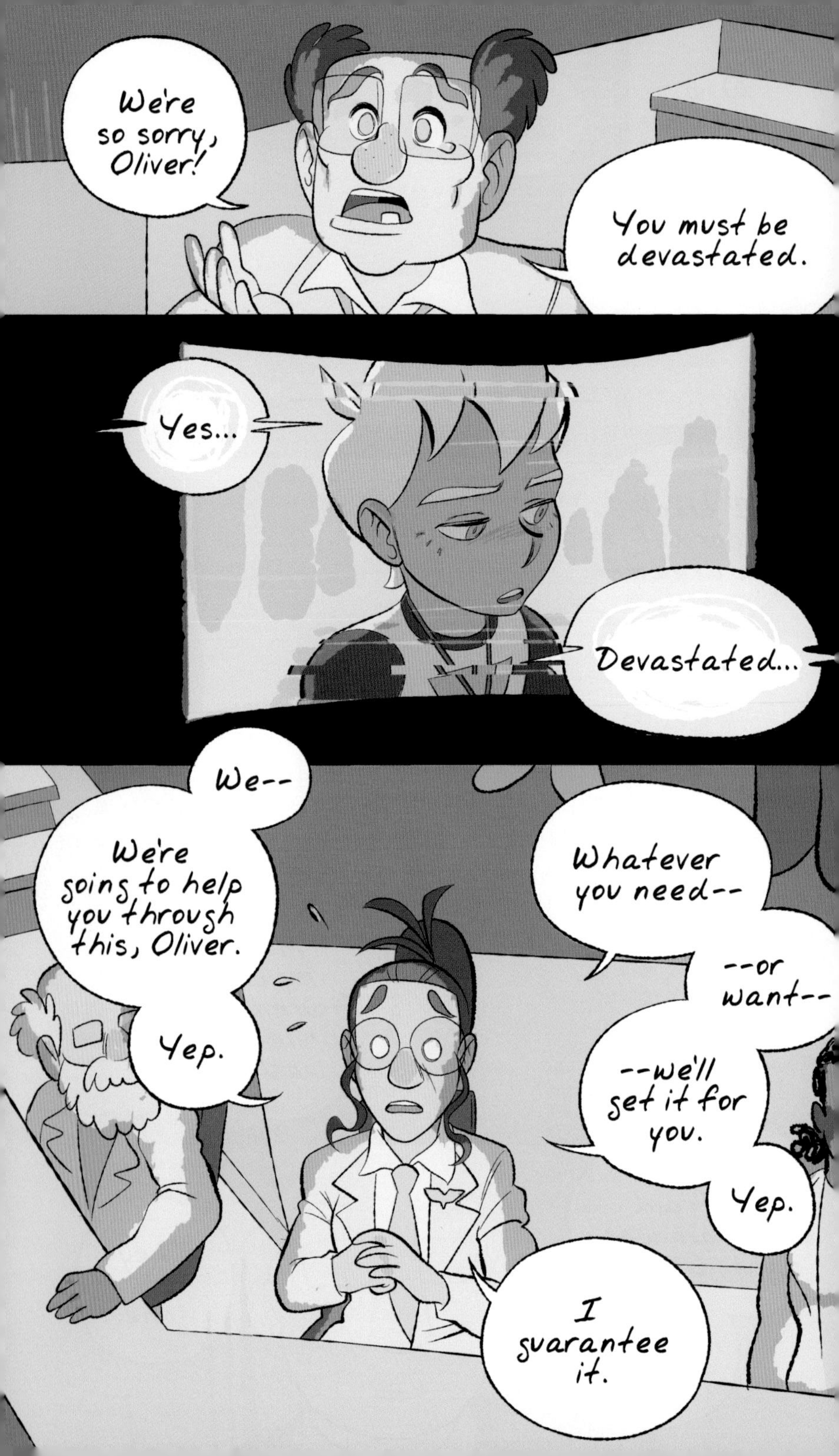
We're so sorry, Oliver!
You must be devastated.
Yes...
Devastated...
We--
We're going to help you through this, Oliver.
Yep.
Whatever you need--
--or want--
--we'll get it for you.
Yep.
I guarantee it.

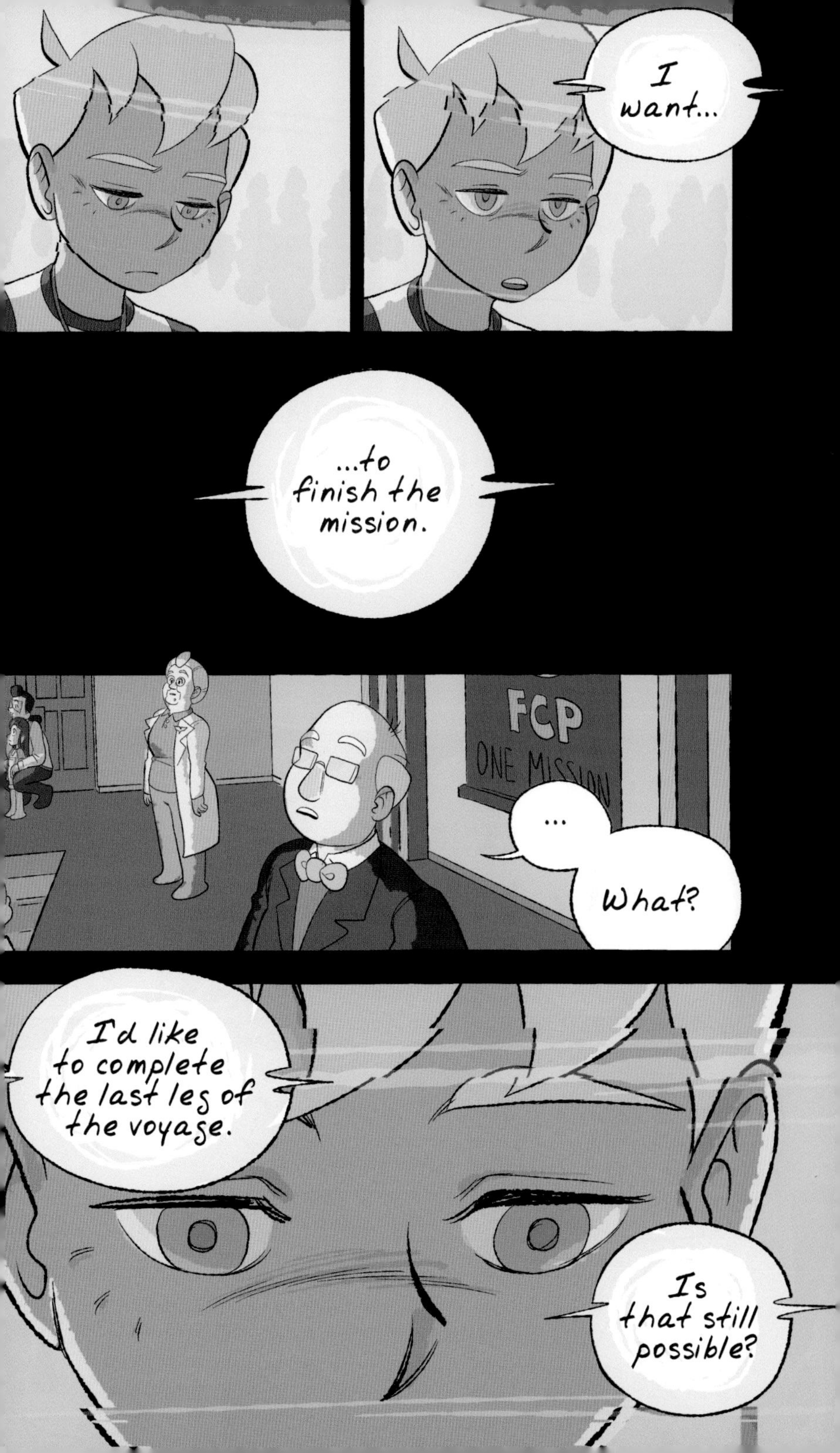
I want...
...to finish the mission.
FCP
ONE MISSION
...
What?
I'd like to complete the last leg of the voyage.
Is that still possible?

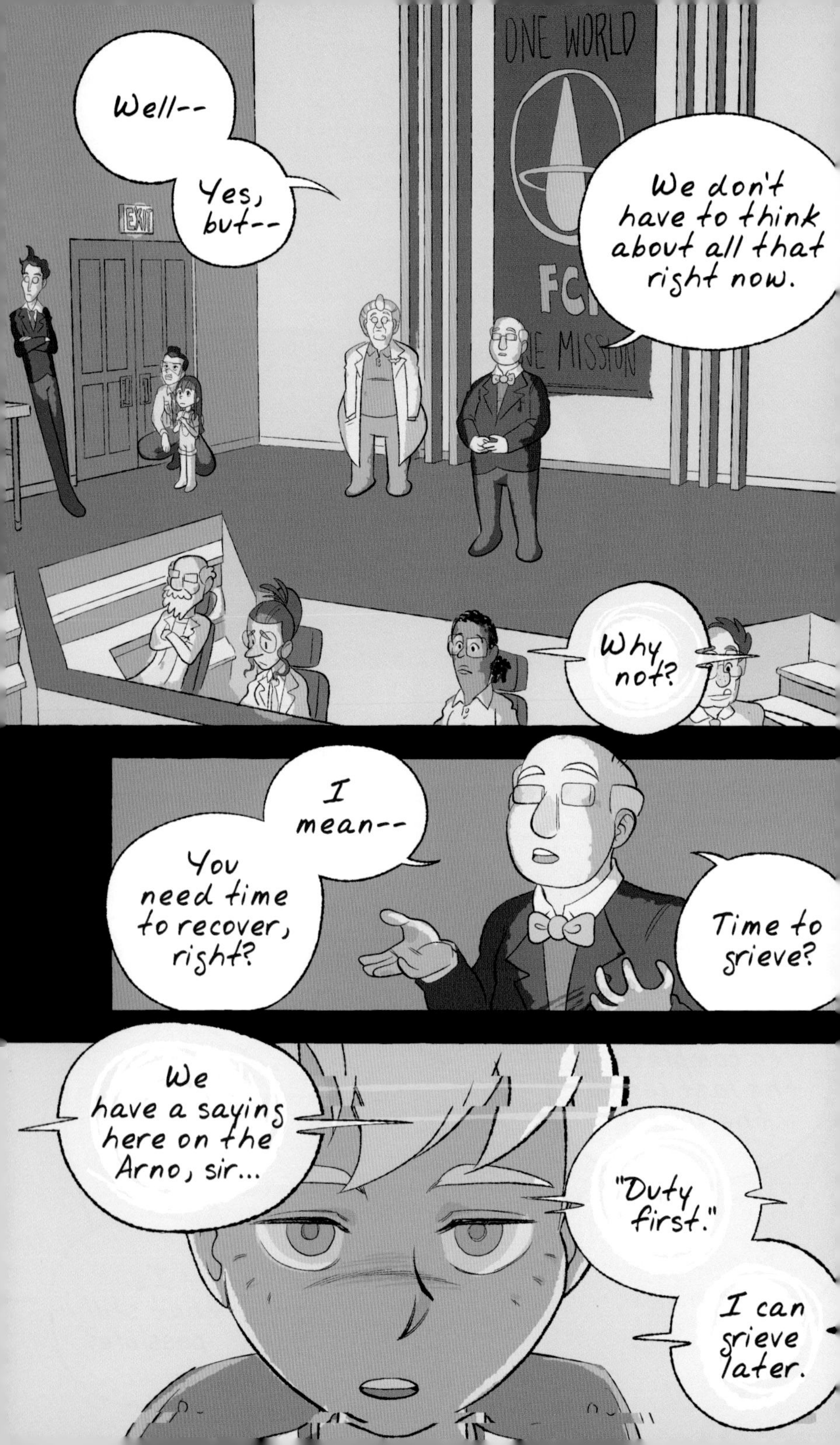
ONE WORLD
FCI
ONE MISSION
EXIT
Well--
Yes, but--
We don't have to think about all that right now.
Why not?
I mean--
You need time to recover, right?
Time to grieve?
We have a saying here on the Arno, sir...
"Duty first."
I can grieve later.

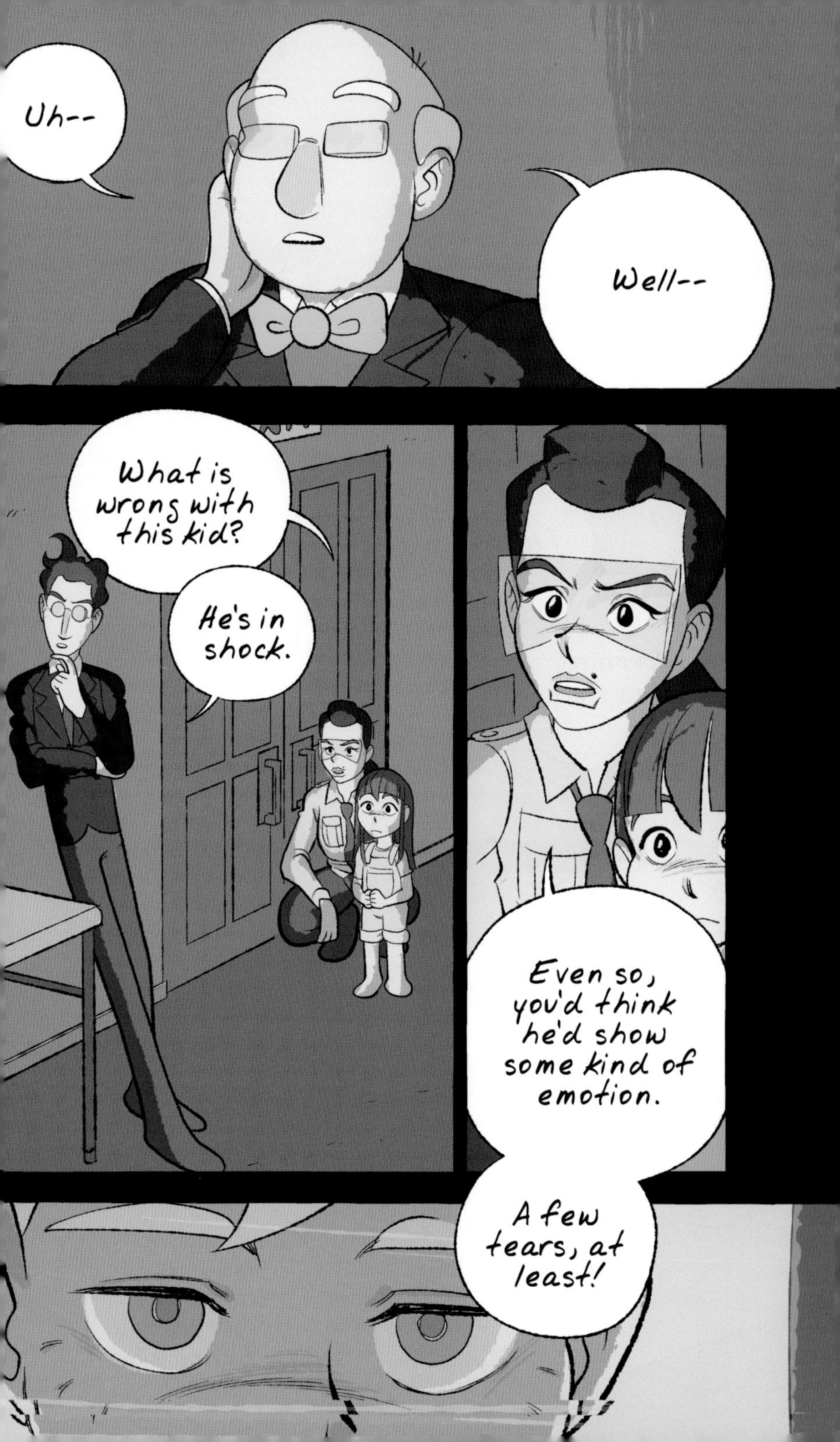
Uh--
Well--
What is wrong with this kid?
He's in shock.
Even so, you'd think he'd show some kind of emotion.
A few tears, at least!

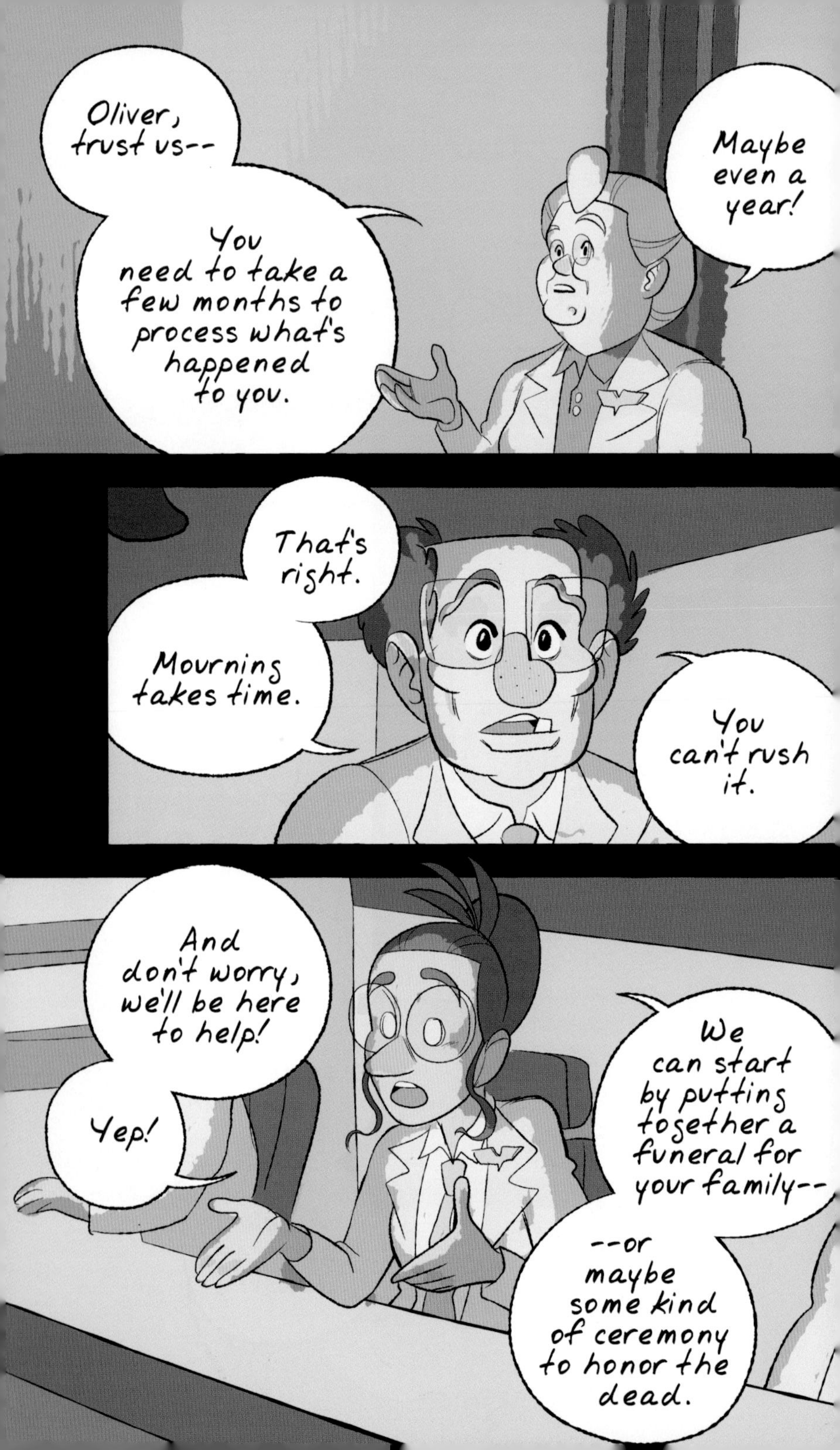
Oliver, trust us--
You need to take a few months to process what's happened to you.
Maybe even a year!
That's right.
Mourning takes time.
You can't rush it.
And don't worry, we'll be here to help!
Yep!
We can start by putting together a funeral for your family--
--or maybe some kind of ceremony to honor the dead.

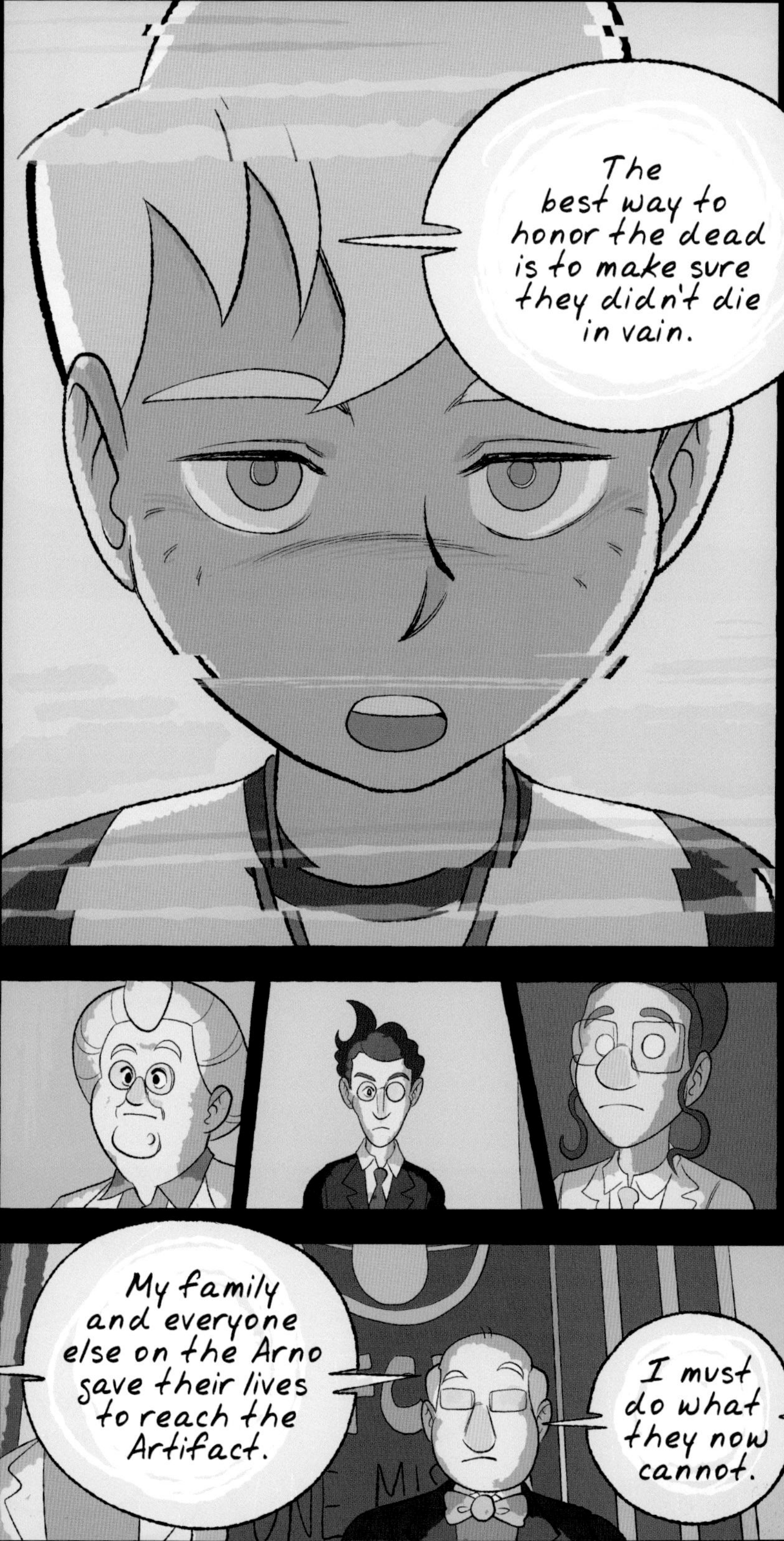
The best way to honor the dead is to make sure they didn't die in vain.
My family and everyone else on the Arno gave their lives to reach the Artifact.
I must do what they now cannot.

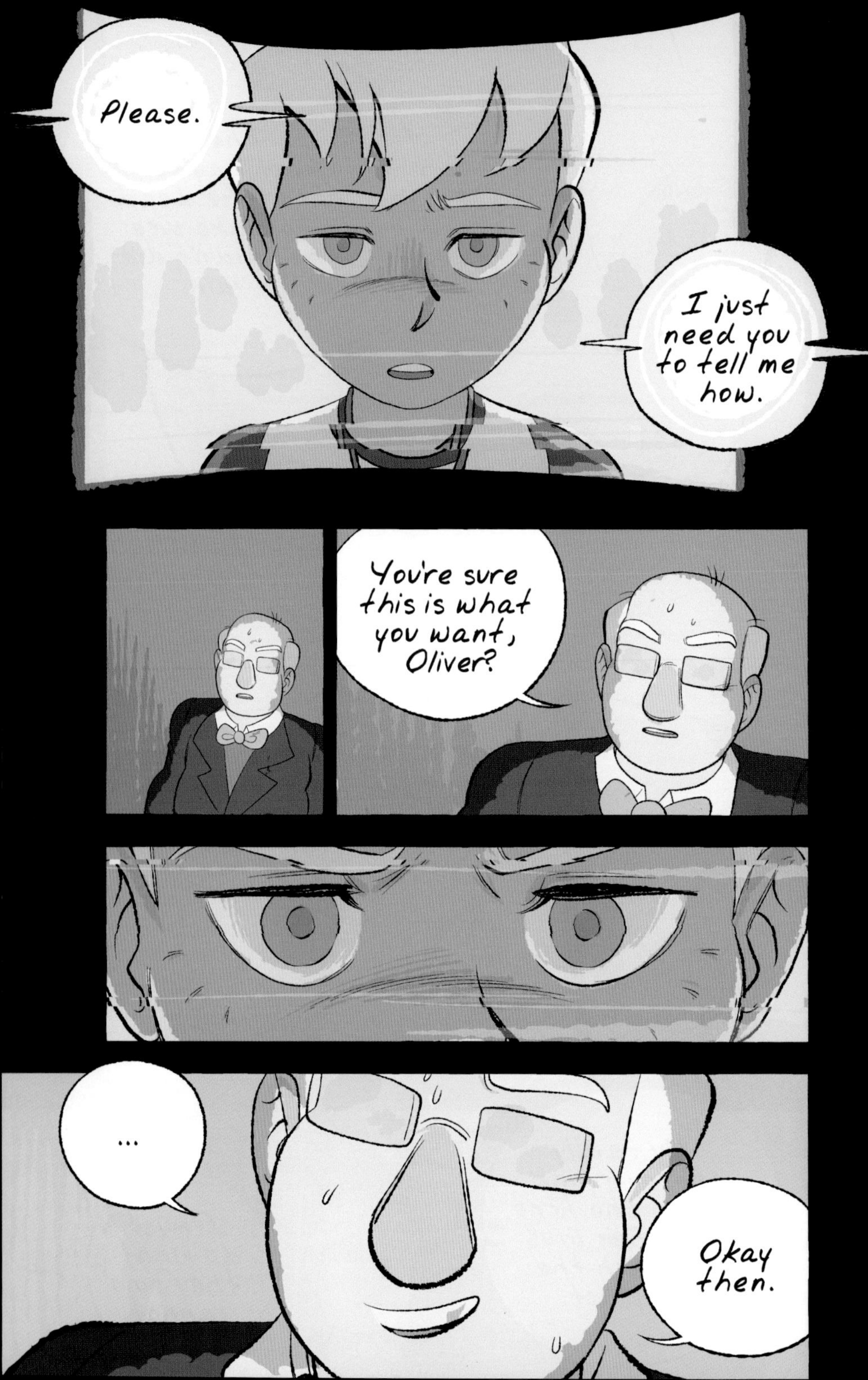
Please.
I just need you to tell me how.
You're sure this is what you want, Oliver?
...
Okay then.

COMING SOON . . .

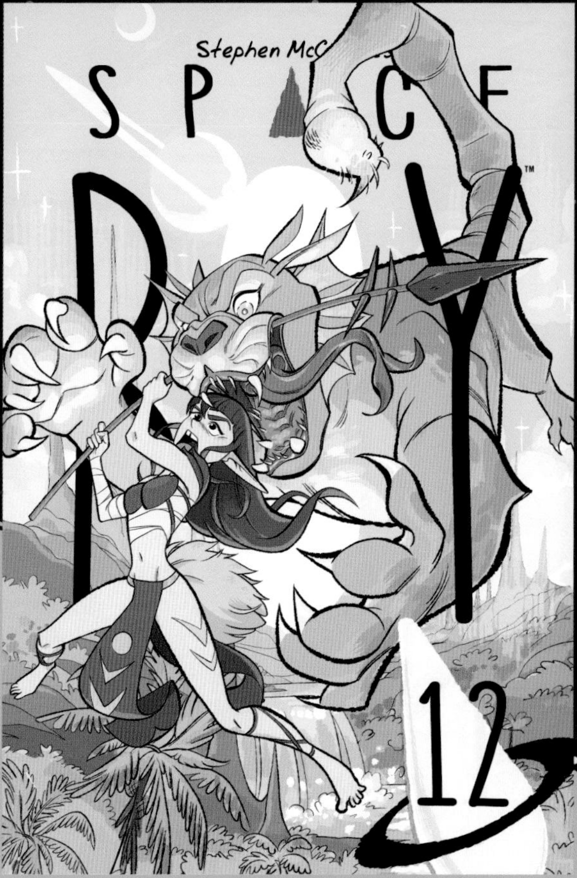

Stephen McC
SPACE BOY
12

Unravel the conspiracy at the heart of the FCP in the latest exciting volume of *Stephen McCranie's Space Boy*!

In the aftermath of the homecoming dance, the students of South Pine are left reeling from the disappearance of one of their friends. As Zeph, Cassie, and David struggle to make sense of the tragedy, Amy begins to adjust to her new life in the FCP, finding unexpected allies as she tries to uncover more about the shadowy organization, and what its goals are for Oliver and herself. Available October 2021!

YOU CAN ALSO READ MORE *SPACE BOY* COMICS ON WEBTOONS.COM!

HAVE YOU READ THEM ALL?

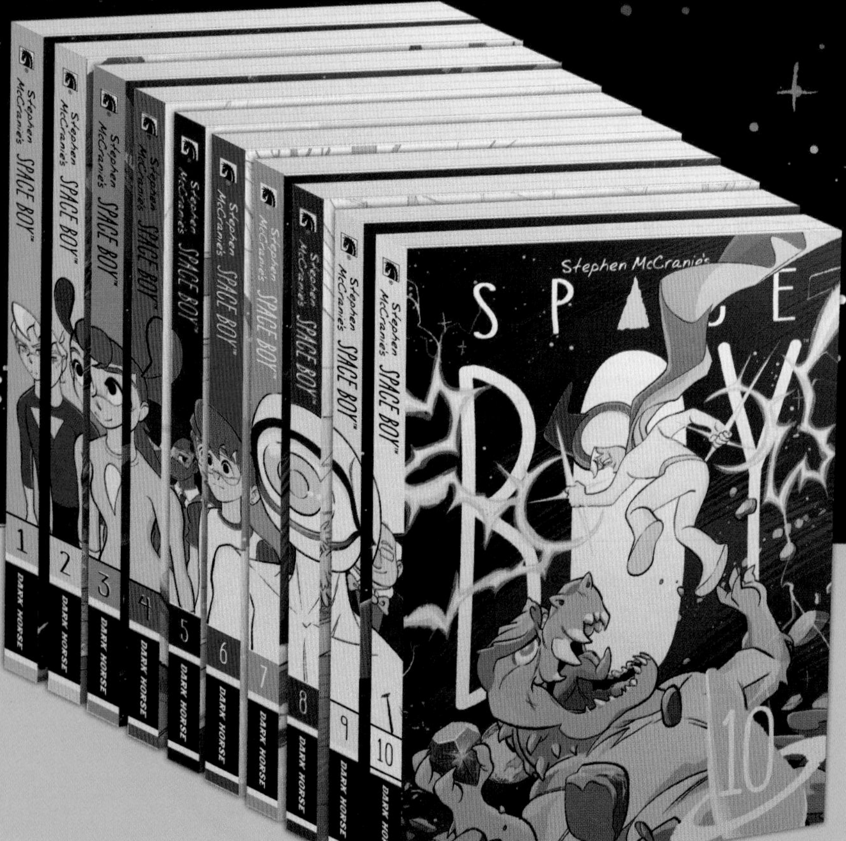
Stephen McCranie's
SPACE BOY
10
DARK HORSE

VOLUME 1
$10.99
ISBN 978-1-50670-648-1

VOLUME 2
$10.99
ISBN 978-1-50670-680-1

VOLUME 3
$10.99
ISBN 978-1-50670-842-3

VOLUME 4
$10.99
ISBN 978-1-50670-843-0

VOLUME 5
$10.99
ISBN 978-1-50671-399-1

VOLUME 6
$10.99
ISBN 978-1-50671-400-4

VOLUME 7
$10.99
ISBN 978-1-50671-401-1

VOLUME 8
$10.99
ISBN 978-1-50671-402-8

VOLUME 9
$10.99
ISBN 978-1-50671-883-5

VOLUME 10
$10.99
ISBN 978-1-50671-884-2

AVAILABLE AT YOUR LOCAL COMICS SHOP OR BOOKSTORE. TO FIND A COMICS SHOP IN YOUR AREA, VISIT COMICSHOPLOCATOR.COM. FOR MORE INFORMATION OR TO ORDER DIRECT, VISIT DARKHORSE.COM.

DARK HORSE BRINGS YOU THE BEST IN WEBCOMICS!

These wildly popular cartoon gems were once only available online, but now can be found through Dark Horse Books with loads of awesome extras!

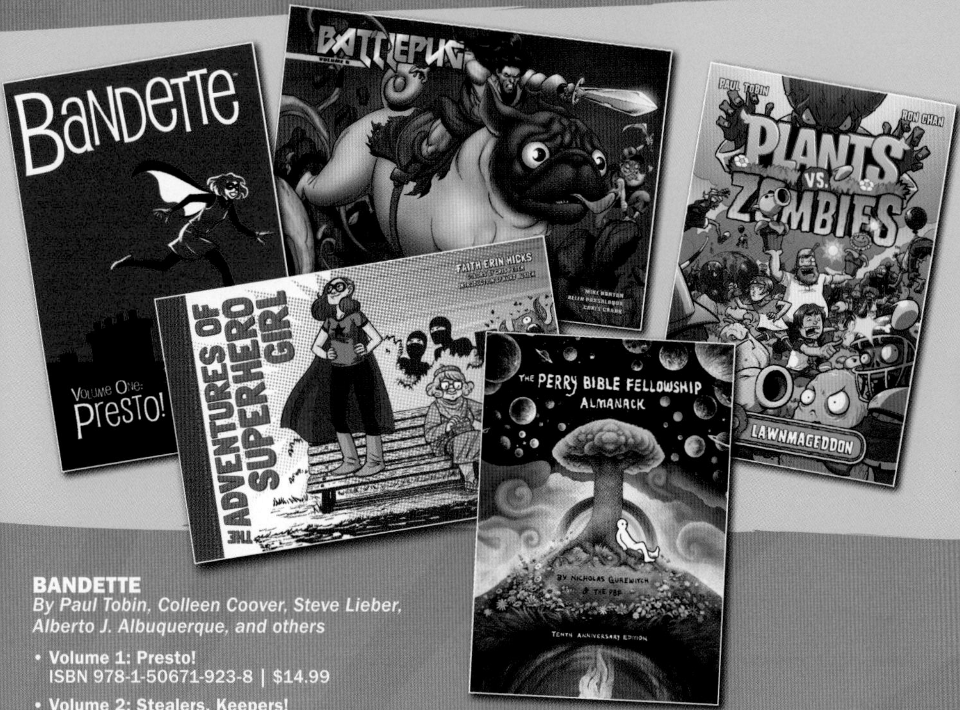
BANDETTE
VOLUME ONE: PRESTO!
BATTLEPUG
MIKE NORTON
ALLEN PASSALAQUA
CHRIS CRANK
FAITH ERIN HICKS
THE ADVENTURES OF SUPERHERO GIRL
PAUL TOBIN
RON CHAN
PLANTS VS. ZOMBIES
LAWNMAGEDDON
THE PERRY BIBLE FELLOWSHIP
ALMANACK
BY NICHOLAS GUREWITCH & THE PBF
TENTH ANNIVERSARY EDITION

BANDETTE
By Paul Tobin, Colleen Coover, Steve Lieber, Alberto J. Albuquerque, and others

- **Volume 1: Presto!**
  ISBN 978-1-50671-923-8 | $14.99
- **Volume 2: Stealers, Keepers!**
  ISBN 978-1-50671-924-5 | $14.99
- **Volume 3: The House of the Green Mask**
  ISBN 978-1-50671-925-2 | $14.99
- **Volume 4: The Six-Finger Secret**
  ISBN 978-1-50671-925-2 | $14.99

MIKE NORTON'S BATTLEPUG
By Mike Norton

- **The Devil's Biscuit**
  ISBN 978-1-61655-864-2 | $14.99
- **The Paws of War**
  ISBN 978-1-50670-114-1 | $14.99

THE ADVENTURES OF SUPERHERO GIRL - EXPANDED EDITION HC
By Faith Erin Hicks
ISBN 978-1-50670-336-7 | $16.99

PLANTS VS. ZOMBIES
By Paul Tobin, Ron Chan, Andie Tong, and others

- **LAWNMAGEDDON**
  ISBN 978-1-61655-192-6 | $10.99
- **BULLY FOR YOU**
  ISBN 978-1-61655-889-5 | $10.99
- **GROWN SWEET HOME**
  ISBN 978-1-61655-971-7 | $10.99
- **RUMBLE AT LAKE GUMBO**
  ISBN 978-1-50670-497-5 | $10.99

THE PERRY BIBLE FELLOWSHIP 10TH ANNIVERSARY EDITION
By Nicholas Gurewitch
ISBN 978-1-50671-588-9 | $24.99

AVAILABLE AT YOUR LOCAL COMICS SHOP OR BOOKSTORE | To find a comics shop in your area, visit comicshoplocator.com. For more information or to order direct, visit DarkHorse.com

DARK HORSE BOOKS